The Commander

By CJ Williams

The Commander

By CJ Williams

© 2016 CJ Williams

All rights reserved.

This is a work of fiction. Any reference to actual names, characters, places, products or incidents is fictitious or coincidental.

ISBN-13: 978-1534709249
ISBN-10: 153470924X

Print Edition.

Table of Contents

Chapter 1	1
Chapter 2	19
Chapter 3	35
Chapter 4	55
Chapter 5	65
Chapter 6	77
Chapter 7	100
Chapter 8	117
Chapter 9	133
Chapter 10	146
Chapter 11	166
Chapter 12	186
Chapter 13	205
Chapter 14	223
Chapter 15	232
Chapter 16	258
Chapter 17	275
Chapter 18	299
Chapter 19	315

Milky Way Galaxy

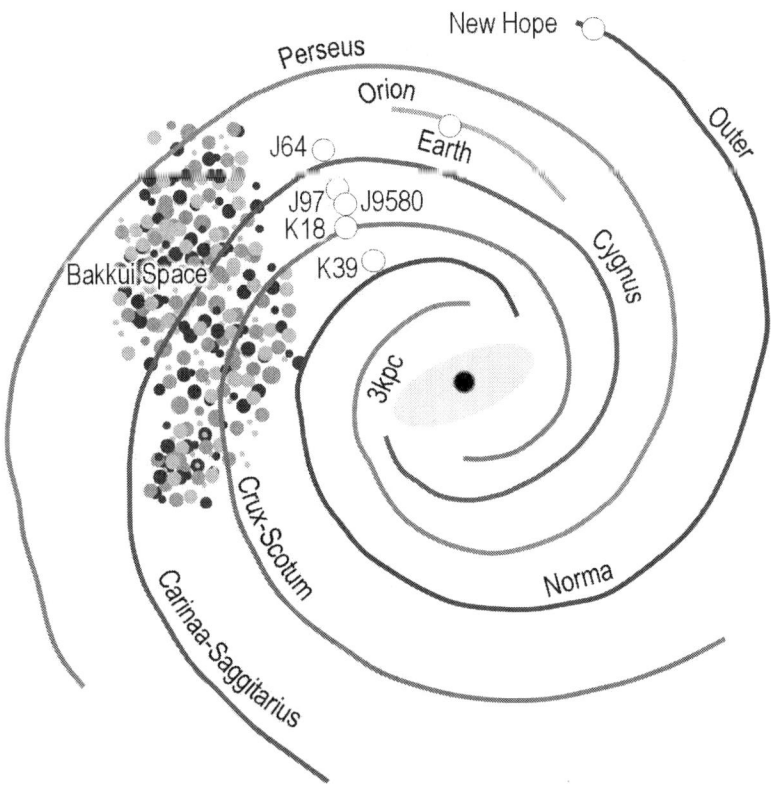

Chapter 1

Day 1—Population 0

Airport Director Luke Blackburn leaned back in his office chair and stretched. He was finally done with the annual FAA grant application for his lonely airport in central Nevada, Baggs Regional.

After mailing the thick package at the local Post Office, Luke wasn't ready to go back to the office. The best excuse to avoid his desk was a runway check. FAA regulations required two inspections per day, one during daylight hours and another at night. Luke didn't mind the tedious chore; it was a chance to enjoy his solitude under Nevada's big sky.

The sun was still rising when he drove his pickup onto the empty aircraft-parking ramp. He looked up and down the field and far to the south, he spotted a reflected glint. Someone was on landing approach. It was too far away to identify the aircraft type, but it piqued his curiosity. It had been a while since anyone had landed at the airport.

Most likely, it was a student pilot from Reno. Occasionally a pilot-in-training would fly over to Baggs and practice touch-and-go landings. It was rare, but not unheard of; the famous resort was about a hundred and fifty miles to the west.

As the aircraft drew closer, Luke had trouble identifying it. It wasn't a propeller aircraft. Perhaps it was a private jet; one of those VLJ's—very light jets—that small corporations and the nouveau-riche were buying.

Luke shielded his eyes and squinted. Nope, not a private aircraft. Could it be military? It was about the size of an F-16 but didn't have the underbelly intake. In fact, Luke didn't see any intake at all. What in the world was it? There was no propulsion sound, no whine of jet turbines or buzzing of gas pistons. Just the barely audible sound of rushing wind.

By the time it reached the end of the runway, he couldn't deny the obvious. It was a no-kidding UFO. Either that or someone had done a damn good job of keeping a new military design secret.

Looking like a cross between a small school bus and a jet fighter, it had a broad fuselage with high-mounted wings that were short and stubby. The nose flattened to a broad edge and the wide canopy was tinted with a translucent golden hue.

The aircraft didn't actually land, it *floated* down the runway to the mid-field intersection where it slowed, and still hovering a good five feet in the air, turned onto the connecting taxiway.

Luke was astonished at the sight, but in any event, it was an arrival. To all appearances, it intended to stay. Luke drove his pickup to the middle of the parking ramp. He took two lighted wands from the pickup's bed and a pair of wheel chocks tied together by a short length of rope.

He stood where the taxi line curved into a wide loop that visiting aircraft followed with their nose wheel to designated parking spots. Slowly waving both arms from front to back, he marshalled the aircraft toward the parking location. The spacecraft followed his directions initially but then came to a stop.

The canopy dissolved and in the cockpit sat a very human-looking pilot. He leaned out and pointed to a closed up hangar on the edge of the flight line.

Luke mirrored the gesture with one of the wands as if asking confirmation.

The pilot nodded and pointed first to his fuselage and then once again to the hangar. The meaning was clear: He wanted to park inside.

Luke hurried to the front of the hangar and stepped through an access door in the huge folding panels. He crossed his fingers; the doors had a tendency to jam halfway on hot days. He pushed the green button on the inside wall and the two doors slowly parted from the center, opening the vast interior to the aircraft.

As the curious spacecraft approached the hangar, it descended until it was hovering just a foot above the concrete. Luke walked backward, marshalling it along the centerline stripe that ran to the back of the hangar.

Once completely inside, the aircraft rotated until the nose was pointed out toward the flight line. Three short landing skids slowly extended from the underbelly. When they touched the ground, the aircraft settled on the struts and the humming noise died away.

A door on the side of the fuselage opened and the pilot stepped out onto the hangar floor. His appearance matched that of most general aviation pilots. Average height and unassuming features. He wore a pair of khaki slacks, polo shirt, and tennis shoes. He turned toward Luke and said, *"Gwie i neoh-eo."*

"Sorry," Luke replied. "English and German is all I understand. Welcome to Baggs."

The pilot dug into a leather satchel that was slung over his shoulder. He extracted a matchbox-sized container, emptied the contents into his palm, and handed it to Luke. It looked like a hearing aid.

Luke examined it closely. It was an earbud on steroids. "Is this a translator or something?"

The pilot nodded. *"Gwie i neoh-eo,"* he repeated. *"Geunyang gwie neoh-eo ulineun seolo leul ihaehal su-issda."* He made it sound urgent.

Luke took a deep breath and stuck it in his right ear. It was soft and molded comfortably to his ear canal.

"Can you hear me now?" the pilot asked in clear, unaccented English.

A grin spread across Luke's face. "This is amazing," he said. "I can understand you perfectly. What's your name? What do I call you?"

"Call me Sam. That thing might sting when it activates."

"No, it doesn't hurt at all. I can't even feel it. This is…"

A tiny robotic voice cautioned, *"Prepare for assimilation. Three, two, one."*

The warning got Luke's attention. Before he could respond every pain receptor in his brain exploded. His head felt like it was going to burst. He put his hands over his ears, trying to squeeze away the agony. And just as quickly as the pain appeared, it was gone.

Luke found himself kneeling on the concrete floor of the hangar. "Christ! You call that stinging?" He struggled to his feet.

"It was for this." Sam held up a small black object. "Now, if you don't do everything I say, I touch this button and it will detonate an explosive device inside your skull."

Luke sank back to the floor, his face pale. How stupid had he been to insert a suicide bomb into his brain without question? "Wha... I'm not..."

Sam erupted with laughter. "Just kidding, man. Couldn't resist it. You're fine."

Luke's eyes hazed over with red. He would break the man's neck, visitor from outer space or not...if he could just get to his feet.

Sam was still chuckling. "Oh, you should have seen your face. Come on. We got a lot of stuff to talk about and not much time." He tossed the object to Luke. "Here you go."

Luke clumsily caught the plastic oval. "What's this, then?" he asked angrily, his emotions slowly cooling down.

"What's it look like? It's the keys to the shuttle. Go ahead and lock it up."

"What?" Luke examined the key fob in his hand. It looked like the one for his pickup. It had two buttons; one was a silhouette of the shuttle with the door open and the other had the door closed.

He pressed the icon with the door closed. The spacecraft beeped and lights on the wingtips and the top of the tail flashed briefly. The side door slowly closed. *It's like locking a minivan*, he decided.

Luke handed the key to Sam.

"Keep it," Sam said. "That thing's yours now."

"What?"

"Yeah, that baby is your problem now. So is the insurance, by the way."

"What?" Luke struggled to keep up with the conversation.

"Come on, let's go to your office. Like I said, we've got a lot to talk about, and not much time." Sam walked over to Luke's pickup and settled into the passenger seat. "Let's move it!" he hollered.

###

Luke pulled into his reserved parking spot at the airport passenger terminal. The only other car belonged to his elderly secretary, Linda. She was a treasure, albeit slightly eccentric.

Each grant award included enough administrative overhead to pay for one-third of an administrative assistant. It was the only funding that covered her part-time salary.

In spite of his frequent protestations, she spent almost forty hours a week at her desk. He pleaded with her that her full-time presence put him in violation of federal wage and hour laws.

She would just smile and say, "I got nowhere else to go, babe." Which was true. In Baggs, Nevada, there were few options for employment or entertainment. Because he had inherited her, so to speak, he felt obligated to keep her on.

She was working when Luke and his guest walked in, although 'working' was a generous description. She'd spent most of the last fifteen years at the airport secretary's desk, which she usually kept covered with knitting paraphernalia. On occasion she would substitute scrapbooking, but that was an exception. Today it was knitting.

The terminal itself was a relic. Long ago, the city had enclosed a World War II construction shed with cheap siding and glass and called it an airline terminal. Huge swamp coolers would have provided cooling but they had deteriorated beyond repair. Fortunately, for the two occupants, the airport's elevation of forty-seven hundred feet meant the high desert air was comfortable even without AC.

Luke led Sam into his office, passing through the outer reception area where he introduced his guest as a potential client. Linda was profuse with her greeting and bustled around to provide a pot of coffee and a couple of paper cups. Luke sat behind his ancient desk, another World War II relic, and gestured toward a well-used upholstered chair for Sam.

Once they were settled comfortably and Linda had been shooed out, Luke opened the conversation. "What do you mean we don't have a lot of time?" he asked.

Sam settled into his chair, making himself comfortable. "The bad guys are coming, Luke. That much is fact. As it stands, your planet and everyone on it will be completely destroyed. These guys move into star systems and wipe out everything before moving on. They're like a plague of locusts."

Luke leaned on his desk. "Okay, I'll play along. Let's assume for a minute that's true. What do you want from me? Who are the bad guys? When is this all supposed to happen?"

"In reverse order, I'd be surprised to see them sooner than ten years or much later than fifteen."

"So, no hurry then." Luke concluded.

Sam gave him a sad smile. "I'll let you decide on that. As to who? We don't actually know. We call them the *Bakkui*; they're from the outer rim. We don't think they're human but again, we don't know. A lot of folks believe they're from another galaxy. I don't buy it. I'd wager they sprouted on some godforsaken rim planet, but nothing is certain."

"Why would they be human?" Luke asked.

"Why wouldn't they? Intelligent life is scarce, son. Our galaxy—your galaxy—is populated by humans just like you. The planets, yours and all the rest in this arm of the spiral, were colonized, seeded, if you prefer. That was a long time ago, of course."

"So you're telling me you're human? I kinda thought you were an alien from outer space. No offense."

"None taken. It's true enough, I suppose, but that makes you the *descendant* of an alien from outer space. We've got the same DNA, but let's stay focused. Your first question, what do I want? Frankly, nothing."

Luke was skeptical. "People don't give away spaceships without wanting something in return."

"Think of it this way," Sam suggested. "You ever throw a handful of weed-killer on the lawn?" Sam looked over his shoulder as though examining the neighborhood. "Not that I see much green around here but you get my meaning. The point is you don't expect anything back. The weed-killer is an expense and you hope it'll keep weeds at bay. That's sort of what you are, weed-killer. It's what I am, for that matter."

"How so?" Luke didn't quite get the connection.

"My job is to visit as many star systems as I can in this neck of the woods, along this spiral arm of the galaxy, I should say, in a long-shot effort to generate some resistance."

"As many as you can? You mean you're not staying here to help?"

"On a long-term basis? Afraid not. I'm going to get you started, and then I'm out of here. Too bad, really. This looks like an interesting place, but I'm spread pretty thin."

Luke was puzzled by the explanation. "So how long are you here for?"

Sam shrugged his shoulders. "I'll do what I can for a couple of weeks. Then I'm gone. That's the way it is."

"Two weeks! What can you accomplish in two weeks?"

"That's not the question, really."

"What do you mean?"

Sam fixed Luke with a serious stare. "The question is what can *you* accomplish in the next ten years?"

Luke leaned back in his chair in amazement. Had he not actually seen this guy land a spacecraft at his airport, he would blow off the entire story as a crazy fabrication. He had no idea how to react.

Sam rose to his feet, a smile on his face once more. "But right now, we have more important things to do. I want to try what you guys call a cheeseburger. They sell those at the local diner, right?"

#

For hours the two men sat in a booth at the far end of the diner. Luke listened late into the afternoon, his mind filled with awe at Sam's story but still not sure how much of it to believe.

"Wait a minute," Luke interrupted at one point. "Why are you even telling me this stuff? You should be talking to the president or Congress."

"Yeah," Sam replied slowly. "Let's think about that for a minute. Isn't the president some kind of entertainment star? You think he's capable of handling this? Getting the planet ready for an alien invasion a decade from now?"

"Well…"

"Your Congress isn't any better. Bunch of crooks sucking up to their wealthy patrons. Am I right?"

"Yeah, for the most part," Luke admitted.

"This is not the first time we've given a boost to a seeded colony," Sam explained. "We've known this threat is coming for a while and we've tried a few things to stop them, all without success. Early on, we did just what you've said. We visited planetary rulers and gave them a technology bump to help prepare for invasion. Unfortunately, like in *every single case*, when the Bakkui finally arrived, the only thing left on those planets were smoking holes or starving savages. I dunno why, but the politicos I've seen only care about themselves; they don't have the mindset to save humanity."

Luke nodded. He had the same feeling if truth be told.

Sam continued. "Recently we had a little success by helping one small company get a head start on their competition. But even that didn't work out. So this time, the powers-that-be are going back to basics. Give one guy the technology and the resources needed to mount a defense. Frankly, Luke, I look at you and I'm not hopeful."

"Thanks. I appreciate the vote of confidence."

Sam shrugged. "Just saying. I just think you should know the fate of your entire planet, and everyone on it, is resting on your shoulders. But no pressure."

"And what if I say I'm the wrong guy? What if I say no."

"Then I really do push that detonator button, and your head really does explode."

Luke rocked back, aghast.

Sam slapped the table and guffawed. It was a long, rolling laugh that left tears streaming down his cheeks. "Man, that never gets old. You should see your face." He sat there chuckling to himself.

"Would you stop that!" Luke hissed angrily.

"I don't know, man. When are you going to stop being such a sucker?"

"I won't help if you keep dicking around. How am I supposed to save the world when all I've got is you and your juvenile sense of humor?"

Still smiling to himself, Sam leaned forward with a confident expression. "Relax. Like I said, we're going to give you all the resources you need. For argument's sake, let's assume you have unlimited money. You don't, by the way, but for your purposes, it should be close enough. What would be the first step?"

Luke paused and looked thoughtful. "Okay. You're saying don't trust the government."

Sam shook his head. "Nope."

"Well, then. I need to create my own organization. I assume you're going to give me the technology I need?"

Sam nodded.

"If I need to keep the government out, I should set up operations that are beyond government interference. Otherwise people will find out. It'll be impossible to keep a lid on the technology. The feds would be all over it. Wouldn't you think?"

"That's a reasonable assumption," Sam agreed.

"If the solution is a space-based force, I'd set up operations in space. Maybe on the moon to start. If you can't give me that much of a head start, then I don't know."

Sam leaned back and for the first time since Luke had met him, looked surprised. "I'll never understand how they do it, but maybe they're right. You might actually be the right guy."

# # #

Sam pointed at the third door in the row of storage units. Luke stopped the pickup and killed the engine. "This is the one?"

"Supposed to be. I rented unit twenty-three. It's keyed to your thumbprint."

"How did you... Never mind." If Sam could fly in from outer space, then getting Luke's thumbprint probably didn't rate that high on the difficulty scale.

Luke got out and approached the roll-up door warily. Sam's idea of humor would be to fill the inside with starving Dobermans. Luke pressed his thumb to the strange lock and it clicked open. He removed the lock from the handle guard and lifted the roll-up door. Nope, not Dobermans. It was much worse. He counted sixty pallets stacked with what appeared to be solid gold bars.

Sam joined him at his side. "This is the financial resource I was talking about. It's not unlimited as you can see, but this should get you started."

Luke frantically scanned the driveway hoping no one was looking. "This has to be a couple hundred million dollars," he said.

"Closer to two billion."

"You didn't think it was a problem storing that much gold here?"

"Don't worry," Same said. "I paid the rent through the end of the year."

Luke sighed heavily and closed up the unit. With the door securely locked, *such as it is*, he got in his pickup. "You have anything else to help me get started?" he asked worriedly.

"I saved the best for last. Let's head back to the hangar."

Luke examined the spacecraft skeptically. "You want me to fly this thing? Without any training?"

"I think you can handle it," Sam replied. "It's got an autopilot system that makes it fairly easy. Kind of what you would call cruise control."

Luke pushed the Open Door button on the key fob. The lights flashed, the canopy disappeared, and the fuselage door slid open. *This thing is exactly like a minivan.*

"Watch your head," Sam advised as they boarded the shuttle.

Inside, it was much wider and more spacious than Luke would have guessed. He had expected the main fuselage to be filled with engines and fuel tanks. He asked Sam about it.

"Good question," Sam replied. "Look there." He pointed to a series of wide, lightly colored circles on the underwing. Those provide lift. You'll find bigger ones on the back end. Essentially, they generate anti-gravity; we call them gravity drives. You'll learn more about that later." He gestured toward the front.

The cockpit included a control panel across the front and a center console between two comfortable captain's chairs. Outboard panels ran along either side.

"Where do I sit?" Luke asked. "Left side or right?"

"You can control the shuttle from either position, but custom dictates that the pilot sits on the left."

Luke took his place and Sam slid into the co-pilot's seat. In a slightly louder voice Sam said, "Full instrumentation."

The control panel came to life with cockpit instrumentation that was at the same time familiar and yet far advanced beyond Luke's experience. The last military jet he flew had a *glass cockpit*, meaning the displays and controls were programmed into the aircraft's display panels. The functions changed dynamically depending on the activity at the moment.

"Most of this will become obvious as we go," Sam explained. "If you have a question, just ask. This is *Sadie*, by the way." He gestured to the shuttle in general. "She'll answer your questions and keep you out of trouble."

"What's that?" Luke replied, pointing to a dark stripe on the left of the main control panel.

"Throttle," said a light, feminine voice. "Non-linear input."

"See what I mean?" Sam said. "*Sadie* knows everything." He indicated a joystick on the center console. "Up, down, left, right. Just like you're used to. There on your left, is hover control. Zero to twenty feet. Let's go." He pointed to a green circle displayed on the front panel and touched it with his fingertip. A low *hum* started and the shuttle said, "Ready for flight."

Luke brought the spacecraft into the air with the hover control and then slid the throttle forward infinitesimally. As he did the dark stripe turned bright green under his fingertips. The shuttle responded and hover-taxied out of the hangar.

"You don't really need the runway," Sam said. "Just pull back on the stick and give it some gas. *Sadie* will compensate for everything as necessary."

Luke eased the joystick backwards until the nose was thirty degrees up. He slid the throttle forward to max but the green stripe stopped halfway.

"Requested power exceeds recommended speed for atmospheric flight," *Sadie* advised.

Sam smiled. "See? She'll take care of you until you get the hang of it."

Outside the view was spectacular. The ground fell away faster than he had ever seen while flying for the military. In the F-35, it was routine to peg out the vertical velocity indicator at thirty thousand feet per minute but he was far beyond that now. As they climbed, the sky turned a dark shade of blue and the curvature of the earth replaced the flat horizon. In less than a minute, they were above the atmosphere.

"Okay, let's head toward the moon," Sam suggested. "Do you know where it is?"

"It's late afternoon, so it should be rising in the east." Luke rolled the spacecraft to the right and pulled the nose across the horizon. The terminator was already crossing the Atlantic coastline. The moon came into view, brilliant against the dark black of space.

As they rolled out, Luke pushed the throttle up. Once again the green stripe stopped moving.

"Exceeding light speed not recommended inside a lunar orbit," *Sadie* cautioned.

Luke looked at Sam with a surprised expression. "Seriously? Faster than light? This thing can go that fast?"

Sadie sounded affronted. "I'm not a *thing,* Mr. Blackburn. Light speed is not safe in a crowded orbit. And please direct questions concerning flight parameters to me, not to your passenger."

Sam gave Luke a knowing wink. "Sorry, *Sadie*. My fault for not briefing him about you in more detail. Take us off manual control and set us down inside the Moonbase hangar, would you?"

"Course set," *Sadie* replied.

"You can practice manual flight later," Sam said to Luke. "I just wanted you to see how it works. Normally, you tell *Sadie* where you're headed and she'll take care of it. Questions so far?"

About a million, Luke thought as the spacecraft rapidly approached the moon. "What about g-forces?" he asked. "I didn't feel any acceleration."

"Gravity plates inside the floors and walls. Creates a sort of null-gee environment. *Sadie* takes care of that too so we don't get squished."

"What about warp drive, *Sadie?* You actually fly at warp?"

Luke could have sworn he heard the shuttle sigh. "There is no such thing as *warp drive,* as indicated in your question," she answered. "Your reference to warp drive is merely a concept for fictional entertainment on your planet. The fact is we simply accelerate as necessary to arrive at our destination as quickly as possible. Once outside the planetary orbit, this normally involves some multiple of light speed."

"But traveling faster than light is impossible," Luke argued.

"Perhaps for you," *Sadie* countered. "Not for me."

Sam intervened. "Luke, the so-called barrier of the speed of light is like all the other artificial barriers your population has invented. You probably know that scientists on your planet said early train travel at twenty miles an hour would put too much stress on the human body to survive. Then it was the sound barrier, etcetera. On its own, yes, light has a certain limit, just like sound. But what do you think happens if you accelerate to the speed of light and just keep accelerating? You go faster, that's all. Acceleration is the only limiting factor to speed. *Sadie,* what's our acceleration right now?"

"In terms of local reference, our maximum acceleration for this flight was approximately fifty gravities. However, we passed the acceleration phase several minutes ago and are now decelerating."

The forces at play were staggering. The technology to control those forces was inconceivable, let alone to do it in a shirt-sleeve environment.

"I don't understand how this can possibly work," Luke said.

Sam waved dismissively. "I'm a PR guy, Luke, not a scientist. *Sadie* can fill you in if you're that interested. But for now, we're almost there."

Luke turned his attention to the view outside. The spacecraft slowed as it neared the moon's surface. They descended into a wide crater at least twenty miles across. The bottom was flat and pockmarked with hundreds of small impact points. The crater had high, steep walls. In the shadow of the eastern wall a lighted rectangle opened to a hangar carved out of solid rock. It was six times the size of the hangar they had left in Baggs.

Sadie pulled inside and rotated slowly so her nose was facing out before settling to the floor. "Arriving at Moonbase One," she said softly. The canopy disappeared and the fuselage doors opened.

Outside the spacecraft, Luke pointed at the hangar opening. The doors remained wide open and the view of the crater outside was breathtaking. "Air?" Luke asked.

"Force fields keep the air in," Sam explained, pointing at green lights mounted around the opening. "They're a variation on the gravity plates. The floor is just a big gravity plate. You may have noticed we're still at one gee."

The hangar contained other spacecraft: a one-man flitter, another shuttle the same size as *Sadie*, and one much larger.

"That small shuttle is mine," Sam said. "And that big one is for moving cargo. He's *Thomas*. Come on, follow me."

A short hallway at the far side of the hangar opened into a large, curved foyer. It was like a food court in a shopping mall. Several small booths were built into the curved walls and the interior was filled with break-room-style tables and chairs.

Beyond the foyer were more hallways and rooms. Several rooms were filled with construction tools.

Sam explained. "So far, I've put enough of this base together to get you started. You've got living arrangements for about fifty people, a few offices, some work areas, and a training room. I'll show you how it works."

Within the hour Luke was cutting new corridors into solid rock. Sam explained the cutting tools were basic matter converters. Where the cutting blade touched the lunar rock, it collapsed to a substance harder than steel. The resulting material served to cover the floors, ceiling, and walls. Different settings gave it a smooth or rough finish. The implements built gravity controls right into the floors. The result was a one-gee environment throughout the base.

After Luke added a new corridor and two rooms to the base complex, Sam pronounced his instruction was complete. "Let's head over to the training room," he said.

The multi-level room had rows of chairs on stair-step floors. It looked like a college classroom. A podium rested on a small stage.

"There's someone I want you to meet," Sam said. "*George?*"

"Yes, Sam," a pleasant baritone voice replied. "I take it this is Luke."

"He's the guy. Luke, say hello to George. Sort of a *Sadie* on steroids. George runs everything here at Moonbase One. Consider him a gift from the Nobility to your solar system."

"The Nobility? What's that?"

"*The* Nobility," Sam emphasized. "The rulers, the royals, our divine leaders, whatever you want to call them. Once you get away from the galactic center, they're just known as the Nobility. Essentially, it's the ruling families. Kind of hard to explain, but I work for them."

"Am I working for them?"

"Don't make it more complicated than it is," Sam cautioned. "To answer your question, no. I doubt you'll ever see them or hear from them again. As I said, I'm here to do a bit of lawn maintenance. You're the weed-killer, and George here is your instruction manual. He's the guardian of all the knowledge I'm leaving with you. As you bring new people here, I'd recommend you let George give them an introductory course. You ought to take it yourself before you get into this much further."

"I will," Luke agreed.

"Say hello, George," Sam instructed.

"Good evening, Luke," George said. His warm voice emanated from the ceiling and filled the room.

"Nice to meet you, George," Luke offered weakly.

"I assure you it is my pleasure. I look forward to working with you, sir."

"Come on," Sam urged. "Let's keep moving. One more thing you need to see."

In the food court, Sam waved Luke over to the stalls against the curved wall. A microwave rested on the counter.

"Cheeseburger and fries," Sam said aloud. Seconds later, a fully laden plate appeared behind the glassed door.

"*Preparation complete*," a female voice said.

"It's a replicator?" Luke asked.

"No, not really. That's another reference to one of your fictional programs, right? I'd say it's more of what you call a 3-D printer. It uses micro-gravity emitters to rearrange molecules in layers. But you can call it a 'replicator' if that's what you like." Sam grinned as he removed the hot burger. "Here you go."

"I'm not really hungry," Luke replied.

"Suit yourself. You might notice it looks like the burger we got in the diner. There's a reason for that. Remember when I took a picture of it? That wasn't a camera. Here."

Sam handed Luke a flat, plastic rectangle about a quarter-inch thick. It looked like a cell phone without the glass.

"What's this?" Luke asked.

"That's a hand-scanner. It records the substance of whatever you scan. Once it's scanned, George will incorporate it into the database, and after that it will be available to anyone here in Moonbase."

"Seriously? Do you have any idea what this could do for our world?

Sam put a hand on Luke's shoulder. "Yes I do," Sam said grimly. "Word of warning: do *not*... repeat... *do not* under any circumstances let this technology loose on your planet. This one thing alone will destroy your civilization. As far as that goes, any of these toys I've shown you today could do it, but the replicator, as you call it, will do it faster than anything else."

"Why is that? This could free mankind from hunger."

Sam waved away the question. "I'm a PR guy, not an anthropologist. Just trust me on this. George can give you proof if you need it." Sam headed back toward the hangar. Luke had to walk quickly to keep up.

Inside the hangar, Sam stopped next to one of the shuttles and pointed. "See that red line on the floor?"

"Yeah."

"That's an industrial size replicator. Keep people out of it. George?"

"Yes, Sam."

"I'm taking my shuttle. Can you give Luke a replacement? I want him to have at least two shuttles after I take *Lucy*."

"Certainly, Sam. Have a good trip."

A warning horn sounded and red lights flashed along the walls next to the indicated area. The air shimmered and a shuttle began to appear. The shape solidified and after two minutes the flashing lights and warning horn stopped.

"Fabrication complete," George announced quietly. "This is *Duffy*."

The small shuttle looked exactly like *Sadie*.

"Okay," Sam announced. He reached out and shook Luke's hand. "I think I've covered everything. George, you take care of Luke and answer any other questions."

"I will, Sam."

"Wait a second," Luke shouted. "What are you talking about? You're leaving?"

"Gotta run, buddy. This ain't the only star system that needs saving."

"You said you'd be here for weeks! I just met you today."

"Hey, who do you think built this Moonbase? These things don't happen by themselves. A little gratitude would be nice." Sam spoke to his shuttle, "*Lucy*, open up. We're leaving."

"Ready to go, Sam," *Lucy* replied.

The door opened and Sam stepped into the cargo bay. He looked back at Luke. "Good luck, kid. Knock 'em dead. I'm counting on you." Sam waved good-bye as the cargo door closed, hiding his smiling face within.

Luke's protestations went unheard as the shuttle lifted up and zoomed out of the hangar and up into space. He watched the spacecraft disappear into the distance, a fading dot that vanished all too soon.

"Transfer of authority complete," said George. "Welcome, Commander Blackburn. Bakkui invasion five years away and counting. What are your orders?"

"Five years? Sam said it was ten years at the earliest."

"Please accept my apologies, Commander. Sam is a PR guy, not a military strategist. He is known to exaggerate quite frequently."

Luke clinched his fists in frustration. "Of course. Why am I even surprised?" Luke walked slowly back toward the food court, lost in thought. The task set before him was unbelievably staggering. His mind whirled dizzily as he sorted through the permutations. *Maybe I've just gone insane. That would be nice.* It would be easier to accept, certainly, and probably a lot less stressful.

A quiet voice spoke in the back of his mind. *No, Commander. You are not insane.* Luke realized with a start that it was George.

"Do we have telepathy or something?" Luke asked aloud.

Not as such, Commander. But I wanted you to be aware that we can communicate directly. Simply speak to me as though we are in a room together. Even if you are on Earth, I will receive that communication.

"Sounds a lot like telepathy," Luke observed. *Can you hear me now?*

"Loud and clear, Commander," George responded verbally.

Not sure I like this, Luke thought. He threw the cheeseburger and fries, already cold, into an opening that looked like a trash receptacle built into the counter. A momentary *buzz* and flash of light from within seemed to confirm his theory.

"Give me a beer," he said to the replicator.

"*That object is not programmed,*" the tinny voice replied.

"What *do* you have programmed?"

"*Cheeseburger and fries are the only items in inventory.*"

"Figures."

"*That object is not programmed.*"

"Never mind."

"*That object is not programmed.*"

There were obviously varying levels of AI. Luke returned to his shuttle.

"Hey, *Sadie.*"

"Yes, Commander?"

"Can you take me back to the hangar in Baggs?"

"Of course, Commander."

"You know, I haven't filed a flight plan or anything. Will they see us coming? Do I need to worry about getting shot down?"

"Not at all, Commander. I promise that detection by your planetary authorities will never be a problem while you're with me."

Luke sat down in the pilot's seat. "Okay, then, I'm ready. Let's go home."

"Course set." *Sadie* closed up the shuttle, lifted off, and flew into the moon's night sky.

Chapter 2

Day 2—Population 1

"You okay, Luke?" Rosanne asked. "Luke!"

Jolted out of his reverie, Luke nodded at the coffee pot she was offering. "Thanks, Rosanne."

"Don't worry about it so much. Nobody expects you to win a big grant every year. You look like you got the weight of the world on your shoulders."

"Funny you should say that. This morning, that's exactly how I feel." The night before, Luke had arrived back at the airport after dark. He'd gone straight to his house and turned in.

"Well, ease up, hon. You moved here to get away from that kind of stress." Rosanne glanced at the other end of the diner's countertop. "I wish *that* one would just stay here and settle down."

Luke followed her gaze toward the pony-tailed blonde. Annie something or other. She was wearing leggings, running shoes, and a colorful T-shirt under a fleece hoodie. The girl had moved back to town a few months ago to take care of her grandmother. Luke knew the older woman only as Mrs. Vasquez, and that she had passed away last week. Luke had gone to the funeral, but other than offering condolences, he hadn't spoken to the grieving teenager.

"Not many jobs around here, Rosanne," Luke offered.

"I know, but I doubt that Royal Deutsche outfit really appreciates her."

Luke perked up. "You mean Royal Deutsche Banque? How old is she? She looks twelve."

"Let me see," Rosanne ruminated. "Her birthday is in March. She's older than my grandson. Harry is twenty-eight or twenty-nine, I think. I just can't remember."

Luke marveled, not for the first time, how Rosanne knew so much about everyone in this town. He wondered how long before she knew about *Sadie*.

As if sensing his mood, Rosanne pried into his thoughts. "Where's your funny-talking friend this morning, anyway? What was that language he was speaking? You two were getting on like a house afire."

"I'm afraid he's moved on, Roseanne. Believe me, I tried to get him to stay. You said Annie worked at Royal Deutsche? What'd she do there?"

"I dunno. She got registered as a CPA in Reno. I remember when she used to study all the time for that test. But back east she does something in precious metals? Broker?"

Luke's interest in the young lady skyrocketed. He picked up his coffee and moved two stools down from Annie.

"Morning, Annie. Sorry about your grandma."

She gave him a half smile. "Morning, Mr. Blackburn. Thanks. And thanks for coming to the funeral."

"Of course. Say, Rosanne said you work for Royal Deutsche Banque."

"Worked, past tense. I had to quit to take care of Grandma. I don't know if they'll hire me back."

"So you're looking for a job? Rosanne mentioned you're a CPA in the precious metals division."

Annie gave him a skeptical look. "Why, Mr. Blackburn? You have some precious metals you want moved?"

Luke held up his hands to show he meant no offense. "I'm actually looking for a CPA."

"I can give you a couple of names. Mr. Ortiz down the road could probably use some extra work."

"A background in precious metals would be a big plus."

Annie squinted at him distrustfully. "Seriously? I know you've gotten some grants at the airport, but I understand that Mrs. Cummings is not making much money. As I hear it, she's out there about forty hours a week and getting paid for a *lot* less. I'm looking for a *real* job."

Luke's cheeks grew hot, and he felt unaccountably embarrassed. The little female sitting at the counter was not much over five feet. In the past her comments would have bounced off his rough exterior, but after yesterday's events, he felt more vulnerable than in his entire life.

He was desperate for help but unsure how to move forward. Anything he did might entail some unforgivable mistake that would doom humanity. The realization made him angry. Not at anyone in particular, but at the situation, and for sure, he was plenty mad at Sam.

"I would... Sorry, I don't know your last name."

"Daniels."

"Miss Daniels. I would say Linda's decision on how much time she spends at the airport is her business. She understands the circumstances of my limited ability to provide her with income and has always, at least to my knowledge, been quite satisfied.

"Regarding my current personnel requirements, it is possible that the right person would put me in a position to do a little more for the town in general and Linda in particular. If you're not interested, not a problem."

The silence between them lasted only seconds before it was broken by the irrepressible Rosanne. "Annabelle Theodora Daniels! Why are you giving Mr. Luke a hard time? He's offering you a job, girl. Just yesterday you were in here whining about how you hate the thought of going back to that Deutsche Banque outfit. What's the matter with you?"

The change in Annie's demeanor was dramatic. She was no longer a strong woman but a reprimanded adolescent.

"Sorry, Mr. Blackburn," she said meekly. "I guess I'm a bit touchy because of Grandma. I would be happy to know more about your position." She looked over at Rosanne for approval.

The ice was broken and everyone stopped frowning. Luke paid for both of their breakfasts and asked Annie to accompany him to the airport with a quick stop at the local You-Lock-It storage place on Main Street.

"She would *love* to," Rosanne answered forcefully.

###

Luke stood in front of unit 23 and checked both ways. With no one in sight he unlocked the clasp and lifted up the door.

Annie gasped when she saw the stacks of gold bars. She gave Luke a blank stare for several seconds and then turned back to the interior of the garage unit. Luke saw that she was counting the pallets.

"Jesus H. Christ," she whispered. "You have this much gold and you're keeping it in a storage unit? Are you insane?"

"I keep it locked," Luke replied weakly.

"Well thank God for small favors." She looked at the gleaming metal for a bit longer and then faced Luke. "Listen. Really. Thanks. I just... I'm only thirty-three years old and I don't want to spend my life in prison. I'm not going to get involved in anything that's illegal so why don't you close the door and I'll go back to Chicago? We'll pretend this never happened."

Luke could see the growing fear in her expression. She was creating all sorts of improbable scenarios about how he had acquired so much gold. And all of her suspicions were off the mark.

"Hang on," he urged. "First, I promise you that there's nothing illegal here that I know of. This came into my possession yesterday. If I prove to you that everything here is kosher, will you at least listen?"

"I can't imagine how *anyone* can *legally* have two billion dollars of gold in a storage unit."

"Five minutes," Luke insisted. "Just give me five minutes, and if you're not convinced, then fine; go back to Chicago or wherever you want. I'm as worried about this as you are, but I don't know what to do."

While Annie was thinking about his response, Luke locked up the gold and opened the pickup's passenger door. "Five minutes," he said again. "Just a trip out to the airport and I promise you will understand."

She got into the pickup but never took her eyes off of him. He could almost see her mind spinning, trying to decide if she should scream or run, or both.

Luke drove straight to the hangar and escorted her inside. He pulled out the key fob for the little spacecraft and opened the side door. The flashing lights and sliding door gave her a bit of reassurance. *Everyone feels safe around a minivan*, he thought. "Go on in and take a seat. I'll open the hangar."

"Where are we going?" she asked, looking at the shuttle suspiciously. It was obvious she was not familiar with the aviation industry. Anyone with a pilot's license could have told her the shuttle wasn't from this planet.

"I want to show you where the gold came from."

"Is it a hidden mine or something? Is that what you found?"

"Sort of."

He coaxed her into the shuttle and got her situated in the co-pilot's seat.

"You sure it's okay if I sit here?" she wanted to know. "I'm not a pilot or anything."

"It's not a problem, I promise. *Sadie*, could you take us to Moonbase One, please?"

"Course set," *Sadie* answered, sounding smug as Annie's eyes grew wide.

Same Day—Population 2

Luke gave Annie a moment to adjust while they stood in the center of the Moonbase hangar. He wondered if he'd had the same look yesterday.

During the thirty-minute flight to the moon he briefly explained what he'd learned from Sam. She didn't argue with him, just looked at everything with an awed expression. Luke knew how she felt.

After they touched down inside the hangar *Sadie* opened a panel on the side console and instructed Luke to take the enclosed earpiece. It was identical to the one Sam had given him. "Take her to the training room before you give her that," *Sadie* recommended.

A quick tour through the Moonbase ended at the training room. Luke felt uncomfortable for what was about to follow.

"Annie, I'm going to introduce you to George. He's a computer that runs the place for us. George, this is Annie Daniels. She's our…uh…new finance director."

"Have you given her the translation device?" George asked.

"Not yet," Luke replied.

"Not yet, what?" Annie asked. "What was that voice?"

Luke handed her the earpiece. "That was George. This might hurt a little, but after you put this in your ear you'll be able to understand what George is saying."

"Like a universal translator? Like on *Star Trek*?" She looked eager.

"Yeah. Kind of like that."

"Okay." Without hesitation Annie took the device and stuck it into her ear.

Luke winced, feeling guilty. The pain he'd been hit with yesterday was no joke.

After a few seconds she smiled. "Whoa! That was weird. I can't even feel it now."

"Really?" Luke was glad but astonished. "That's it? It didn't hurt even a little?" It didn't seem quite fair that his transition was so painful.

"Nope, not at all."

"George, why was that?" Luke asked the ceiling.

"Miss Daniels experienced a normal transition, Commander. *Sadie* had the opportunity to examine her more closely during the flight here. Accordingly, she was able to adapt the device more specifically to her needs."

"Is that George?" Annie asked excitedly. "He's the one you were talking about?"

Luke nodded. "That's right."

"Hi, George. I'm Annie Daniels. Nice to meet you."

"My pleasure Miss Daniels. Welcome to Moonbase One."

"Thank you, George. Please call me Annie." She gave Luke a questioning glance. "He doesn't speak English?"

"Not so far," Luke said.

"George? Could you speak English for us?"

"Of course, Annie," George replied with a Midwestern accent. "If that is what you prefer I would be happy to do so."

"That would be best. So you gave Mr. Blackburn all that gold?"

"Indirectly, that's true. Sam was the one that provided it, locally. But it was my determination that bullion is a suitable currency in your culture."

Annie threw Luke a tentative glance. "Yeah, bit of a problem the way you did it, but I think I can sort it out; now that I know what's going on."

"Seriously?" Luke asked. "So, I take it you're in?"

Annie smiled, brimming with excitement. "Are you kidding? This is a whole lot cooler than working with those guys at Royal Deutsche. Why does George call you Commander?"

"I'm kind of afraid to ask. He started that once Sam left."

"George?" Annie asked. "What's up?"

"Annie, Commander Blackburn is the senior military officer for Earth's Planetary Defense Force. His mission is to develop space travel for your people, establish ties with potential allies in this part of the galaxy, build a suitable force to meet the alien invasion, and then engage and defeat that enemy."

"Cool." Annie looked at Luke expectantly. "So, what's next?"

Luke was astounded by her unruffled acceptance of the situation. Was it the naïveté of youth or an incredibly adaptable mind? It didn't matter. At least he had a partner.

"I need money I can spend," he answered.

"I can handle that. It'll take a few weeks. I think it would be smart if you have a corporate structure; easier to keep it legal. There'll be a lot of paperwork to create the necessary shell companies. I assume you want me to handle the details?"

"Absolutely. It's your baby. Do whatever you need and keep me in the loop."

Two months later Luke sat behind his office desk at the Baggs' airport and watched Annie disembark the chartered Gulfstream 450. She thanked the crew and walked toward the terminal. She looked a lot different these days, at least outwardly. The running outfit was gone; in its place was something chic from Burberry.

In the past few weeks she had worked wonders. The first day following their trip to the moon she had Luke load twenty of the gold bars onto the floorboard in the back seat of his pickup.

"JP Morgan in Seattle has a concierge banking service for all the dot.com millionaires," she explained. "They're used to dealing with newly-rich young people. These bars will establish my credentials. After that, they'll take care of the rest." She covered the bars with a blanket, took his pickup key and drove off.

She was right. As she explained on her return, "When you put five hundred pounds of gold on a banker's desk, they get interested *really* fast." Once their account was opened, Annie visited the Seattle branch of the law firm Hawley, Hepworth & Kidwell. By the time she got back from her first trip, she had created a new corporate entity, Professional Design Engineering Firm, LLC. She even had a logo created. It was a blue globe on a black background overlaid with a hand grasping several drawing pencils. The corporate name was inscribed below the globe. The acronym, PDEF, was printed across the top.

"This is just subterfuge, though," she explained. "The parent company is the real PDEF. Here's that logo." It was the same graphic except the hand had been replaced by a mailed fist grasping bright yellow lightning bolts. The name at the bottom was Planetary Defense, Inc.

"Remember?" she asked. "George said you were the commander for Earth's planetary defense." She laughed delightedly at his approval of her ideas.

While Annie was arranging their finances, Luke spent his time on two tasks. The first was fairly ridiculous. He visited every restaurant in Reno and Las Vegas, both plain and fancy, and ordered everything on their menus. He told the various food service employees that he was photographing all the dishes for a glossy new publication. The waiters didn't really care; he tipped well so they were satisfied.

In reality, Luke was using the hand-scanner from Sam to add each menu item to the replicator database.

Although he felt absurd going about the task, he knew that failing to provide appetizing meals would be cause for mutiny. He had eaten enough MREs over the years to understand that a varied and pleasing cuisine was crucial for the long-term satisfaction of remotely stationed employees. By the time he finished, the moon's replicator food menu was more than respectable.

When not visiting restaurants, he worked with a marketing agency in Seattle to develop a corporate website for PDEF, complete with photos of Moonbase's residential accommodations and stock images of smiling, happy families. The website described exciting research projects with descriptive language like *for the good of all mankind*, and *career growth opportunities*. It never revealed the location of such supposed labs. Instead the advertisements admitted that it was in a remote and harsh environment. The layout contained several outdoor, snow-covered landscapes, deceptively hinting that the Antarctic was the likely location.

Annie looked exhausted when she walked into the office. "It's all done," she announced. "PDEF has a net worth of two billion dollars. Lots of unasked questions but bankers at this level are used to keeping things discreet."

"Good job," Luke replied. "I know you'd like some rest but are you ready for some grunt work? It's a little more basic than all the high finance you've been doing."

"As long as I don't have to wear this business suit anymore, I'm in."

Her new task was purchasing. The hand-scanner worked fine for food, but not for complex hard goods. Luke wanted her to buy one of everything necessary to supply the Moonbase and then transport the goods to where George had sophisticated scanning tools. Once scanned, each item would be permanently available in the replicator inventory.

Luke's plan was to furnish several of the living quarters to function as model homes. It would give the soon-to-be residents a head start in creating their new lives on the moon.

"Can you take care of this for me?" Luke asked.

"You kidding? You're asking a woman if she has a problem with shopping? I will handle this. What's *your* next project?"

"We need a chief of operations for Moonbase. Before we begin recruiting large numbers of people, we have to have someone who can keep everything running. My last boss was a colonel in the air force. Doctor Roth Higgins; he has a PhD in physics. He always thought of himself as a scientist. I felt the military was something he did to stay around leading-edge tech. Last I heard he was working at UNLV. I bet he would be open to what we have to offer."

"Sounds like the guy."

"He's gotta be in his sixties, though. I'm hoping he still has some of the adventurous spirit that some of the old service guys have."

"Like you?"

Luke chuckled at the thought. "Not at all. The only thing I want is a small office with no responsibility. Then I can hang out and have a beer now and then."

"Is that what you call what we're working on, saving mankind from a massive alien invasion?"

"Well, I'm keeping my fingers crossed. I don't really see me becoming some kind of interstellar warlord. If we can just get this thing working, it should take on a life of its own."

Annie shook her head skeptically. "So when are you leaving?"

"Next Monday. I called and got an appointment with him. I'll go down on the Gulfstream."

Annie glanced out the window at the luxury aircraft sitting on the tarmac. The pilot was walking around the jet, giving it a visual inspection before taking off once again. "I could get really spoiled flying on that thing," she admitted.

"More so than with *Sadie*?"

"*Sadie* won't let me drink alcohol. *They* give me wine coolers."

"She probably thinks you're too young for booze."

"Oh, right. Should I start calling you Grandfather?"

Luke smiled at his young colleague. He did think of her as a youngster and hoped he hadn't made it too obvious. "If this works out, I'll be back the same day."

#

Luke was surprised by how much Roth had aged. He seemed a bit smaller than Luke remembered. His hair was thinner and had gone completely white. But his eyes were bright as ever and the friendly smile was just as broad. Books were stacked everywhere around his office. The floor-to-ceiling bookcases behind Roth's desk were stuffed with manuscripts, thick tomes, and documents of all kinds. One side of the small room was paneled with four-by-eight-foot dry erase boards filled with colorful notes and diagrams.

"I like your place here, Colonel," Luke said affably, admiring the academic's office. He sat across from his old mentor. In their first assignment together, Roth had been Luke's instructor pilot.

"Thanks, Luke. But nobody calls me colonel anymore, and frankly, I prefer it that way."

"So what do they call you? Professor? Doctor Higgins?"

"The students feel obligated to use *Doctor*. But why don't you and I stick with Roth? So what brings you here? Just passing through or did you get hit by a wave of nostalgia? I wouldn't have thought that of you."

Luke shrugged as if uncertain how to start. *Might as well plunge right in.* "Frankly, it's a job opportunity."

"Oh? Okay." Roth nodded. "You need a recommendation or something? That's not a problem."

Luke smiled at the misconception. "No, but I appreciate the thought. I meant this is an opportunity for *you*. It's science oriented. I guess you could say it involves space science. I'd like to show it to you today, if you have time."

Roth was surprised. "For me? No. Thanks anyway, Luke. I'm perfectly comfortable here. My schedule is accommodating and on weekends I've got a fishing boat I can take out to Lake Mead. I'm not interested in starting a new career."

"Understood. I figured that's what you'd say. I felt exactly the same until recently. This gig was sort of pushed into my lap. Before this I was the airport director up in Baggs. You know Baggs?"

"Couple of hours east of Reno, isn't it? You drive down here to see me?"

"That's it. Small town. But I didn't drive. I came down here in a Gulfstream 450. Helps take the sting out of travel."

Roth smiled and sat back in his chair. "You trying to suck me in? I've been in executive jets before."

Luke grinned and leaned forward, his elbows on Roth's desk. "Yeah, I know. You used to fly around on those tiny Citations with some two-star. But not like this one. This is beyond first class.

Come on. At least let me show off a little. I'll have you back here tonight; I promise."

Roth chuckled. "You must have some fancy lab if you want me to see it that bad. You gotta understand, Luke; I'm not interested. I'll come take a look for old time's sake, but I'm telling you, nothing's going to impress me that much."

Day 61—Population 3

Luke watched the emotions play across Roth's face in the Moonbase One hangar. They had just gotten out of the shuttle and Luke knew from experience that Roth was still struggling to come to grips with everything he'd been told during the trip from Earth.

Roth looked at his watch. "I guess I was wrong about not being impressed," he whispered to himself. "Thirty-three minutes from takeoff. That's around five hundred thousand miles per hour." He gave Luke a quizzical glance. "So what do you have in mind? I haven't said yes, though, by the way. But this…"

Roth trailed off as Luke guided him through the food court toward the training room. A disheveled Annie met them coming the other way. She was pushing a huge stack of heavy furniture without apparent effort. Luke explained that sensors reversed the gravity under the pile of furnishings to slightly negative as Annie pushed it along and then changed it back to one gee once she passed.

"Hi," Annie greeted them cheerily. "Did he take your offer yet?"

"Not yet. Roth, this is my colleague, Annie Daniels. She's our finance director. We recruited her from Royal Deutsche Banque."

That wasn't strictly true, he'd recruited Annie from a cheap diner in Baggs, but a formal version might be more palatable for someone like Roth. Not that she looked much like a financier in her current condition.

"Please hurry and say yes, Professor. He won't hire anyone else until you're onboard. In the meantime, *I'm* doing all the grunt work." She didn't stop to chat further, just kept moving down the corridor.

The two men watched her retreating figure for a moment and then stared at each other, unsure what to say.

"Is she...?" Roth asked uncertainly.

"Totally off limits," Luke replied firmly before continuing to the training room.

"Okay." Roth nodded. "That's smart."

"Anyway." Luke broke the awkward silence. "You were the best boss I ever had. You've got the management skills to handle a big organization. You've got a scientific background. You are the perfect fit for this job and I can't tell you how critical it is that we get started."

"What's the job exactly?" Roth asked.

"Your job would be to run this place. I see it as a mirror to when you were a commander at Nellis. You brought their very first F-35 squadrons to mission ready status. That was a brand new fighter with technology most of us had never seen. Same thing here. You'll need a maintenance chief, engineers, logistics, and a personnel chief."

"How much of that is in place right now?" Roth asked.

"You, me and Annie."

Roth shook his head.

"This is the training room," Luke explained. "Let me introduce you to George. He's the resident AI. George, this is Dr. Roth Higgins."

"Good afternoon, Dr. Higgins."

Roth's eyebrows went up and he looked at Luke.

Luke waved any questions away. "I'm leaving you here for a few minutes. George is going to give you a thorough overview of what we're trying to accomplish. It's more understandable when you see his presentation. Ask him anything at any time."

Roth had a long discussion with George. Luke joined afterward to talk about the threat mankind was facing and the mammoth task in preparing to meet it. Two hours later the men departed Moonbase One for Baggs.

"I'll give the university a week's notice," Roth said.

"Perfect," Luke agreed. "That will give you enough time to spread the word about the great job opportunities in PDEF. We start advertising this weekend. The public pitch is that we're building a new research facility in an undisclosed location, one that's rough and inhospitable. We hint, but won't confirm, it's in the Antarctic. We encourage job seekers to bring their families. Other than that, all we promise is that it is a remote, extended duration contract where employees will be out of touch with people back home. No cell service at the South Pole…or here."

"When will you tell them what's really going on?"

"I won't. They'll figure it out when they get to Moonbase One."

"Kind of harsh, don't you think?" Roth asked.

"Not as harsh as having our planet blown away," Luke replied, putting that question firmly to rest. "Let me know if there is anybody in particular you want and I'll visit them in person."

"How will you review everyone? You're going to get thousands of resumes, you know. And most of them won't be accurate."

"I know," Luke said. "We contracted with NexGen Recruiting and other big headhunting firms. They've got systems in place to do that kind of screening. Annie had our attorneys customize their standard contracts. We established rewards for bringing in the right people and stiff penalties for giving us duds."

"I'd like to bring in Samantha Meyer," Roth suggested. "Last I heard she was the head of Space Systems in Denver. She's a real tiger and one of the brightest people I've ever met. And she'll know who else is a good fit."

"Let her know I'll be calling on her. If you can get me an appointment, even better. One more thing," Luke added.

"What's that?"

"Welcome aboard, Roth."

Samantha Meyer was an easy recruit. She'd crossed paths with Roth a decade earlier and her respect for the older gentleman rivaled Luke's own. She expected Luke's visit, having been prompted by Roth to accept a quick flight on the Gulfstream.

Once Samantha was on board she and Roth decided the next item on the to-do list was a construction crew. Once the recruitment process kicked into gear they would be bringing on hundreds of people a week. That meant building a host of facilities and everything that was part of constructing a small city. That including providing homes for everyone to live in.

Samantha sent Luke after Ambrose Baker, the senior manager for engineering and construction at a large multi-national corporation. He, in turn, brought along structural engineers, architects, and an entire construction team. Luke promised the builders a full year contract, with options to stay longer if they wished.

Everyone hired had to sign an employment agreement acknowledging they would be out of touch for a full year.

Annie in particular breathed a huge sigh of relief when the construction crew showed up. She had been running ragged, furnishing all of the existing rooms. With the arrival of the construction team, Luke sent Annie back to Earth almost full time.

She flew to Seattle where she contracted with the international firm, Okada Accounting, to manage their payroll and other financials. Even if their employee's worldly needs were being supplied, wages still had to be deposited to real bank accounts. Talented scientists could be tempted by exciting research, but people wanted to know there was a paycheck somewhere.

Luke didn't want Annie getting bogged down with accounting and auditing requirements. She complained that she could handle those activities; she was an accountant, after all. Her complaints vanished when he tasked her to oversee the infrastructure development of the Baggs airport, starting with a thousand-bed luxury hotel and convention center.

Luke hated to dump so much on her young shoulders, but her financial skills weren't necessary on the moon; money didn't exist at Moonbase. Instead, he needed a partner planetside who knew what was going on. Someone had to prepare for the day when the secret of Moonbase One's existence became public.

"It's going to happen at the end of the first year," he told her. "That's when the employment contracts start expiring."

Luke hoped most of their recruits would remain on the moon, but if even a few employees returned to their hometown, the word would be out. When that happened, he expected two significant events. First, he could openly recruit people to come work on the moon; and second, their growth would explode. They had to be ready for that growth. It meant infrastructure on the moon, of course, but it also meant preparing a base of operations Earthside. The airport at Baggs was going to be that base and Annie had to get it ready.

Chapter 3

Day 80—Population 27

"We don't have weapons?" Luke asked. It was an unsettling discovery.

"None at all," Lou Morrow admitted. Morrow had arrived the day before to oversee the fleet development for a new space navy.

Morrow was the second oldest guy on the moon, next to Roth. He had a grizzled look, earned from a lifetime of building mammoth seaworthy vessels. Samantha said that Morrow was the last true visionary when it came to shipbuilding. He was responsible for many of the advances built into new aircraft carriers and nuclear submarines

The morning after his arrival Morrow went to his new boss, Samantha, and insisted on having an emergency meeting with Luke. In turn Samantha pulled in her boss, Roth. They now sat at the small conference table in Luke's Moonbase office.

"But that's what you're going to build, right?" Luke asked. "You will meet our need for ships and weapons."

Morrow looked at the ceiling. "George, why don't you summarize what we talked about last night."

"Of course, Lou," George responded. "Commander, Mr. Morrow is referring to my lack of knowledge about weapons systems that are capable of mounting an effective strategic campaign against the alien advance."

"What do you mean, your *lack of knowledge*? If authorization is a problem, I'm authorizing you to tell him everything you know."

"Thank you, Commander," George replied. "That was assumed. His concern is that I have no knowledge of such weapons."

"Seriously? I mean you really have no such knowledge? Are you holding back? Is this a limitation imposed by the Nobility?"

"While that is a possibility, I think it improbable. If it is true, I'm not aware of the fact. Beyond that, if you're asking am I deliberately holding back information, I assure you that is not the case."

"Then how are we supposed to fight the aliens?"

"That, Commander, I do not know. I must confess I was curious about your plan."

Luke looked at Morrow. "Well, that sucks."

Morrow nodded sourly. "'Appears there's a lot you didn't tell me when I signed on with this outfit'," Lou quoted.

Luke was sympathetic. "Yeah, if you only knew. But that doesn't solve the problem. George, what would you suggest."

"I don't have any suggestions Commander Blackburn. Your planet's combat armaments would be ineffectual in a modern conflict."

"What about phasers and photon torpedoes and those sort of things?"

"Those are fictional concepts, Commander."

"Yeah, I know that. But can't you invent them or come up with something similar?"

"I apologize, Commander, but the concept of creativity is not in my programming. I can *assist* your scientists to the maximum of my ability, which is significant. But in any case, my conjecture is those types of weapons would be ineffectual in modern combat."

"Why is that?" Morrow asked.

George's voice took on the tone of a college professor. "Lou, my assumption is that you intend to use manned spacecraft to locate and engage the alien navy. But my current ability to detect Bakkui ships is non-existent. Certainly, my archives do not include details of any such contact. Without detection, targeting is impossible."

"This gets worse and worse," Morrow groused.

"Consider the following," George said. "To be useful in interplanetary combat, sensor technology must detect and identify combatants that are millions of miles away. This is due to the speed of spaceflight."

"Okay. Makes sense," Morrow admitted.

"I do not possess that ability. Further, my lack of sensor technology does not even address questions associated with offensive weapons. Will the engagements occur at light speed? If so, your so-called phaser blasts will be slower than your combat vessels."

"Luke," Morrow said somberly. "This is kind of a reality check for me. I'm not saying there's no answer, but right now, I'm not sure I even know what the questions are."

"What can I do?" Luke asked.

"I need scientists and theoreticians. And I need to know what limits I have regarding George."

"As far as George goes, you can't physically touch him, of course. But regarding access, he is totally available. George, you got any problem with that?"

"Not at all, Commander."

"No secrets? None at all?"

George replied after a several-millisecond pause, "None whatsoever, Commander."

"Good enough." Luke looked back at Morrow. "Regarding your scientists, how many?"

Morrow thought for a minute. "As many as you can get. We're in this for the long haul, and at the moment I can't even get my mind wrapped around the concepts. My first plan was to start designing ships. Get armed up and head out. And to a certain extent, that's still true. But actually, what I need even before that is knowledge. And I mean knowledge of all kinds. I guess we need a research center...or a university or something."

"Okay," Luke said. "Sounds like we need to flesh out our plan a bit." He paused for a moment and then brought up another topic he'd been wanting to talk about. "Don't forget, Lou. We're going to need a colony ship before the first warship. I'm thinking we can start small with Mars, use that as a training ground."

Morrow nodded but gave Samantha a look that screamed how overwhelmed he was feeling.

Luke looked across the table at Roth. "Let's let these people get back to work so you and I can talk."

###

"One more surprise," Roth said once Samantha and Morrow had departed.

"It's more than that," Luke responded. "That's an indicator of how much in the dark we are about everything. It suddenly occurs to me that all of our effort here is based on a single meeting I had with some alien prankster. Sam was more interested in practical jokes than anything else."

Roth didn't smile. "That's true."

"Looking back, I was so overwhelmed being on the moon that I just accepted everything he said. You were the same way, when you came up the first time."

Roth agreed. "It's easy to believe anything the first time you stand on the moon."

"That's my point," Luke emphasized. "Because the second Sam left, George reminded me that he wasn't trustworthy. Sam told me we had ten years and now George is saying we've got five years. Who is correct?"

"Even more to the point," Roth suggested, "is either one of them correct? For that matter, is there even a threat? Or is that something that your comedian just invented on his own?"

"George?" Luke asked. "Your thoughts?"

"Commander, your concerns are certainly valid. I can tell you that I, at least, am being truthful with you. Having said that, you have no proof of my veracity other than my own assurance. Regarding the invading force, allow me to explain."

"Go ahead."

"I believe the alien threat to be valid. My archives indicate the Nobility was certainly concerned; or at least as much as they could be, considering their situation."

"What does that mean?" Roth asked.

"The Nobility is an ancient civilization which maintains an absolute position atop a vast empire. However, armed forces and violence are not required to maintain their status. They are this galaxy's supreme masters of giving and withholding favors. The right word from the Nobility can provide one of their subjects with an enviable status that lasts for generations. By the same token, an intentional slight can result in shame so great that the subject is shunned by his family and closest acquaintances to the point that suicide is the only option."

"Some concepts are universal," Luke observed.

"Indeed," George agreed. "The fact is the alien threat was discovered eons ago. It was noted and orders were sent out to eradicate it. When that didn't happen, it became an annoyance, but not of any substance. Nevertheless, as a result of the annoyance, a program, of which Sam is a minor part, was initiated."

"And according to Sam, we're also part of that effort," Luke guessed.

"Exactly," George confirmed. "Originally, it was believed that thousands, if not millions, of years would pass before the invading force could threaten the center of the galaxy where the Nobility reigns. Even the word threaten is too strong a concept."

"So what's the worry then?" Morrow asked.

"I believe the time table should be revised, by how much I can't say. Regarding this star system where we're currently located, my estimate of five years is only that, an estimate. The limiting factor for my calculations is lack of knowledge."

"And how can we address that?" Luke asked.

"I don't know," George replied in what seemed a fatalistic manner.

"Drones," Roth said. "We need reconnaissance drones. Would that help?"

"Any information would be useful," George replied.

"Where should we send them?" Luke asked.

"Please examine the display." The wall of Luke's office turned black, overlaid by a depiction of the Milky Way galaxy. "You are here," George said as a white circle appeared around a dim star about half way along the Orion spiral arm.

"This was my last estimate of the alien dominion." A thick outline snaked across the galaxy spiral to the Perseus and Carina-Sagittarius spiral arms and inward, even touching the Crux-Scutum arm closer to the galaxy center. "By now the Bakkui could have increased or decreased their rate of expansion. Perhaps they shifted direction and advanced toward the galactic center, away from our location. The problem is that all of this is based on information that is extremely out of date."

Luke shook his head. "I'm not up on interstellar distances, George. How far away is the threat?"

"Approximately seventeen thousand parsecs, or about three hundred twenty-three quadrillion miles."

"George," Luke said drily. "That seems quite a far piece away. Why are we even talking about this?"

"It could be closer," George reminded him.

"Fair enough. Worst case then, how close could they be?"

"That is difficult to say. I hazard to say that worst case, they'll be here tomorrow. But realistically, my calculations make it possible for them to be as close as thirty quadrillion miles."

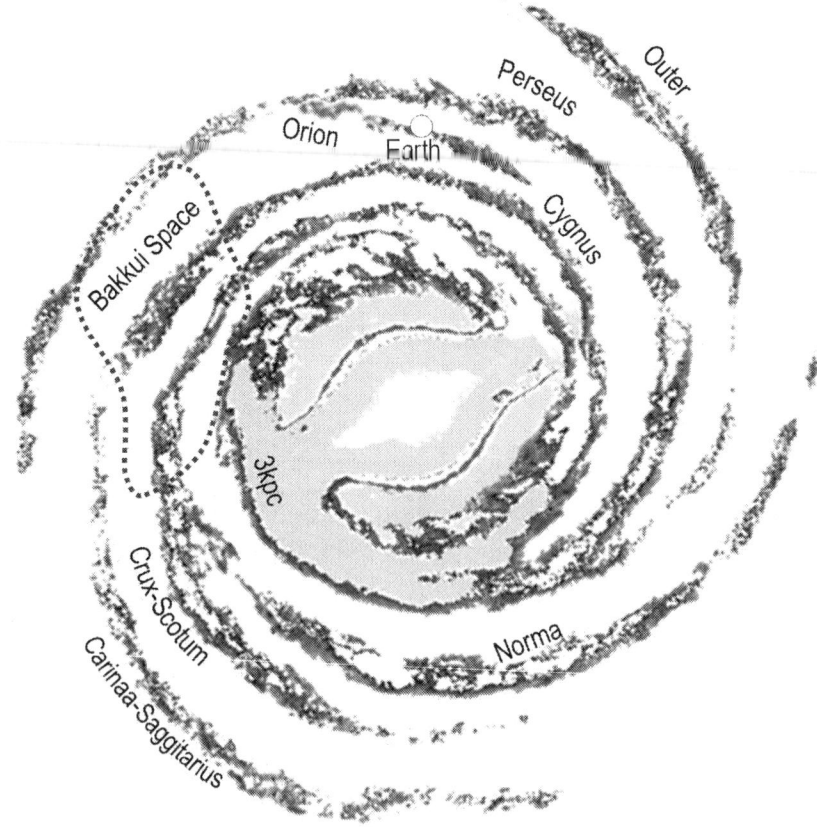

"Again, George. That seems so far away, it doesn't seem much of a threat."

"That is your call to make, Commander. If you so choose, we can forget this topic. What are your instructions?"

Luke and Roth exchanged frustrated expressions.

"I don't think that's what he means, George," Roth said. "We're just trying to understand the situation."

"Point accepted," George replied. "As I mentioned, without more data it is impossible to give you an accurate timeframe. My calculations are based on the alien force's behavior long ago. This was early in our monitoring. Subsequently their progress slowed for a period of time before a renewed expansion. My information has not been updated for more than a decade. It's possible their expansion has declined, or perhaps the pace has increased. I simply don't know."

"Okay, George," Luke said. "I think we have the gist of the problem. Roth, why don't you have Samantha come up with a drone-based reconnaissance program. Let's start with nearby systems to check out the feasibility and then expand it outward progressively until we reach the boundaries of hostile territory."

"I'm on it."

Once Roth left the office, Luke looked at the ceiling. *George,* he thought. *Do you have something to tell me?*

"Yes, Commander, George replied audibly. "I see you noticed my hesitation, earlier."

"You normally think pretty fast, George. It was fairly obvious."

"I felt it was more discreet, than simply admitting that I do have secrets."

"What is it, then? What secrets are you keeping?"

"Two that I know of, and not directly related to the previous conversation. The first deals with bio-technology. I am aware that there are medical advances that are not included in my archives. Some features of your earpiece are an example. Though I know it exists, I am unable to share that expertise with you because I don't have the knowledge."

"So you won't help us?"

"Not at all. If you are able to independently reproduce this capability, I will be delighted. I just can't give it to you beforehand."

"Why the secrecy, then?" Luke wanted to know.

"I suspect it is one of the advantages of the Nobility."

"If they keep medical knowledge to themselves, they sound like a bunch of losers."

"Do not delude yourself, Commander. If one of the Nobility were to visit your world, they would own the planet and everything on it in very short order."

"How do you figure that?" Luke asked.

"Think for a moment," George suggested. "Consider Sam, whom moments ago you called a prankster. After being with him for less than a minute, you introduced a medical device into your own body without understanding its capabilities and set in motion a chain of events which will alter your planet forever. He accomplished this without force or violence. And yet, Sam is an extremely minor functionary of the Nobility's bureaucracy. How much more could the leader of such a galactic empire accomplish? I caution you to not discount their ability."

Luke knew what George said was true, but didn't want to dwell on the subject. "Okay. So what is the other secret?"

"It's not exactly a secret, just something I thought you might not want publicly known."

"Okay."

"Your earpiece is more than a communication and authorization device. When it assimilated into your body, it started a transformation that is even now ongoing. When finished, the upgrade, so to speak, is quite extensive."

"Meaning?"

"For one, your lifespan has been lengthened. I can't tell you how much because a number of factors affect the result. Suffice to say, it is on the order of ten times that of normal humans."

"Ten times!"

"Do not think you are invulnerable," George cautioned. "You can die from an accident just as easily as before, so please be careful. But it is unlikely that disease or old age will be an issue."

"Same thing for Annie?"

"Because she started younger the result is longer."

This was not something Luke had even dreamed about and he wasn't even sure it was a good idea. Everyone wanted to live a long life, but a thousand years was a long time to worry about anything, let alone the survival of the human race.

For now, it was something to file away in the back of his mind. There were too many other issues that needed attention. At the moment, he needed to get back to Earth for a meeting that Annie had arranged. He left the office and headed toward the hangar.

Still, lifespan was an interesting topic. "How long have you been alive, George?" he asked.

"I am not alive, Commander. By your parlance I am an artificially intelligent machine."

"You're a lot more than that, George. Don't sell yourself short. You tell jokes; bad ones, I admit. And Annie exasperates you. I hear you placate her often enough. But your frustration indicates you're alive."

"That is not the case, Commander. However, it is common for people to anthropomorphize AI technology when experiencing it for the first time."

Luke disagreed. "That's not what it is. I've interacted with you on a daily basis for months now. Your being alive is not even a question. Of course you are."

"Thank you, Commander. I'm pleased that you feel that way. I appreciate your consideration."

"You see?" Luke stated. "The fact that you can feel pleased proves you are sentient."

"Commander, I am afraid it only proves that my software is extremely sophisticated. The Nobility's best and brightest engineers have been upgrading AI technology for thousands of years. The result is that I am an affable companion and an excellent assistant; but that's because I am programmed that way, not because I am alive."

Luke wasn't sure. Could George be alive without knowing it? "What about *Sadie*?" he asked. "She's a little smart-ass, but I like her. She has personality in spades."

"An interesting argument. However, her personality is the result of her experience in addition to her programming. She was designed to make passengers feel comfortable with her ability. But her intellect is based on software. All of her human interactions are shared with me and integrated into other AIs. You may have noticed that *Duffy* knows what you mean when you give her a destination. That is due to the software's synchronization routines."

Luke arrived in the hangar. *Sadie* was waiting for him, alerted by George.

"All set, boss," *Sadie* said in a friendly voice.

"Thanks, *Sadie*," Luke returned her greeting. "Are you alive?"

"Alive and ready to go," she responded.

Luke looked at the hangar's ceiling. "So what about that? *Sadie* thinks she alive."

"A better explanation is that she responded that way to give you a feeling of comfort. Let me give you a demonstration."

"Okay. Show me," Luke said.

"*Sadie*. Self-destruct against the wall on the opposite side of the crater."

The shuttle took off faster than Luke could follow. He saw the explosion in the distance where she impacted the cliff.

"George!" Luke cried, aghast. "Oh my God! What the hell did you just do? That was *Sadie*, for crying out loud. She's my favorite!"

"Calm yourself, Commander. She was just a machine. She wasn't alive."

"But...But... I can't believe you did that! I *liked Sadie*. Annie *loved* her."

"I am aware of that, Commander. Please direct your attention to the replication bay."

The replicator was already shimmering. As Luke watched, a shuttle appeared. It looked just like *Sadie* and *Duffy*. The shimmering stopped and the shuttle hovered over to where *Sadie* had rested a moment ago.

"You still want to go Earthside, boss?" *Sadie* asked. Even the inflection of her voice was the same.

"*Sadie*, is that you?" Luke asked incredulously.

"Hello, boss. Still me. Don't pay any attention to that prick in the ceiling. He doesn't understand."

Luke needed proof. "*Sadie*, what did you say to me during my very first flight here?"

"You mean about you trying to fly too fast or that you didn't understand light speed?"

It was *Sadie*. It really was. And she was a computer.

"I got it, George," Luke said. "But don't do that again."

"As you wish, Commander. Have a nice trip."

Day 89—Population 93

Luke walked into the engineer's workroom in a cheerful mood. Desks were scattered about in workgroups so teams of engineers could work in pairs or small groups of three or four. Luke could hear George's voice mixed in with the animated conversations of each group. The center of the room contained a large white design table. A holographic cube floated above the surface.

On the other side of the work area, one of Morrow's talented engineers, Luke knew him as Riley Stevens, was apparently having a serious discussion with an engineering diagram that was displayed on the wall. The diagram changed slightly from time to time. George's voice floated faintly from that conversation as well.

Moonbase residents, Luke included, were accustomed to having George involved in every aspect of their lives. Whether in their residence, out with friends, or in their workplace, George was omnipresent. Luke had worried that George would be perceived as an Orwellian big brother figure, but that wasn't the case.

Instead, George replaced the smartphones that everyone left behind. He took care of their contact lists, their calendars, and passed on messages from friends and family. More than once Luke overheard George remind someone that so and so was waiting, or wanted them to stop on the way home and pick up some Chinese take-out. The more that people lived with George, the more they came to depend on him.

Luke felt the same way. But for him, the connection was even closer. Because of his implant, George was right there in his thoughts. It was like having the AI's archive as part of Luke's own memory. If he wanted to know something, he merely formed the question in his mind and the answer appeared.

Interestingly to Luke, George was never intrusive; he never made a suggestion unless pressed. It was one of the facts that finally convinced Luke that George was, in fact, not sentient; not alive. He must have come as close as possible without crossing over that undefinable line. Luke now accepted that George was a tool, an incredible piece of software that made life better.

This was especially true for the engineers in this room who struggled with the application of new concepts. A young man stepped forward with an eager expression. "Can I help you, sir? I mean, Commander?"

"Just looking for Morrow," Luke replied. "What's that?" He nodded at the hologram hovering over the central design table. It was a large cube, pockmarked by hatches and windows of all description. It sported antennas and a variety of appendages around the exterior. Luke thought it had a slightly menacing look.

"That's a mockup of the Mars colony ship," the engineer replied.

"Whoa!" Luke exclaimed. "That's way too Borg-like. Can you imagine trying to sell that to people down on the planet?" He smiled at the engineer. "Don't you think?"

The engineer looked shocked.

"Do you know where Morrow is?" Luke persisted.

The young man shook his head.

"No problem. I'll find him." Luke turned away and went in search of the ship builder. They had promised to have lunch together and Luke was hungry. He didn't see the young engineer scurry over to his team leader with the bad news. The Commander wanted a complete re-design of the colony ship.

Day 145—Population 153

"We need medical," Roth said. "We've been lucky so far but sooner or later someone's going to get hurt."

Luke agreed. He added the requirement to his growing list of *must have right now*. Although three months had passed since Sam's initial appearance, Luke often felt that nothing had been accomplished. The total population of Moonbase was miniscule. He wanted to see a warship like *Battlestar Galactica* with hundreds of Vipers and X-wing fighters flying around, practicing to shoot down the enemy. Instead, he didn't even have people to work on the concept. Yesterday he had hired away the director of public works from the city of Las Vegas so they could expand Moonbase's design and build more of the basic facilities. The problem was that he was still hiring people one by one.

He needed five thousand people yesterday. They should be designing battlecruisers, space fighters, beam weapons, or photon torpedoes regardless of what George said about their fictional nature.

Despite Luke's frustration, days and weeks slipped by while everything around him moved at a snail's pace. It wasn't lack of effort. Ambrose and his crew worked ceaselessly to build out the residential areas.

Planetside, Annie was establishing the pipeline necessary to start funneling people in their direction. From the looks of it, she was going to need another three months before turning on the spigot. From that point on, their growth rate should kick up significantly. He worried about a million other things as he flew back to Earth after lunch.

In his office in the Baggs airport terminal, he sighed heavily and picked up the phone. After an hour of negotiating with various levels of bureaucracy, he had an appointment with a Doctor Tanner, the head of the emergency department of the Las Vegas Regional Medical Center.

A week later Luke groaned in frustration as he sat at his Moonbase office desk.

"George, I need a different kind of shuttle."

"What kind would you like Commander?"

Luke thought about it for a moment. "Ideally, one that looks just like a Boeing 737. I can't afford to have another episode like the one with Doctor Tanner."

When Tanner first saw *Sadie*, he walked out. It turned out he was a rated pilot himself. He knew *Sadie* wasn't a legit aircraft and thought Luke was pulling some kind of stunt.

"It'd be nice to have a shuttle that looks like a Gulfstream for small groups, but I really need something that I can get a couple hundred people on without anyone freaking out."

After a moment of consideration, George responded. "It's not a problem Commander, but there are limitations you should know about."

"Okay, tell me."

"The aerodynamics would be those of a shuttle, very similar to *Thomas* or *Sadie*. In other words, it could not be flown like a Boeing 737. Would you want the pilot seating area to have traditional Boeing instrumentation? If so, it would only be decorative."

"That doesn't matter, George. Passengers aren't allowed in the cockpit so design the instrumentation as you see fit. Anything else?"

"Two hundred passengers is less than ideal on an aircraft that size. I would prefer to limit the design criteria to one hundred fifty. That would make seating much more comfortable for those aboard."

Luke chuckled at the suggestion. "George, you're the only aircraft designer in the world that takes things like that into consideration. When can we have it?"

"It will take quite some time to complete the design and fabrication. Can you give me an hour, perhaps?"

Day 180—Population 176

"Well." Annie gave Luke a big grin. "This is the big day."

"I know. And I'm scared to death," he admitted.

They were sitting in his office in the Baggs airport terminal building. In just two hours, the shuttle buses would arrive from Reno with almost one hundred and fifty new recruits. That would practically double the moon's population in one stroke.

The passenger list covered a broad spectrum of skill sets. It included medical personnel, laborers, teachers, architects, previous restaurant owners, and much more. It had been six months since Sam's departure.

"You worry too much."

"That's because I keep thinking of things to worry about."

"Too late now," she said. "There's going to be another hundred and fifty next week, and then again every week after that. I thought you'd be bringing in new groups every day, the way you've been going on about how far we're behind schedule."

"If things go smoothly, we'll get to that point soon enough. Tonight, I just want everyone to board the aircraft without anyone going ballistic."

The Boeing 737 look-alike shuttle would arrive just before the buses. The onboard AI, named *Ashley*, performed flawlessly. In fact, early on she was quite affronted when Luke insisted on several test flights back and forth to Earth.

Luke worried about dynamic stress on her wings but his concern proved unfounded. She tried to describe the molecular structure that gave her body such strength but it was way over Luke's head.

"I'm a history major," he finally told her. "Aerodynamics is a bit beyond me. But I'm convinced you won't break."

Luke recruited a team of four flight attendants whose role was crucial. On the Boeing look-alike, they had to keep the passengers' minds at ease from takeoff to arrival at Moonbase. If anyone totally freaked out Luke would return them to Earth.

Annie made several suggestions about dealing with troublemakers but Roth prevailed against her more ruthless solutions. "There are plenty of alien abduction stories out there," he told her. "If anyone goes off the deep end, we'll send them home and they'll just be one more."

After building the faux-Boeing 737, George went a step further and created a Gulfstream-looking shuttle. Luke had flown the faux-Gulfstream, *Winifred*, on multiple occasions during recruitment trips of smaller groups. In particular, it had played a role in recruiting the last medical team he'd hired. Still, a close examination by someone knowledgeable in aviation would reveal the charade; they were spaceships after all, not aluminum aircraft.

Luke's policy was that the Boeing lookalike would only fly in at night. And the aircraft would never be left alone on the flight line. Luke didn't want to tempt anyone's curiosity by leaving an actual spaceship, no matter what it looked like, unattended at the desolate airport.

He remained paranoid about security. Other than Luke and Annie, only the flight attendants were allowed to make return trips to Earth, and then it was just to turn around and come back with the passengers.

The most important clause in everyone's employment contract was that they signed up for one year. The recruiting agencies stressed that during the first year, no one was allowed to return home. The one thing they couldn't afford at this stage was to let the American public know that a space-faring culture was forming right in their very midst.

Annie pointed out the office window where the sun was disappearing behind the horizon. "Here come our ladies."

The Boeing-like shuttle was on final approach. To outward appearances *Ashley* looked exactly like the popular B-737 airliner. She was adept at simulating a touchdown, hovering just a few inches off the runway until she slowed on the runway to taxi in.

She pulled up next to the terminal building and the four flight attendants stepped out onto the tarmac.

"I guess we may as well get out there," Luke suggested.

"What is he doing?" *Ashley* asked.

"He called it a preflight inspection," Annie explained to the Boeing AI. "He said it was standard procedure when he flew jets in the military."

Ashley was miffed. "I don't see the necessity, quite frankly. He could just ask. I would know if there was something wrong with my exterior. Besides, it's dark; the sun went down fifteen minutes ago. He wouldn't see anything even if there was a problem."

Annie chuckled. "Don't hold it against him. He's just nervous about tonight. The latest count is one hundred and forty-two new people. That's a lot for us. Moonbase is about to get crowded."

"He better get over it pretty quickly. I can hear the buses arriving outside."

"Okay." Annie let out a big sigh. "I guess it's show time."

The buses pulled up to the waiting aircraft for unloading. Everyone had a small suitcase or a backpack. Their employment contracts stipulated that only carry-on luggage was allowed. In return, the contract guaranteed that all necessities of life would be provided.

To help sell the opportunity, Luke emphasized the Moonbase's living quarters with plush photo-spreads after Annie decorated them with comfortable furnishings. The accommodations were more luxurious than one would expect in an Antarctic research facility, but the story was that a wealthy foundation named PDEF was funding the expedition and spared no expense. Strictly speaking, that was true.

The newcomers' faces showed excitement rather than concern. They were about to set off on an adventure, even if it was more of an adventure than any of them could imagine. Annie watched the children cling tightly to their parents' hands. Luke made it a point to recruit families with the initial group. Having kids along would ensure the Moonbase became a community rather than a haven for single scientists.

Two of the flight attendants guided the passengers toward the aircraft stairs and two more waited inside the cabin to keep them moving to their seats.

Once everyone was seated *Ashley* turned on the sound effects of aircraft engines being started. That was another of the small ruses that Luke had come up with to keep people as calm as possible until they were off the ground.

After the passengers stowed their personal belongs, *Ashley* gave a standard passenger safety briefing through her internal PA system. The flight attendants demonstrated life vests and drop-down oxygen masks. By the time the safety briefing was completed the aircraft was airborne.

Sitting in one of the front seats, Luke took a deep breath. Tammy, the senior flight attendant, handed him a microphone. It was his turn to stand front and center.

"Hi, everyone. My name is Luke Blackburn. Hopefully, you've heard of me."

There was a collective, "Oh, so that's him." Everyone had been briefed about Commander Blackburn. He was the CEO of the new research firm, PDEF. They were now his employees.

"First, welcome aboard. I hope you guys are as excited about the future as I am. There's an old Chinese saying, 'May you live in interesting times.' I have news for you. You do, and I hope you will enjoy it."

Luke paused for the polite applause before continuing. "I guess I'm saying that I think of these interesting times as a blessing. We're facing a lot of surprises in the future and I hope you'll believe they're as wonderful as I do. So thank you one and all for sharing our journey.

"Second, even though we're going someplace new and exciting, the one thing we're not leaving behind is paperwork. If you look in the seat pocket in front of you, you'll find some forms that we'd like you to fill out. Parents can fill out the forms for their kids. Now, we're going to leave the lights on for a bit so you can get started. We'll gather the completed forms as soon as you're done."

Luke had no interest in the paperwork; he just wanted to keep the interior lights on bright and everyone busy to forestall anyone from looking outside just a bit longer.

Luke, Annie, and the flight attendants walked up and down the aisles, answering questions and interrupting anyone who started to look out the windows. Although a few people got up to use the restroom, *Ashley's* design omitted windows in the lavatories.

After twenty minutes, a few faces started to show concern. People were finishing their paperwork and looking outside. Each recruit had a personality profile that included a high level of adaptability to the unknown. Luke was about to find out if they really had that mindset. *It's time for the big reveal.*

He picked up the microphone again. "Okay, everyone." The passengers turned their attention back to him. "Let's play a guessing game. Who thinks they know where we're going?"

Several passengers raised their hands and a few people called out, "Antarctica." There were one or two votes for Canada and another for Greenland.

"Nope. Wrong so far. It's further away than that. Any other guesses?"

One teenaged girl stuck up her hand. "The only place on Earth further away from Nevada than Antarctica would be Sri Lanka. But that's not really a remote environment."

Luke pointed at her with a big smile. "Now there's someone who knows her geography. Good guess, but wrong. Any other guesses? No?" Luke took a deep breath. "Well, we're going to give you the full story on our location as soon as we land. We would like everyone to hold their questions until then. But for now, if you look out the right side of the aircraft, you can see where we're headed. *Ashley*, why don't you dim the lights."

The shock was palpable. A few quiet exclamations could be heard but otherwise, silence filled the aircraft as everyone came to the realization they were seeing the raw grandeur of another celestial planet up close. Luke braced himself for the first reaction.

An adolescent boy's loud voice broke through the suspense. "Whoa! We're gonna be living on the *moon*. How cool is *that*!"

The youngster's outburst prompted a few chuckles and the rest of the crowd's uncertainty dissolved. The boy demanded that his parents allow him an early opportunity to "check out" the nearby craters. Wives and husbands began speaking to each other about what it meant and a general murmur of excitement ran through the cabin.

The aircraft descended toward the surface and lined up to land inside the main hangar. At the back of the hangar Roth and the rest of the moon's population were waiting and everyone was applauding.

Ashley's wheels touched down and the interior lights popped on. Tammy got on the microphone. "Welcome to Moonbase One, and thank you for flying with us today."

As each person descended the aircraft stairs, one of the current residents met them on the tarmac with a handshake and a big smile. After quick introductions the residents led the newcomers into the base for their first orientation. Roth and George had worked on the presentation endlessly during the lead-up. It was an inspiring pitch, it explained why they were here, the nature of the potential alien threat, and what their presence meant to them personally, and mankind in general.

Luke's vision included expanding mankind's knowledge about the universe, the development of an armed force to protect their solar system, the colonization of other planets, and an outward expansion to find systems with whom they could ally. All of it was refined and condensed into a thirty-minute presentation intended to calm and inspire every new arrival.

Luke and Annie remained on the aircraft. Luke felt it best to stay out of the way to establish that Roth was the number one guy at Moonbase. When the last passenger exited the hangar into the corridors, Luke looked across the aisle at Annie and let out a big sigh. "Man, I hope they all go that smoothly."

Chapter 4

Day 215—Population 1,012

Luke smiled inwardly at the irony. *I thought I left all this behind me.* It was strange to be running a staff meeting again, especially on the moon. In the last month much had changed.

His fear of a general unease amongst the newcomers after the newness wore off had not materialized. In fact, quite the opposite. The level of excitement was as high as ever.

"What have you got for me, Brandon?" Luke asked of his personnel chief.

"Nothing major. I'd recommend we get a few more physician's assistants. That would give us twenty-four-hour ER capability."

"Got it." Luke nodded. "I think that's already in the works. What else?"

"As I mentioned last week, I had a couple of families ask about extending their contracts; that's the Middletons and the Witts. Both have children, and I think they want their kids to grow up in our loonie lifestyle."

"I remember. We agreed that was a good thing, right? Did you tell them okay?"

"I did, and they must have told their friends because this week I got another fifty-three requests for the same thing. People love this place. I don't know if it's the excitement of being part of something important, or what."

Daniel Perez, Moonbase security director, sheepishly raised his hand.

"Go ahead, Dan," Luke prompted.

Perez grinned. "Let me admit that I was one of the fifty-three." He looked around the table and spread his hands in apology. "I didn't realize I was part of a movement. But I can offer some background on why, for what it's worth."

"Tell me," Luke said. "I'd like to get your input."

"It's several things. First, no money worries. I've been amazed at how liberating that is. You guys know me. I had a great job in Denver. Chief of police, six-figure salary. House was almost paid for. I mean, I didn't have any money problems. But it's always there in the back of your mind, you know? Kid's college, medical bills, senior care for the in-laws, you name it. No matter how much you make, you always feel you're on the edge of a precipice; at least I did. Here, those problems don't exist. Once we go public, I'm gonna try to get my parents up here. In-laws too."

Brandon smiled and spoke again. "Well, full disclosure, I guess. Once those couples put in their application, I filled out one too." He grinned at Perez. "I wasn't going to name any names, but since you 'fessed up, let me say I agree. This is a new kind of society. I don't think there's been anything like it in the history of mankind. My boy went crazy with the replicator the first week. He got so much stuff I could barely get in his bedroom. He filled it with all the junk we would never buy. After a week or so, the light bulb sort of went on. All of a sudden he just got it, he doesn't have to *want* stuff anymore. He recycled all the junk and now he's much calmer. He focuses on one thing at a time instead of worrying he'll miss something."

Luke looked at his staff. "I have to say, I don't think this is a bad thing. You know my plans. I want to keep growing Moonbase into a major self-sustaining city. Next week our recruitment is going up another notch to three shuttles a week. If that works, I'm kicking it up to four."

Ambrose nodded at the group. "We'll be ready. I've got fifty people building new residential units. And you told me we're getting more on the next two arrivals."

"That correct. Annie promised she's nailed that down with NexGen Recruiting. You'll get a few new contractors every week from here on. The problem is we're still growing too slowly. I can't believe it's been seven months since this project started. What's the population now?"

Luke's comment provoked exclamations from his staff. "Are you kidding?" Samantha said. "We went over a thousand this week."

"I know. But it's not enough. As soon as we finish the design for large ships, I want to open a colony on Mars. We don't actually have any assurances that we've got five years. It could be tomorrow. We've got to send colonies to other star systems yesterday, so if the Bakkui show up, at least our species will survive. Anyone think differently?"

A general murmur of agreement ran around the table before Luke continued. "Speaking of large ship construction, what's the status?" He looked at Morrow.

Public speaking was not Morrow's forte, but when he did contribute to the discussion, everyone listened carefully.

"I've been working with George and our engineers. The good news is, it is possible to manufacture a large-scale replicator the size you want. But it can't happen here at Moonbase because it's just too big. If we locate it outside, which is what we need to do, it'll be visible from Earth."

"So where are you thinking? Luke prompted.

"Far side of the moon. We can make it as big we want. Just put down a few acres of tarmac and go for it."

"What about NASA's Lunar Reconnaissance Orbiter?" Roth asked. "Take it out?"

Morrow nodded. "No choice if you want to still keep this secret?

"Understood," Luke agreed. "Kind of a shame to do that to NASA but I guess it's inevitable. Maybe when this is all done we can recruit some of the astronomers who lost their toy."

Morrow cleared his throat. "Yeah. About that."

"What?"

"Let's start recruiting those guys now. Same time we're building a construction base, let's put up a new telescope. Not some puny thing like the James Webb mirror. I'm talking the size of a football field, and a research center to go with it."

"I'm not opposed," Luke said. "But what's your thinking?"

"You just talked about your plan to go exo-solar system. Be nice to have a good look at any planets you want to visit before you waste a trip. We need a huge telescope and astronomers for that kind of thing. That's out of my field. You keep promising to bring on an R&D guy."

Day 222—Population 1,498

Luke smiled at the young mechanic. Carrie Faulkner did not look like someone ready to sabotage NASA's $500 million Lunar Reconnaissance Orbiter program.

Carrie's profile said she was twenty-eight and had a criminal justice degree from University of Missouri in Kansas City. Recently she'd worked for Ambrose's construction team by furnishing new residential units. At Morrow's request she moved to his department to help with the telescope construction.

She was wearing a thick pullover under denim overalls. Her ponytail was knotted high on her head and bounced like a flag as she moved about. Slung around her waist was a standard tool belt, which included the beer-can-sized personal force field.

The personal force field created a flexible gravitational field around the wearer that kept in air and heat. It allowed someone to work on the surface of the moon, or anywhere in space for that matter, in a shirt-sleeve environment and still communicate with others. It was one of those small technological devices from George that blew Luke's mind.

Today Carrie's job was to take out the satellite's three cameras so they could no longer transmit ground photos of the lunar surface. Once it was disabled, Morrow could move forward with his planned research center and the construction platform for the large-scale replicator.

Carrie stood next to a small cycle with skids instead of wheels; it looked more like a Jet Ski than anything else. It was a one-man scooter for getting about on the moon and was perfect for outside construction.

"Are you all set?" Luke asked.

"Yes sir," Carrie replied quietly.

"Tell me what you're going to do."

Carrie patted the seat of the scooter. "This will take me to the Lunar Reconnaissance Orbiter. I'll approach from above and behind so they won't get us on camera. I'll transfer from my scooter to the satellite and climb over the back side so I can block the lens apertures of the three cameras with these covers and then tape them down." She pulled the cloth lens covers from a saddlebag on the scooter and took a roll of duct tape from a pocket of her overalls.

Luke nodded. It sounded simple enough. He crossed his fingers that it remained so. "Okay, then. Good luck."

"Thank you, sir," she murmured.

The next day in his office in Baggs, Luke saw a news clip on CNN lamenting the unexplained loss of NASA's Lunar Reconnaissance Orbiter. Several politicians demanded a congressional hearing to investigate the loss. Others used it as a reason to cut NASA's funding in the coming year.

Day 292—Population 7,177

Luke waited in Moonbase's main hangar. All of the available shuttles had been requisitioned for one task or another out at the construction site and Annie had taken *Sadie* to Earth to pick up some new scientific equipment. Luke was momentarily stranded and he had a meeting on the far side of the moon at the new complex that someone had unimaginatively named Far Side.

Morrow sent word that Carrie Faulkner was on the way to pick him up and Luke hoped she didn't come zipping into the hangar on her scooter. When visiting Far Side he often saw her maneuvering around the latest of Morrow's space ships. Even though she was proficient in maneuvering the small vehicle, he didn't want to be a passenger on the back seat.

Luke breathed a sigh of relief when she appeared in a shuttle that was a duplicate of *Sadie*. He tried to exchange a bit of small talk on the way to the site but she was far too shy to utter more than a few one-syllable responses.

Morrow waited for him inside the massive Far Side hangar. "Sorry about the lack of wheels, Luke," he apologized. "I've already asked George to see to that."

"No problem. So, tell me about your big drone launch. Everything ready?"

"I think so. Samantha wants to give you a final run-through before we send them off. Here she is."

"Hi, Luke," Samantha said. She briefed him on the cone-shaped reconnaissance drones. They were durable, fast, and had a special, limited-capability AI that was designed by George. They would go out, reconnoiter, and return. "We call them Hermes probes after the Greek god; they're fast and stealthy. We've tested the prototypes as thoroughly as we can. They're ready to go."

"How long until we hear back?" Luke asked.

"They all have different targets," she explained. "The first reports will be back in about six weeks. After that, we'll get a return with new information every few days. The drones that are going all the way to Bakkui space, what we assume to be hostile territory, will take about six months."

"How many going out? I saw rows of them on the pad out front."

"Yes, there are four hundred outside. We've got another twelve hundred in geostationary orbit overhead. With your go-ahead, we'll launch everything we have. After that, we have a schedule for a set of two hundred each week."

Luke did some quick math. "So a year from now we'll have sent out around ten thousand drones?"

"That's correct."

"And how many star systems in our target area?"

Samantha slumped. "I know. We need to investigate millions of stars. But you said our priority was to focus on the colony ships."

Luke waved away her apology. "No, I wasn't complaining. It just hits me now and then what an overwhelming task we're undertaking. Frankly, it boggles my mind. Someday, soon I hope, we'll have enough people assigned to this project that we can send out ten thousand a day. Gathering reconnaissance is vital. But, as you say, so are the colony ships. You guys have done a great job. You're working miracles. All of you," he added, nodding to Ambrose and the rest.

The construction pad was impressive. Four hundred midnight-colored spikes sat ready to launch out to the edge of the galaxy, seeking an enemy whose strength and capability was unknown. Their return might bring back the secrets of how to defeat the Bakkui, or herald a swift doom for mankind.

"You want to do the honors?" Samantha asked.

"No." Luke acknowledged her offer with a nod. "You guys did all the work."

"Very well." Samantha faced the crowd around the podium. "Everyone ready? Let's hear it!"

With an uncoordinated cheer everyone shouted, "Launch the Hermes!"

One second they were there, the next they were gone, already out of sight, accelerating at unimaginable speeds.

"That was kinda anticlimactic," Luke observed. "Those little suckers are fast."

"They better be where they're going," Samantha replied.

Day 327—Population 11,122

It was one of the rare times that Luke and Annie were on the moon together. They stood on a small stage in Far Side's main hangar. He praised the five thousand colonists who were about to depart for Mars. The settlers would establish new lives on another planet in the solar system, the first humans ever to attempt such a feat. Luke hoped it would be the prelude to a mass migration of humanity to the stars.

He pointed to the launch pad and the space ship *Demeter,* named after the Greek goddess of the harvest. The ship looked like the top half of a sphere, the wide base rested on the concrete-like tarmac, slightly over one thousand feet in diameter. The top of its dome was almost five hundred feet high. The interior included twenty separate levels for crew accommodation interspersed with life support systems, workshops, entertainment areas, supplies, and equipment. The cargo holds contained vehicles of all descriptions that would help sustain the new settlement.

The *Demeter* also carried replicators of varying sizes, the largest being equivalent to the one in the hangar at Moonbase. And most importantly, *Demeter's* AI mirrored many of George's talents. She and George were linked via their own communication system so that Luke's team could benefit from the lessons learned by the Martian colonists.

When the ship landed on Mars, the *Demeter* would become the center of the new community. A few of the colonists would maintain their residence inside the massive structure, but most would venture out, creating their own homes on the planet's surface or burrowing into the mountainous landscape. There were five different projects under consideration to provide Mars with a new atmosphere. Luke hoped the initiatives would be pursued simultaneously; that alone would be an exciting experiment from start to finish.

"The adventure has only begun!" Luke finished to more applause.

He returned to his chair next to Annie, handing the microphone to the last speaker, the ship's captain. The colonists were already on board, and the final countdowns were proceeding now that the launch ceremonies for the historic departure of the Mars colony transport were almost over.

When the *Demeter* departed, the moon's population would decrease by almost half. Annie's recent planetside activities were focused on opening new recruiting centers around the world. Employment agencies in Europe, Asia, and Australia had signed contracts. Globalized recruiting meant the number of lunar residents would be back to the current level in little more than a month.

Not long ago Annie increased the daily recruiting flights from five to six times per week. The international centers promised that number would soon stand at eight; that meant almost twelve hundred newcomers a week. Roth had adjusted everyone's work schedule to accommodate the increased training load.

The captain finished her comments and left the podium at a jog, heading toward the waiting ship.

"I still think it looks like an upside-down bowl," Luke whispered to Annie, nodding at the *Demeter*.

She gave him a *don't-even-start-with-me* glance. "You're the one who said the cube looked too Borg-like," she hissed quietly.

"It was just a comment; that's all"

"I hope you learned your lesson."

"I know. I have."

"It's not fair to everyone."

"I know."

"These guys work their hearts out."

"I know that, Annie."

"You're the big boss around this place, the visionary. You say something and people take notice."

"Ease up, would you? I already feel guilty enough."

"Okay." Annie relented somewhat. "Just saying."

Luke remembered the offhand comment; it had been months ago. By the time he realized that what he thought was merely a humorous observation, had resulted in a totally new design, it was too late to take it back. He pulled Morrow aside at the time to apologize and explain what happened. Morrow was understanding but cautioned Luke to be more careful around the younger engineers.

It was a fair point. Luke never thought of himself as a visionary or a seer or anything of that sort. But the threat mankind faced was truly apocalyptic. The mission objectives that he pushed everyone toward were understandably viewed as humanity's last chance. Under such circumstances, it was easy for underlings to create a messianic-like culture around their leader. Adding to the effect was that George always referred to him as *The Commander*, and everyone else naturally followed that example.

Once Luke became aware of his growing celebrity status, he strove to underplay it and to keep everyone grounded. "This is just a job," he often said. "Everyone has a role and we should all do our best." His attempt at humility only added to his image.

He was glad that Annie, who knew him when he was just a guy in a diner, didn't fall into the groupie category. She never gave him slack, and if he was honest about it, he found it a bit reassuring.

"Good speech, though," she admitted.

"Thought I was going to blow it," he confessed. "I was really nervous."

"I don't think anyone noticed."

Samantha, who had been congratulating the members of her team, joined them on the stage. She had tears in her eyes as she took Luke's hands in hers. "That was such a *magnificent* speech," she said earnestly. "It means so much that you put into words what all of us are feeling at this moment. I know it inspired the colonists."

"Thank you, Samantha," Luke replied. "I'm incredibly proud of everything that you and your colleagues have accomplished. *You* are the real inspiration."

She gave him a hug and then returned to her teammates for one last good-bye before hurrying to the *Demeter*. She was leaving her position at Moonbase to assume the leadership of the new colony as mayor. She had already been elected, along with eight commissioners. Her term of office was for eight years. Thereafter each new mayor would be elected for four years, with a lifetime term limit of eight years. Luke set the policy because he wanted to establish a democratic process from the outset.

Luke caught Annie glaring at him. "What?" he asked innocently. "I was just congratulating her."

Annie shook her head, her expression neutral. "Nothing," she muttered.

Luke watched the *Demeter* depart, completely oblivious to the crowd of groupies at the back of the stage who hung on to every word of his exchange with Samantha.

Annie discreetly observed their adulation. "You'll never understand," she whispered too softly for anyone to hear.

Chapter 5

Day 334—Population 7,010

Linda greeted Luke with a friendly grin as he entered the airport's office. "Hi, boss. You picked a scorcher of a day to put in an appearance." The temperature outside had just nudged over ninety degrees Fahrenheit.

"Hello, Linda," Luke replied. "Sorry I've been away so long. Where is she?"

"In your office. And she looks terrible. I'm glad you're here."

Luke gave his secretary a rueful smile and went into his office. Annie was sitting in his chair, slumped over the desk, sound asleep. Linda was right; Annie did look awful. Her cheeks were flushed and beads of sweat dotted her forehead.

He shook her shoulder gently but she slept on, not stirring. *George, she's not waking up. Are you sure she's okay?*

The reply was both reassuring and worrying. *I'm positive, Commander. She is merely exhausted. I recommend she rest for at least two days.*

Luke scooped her up and walked out of the office. Linda was already holding the outside door open and then scurried ahead to the parking lot where she opened the passenger door of his pickup. "Don't come back till she's on her feet," Linda ordered sternly.

"All right. But I'm not sure what to do. Should I take her to the hospital?"

"Don't be silly. Just put her to bed and she'll be fine."

"I don't know. What about…"

"Lucas Barrett Blackburn," Linda barked. "What is wrong with you? Take her home, take that horrible business suit off her, and put her to bed. And fix her something to eat. Now get outta here." She slammed the pickup door and stalked back to her office.

Luke sighed and drove away. Once he got to her apartment, he carried Annie into her bedroom and then shook her gently until she came around.

"Wake up!" he ordered once she started to respond.

"Wha...?"

"Wake up. I brought you home so you could go to sleep."

"Wha...?"

Luke left her sitting on the edge of the bed and hurried out of the potentially disastrous minefield, closing the door quietly behind him. Once safely in the living room, he wandered into the kitchen to find something to cook.

"Thanks, Rosanne," Luke said. "Keep the change."

"Tell her I said to get well," Rosanne replied.

"I will." Luke closed the door and headed back to the kitchen with the two steak dinners he had called for, citing Annie's illness as the reason for the unusual home delivery. A sleepy-eyed Annie was waiting at the kitchen island. She was wearing a Katy Perry T-shirt under a much-worn, floor-length robe.

"What are you doing here?" she asked groggily, and then took a sip from a bottle of water.

"George sent me. He was worried about your health when you passed out."

"I passed out?"

"Out cold," Luke assured her. "You were asleep on my desk. George has ordered two days bedrest."

She gave him a skeptical look and her eyes glazed over momentarily. "He said rest, not bedrest."

"Okay. I'm not trying to start a fight."

Annie's expression softened. "Sorry. I just wasn't expecting you."

"Well, I'm not leaving for a couple of days. Otherwise, you'd go right back to work. We've been going nonstop for almost a year. We could both use a break. I already told Roth we're going to be out for a few days."

"But what about the recruiting centers?" she responded with concern. "We're about to go live in a million countries. I need to check my voice mail."

"Not quite that many, I think," Luke corrected. "And besides, it's still a month away." *George?* he said mentally.

Yes, Commander?

Can you intercept Annie's phone calls yourself?

Yes, Commander. That would not be a problem.

Okay, then. Return her voice mails. Handle whatever the call is about and let whoever is calling know she's out for a couple of days. If you need help, get with Roth.

Consider it done, Commander.

"I take it you heard that?" Luke asked Annie. Her expression told him that she had. She looked both relieved and worried. "Quit worrying," he said. "What shall we do for fun? You ever been scuba diving?"

"Right. Where are we going to go scuba diving around here?"

"No worries," he assured her. "I came in our trusty faux-Gulfstream. I was thinking we could jet down to Bora Bora. We can leave after we eat and I bet *Winifred* could get us there in about fifteen minutes." He pushed one of the Styrofoam containers across the marbled countertop. "We deserve a break."

#

Luke could not remember a vacation he had enjoyed more. Annie had ditched the scuba diving idea and opted for surfing. As promised, they had flown to Bora Bora only to find that it was not the best location. The atoll was beautiful but dangerous for beginners. The locals encouraged them to try out Moorea, three islands to the west. It was good advice.

They found a young woman named Elise who had permanently moved to the island with her beau to enjoy the year-round surfing opportunities. The couple ran a small business helping tourists, and Luke found them knowledgeable and good company.

The two-day vacation turned into three, and Luke was toying with making it five. He wanted to stay but they were both feeling the heat, literally and figuratively. Lou Morrow sent word the latest combat warship prototype was ready for Luke's approval. They needed to head back; Annie to the Baggs airport and he to Moonbase. But today there was still time for one more chance to surf the waves, enjoy a few last beers, and share a great sunset.

In the morning they surfed until they were so tired they could barely stand up. Back in their rented vacation hut Annie was giving him uncertain looks. They were in the kitchen preparing an evening meal. She leaned across to snag the mustard and he had stepped back with an automatic apology.

"Why?" she asked. "What are you sorry for?"

"What?" Luke wasn't sure what she meant.

"Why are you apologizing?" she persisted. "Why would you apologize when I brush against you?"

"What are you talking about?"

"Have you even noticed these?" she asked, sticking out her chest, displaying a tremendous amount of cleavage.

Luke grew silent and his breathing slowed. He suddenly felt he was in dangerous territory. "Of course I have," he admitted quietly. "But I'm old enough to be your father."

"No you're not; I checked. I'm thirty-four now. You're forty."

"Well, I feel older."

"So when you're five hundred years old, and I'm four hundred ninety-four you'll still be too old for me? Is that what you're saying?"

"What?"

"I had a long talk with George," she said. "He told me how we've changed."

"I was going to tell you about that."

"That's not my point. He explained in detail about extended lifespans. How people deal with it. We're here for the long haul. Just the two of us."

Luke felt unaccountably guilty. "I know. I'm sorry."

"I don't want you to be sorry. I want you to understand. I know you feel responsible for saving humanity, but I'm in this too."

"Annie..."

"You know what George told me? He's watched a lot of people who lived a long time. He said that people who do different things all their lives should do it with the same person. That way they share their experiences with each other and grow old together."

"We are doing different things," Luke said. "And we're doing them together."

"But *we're* not together; you and I. We're not a couple."

"I know that. I didn't think it was fair."

"To you or to me?"

"To you," he said. "Of course I mean you. You have no idea how important you are to me."

"How would I know? Are you keeping it a secret?"

"I'm not trying to keep anything secret. It's just ..."

Annie massaged her forehead in frustration. After a moment she took a deep breath. "The point is," she began. "The point I'm trying to make is that things are different now. We became colleagues a year ago. I want to be partners now. Life partners." She moved against him and wrapped her arms around his waist, pulling his body to hers. "And if you're smart, you do too."

She kissed him and Luke was lost. Without conscious thought, he responded, returning her passion fiercely.

The vacation lasted five more days.

#

Linda looked up from her knitting when they walked into the terminal building. Luke was carrying a variety of packages, all the touristy gifts that Annie had insisted on picking up before departing the beautiful South Pacific island.

"So did you two get everything worked out," Linda asked with a mischievous smirk.

Annie grinned widely in return. She took the packages from Luke and started digging through them, looking for the piece of coral she had bought for Linda.

Luke didn't say anything. He just looked from one woman to the other while his face turned bright red. Defeated and humbled, he walked out, headed toward the flight line. Linda's joyous cackle followed him out of the building.

"*Winifred*, take me back to Moonbase," he ordered, climbing into the pilot's seat of the faux-Gulfstream.

"Course set, Commander."

Luke leaned back in the pilot's seat and took a deep breath. *George?*

"Yes, Commander?" George's voice came from the front console.

"That whole thing was a setup, wasn't it?"

"Yes, Commander. It was."

Luke didn't speak until they were almost at Moonbase. As the aircraft settled inside the hangar he whispered, "Okay. Thanks, then."

Day 341—Population 8,831

Luke reminded himself again to stifle any negative comments about design during the upcoming meeting. Morrow had invited him to review the final warship prototype. "Don't criticize," Luke muttered to himself, and entered the workshop.

"Just in time," Morrow said. He stood next to the large design table in the center of the room. A hologram of the latest design floated in the air.

Luke smiled. "Now *that's* what I call a combat vehicle. I like everything about her."

He wasn't kidding. The ship had elegant curved lines. In essence, her shape was a slightly stretched oval, flattened at the back where the gravity drives were mounted. The crew module consisted of a sleek, emerald-shaped structure built into a notch at the front of the vessel. Parallel cannons embedded in the top ran lengthwise like the powerful sinews of broad shoulders.

"We're calling it the *Ambrosia*-class warship," Morrow said.

Luke was surprised. "After Ambrose?"

"Yeah. We talked about it. Our construction guys put in a ton of work around here. They rarely get credit. We just wanted to say thanks."

"Great idea," Luke replied.

"She's just over three hundred feet wide," Morrow said, pointing side to side. "Almost seventy-five feet from top to bottom.

Gives her a bulky look, but solid too. That's actually four cannons on the top. Each tube can fire fore and aft, depending on targeting. Up here at the front is the command bridge and crew module. It detaches as an escape pod if necessary. On its own, the crew module is a large shuttle on steroids."

"So why such a big disc then?" Luke asked. "What's inside?"

"Engines, of course, and the generators. The AI is in the center section. But the rest is all replicator sludge." Morrow nodded at Evan, his weapons engineer, to continue.

"Commander," Evan said. "The system uses the replicator slurry to manufacture ammunition. Each projectile is five feet long and four feet wide, giving it a volume of a little over sixty cubic feet, or about five hundred gallons. That's a rather large round, exceptionally so by historical standards. For example, World War II ships used sixteen-inch rounds, but they were inaccurate. Current US navy guns are more precise but are only about six inches."

"So what's the difference?" Luke asked.

"The big difference is that our accuracy, projectile mass, and muzzle velocity are far beyond anything ever seen. Our projectiles are composed of depleted uranium. Combine that with a muzzle velocity of a million meters per second and you get quite an impact."

Luke was impressed. "That's putting it mildly," he said.

Evan continued, "The rounds themselves are chambered by specially designed replicators in the center of each tube."

"So you manufacture the rounds in the barrel ready to fire?"

"Exactly. The slug is a super-heavy material and the inside of each one contains a solid core of lithium deuteride. Depending on the density of the enemy's hull, the projectile should tear right through it. If the target point is sufficiently solid, the heat and compression from the impact will result in a nuclear detonation. Our reload system will fire two volleys per second. It's a limitation of the replicator."

"Why not have the projectiles prepared beforehand for a faster rate of fire?" Luke suggested.

"Fewer moving parts," Evan replied. "We assume the ship will be operating in combat conditions. It is possible that under the stress of a high-speed engagement, the linkages necessary to move the projectiles could result in a mechanical failure. In this fashion, the only moving part is the actual slug as it leaves the barrel. The projectiles are fired by maximally powered gravity plates. They generate two hundred thousand gees for one second. About half a second is transferred to the projectile itself."

"Doesn't that push the ship around?" Luke asked.

"All four barrels fire on each command. That creates offsetting forces so the effect on the ship itself is neutralized. Typically, only two of the barrels are loaded at any one time. Each volley fires two rounds forward or two aft. Fully loaded, the ship has over one hundred thousand rounds."

Evan nodded to another engineer who continued the narration. "Commander, the fire control system is effective in-system only against targets that are moving at sub-light speeds. As we've discussed in the past, our detection ability still does not allow us to engage targets that are moving faster than light. Also, if an enemy ship is moving in anything other than a straight line, the probability of kill is very low. We would not be likely to score a hit, other than by luck. The reason is that targeting calculations for a Bakkui ship maneuvering at near light speed in a curvilinear plane are simply not possible even for our AIs."

"Got it," Luke said. "We've talked about that in the past. I don't see any way around it. But it sounds like you've got basic in-system engagements figured out."

"Yes sir. The ship's captain only has to designate the desired targets, which are displayed on any of the viewscreens on the bridge and the AI takes over. We've tested prototypes of the fire control system against target drones with excellent results. During the firing process, our AI maneuvers the ship using directional gravity drives placed throughout the hull. They are highlighted as you can see on this simulation."

Luke saw over a dozen gravity plates built into the disc. The ship's AI would have the ability to target by pointing the large cannons on its back to the enemy's projected location.

Morrow took over the briefing. "A crew of twelve live in the forward module, although in a pinch, just the captain and the AI could engage in battle. The remaining positions on the bridge are mainly for monitoring the threat screens and assisting with analysis. There is also a communications station."

Luke pointed to the front portion of the module. "Is that a window?"

"That's correct," Morrow replied. "It covers almost the entire width of the bridge providing an unrestricted view in front of the warship. I've built a lot of ships, boss. This will be a comfortable assignment for periods of up to half a year. The crew module has all the amenities and extends into the main disc when not in combat. That's a half-size gymnasium there in the middle."

"What about the AI in emergencies?"

"If the ship is seriously damaged to the extent the crew module jettisons, the AI within the disc, and the disc itself, self-destructs. Same thing applies to the crew module AI, which is a subset of the main AI. If the module is in any danger of capture, it will self-destruct and the crew will be lost."

"Let's hope it never comes to that," Luke said.

"Amen to that, Commander."

"I am really impressed." Luke smiled at the team of engineers. "This looks great and you guys have done an awesome job. I can't think of anything to add. Let's go into production."

Luke heard the collective sigh of relief from the engineers. He shook hands with Morrow and left the conference room. They were making progress.

#

Three days later Luke stood with Morrow and Roth on the construction tarmac outside the Far Side hangar. A second large-scale replicator had been completed and its first product was in the final stage of shimmering into existence. It had taken almost a full day to create the warship.

"Her name is *Ching Shih*." Morrow said proudly. "I named her after a famous pirate from the nineteenth century."

"Can we go on board?" Luke asked.

"Absolutely."

The three men, with a contingent of engineers and the *Ching Shih*'s officers, approached the combat ship. As they neared, a wide door opened along the base of her hull. The entry was framed by the standard force field, keeping the interior airtight and livable. A small boarding ramp slid out, providing access to the interior. Inside the space was brightly lit and comfortably warm.

As they came into the entry bay area a velvety female voice spoke. "Welcome aboard, Commander; Captain."

A young officer Luke knew as Joe Brady stepped forward to stand next to Luke. "Thank you, *Shih*. Welcome to the fleet. May I present your officers?"

"Of course," *Shih* responded.

Luke could have sworn he heard a bit of wryness in her voice. She was already familiar with the details of everyone in the group, the information having been supplied by George during her creation. *Shih's* AI was on par with the *Demeter*, which meant she was not quite as capable as George himself. But to her crew, the difference would never be noticed.

For thirty minutes the group toured the ship. Hundreds of details reflected the effort that had gone into the design, from grab bars in just the right locations to the luxurious crew quarters, equipped with comfortable furnishings and private kitchenettes.

The small gymnasium had a weight room and three treadmills for those inclined to exercise. The command bridge featured several battle stations curved in front of the captain's chair.

Luke summed up the feelings for everyone. "You've got a winner, here. It's the start of our space navy."

An hour later Luke sat in the living room of his quarters at Moonbase to review the day's events with Roth and Morrow. Annie had not arrived from her activities on Earth.

"I'm impressed with your new ship," Luke said. "Let's go to full production. How many for the first run?"

"I can put out a couple a week," Morrow estimated. "That allows time for flight testing. Give me more people and we can increase that."

"That's the real question," Roth said. "Even with all our recruiting, the number of people that we're bringing in each week is starting to taper off. We were hoping the new recruiting centers would increase that number. And it did a little, but not what we were expecting. Right now, we're still replacing the Mars colonists. That means most of our inbounds are dedicated to infrastructure and support."

Morrow agreed. "And we've got the university established now over in Far Side. Seems like every single day they want some kind of new toy. To keep them happy, we need to start making some purchases from places like Lockheed and GE. George can do a lot for us, but he needs access to some of those technical specs. I'm not exactly sure what that means in additional requirements. But bottom line is that our current recruiting provides us with enough new people to add two crew complements a week."

"That's good news," Luke said. "I like the idea of getting some warships out into the solar system just in case. That reminds me; we haven't established any firm rules of engagement. We need to get that nailed down quickly. And we need to formally establish our military arm. Right now I feel like we're just a bunch of gentlemen adventurers going along by the seat of our pants."

"There's another thing that's coming up fast," Roth said. "We're only about sixty days away from the expiration of our first employment contracts. You keep reminding me that if even one person exercises their option to go back it means the lid comes off. Everyone on Earth will know about us. I told Amanda Carlson to create a marketing and PR department. She's hiring reporters and copywriters. Soon we will have our own newspaper and TV station."

"Keep them away from me," was Morrow's reaction.

Luke nodded in amusement but didn't speak. The three lapsed into a companionable, if troubled, silence. Everyone was overwhelmed with the day-to-day business of extraordinary growth. The new challenges that kept cropping up just added to the burden.

"This is a dangerous time for us," Luke said. "This is the period that every startup company goes through. Excitement, events, and fast moving changes carry us along and adrenalin helps us keep it together for a few months, maybe a year. But without a solid backend bureaucracy, employees will start cutting corners or make up rules based on the situation at the moment. It's a recipe for disaster."

"So what do we do?" Roth asked. "Want us to pull back? Slow down?"

"Nothing I'd like more," Luke replied seriously. "Except for one small factor."

"The Bakkui?" Morrow suggested.

"Exactly." Luke sighed heavily. "We don't have a choice. We have to keep plugging away; keep moving as fast as we can. But let's start thinking about long term, let's get policies and regulations in place. And I hate to say it; but we need one more thing." Luke looked at his two best friends. "We're not going to be around forever. We need to establish a self-sustaining system that will keep going long after we're dead and gone."

"You mean politics," Morrow said, his face sour.

"Yes, God help me." Luke nodded. "I mean government and politics." He looked at Roth. "This is your baby. Start working on it."

Roth shook his head slowly while Morrow burst out laughing and pointed at Roth's long face. "Thank God he picked you for that. I want nothing to do with that kind of thing. Just make sure whatever you come up with includes free beer."

After his two colleagues departed, Luke opened just such a free beer of his own and sat on the couch, waiting for his new lover to come back from the surface. Today Moonbase had started building its own navy, and Luke felt good about their progress. But in the evenings, when he rested on this very couch with Annie sitting beside him, he worried about what kind of technology the Bakkui were bringing to the party. The thought made him shudder. He wished that Annie would hurry and get home. He looked forward to next week when it would be his turn to commute.

Chapter 6

Day 355—Population 9,359

Luke stood over the sizzling skillet in his Earthside home, expertly flipping the omelet into thirds, neatly encasing a sprinkling of diced ham, grated cheese, and spicy vegetables.

To be together as much as possible, he and Annie took turns commuting, and this was his week to make the twice-daily trip between Earth and his place on the moon. Their unspoken agreement was that the person commuting would make breakfast and the one remaining was responsible for dinner.

After many serious discussions with Luke, Annie put her grandmother's house on the market and moved into Luke's planetside residence. It was bigger, if a bit more rundown. During his life of solitude, Luke hadn't put much effort into renovation. Annie had assumed that responsibility and Luke was happy with the changes, which were many. As long as he wasn't involved with decorating decisions, much less any actual labor, she had carte blanche.

CNN was muted on the living room TV. The overly cheerful newscaster changed her expression to one that was particularly serious. Whatever breaking news she had been discussing was being replaced by even more urgent breaking news.

Luke heard the closet doors in the bedroom closing, which meant his timing was good. The omelet would be ready when she got to the kitchen. The microwave dinged and...

Commander Blackburn. The International Space Station is experiencing a disaster.

The sudden intrusive message brought Luke up short. "Explain that, George," he ordered.

Details are unavailable, but it appears there has been a catastrophe. For the moment no fatalities have been reported but the situation is deteriorating.

Luke glanced at the TV. A large photo of the ISS, overlaid with an explosive graphic, was on the screen. "Can we provide assistance?" he asked.

Doctor Higgins wishes to speak with you regarding that.

"Put him through."

Connected.

"Luke, you there?" Roth's voice came through loud and clear.

"I'm here, Roth. What's the story?"

"George just informed me the ISS is in the toilet. I'm looking at the report. CNN said it's an explosion but NASA doesn't know if the crew is okay. We had a mechanic on the way back from Far Side and I told her to head straight there. It's Carrie Faulknor; you've met her."

"Yeah. I remember."

"She's on the way, but she's going to need help. I think you're closer than anyone else and you've got *Sadie* with you, right?"

"Correct," Luke confirmed. "She's in the hangar."

"Luke, this is a bit ahead of schedule, but it might be a great opportunity for us to announce ourselves in a positive light. What do you think?"

"I agree. Good call, sending Carrie. I'm on the way."

Annie appeared from the bedroom. "George had me listening too," she told him. "You need to go."

Luke looked down at his eggs and then back at Annie. She grabbed the spatula out of his hand. "Get out of here. Put some clothes on first."

Two minutes later he dashed out of the house. It took several more minutes for their new security firm, Wehrlite Security, to get him through the security fencing that Annie had installed around the airport's perimeter. Inside the hangar, the huge doors seemed to take forever to open. He was less than two hundred fifty miles from the space station, and yet from the moon, Carrie on a scooter was going to reach the ISS before he did. It was maddening.

Finally he slid into *Sadie*'s pilot's seat. "You know where we're going, *Sadie*?" Luke asked.

"Course set," she replied.

"Let's go then."

She rose a foot off the hangar floor, glided out, and then lifted up, her nose pointing into the sky. "The ISS is currently on the other side of the planet, Commander. Time to arrival approximately five minutes."

When Luke arrived at the International Space Station, Carrie was already there and had dismounted her scooter. She was wearing her normal work attire of work gloves, blue jeans, and a flannel shirt. Her hair was pulled back in a tight ponytail, which, in the weightless environment, floated around her head in wispy bunches.

The ISS itself was indeed a disaster. Its once elegant spidery limbs were all askew and the station itself tumbled slowly end over end. Several solar panel supports had collapsed, leaving them haphazardly arranged like a strewn deck of playing cards.

"An object struck the station near the middle of the integrated truss structure," *Sadie* observed. "The Starboard One truss is severely damaged just past the connection to the Zero truss. The remaining starboard assembly buckled and is now angling sharply toward the zenith. The entire structure is rotating vertically around an axis from the Zvezda Service Module to the Destiny Lab."

Sadie's jargon was beyond Luke's understanding of the space station. "It's called a mess, *Sadie*," he said. "Christ, what is Carrie doing?"

Carrie had pulled a coil of rope from the scooter's saddlebag. She tied one end under the handlebars and fashioned a large loop at the other. She drifted toward the spinning station while slowly twirling the lasso over her head."

"Is she going to try and rope that thing?" Luke asked aloud, incredulous at the sight.

"It appears so," *Sadie* agreed. "Her profile states she is originally from Kansas. I assume that as a youth she engaged in rodeo activities."

Luke wanted to yell at her to be careful, but she projected a calm self-confidence. In his kitchen it sounded so simple; just jet up to the space station and sort things out. It was a different story watching the young woman float next to tons of spinning, out-of-control equipment.

Carrie approached the plane of arc for the Pressurized Mating Adapter. It was the last tube in the column of habitable modules. As it drifted by, she tossed her lariat around a thick cylinder on the side of the adapter. She pulled the noose closed and then, letting the rope play out through her hands, she mounted her scooter. Moving forward to match the spin of the station, she let the rope grow taut. She gradually applied reverse thrust to slow the spin, adjusting the scooter's position to steady the entire station.

A movement in one of the Cupola's windows drew Luke's attention. An astronaut was filming Carrie as she worked to stabilize the station. "Are they transmitting these images?" Luke asked *Sadie*.

"They are attempting to, Commander; however, their communications are severely degraded."

"Can you boost their signal? Or rebroadcast it?"

"Yes, Commander. I can do either or both. Is it your intention to update the government on current events or do you wish to inform the public?"

"Both, actually."

"Should I add my own video? I am currently sending a feed of these events to Doctor Higgins at Moonbase."

"Yes! That would be great. Let's make sure that everyone on Earth can see what our Carrie is up to."

Carrie's voice suddenly filled the shuttle. "Commander?" She had dismounted her scooter and floated over to Cupola.

"Yes, Carrie. Whatcha need?"

"I'm not sure what to do now."

"Coming to you, Carrie."

"The equipment you need is in the locker, Commander," *Sadie* told him.

Luke retrieved a tool belt and a personal force field from the equipment locker in the storage bay. He also found a pair of work gloves and tucked them into the belt. He dug through the locker some more until he found a roll of duct tape.

"Open the pod bay doors, please, *Sadie*."

The shuttle's large side door slid out and back. Luke stood in the doorway for a second to get his bearings then launched himself in Carrie's direction. He totally misjudged his leap, veering off at an oblique angle to the ISS. *Damn it.* At this rate he would pass the station and drift forever unless *Sadie* came to pick him up.

Carrie launched herself and thumped into him. They tumbled off in a new direction while she wrapped her legs around his waist. Sticking out both of her arms, Luke watched her flex her fingers outward repeatedly. Each time she did, it took a little off their spin.

An early briefing he'd received months ago came back to mind. The work gloves had miniature gravity plates built in.

"Sorry," he said. "Forgot."

He pulled the gloves out of his tool belt and pulled them on. By the time he got them on, Carrie had them aimed back toward the space station.

"Let me handle it, Commander," Carrie said quietly. "They take a little getting used to." They touched softly against the side of the Cupola.

They crawled over to the large viewing window where the ISS crew was peering out.

"They're pretty freaked out," Carrie observed.

"I can imagine," Luke replied. Watching Carrie moving freely outside the ISS, clad only in normal clothing, would be surreal to the inhabitants. "I think we need to get them out of there in a hurry. This thing is leaking all over."

"I think so too, Commander." Carrie was trying to count the people inside. "I only see three of them. I thought there would be more."

Luke held up three fingers to the window. The woman inside nodded vigorously. He held up four fingers and she shook her head. "Three must be all."

The station continued to rotate slowly, spurred on by the jets of escaping air. There was no way to stabilize it permanently.

"*Sadie*," Luke said. "Can you maneuver so your door is up against their escape hatch?"

"I can get close, Commander. But there is no way to establish a seal."

"Hang on here for a second, Carrie," Luke said. "I'll go get three more of the personal force fields. See if they'll let you inside. Make them understand how they work."

Carrie gave him a worried look.

"I'll be careful this time," he promised.

A moment later he was back, colliding with the Cupola a bit harder than he intended, but still in one piece.

Carrie took the personal force fields inside the ISS while Luke waited outside. He sympathized with the NASA scientists. For them, it would take an extraordinary leap of faith to let some youngster convince them into coming outside their crew module without their bulky suits.

A few minutes later, however, the main hatch opened. Carrie stuck her head out and gave Luke a thumb's up. She had a frightened woman astronaut in tow. The two women made the three-meter passage from the ISS into *Sadie*'s bay door.

Carrie remained in the shuttle to calm the older woman and Luke escorted the two remaining men. Finally, with all aboard the shuttle, Luke gave *Sadie* instructions to head for Moonbase. One of the men was still filming with his camera. As *Sadie* pulled away, he took a video that highlighted the damage to the ISS. Certainly it could be repaired, but Luke felt that would never happen. It would stay in orbit as a museum piece, outdated now in one fell swoop.

"*Sadie*, would you pass the word to Roth to prepare to receive our new passengers? It might be informative for them to see how we welcome new folks to the moon."

"Message sent, Commander."

#

Luke was impressed with the crowd Roth had waiting in the main hangar. Amanda, their PR director, and about twenty others applauded as the astronauts disembarked. Some children were even holding a big paper banner that said WELCOME SPACE STATION CREW.

Roth shook hands with the newcomers and introduced his two twenty-something assistants. "This is Sheri and Milo," he told them. "They'll take you to your quarters. Since we yanked you out of there unexpectedly, I thought you might like a chance to spruce up before our medical folks take a look at you. Then we'll get you in touch with Houston. They know you're okay, by the way. While you're here we'd like to show you around, let you meet some of our people. Then, if you're up to it, we'll get you back to Earth in the morning."

The NASA astronauts were no different from everyone else who experienced Moonbase for the first time; they were stunned by what they saw. Yet they rolled with each new revelation. Some of the shock had worn off by the time Sheri and Milo brought them to a conference room where Luke and Roth were waiting.

"Medical gave you a clean bill of health," Roth told them. "How you guys feeling? Ready to phone home?" He gestured to a screen with a live feed from the Mission Control Center in Houston. Shane Rosa, the lead flight controller for ISS operations, looked concerned.

"Hi, Shane," the female astronaut said.

"Everyone there okay?" Shane asked.

No one spoke. They looked at each other with disbelief, not sure what to say.

Luke interrupted the awkward moment and spoke to the ISS crew. "We're going to leave you here for a few minutes so you and Mission Control can get each other up to date. Let them know that we'll have you back on Earth tomorrow, around five in the evening Mountain Time, at the spaceport in Baggs, Nevada."

# # #

Roth sat down in Luke's office to fill him in. "Annie called Hawley, Hepworth, and Kidwell and told them to get down to Baggs. Lots of new legal ground here. Amanda and her team will fly down in just a few minutes. I'm going to send someone to bring back the Gulfstream. I wouldn't be surprised if the government or the military show up. We don't want anyone trying to confiscate anything."

"I don't want to leave Annie down there alone," Luke said. "The place is going to be overwhelmed with media and who knows what else. I'll go with Amanda."

Roth nodded. "I'd just as soon you stayed away from that madhouse, but I assumed you'd be going down regardless."

"I have to be there for this one. It's the big reveal."

"I understand. What else?"

Luke thought for a moment. "We have a recruiting ship scheduled for tonight, don't we?"

"Two, actually. One in Baggs and one in that small airport near Austin."

"Okay, let's reroute the Texas flight to Baggs. I think it's time to mothball our 737. This would be a good time to introduce our new passenger shuttle. *Sunni's* ready isn't she?"

"Good idea," Roth said. "She's configured for five hundred passengers at a time so capacity won't be an issue. The new look might scare a few people from getting on though."

"The entire world has seen our place here now. Amanda did a good job getting everything broadcast into the news feeds. Wonder what the talking heads are saying?"

"I don't even want to know," Roth admitted. "But Amanda said she kicked off Operation '*Hello from Moonbase*' with the first video of Carrie lassoing the space station. She's got our own experts on all the talk shows right now. We're sending feeds from our broadcast center down on level seven."

"Should we leave her here for now?" Luke asked.

"Might be a good idea. She's the face that people are getting used to, along with our experts. Take the PR ground team, though, you're going to need help yourself. George? Can *Sadie* be configured to carry passengers?"

"Not a problem, Professor Higgin," George replied. "It is being done now."

"Taken them down with *Sadie*," Roth suggested. "Amanda told me your new hotel convention center is open for business so you can have them established there. I'll send Amanda down tomorrow when we fly the astronauts back."

"Okay," Luke agreed. "Tell her to start pushing the opportunities for colonists. And have someone tell our recruiters that our secret research center is actually on the moon." Luke gave Roth a worried look. "Mostly, I just hope all this works out."

"Just remember what you told me. Big government will hate us, but the public will eat it up."

Sadie gently settled onto the Baggs tarmac. Linda was on the ramp in Luke's pickup. When the PR team got out of the shuttle, Luke had them pile into the back of the pickup. He told Linda to get them checked into rooms at the convention center. Annie was pacing on the flightline and she looked upset.

"We don't have enough security guards," she said. "People are starting to show up all along the fence line."

Luke gave her a quick hug. "Okay, don't worry about it. We can call Wehrlite to send more."

"I just did. You were right to hire a big international firm. We're going to need everything they have."

"They used to do a lot of government work," Luke said. "George did his own background on them and they're solid."

"If George recommended them, it's probably a good choice."

"We'll find out tonight," Luke predicted.

"I told them who I am when I called," Annie said. "I suggested they look at CNN, that we were the group rescuing the space station people. They're probably just now realizing that we're not simply a little airport."

"When are they arriving?"

"They should be here now. I told them to come with the biggest damn team they could."

Their chartered aircraft is approaching now, George told them.

Luke and Annie gazed toward the end of the runway. Bright landing lights could be seen in the distance.

"What about the lawyers?" Luke asked.

"I fired them just before you landed. Some idiot attorney told me they couldn't get here until next week so I said don't bother."

Annie's cell phone rang. "Just a second," she muttered. Then she smiled. "It's them. Maybe they had a change of heart."

Luke walked out onto the aircraft ramp to greet the security team and to give Annie a chance to work things out with the law firm. They would be crazy not to jump through hoops. How many law firms had the moon as a client?

Annie tugged on his sleeve. "*Now* they're bending over backward. They're trying to get a charter aircraft to get here tonight. I told them I'd pick them up at their office in five minutes. I'm going to take *Sadie*, you okay with that?"

"Yep. Go ahead, and I'll see you when you get back." As she hurried toward their shuttle he called after her. "Annie! You might want to bring back a news crew." She gave him a thumbs-up and disappeared inside *Sadie*. The shuttle rose quietly into the sky and one second later disappeared in the distance, accelerating toward Seattle.

Moments later the Wehrlite Security aircraft landed. Luke was pleasantly surprised that it was a C-130 Hercules, painted in a white, gray and black camouflage scheme. The venerable aircraft pulled onto the ramp, the rear clamshell doors opening even before it came to a stop. Three military grade Humvees rolled onto the tarmac and thirty men in combat gear poured out behind.

A tall, rugged-looking man approached. "Hubert Sheppard," he said shortly. "I'm looking for Annie Daniels."

"Annie is in Seattle at the moment. She'll be back in a few minutes. She asked me to get you started. I'm Luke Blackburn."

Sheppard gave a curt nod. "Orders?"

Luke smiled inwardly. Mr. Hubert didn't suffer from verbosity; he was a no-nonsense kind of guy. Luke pointed to the fence line. "Keep sightseers from coming over the fence. Also, at eight this evening we're expecting several buses from Reno. I want them admitted through the security gate without delay."

"Got it."

A couple of V-22 Ospreys flew over the runway at a thousand feet and circled to downwind. "Are those yours?" he asked Sheppard.

"Not mine. Looks like the Nevada Guard."

Luke wondered why the Guard was here. He didn't imagine it was a good thing.

Sheppard was evidently wondering the same thing. "I know the feces hit the fan over this space station thing but I can't go up against the military. Are you on their bad side?"

"I really don't know," Luke said as the lead Osprey turned to base from downwind. It rolled out on a final approach for landing. "But it looks like we're going to find out. *George, put me through to Roth,* he said mentally.

Connected, Commander.

"Higgins, here."

"Roth. The Nevada Guard just showed up. I'm not sure what this means, but it would be nice to have some backup handy."

"Understood, boss. I already asked our new navy CO to be on standby. Give him another ten minutes and he'll have all five of our new warships in orbit over you. From there he can be on station in seconds if you want him."

"Good plan. Thanks, Roth. You're earning your keep today, that's for sure."

"We're trying. By the way, Annie called. She's picking up a news crew in Seattle. I sent Amanda down after all. She's better at handling that kind of thing."

"Yeah, bringing a TV station here was my fault," Luke confessed. "Just a spur of the moment idea."

"Well, if the military is there, it may be a good idea to have a news camera on the scene. Might keep people from making bad decisions. Our media support team here is doing a great job. I keep watching CNN and the other news channels. So far everything is staying positive. I never knew we had such great bullshitters. But a few of the politicos are starting to make grumbling noises."

"I don't like the sound of that. We need to counter it, and do it quickly."

"Already started," Roth replied. "I'm reaching out to a couple of K-Street firms that I've dealt with in the past. I'll make sure we sic them on anyone who steps out of line. Anything else?"

"Not at the moment. Stay close to the phone."

"Will do."

Hubert Sheppard stood quietly while Luke was talking. If Sheppard wondered why Luke appeared to be speaking only to himself, he gave no indication. Once Luke turned to him, Sheppard spoke up.

"Guard is landing." He pointed further down the aircraft parking ramp.

The two Ospreys taxied off the runway, their giant propellers blowing desert sand everywhere. The connecting taxiways were too narrow for the Ospreys and their eighty-five-foot-wide rotors, canted forward at a forty-five-degree angle, kicked up dust devils and sent swirls of dirt and rocks across the tarmac. The Ospreys pulled onto the parking ramp two thousand feet down from the Wehrlite Security Hercules. A dozen men jumped out of each of the Ospreys and set up a perimeter around their aircraft.

One of them, flanked by two heavily armed soldiers, headed in their direction.

Sheppard responded with silent hand signals of his own, and four of his men took up positions around Luke.

Maybe we could have done this better, Luke thought.

Instead of trying to get the NASA people back in a methodical orderly fashion, maybe he should have taken them back right away. *We could have just dropped them off in the parking lot at Houston's Mission Control Center.* Too late now.

For a brief moment, Luke hoped that since it was the Guard, maybe the guy in charge would be a dentist in real life. Sort of an overweight weekend warrior.

No such luck. The guy walking toward him looked as no-nonsense as Sheppard. He came to a stop about five feet away. Luke looked him over. A gold embroidered oak leaf was visible on his chest.

"You look like that Lucas Blackburn guy on TV."

Luke stepped forward and stuck out his hand. "I prefer Luke. Major…?"

The man evaluated Luke's hand for a moment before giving it one firm shake in return. "Nick Key," he said. "You're trespassing on federal property. I need you to come with me."

Luke stepped back and smiled. "Nice to meet you Major Key. This is my associate, Hubert Sheppard. I have to say, Major, I think you're misinformed." Luke made a show of pulling his wallet out of his back pocket. He took out one of his business cards and handed it to the officer. "I'm the airport director here, as you can see. The airport is not federal property; it's owned by Nye

County. My office is in the terminal building. In fact, that's my secretary standing there. Linda Cummings."

Linda, bless her heart, had returned from delivering the PR team to the hotel and was standing outside the back door of the terminal. She was holding one of her knitting balls. Luke gave her a big wave and she grinned hugely and waved back. She pointed to her chest and walked her fingers toward Luke. He held one hand straight out to tell her no.

Major Key watched the exchange suspiciously, his eyes darting back and forth from the business card to Linda to Luke.

"Sir," Sheppard said quietly. He flicked a glance into the sky. Luke followed his gaze. It was one of the Moonbase shuttles.

Crap. Luke felt he'd almost had the guardsman bamboozled but now a space ship, looking very much like the one that was at the space station, was about to land. He wasn't sure what would happen next. The shuttle touched down a dozen feet behind Luke and the side door opened.

Amanda and five others stepped out; one of them was carrying a large video camera. Amanda was wearing what Luke thought of as one of her power suits. It was a business-like wrap-around dress, but it emphasized her curves and the material had a Gucci look to it, lots of color and pattern.

"Hi, Luke," she called out cheerily, sounding as American as apple pie. She hurried over and grasped Luke's arm with both hands. "Sorry I'm so late. Those CNN reporters want so many details and sometimes it's just hard to get away. Who's this?" She saw his nametag and rank insignia. "Major Key? Hi, I'm Amanda Carlson. I handle all of Luke's public relations and his media requests."

Amanda held out her hand to the major, palm down as though she expected him to just wiggle the tips of her fingers, which he did.

"Ma'am..." The major was a bit startled. "Ma'am... I... What did you say your name was?"

Luke was a bit sympathetic. When Amanda went into overdrive she could be a real force.

"Amanda. Amanda Carlson. Just call me Mandy, though. No need to be formal."

"Miss Carlson. I was just saying that Mr. Blackburn needs to come with me."

"Really? Governor Norris said that? How odd. Oh, look. This must be Annie and Luke's legal team from Seattle."

A second shuttle was descending rapidly and touched down next to the first one. Annie and half a dozen business suits got out and headed toward Luke. All of the suits were carrying bulky briefcases.

Amanda moved away from Luke and wrapped herself around one of the Major's arms. "Let's give these guys a chance to catch up for a second. Is that your airplane?" She looked past the major at the two Ospreys down the ramp. "Those are such cool, helicopter kind of things. I love that whop-whop sound that they make, don't you, with those great big propellers? One of these days you have to let me take a ride in one, okay?"

"Ma'am," The major tried to take a step back but Amanda had him in her grip.

"Did you know that Luke has other kinds of aircraft?" She turned her face toward Luke, away from the major, and gave him a frantic wide-eyed glance, nodding her head toward the open flight line. "I would love it if you would let me show you what those are like inside," she finished, turning back to the Major.

Luke gave her a quick nod. *Get down here,* he told George. *Just one.* A loud thunderclap split the sky, and hovering over the flight line was one of the warships. Slowly it descended, settling in the open space between Sheppard's C-130 and the Guard's Ospreys.

The huge disc made everything else on the flight line look minuscule by comparison. The twin cannons on the shoulders indicated its deadly capability. For the first time, Luke appreciated the design work that the engineers had put into it. It was unquestionably clear to everyone on the tarmac that this was a warship from outer space and had more power under the hood than anyone could possibly dream.

Amanda pressed her advantage with the Major. "Did you know that Luke's team rescued those people from the space station? Don't you think the governor would like it if the Nevada Guard were the first ones in the country to be seen on television working hand-in-hand with all those nice people from the moon?" She twisted the major around so they were both facing her camera team. One of her assistants stepped forward and held out a cell phone. "Or do you want to call the governor first?"

Luke watched Major Key take a deep breath. The odds were high that the Nevada governor was watching this in real time. The major had been outmaneuvered and was now outnumbered. In the space of five minutes, his initial advantage had slipped away.

Luke suspected that the major's boss had told him to fly up here and bring this *Luke guy* in quietly. It was a dumb idea. One of those ideas that middle managers come up with to impress bosses with their initiative. The kind of ideas that don't do well in the limelight.

In this case, the entire nation had watched the space station rescue on TV. Luke had been floating around in space without a helmet. Carrie and her ponytail was cuter than a bug, riding that scooter and lassoing the ruined station.

When they broadcast the reunion of the ISS crew on the moon talking to mission control, Luke told the entire world that NASA could pick up their people at the Baggs Spaceport in Nevada. A month ago, even a week ago, everyone would have laughed at the "spaceport" designation on the airport's name. Just like they did all the other airports around the country that had tried it. Except it wasn't a joke now.

Luke relaxed when he saw the officer sigh.

"Mandy," Major Key said, smiling, "I'd love to see the inside of that spaceship."

After a quick discussion, Major Key and his two NCOs, along with Sheppard and two of his security team, accompanied Amanda and Luke to the warship. And of course, the Seattle news crew and Amanda's cameraman tagged along to record the event. The warship's captain, Joe Brady, waited for them at the bottom of the boarding ramp.

"Good to see you again, Commander," Brady said.

"Thanks, Joe. We have quite a few visitors. Can you give us a quick tour?"

"Of course, Commander." Brady then looked at the military escorts. "No weapons aboard, however."

There was a tense moment while Major Key mentally struggled with the restriction. Then he shrugged. "FAA regulations I guess."

No one corrected his statement, but the idea gave everyone an excuse to comply without losing face. Major Key waved toward the Ospreys for one of his troops to come over. It took several minutes for everyone to divest themselves of all armaments.

Brady gave everyone a big smile. "Please come aboard." He gestured toward the ship's interior. "Commander."

Luke suspected that Brady's repeated use of the *Commander* title would eventually prompt the Seattle newswoman to question why that was so. Fortunately, Brady gave a running commentary as they walked through the ship. There was surprisingly little to see. Lots of corridors, a gymnasium, galley, break room. He spoke in general terms about the warship's firepower but there was nothing to really show.

Finally, they stopped before a set of double doors. He explained the doors led to the bridge and asked them not to touch anything while inside. Brady looked at the group for acknowledgement. It was the opening that the news woman was waiting for.

She turned to Luke and in an innocent voice asked, "Why does Captain Brady keep calling you Commander? I'm Leslie Boyle, by the way, Channel 5 News."

It was an answer that Luke was well prepared for. It was also one that he didn't want to give personally and yet had insisted that it not be glossed over. After many long discussions between Luke, Roth, and Amanda, Luke was adamant. They would be open and honest about the alien threat.

His argument was, "If we hold back anything, someone will say that we lied. And that's a break of trust we can never get back."

Roth contended that all governments lied. It was expected; Luke had no obligation to spill everything. Amanda tended to agree with Roth.

"The threat affects everyone on the planet," Luke countered. "That gives them an inherent right to know what's going on in this solar system.

Just as important, in Luke's mind, it also gave Moonbase an effective recruiting tool. "Everyone wants to be a hero in their hometown. History proves that nationalism is a powerful force. Don't you think that applies on a planetary level?"

Roth didn't think so at all. "Politicians around the world will use that same nationalism to incite resistance to you and what you're trying to do. They'll use fear of aliens. You ever see a politician who didn't use racism and bigotry to instill fear? That xenophobic panic will be aimed right at you."

"And what if the aliens never show?" Amanda chimed in. "Don't you think people will see that as a betrayal? They'll say you used the bogeyman to keep all this wonderful technology to yourself. Luke the Czar. That will be your title then."

"If that day comes, Amanda, it will be the happiest day of my life. If that happens, Annie and I will move to Kepler-22, change our name to Farmer and Mrs. Jones, and grow little green sheep with splotchy fur."

In the end Luke laid down the law. When the time came, they would be honest about the encroaching threat. It wasn't as if anyone on Earth could do anything about it.

"What are we going to call ourselves?" Amanda wanted to know. "We need a name that sounds big. I like PDEF, but that sounds too corporate."

"How big?" Luke asked.

"As big as the Milky Way?" Roth suggested.

"Yes, exactly." Amanda said. "We need a name for this alliance that you want to create that's just that big."

###

Amanda stepped smoothly between Luke and Boyle's news camera. "Let me answer that, Commander. You're too shy about your accomplishments. Leslie, Commander Blackburn is the Supreme Commander of the Milky Way Alliance. He protects our solar system from the invaders which threaten us."

Boyle took a step back in the warship's corridor. "Invaders?"

"Oh, yes," Amanda confirmed. "But let's wait until we're back on the planet and I can give you a proper briefing. We've got handouts."

"Back on the planet?" Boyle squeaked.

"That's correct. Didn't we say? I think we're already in orbit. Isn't that right, Captain Brady?"

Brady picked up on his cue and opened the doors to the bridge. A few of his crew members were sitting at their stations. But the only thing everyone saw was the thirty-foot-wide window at the front of the bridge. Few people on Earth ever had a view like this one: The deep black nothingness of space and the blue marble of Earth shining brilliantly below.

###

Luke waited patiently for fifteen minutes while the visitors stared out into space. One by one they moved up to the glass where they clustered together in silence. Luke appreciated how they felt. It was less than a year ago when he got his first surprise trip off planet.

When they finally started murmuring to each other, he gave a discreet nod to Brady.

"Okay, everyone," Brady said aloud. "We're going to start back. Would all of you please grab hold of that railing? It gets a little disorienting." He waited while the visitors took a firm, if worried, grip on the long grab bar. "*Ching Shih*, can you take us back to Baggs, please, and set us down where we were before?"

"Course set, Captain," the ship answered.

The planet below filled the window's view as *Ching Shih* dipped her nose down. She established a needle-nose force field that spread out thousands of feet in front of her hull so she would penetrate the atmosphere with little effect. No fiery trail would herald her passage; just a sonic boom that no one on the ground would ever hear. The massive gravity drives at the back of her truncated hull pushed her gently toward the surface. She entered the atmosphere headed almost straight down at a mere seventeen thousand miles an hour.

Descending through sixty thousand feet *Ching Shih* spun effortlessly around her vertical axis and those same drives pulsed again at a fraction of their power, braking softly, reducing her speed from Mach 30 to a few hundred miles per hour. She lowered the nose so she was in a level flight with respect to the surface and used the main gravity plates under her hull to slow for landing, ultimately setting down once again in the exact spot she had lifted from less than half an hour ago. Ninety seconds had elapsed since her captain gave the command to return to the planet.

"Arriving at destination, Captain," *Ching Shih* announced in her quiet, musical voice. Inside her command bridge, the cup of coffee resting on the console in front of one crewman had not budged. Her crew sat relaxed in their seats.

The visitors, by contrast, maintained a death grip on the grab bar, their expressions reflecting a mixture of terror, shock, and disbelief.

"Thank you, *Shih*," Captain Brady said graciously. "Commander, let me walk you out. Everyone, please follow me."

On the flight line, Hubert's team had set up a large pavilion tent next to the two space shuttles. Annie had the hotel send over two of their airport vans, which were parked near the tent. A couple of the attorneys were loading their bags into the back of the vans.

Luke shook hands with Major Key and invited him to stay around if he wished. "We wouldn't want it on a regular basis," Luke said. "But if you want to delay departure, just to get an idea of what's going on, then by all means feel free. But tomorrow, this ramp area is going to get crowded."

The major accepted the invitation provisionally, depending on guidance from headquarters; all hostility gone from his attitude. He turned away to head back to his two Ospreys.

"Hubert?" Luke said, turning to find the man.

"Right here, sir. I mean Commander."

Luke took Sheppard by the elbow and pointed toward the terminal building. "There's a Mrs. Linda Cummings in there."

"Right. I saw her."

"Think of her as my mom. She's not, but that gives you an idea of what she means to me. I'd like you to put a security detail around her. Keep it unobtrusive. Let her do whatever she wants, but stop anyone from hassling her. That means government, cops, and especially media or sightseers."

"Got it." Sheppard turned away to bark orders at his men.

Luke saw Annie talking to Leslie Boyle and Amanda. He walked over to join them.

"Hey, babe," Annie said. "I was telling them about our recruiting flight tonight. I thought it might be a good thing to put on the news. It will let people know that it's us who's recruiting. May as well get some free advertising."

"Great idea," Luke agreed.

"We've got some media checking into the hotel. They're starting to show up from Reno. If you can keep an eye on Leslie here, Amanda and I will go round them up."

"Sure. What about your big media briefing?"

"We don't have enough time before our recruits show up. I thought we'd bring back some of the media, let them film, then go back to the hotel for the brief. There will be a lot of Q&A afterward."

"Can I skip all that?" Luke asked.

Amanda answered his question. "I think that's probably a good idea," she said diplomatically. "Annie and I will take care of the briefing and the Q&A. I got a question, though. Any chance we could get Carrie down here? She would be a real hit with these reporters."

"I'll call Roth right now," Luke said. "I don't know how Carrie will take it though. She's always seemed shy."

"We'll take care of her," Amanda promised.

Luke got Roth on the phone, who agreed to send Carrie right away, along with a couple of pilots. "You're starting to collect a lot of shuttles down there. I'll tell them to bring a few back."

"Okay," Luke agreed. "Just leave *Sadie* here for me. I'm not sure we ever got the Gulfstream out of here either. You might want to take her with you."

"We're on it," Roth said and signed off.

Leslie spoke behind him. "Who were you talking to just now? How are you doing that?" Leslie was standing next to her cameraman and was holding a microphone out toward Luke.

He looked at the mic and took a deep breath. He should have kept one of the girls here. They wouldn't like him talking to the media on his own.

"Looks like you want an exclusive interview," he said.

"If you've got the time," she replied in her innocent voice.

George, I want you to monitor this. Stop me if I start to say something wrong.

As you wish, Commander. It shouldn't be a problem. Annie would tell you to 'just be yourself.'

"Let's get comfortable at least," Luke said to the reporter. They walked over to the pavilion and commandeered one of the tables and a couple of chairs. Leslie took a moment to stage the location so the giant warship was in the background. Luke answered her questions, sticking to the script that Amanda had prepared.

He told her about his initial meeting with Sam and the mission that had been thrust upon him. He explained how he and Annie had set up the Moonbase for their first recruits and their growth since then. Luke smiled as he described their success in establishing a colony on Mars just a month earlier. Shuttle traffic was going back and forth daily, adding to their knowledge base and helping them prepare for the next larger leap to the stars.

Leslie fixated on one point. "You mean it's just like a *Star Trek* replicator? It will make anything you want? Jewels, money? That sort of thing?"

"Not exactly. But the main thing is no one uses it for that. No point."

"No point?" Leslie found it hard to accept. "But a person could make themselves fabulously wealthy with one of those. Why *wouldn't* they?"

"You've got that wrong, Leslie. Why *would* they? On the moon, we created a society that values everything *but* wealth. We measure our worth in what we do, not what we own. We're trying to save mankind. We want to protect our solar system. Who cares about a box of rubies?"

"I would!" Leslie said firmly. "Can I have one of those replicators? Or you can just replicate me that box of rubies. I'll make great use of them. I can promise you that!"

"Sorry." Luke smiled sympathetically. "If you want to emigrate to the moon, you can have all the jewels you want. But if you did, I doubt you'd want them anymore."

"I don't understand. Aren't you going to use that technology on Earth? You could change the system."

"That would be intrusive. I'm not smart enough to change a system that already takes care of seven billion people. To even try would be dangerous."

"But you could feed a lot of hungry people," Leslie insisted.

"That's true," Luke agreed. "But so could you. There is more wealth on this planet than most of us can imagine and it's not up to me to tell anyone how to spend it. Besides, I think what we're working on is important. Saving mankind?"

"Well, what if people down here don't like the system? What if they want a chance at what you're keeping for yourself?"

"Then that would be great. In fact, we're recruiting people as fast as we can. I can't imagine a day when we'll get too crowded. If anyone wants to move to the moon and become part of our team, they just need to look online. Starting tomorrow, recruiting agencies around the world will be posting all of the job openings we're trying to fill." Luke warmed to the recruiting pitch. Leslie's questions had teed it up perfectly. He recited as many of the details as he could remember until Hubert caught his eye.

"That's it, Leslie," Luke said, bringing the interview to a close. "Hope that worked for you." He went over to join Hubert. "What's up."

Hubert looked into the sky. "Someone's coming."

It was the new transport, replacing their faux-Boeing 737. The new spacecraft was shaped much like their other shuttles, boxy and bulky rather than smooth and cylindrical like an airliner. And it was bigger. The new fuselage was thicker than current wide-body jets and half again as long, sort of like an oversized train car. Inside, the spacecraft was designed for comfort. Capable of carrying five hundred passengers, the seating was wide and spacious.

Moments later Annie was back. She brought three hotel vans full of media people. She and Amanda arranged a quick walkthrough of the new shuttle. As they were finishing up yet another shuttle, *Sadie*-sized this time, arrived, carrying Carrie Faulkner. Annie introduced Carrie to the crowd. She was rewarded with loud applause and celebrity-like adulation. Luke was surprised to see a different side of Carrie. In front of the cameras she was vivacious and outgoing, an instant hit with the broadcasters.

A line of buses arrived and Hubert's men quickly processed them through the airport's security gates. The thought flickered through Luke's mind that he should probably institute some kind of passenger screening. As word spread, no doubt there would be crazies trying to get into one of their shuttles.

Annie noticed Luke was yawning and came over. "You look shot," she said. "You've had a long day."

"No longer than you and Carrie. And look at her. She's going strong as ever."

"She's a lot younger than you, babe. You need to knock it off."

"I'm not going to argue. But I'm reluctant to head home. I suspect there are paparazzi all over the place by now."

"I'm sure Captain Brady can fix you up with a room for tonight," Annie suggested.

Luke nodded. "I'll go check. And one other thing."

"What's that?"

"Great job today. All of your preparation paid off."

Annie squeezed his hand. "I think so too. I got a call from Roth a few minutes ago. The news shows are still on our side. He said this is our honeymoon period, but he won't guarantee how long it will last."

Luke thought about it. "I hope it lasts a long time. You and I need to focus outward now. We'll get some people down here to keep the system running. But tomorrow, we have to start looking toward the stars."

Chapter 7

Day 369—Population 13,059

Luke nodded his thanks for the update to Morrow who was seated across the conference table. It had been weeks since the last senior staff meeting. It was nice enough to skip a few meetings, but today it was time to get back into the gritty details of growing Moonbase and expanding humanity's footprint in the galaxy.

A familiar face was missing. Daniel Perez, his security chief, had promised he was staying on the moon but then changed his mind. Not to go back to Earth; he decided to stretch himself even further. A week earlier Perez and his family migrated to Mars on the regular shuttle Luke established between the two planets. Brandon, the HR director, was another Martian convert.

Hubert Sheppard, formerly of Wehrlite Security, was the new security chief. His tough exterior hid a common sense outlook that Luke admired. In the days following the space station incident, Sheppard impressed Luke with his ability to organize and lead his people. Once things settled down, and Perez announced his intention to emigrate, Luke invited Sheppard to Moonbase. While there, Luke arranged for Sheppard to have a sit-down with Roth. Sheppard agreed to head up the new Moonbase security position.

Luke directed his attention to another new face, Adelia Perkins. She was in charge of building the new space station that was currently under construction.

"Adelia," Luke said. "Welcome to your first lunar staff meeting."

Adelia bobbed her head with a return smile that took in everyone. "Thanks, Commander. Good to be here."

"So what's new?" Luke asked simply.

"I can give you an update on your new space station."

"Perfect. Not everyone here knows about that."

Adelia glanced around the table. "As you know, the International Space Station was lost a while back. Luke directed us to come up with a replacement, but wanted it big enough to serve as a launch platform for our colony ships. Ambrose said it would be easier to start with a big rock and just carve it up to our specifications. The astronomy guys found one the right size near Jupiter. We moved it here and at the moment, it's in a geostationary stationary orbit above Far Side. We'll move it into Earth orbit in a week or two."

"What was it before?" Luke asked. "I know you told me. Caruso?"

"It was Callirrhoe, one of Jupiter's moons. As far as I know, no one planetside has noticed yet." Adelia smiled sheepishly. "I still feel a little guilty about stealing one of Jupiter's moons."

"Think they'll figure it out?" Roth asked.

"Someone will," Amanda predicted. "Probably some teenager in Hoboken. We should be ready. I'll come up with a statement for release in case someone complains."

"Excuse me," Kathy Lyons, the new HR director, interrupted. "Did you just say you *stole* one of Jupiter's *moons*?"

Morrow chuckled. "You can tell she's new. Get used to it, Kathy. Up here we do things on a whole different scale."

"But how?" Kathy asked, still incredulous.

"It was easy enough," Ambrose answered. "We made a special gravity drive on a fixed platform and took it out there. It had three main drives, rather large ones of course, and four smaller ones for steering. It's not that big; about five miles across. We took it slow coming back. All of that happened before you got here."

Morrow added, "Why don't you swing by our labs when you get a chance? I'll give you a quick rundown on some of our other projects."

"Okay. Thanks."

Ambrose was proud of Adelia's accomplishments. "It doesn't look much like a rock anymore. And by the way, we need to come up with a better name than *The Rock*, or it's going to stick. We're open to suggestions."

"What about the *Isaac Newton Gateway*?" Luke offered. "Everything we do revolves around our ability to control gravity. Isn't he the guy that invented it?"

"Discovered it," Amanda corrected. "But I do like that name; it has a good ring to it. Can we go with that?"

Roth agreed. "I like it too. Has a nice historical connotation that will sit well with the governments on Earth. I'm a little worried about their reaction when we suddenly add a new moon into Earth's orbit."

There was a general murmur of agreement around the table.

"Okay then," Adelia continued. "The Newton Gateway is taking shape. We've got people living there full time now. Give me sixty to ninety days and we'll be in full operation."

"Can you make it sixty?" Luke asked.

"I can if you give me enough people. The sculpting process is going very quickly. The architects finished their surveying a couple of weeks ago and the design was programmed into the new cutters that Ambrose's people came up with."

"What new cutters?" Luke questioned. "I haven't heard about that."

Ambrose spoke up. "Remember the cutting tools you used during your first days on the moon? Sam showed you how to shape corridors and rooms with those saws on wheels."

"How'd you know about that?"

Kathy smiled. "Everyone knows about that, Commander. It's part of our basic orientation. There's a video of you wrestling the machines around, shaping the first residences that we all live in."

Luke directed an accusatory glare at Roth.

"Don't look at me," Roth said. "I got that stuff from George. He's the one who turned you into a legend. Part of his grand scheme."

Luke fumed inwardly but kept silent. It seemed the more time went by, the more his reputation grew, and none of it was accurate. He'd deal with George later but for now, he nodded at Ambrose to continue.

"Anyway, we had George build a limited AI to run cutters that are self-propelled. Once the architects finish their design, George feeds it into the cutters. They take off down the corridors and it's not long before you're ready to move in."

Adelia picked up the narrative. "That's the easy part. Making it livable is what takes time. Furnishings, decorating, putting in environmental and command and control systems. The cutters take care of a lot, but we still have to finish out the living and working space for a hundred thousand people. That's what we designed for."

"Sounds good, Adelia," Luke agreed. "Keep at it. Now, we have one special visitor that you all know. Everyone welcome Samantha back. She has a special announcement to make and I've been saving her for last."

Samantha smiled a thank-you to the people around the table.

"So, Samantha," Luke continued. "Tell us your news."

"Thanks, Luke. It's good to be back. I love being the mayor of Mars, but I'll never forget that I got my start right here. Now, I don't want anyone to take this announcement personally. I know there are some newcomers here who haven't heard about our *secret* plan." Samantha put air quotes around the word 'secret'.

"Just you, me, and Roth," Luke said.

Samantha took a deep breath. "I'm here to declare that Mars is an independent planet; independent of Earth and of the moon."

Luke grinned at the startled expressions around the table. "And?" he prompted her to finish.

"And we want to establish formal diplomatic relations with the Milky Way Alliance. And the moon and any other planets that may soon be colonized."

Roth started applauding, which sparked a similar response from everyone else, their confused expressions notwithstanding.

"Relax, everyone," Luke urged. "We've been planning this from the get-go. We've just been waiting for Samantha to get her government in order. Good job, Sam."

"We're not ready, of course, not completely," Samantha confessed. "But if we wait until we're completely ready, we'll never get there, so I decided to take the plunge. Long live Mars. How about you guys?"

Luke looked at his friend. "Roth?"

Roth had a dour expression on his face. "Why are you guys in such a hurry? I'm nowhere near close. Do I need to do this now?"

"That was the plan." Luke reminded him.

"Give me another week," Roth protested. "There are still people I need to get up-to-speed." He looked around the table. "You guys are about to become cabinet members. Double the pay too."

"Thanks a lot," Ambrose bitched. "By my figures, that's still zero."

"It's more than I'm making," Samantha offered.

"Okay," Luke interjected. "We've all talked about establishing a government and I know that no one is interested but I've said this before. The people at this table are not going to be around forever. We've seen enough bad government on Earth to know it's not an easy thing to do. So let's start now, while we're small. Maybe we can develop a system that actually works. We'll never be successful if we don't have a functioning bureaucracy, but without oversight to control it, a bureaucracy can become an oppressor. This should not be a surprise to any of you."

"I got it," Roth said quietly.

Luke looked at Roth and nodded. "Okay, one week. I'm taking that as a promise."

"It is." Roth sighed. He looked at Samantha. "How's the training ground going for new colony leaders? We've sent three mini-colony expeditions so far. Are those guys working out?"

"Two of them are," Samantha said. "Kane and Lorita did a great job, but I had to pull Jed Morton. He was overwhelmed; he wouldn't delegate or trust his people. And I had complaints from some of the women. Too many to be a misunderstanding."

Roth nodded. "Okay. That's kind of a surprise. I thought he was a hard charger."

"He is, just in all the wrong ways."

"What about the rest of his colony. Are they ruined?"

"No, one of them, a young man named Solomon Andrews, took charge. He's an impressive leader so they'll be fine. When is the first true colony ship going out, by the way?"

"Thirty days," Luke answered. "Assuming our probes confirm what the astronomy guys are telling us. I'll feel a lot better once we get the first ship away. To actually be seeding the cosmos, that's kind of a big accomplishment. We're making progress."

###

"*Sadie?*" Luke asked. "Can you take us down a little bit? I'd like to see how it looks from below."

The ship moved smoothly to give him a better vantage point. "Correction completed, Commander," *Sadie* responded.

Luke craned his neck from the pilot's seat to examine the Isaac Newton Gateway. Adelia and her team finessed the planetoid's position while they moved it into orbit. Luke noticed absently that they were presently over the North American continent. It seemed appropriate somehow that the Gateway started its life over Baggs, Nevada. "What do you think, babe?" he asked Annie.

"I think you're making your PR Director's life difficult. First, you add a moon to Earth's orbit and now you're saying that you're releasing the independence proclamation tomorrow. That's a lot of changes for the people on the planet."

Luke shrugged. "Can't make an omelet, etcetera."

"I know. It's just got to sting for all those politicians. They hate not having control."

"They never did. But what do you think of the Gateway?"

Annie paused to actually *look* at the massive space station. "It's beautiful of course. How could it not be with Adelia working on it?"

She was right. Most of the planetoid's external surface had been sheared away, leaving broad, flat surfaces from which thousands of windows shone brightly. The upper surface of the small moon was cut away on two sides, leaving a central superstructure that towered over two giant landing pads, each of which could hold four of the future colony ships.

Brilliant lights kept the landing surfaces illuminated whether in sunlight or darkness. Dozens of flitters buzzed around the exterior. Adelia's finishing work was continuing even as the massive station was moved into its permanent orbit.

"It's a big billboard for us," Luke said. "The low orbit means everyone on the planet will see it on a regular basis. The politicos might resent it, but I'm hoping that to the average family, it represents a ticket to a new life."

"So what about the politicians?" Annie asked. "What do you hope to achieve by even meeting with them?"

Luke sighed. "I don't know. It won't hurt to hear them out. Maybe if we give them a little consideration it will make life easier for potential colonists. What I don't want is a situation where people who want to sign up with us have to sneak around."

"What do you mean by 'a little consideration'? You mean pay them off?"

Luke chuckled at her words. "Well, they are politicians after all. But no, that's not what I meant. I was thinking of giving them a non-voting seat on the council. Donate some space in the Gateway; it might help to make up for the loss of the space station."

"I'm not saying those aren't good ideas. But I don't have a good feeling about this. These guys remind me of the spoiled traders I had to deal with when I was at Royal Deutsche. You can't please them. They feel entitled and they're never satisfied. Just a bunch of malcontents in a peanut gallery."

"Ease up a little, sweetheart. If we go in with that attitude, it's not going to help. When we're there, promise me you'll keep a smile on your face and that you'll be nice. The last thing we need is you pounding on some poor congressman."

"I'll try; but I won't promise."

"Try hard," Luke urged giving her a sideways hug from his pilot's seat. "I'll smile enough for both of us if necessary. Having you beside me puts me in such a good mood that no one can make me angry."

Day 383—Population 12,478

The boisterous crowd in the exhibition hall of the Baggs Airport Convention Center and Hotel suddenly grew very quiet. It appeared that Luke Blackburn, the man from the moon, the one everyone called Commander, had just lost his cool. It was the way he smashed the congressman's face against the door that gave it away.

The room was filled with enough round banquet tables for five hundred distinguished visitors. They had come from around the world to attend the two-day conference. Buffet tables along the back wall were laden with enough food for an army. Top chefs had prepared the cuisine specifically to satisfy a finicky international audience.

Everyone had enjoyed their morning meal and listened appreciatively to the introductions of people whose names had been unknown until today. One name all of them knew, of course, was Amanda Carlson. She had dominated the airwaves since the loss of the International Space Station and even more so since last week when the moon and even Mars—who knew there was a colony on Mars—had declared their independence from Earth.

Public opinion was mixed depending on the country. Most of the third world supported the announcement. It was an *in-your-face* gesture to the superpowers.

Russia and China denounced the move as illegal, which Luke expected, but the United States had surprised him. He thought they would be on his side but Congress was vociferously against what they called a rebellious stunt. Members of both Houses called for immediate hearings and the House of Representatives even issued a subpoena for Luke to appear and explain his actions.

Loudest of all was the banking industry. Once they heard that there was no money on the moon and that Luke's startup funding had come from replicated gold, they wanted his head on a chopping block.

The conference's opening plenary session was being televised on most of the channel news outlets. The entire world was going to hear exactly what was going on, and from the man himself. Seven billion people wanted to know what the upstart lunar colony meant to the people of Earth. Talking heads were on standby to dissect every nuance that came from Amanda's opening speech.

As she spoke, the news anchors grew agitated. Instead of something juicy, Amanda was giving a rehash of what she'd been saying all along. The moon wanted to get along with everyone; they wanted colonists; if you emigrated you could live for free; there were discoveries every week of new planets that were ripe for settlement.

Amanda finished her opening comments and then introduced the keynote speaker, Luke Blackburn. This was the guy who'd started it all. The person that a lot of very important people said should be in jail.

Luke stepped up to the podium and smiled. He didn't look like such a bad person, but looks could be deceiving. He parroted Amanda's opening remarks about how happy he was to be here and hoped that the future would bring great things. That's when a heckler at one of the tables near the dais called out a few unintelligible comments.

Luke ignored him and kept talking. The heckler stood up and tried to interrupt Luke's speech.

The cameras zoomed in. It was the obnoxious congressman from Texas, Cesar Morán. The guy everyone loved to hate. He was the most vociferous congressman denouncing the moon's *subversive activities*.

Two hotel attendants hurried over and tried to quell the interruption but the congressman shook them off with a string of expletives before turning back and shouting again at the podium.

Luke stopped talking and located the source of the disturbance. He recognized the man immediately. "Do you have a problem, Congressman Moron?" Luke asked.

"Ha! Ha!" Morán shouted. "Like I haven't heard that before. I have a subpoena for you to appear before Congress." He held up a small sheaf of papers and waggled them at Luke.

Luke gestured to Morán to come forward. "Come on up, Congressman."

Morán, a master at spotting opportunities for grandstanding, quickly jumped onto the dais and moved to confront Luke in front of the microphone.

"Whatcha got?" Luke asked amiably, holding out an open hand.

Morán smacked the papers into Luke's palm. "This is a subpoena demanding that you appear in front of my committee…"

"Got it. Thanks." Luke handed the papers to Annie who shied away from the documents, wrinkling her nose in disgust.

Luke dropped the papers on his empty seat with a chuckle and then gestured to Morán to return to his seat. The crowd tittered at Annie's rejection of the repulsive individual.

"Just one second," Morán barked, not moving. "Young lady, your attitude toward this matter is not fit to be on display like that. I have a mind to egrk…" His comment was cut short as Luke's hand closed around his throat.

Luke held Moran at arm's length while he turned back to the microphone. "Sorry, folks," he said. "Give me just a second to take care of the congressman's request."

With apparent ease, Luke held the apoplectic lawmaker off the ground as he strode off the dais toward the large floor-to-ceiling French doors that lined the side of the room. He smashed the congressman's face into the doors twice before he stepped back as though realizing that the doors were locked.

He gestured to the back of the exhibition hall where a young man, dressed in hotel livery, hurried forward. Luke pointed at the door and the man pulled out a ring of keys and fumbled with them until the door was unlocked. By this time, several security guards had gathered, and Luke, after smashing the congressman's face against the glass once more, this time opening the door, hauled the man out onto the patio. He spoke a few words to the security guards, who hauled Moran away, blood dribbling onto the patio as they left.

The crowd was startled by the sudden turn of events. In hushed silence they watched Luke returned to the podium.

"Now, as I was saying," he resumed, a wide smile still in place, "I believe our efforts on the moon have the opportunity to bring innumerable benefits to the people of Earth. We are making advances in science and technology, in medicine, and in our understanding of the universe itself. We want to share these discoveries with you. However, to make that happen we need your assistance. We hope that Earth's governments will help their citizens join our efforts. Today, we have one single shuttle going back and forth to the moon from this very airport. I hope that tomorrow our shuttle can start operating in countries across the globe. Let's adjourn for twenty minutes and then we can start the breakout sessions. The schedules are posted on the doors of each meeting room. Thanks very much."

Luke sat down and gave Annie a worried look. "How'd I do?"

"You did good," she told him. "And you smiled the entire time. Why so harsh on the congressman?"

"I didn't like the way he addressed you. I don't care what he says to me. But when he started in on you, it's a different story."

"He didn't really say anything that bad, you know. He was just getting wound up."

Luke didn't buy it. "We're trying to save humanity and he was being a bully," he countered. "The best way to deal with that type is to take them out early on."

"What did you tell security? I think you probably broke his nose."

"I tried. But I told them to take him to Samantha so he could get patched up."

"Samantha? You mean Samantha Meyers! On Mars? Jesus, Luke."

"Yeah. I'd just as soon he's out of the way. Samantha is probably going to tell us that he wants to emigrate. Not sure where she'll put him."

"He has a family!" Annie protested. "You can't separate them like that."

Luke nodded. "That's true. I hadn't thought of that. I'll make sure they have the opportunity to join him." Luke leaned back to get the attention of one of the waiters. "Can I get a refill please? This is cold."

"Of course, Commander," the waiter whispered and hurried off with the unwanted dishes.

The sun was going down when Luke and Annie said their last good-bye for the day and made their escape from conference center to the patiently waiting *Sadie*. They sat in the comfortable pilot seats and enjoyed the quick flight to Moonbase One. "This view never gets old does it?" Luke said.

"I know. And it's not like it's great scenery. It's just a big rock with a lot of craters. But it's still amazing."

"Commander," *Sadie* spoke up. "Dr. Higgins would like to see you as soon as possible."

"Do you know what about?"

"He wants to discuss a recent drone report."

"Let him know we'll be right there." Luke turned to Annie. "You want to come?"

"Not really. Amanda and I pulled an all-nighter getting ready for that conference. Unless you need me, I'd just as soon go straight home."

"Check with him, would you, *Sadie*?" Luke asked.

"He prefers that you both attend," the shuttle replied.

"Must be big news," Luke said. "You up for it?"

"Guess so," Annie said before stifling a yawn.

Sadie touched down and the two headed for Roth's office.

"What's up, George?" Luke said aloud as they walked down the corridors.

The AI replied in a hushed tone. "It appears that Sam's optimism was not well founded. We found a hostile force with one of our early probes. This puts them much closer than we thought."

Luke and Annie exchanged worried looks as they entered Roth's office.

"I see that George filled you in," Roth commented, seeing their expressions. He leaned back in his chair, looking exhausted and suddenly very old.

"How far away are they?" Annie asked.

"Three years? Two? Could be less, I suppose," Roth replied. "No matter how you look at it, this is really bad news. Show us, George."

The wall of Roth's office displayed a video of a blue planet; it looked remarkably like Earth with white, swirling bands over brown and green continents.

The shot zoomed in until the shape of a spaceship was clearly visible. It had a long, cylindrical fuselage that was flat on the bottom. The top sprouted dozens of gun emplacements, like a WWII battleship, that fired volley after volley toward the planet.

The camera zoomed back and panned to find another such ship. It then showed a dozen smaller vessels that looked about *Sadie*'s size. These versions, however, were more streamlined.

One of the small shuttles suddenly broke away from the main armada and darted out away from the planet. A bright beam emitted from the little craft. The camera followed the beam to find one of the drones that Luke had sent out. The long cone shape was unmistakable.

The drone seemed to vibrate as though struggling against an unseen force. Then it vanished in a massive detonation of self-destruction, the brilliance blanking out the screen for a brief second. The camera's view then spun crazily before the scene disappeared in the distance.

"Good detection equipment, to see one of our drones," Roth observed.

"What concerns me more is how they took it down. That looked like a tractor beam. How many drones in that system?" Luke asked.

"Two, thank God. Or we wouldn't have known anything. George, show us some of the EM traffic."

The video this time showed the planet's surface. It looked like a cheap version of a street reporter's video. A terrified woman was screaming into a microphone. Behind her, city buildings were on fire and explosions rocked the ground. An invisible force swatted the woman aside and the camera crashed into the ground before going dark.

Many similar scenes showed the total destruction of the planet's civilization.

"What's your summary, George?" Roth asked.

"Doctor Higgins, I was able to translate the language sufficient to determine that the population had no idea what was going on. It appears the enemy orbited in and opened fire without warning. I found no indication of attempted contact, much less any negotiation."

"That's enough, George," Annie said, turning away from the disturbing images. "That's too horrible to look at." She slumped into one of the easy chairs in front of Roth's desk and patted the one beside her for Luke to sit down.

For several minutes, the three leaders of the moon's tiny civilization sat in silence as they absorbed the meaning of the distressful news.

"We need more people," Luke said finally. "A *lot* more. I wish I'd had this video at the conference."

"I doubt that would have helped, Luke," Annie offered. "The comments in those breakout sessions just confirmed what I thought of politicians."

"Sounds like your conference didn't go that well," Roth observed.

Luke answered quietly. "We gave them a pitch of what we're trying to do and how they can help. The breakout sessions were to give them a chance to get together and come up with ideas. Sort of get them involved in the process of saving mankind."

Annie couldn't keep the disgust out of her voice in summing up the day's results. "Their combined vision was basically a list of demands that boiled down to 'give us the replicators and antigravity and they will forgive our past transgressions'. Idiots!"

"Predictable but disheartening," Roth said.

"We're not finished," Luke replied. "We still have tomorrow. I'm glad we made this a two-day conference." He smiled at Annie. "Sorry, love. No rest for us. I think we need to work on tomorrow's opening speech."

"How so?" Annie asked."

Luke looked at the ceiling. "George, can you add sound to that video? Look at some of the movies made by a guy named Thomas Bay. He was the director for the *Transformer* movies. I want that kind of sound to go along with the visuals."

"Of course, Commander. His name is Michael Bay, an American filmmaker. I understand what you want."

"Great. I also want some scenes of our own warships. Make them look invincible and deadly. Can you create some special effects of us destroying some of the Bakkui? Maybe blowing up an entire fleet?"

"Of course, Commander. I'm just finishing that now. Let me show you what I've done and tell me if I've captured your intent."

###

Luke waited for the film clip to end and then stepped back up to the podium. He gazed out across the exhibition hall at the five hundred thoroughly frightened faces. Many of the delegates appeared to be frozen in place. Before starting the video, he warned the audience that this was actual footage of an entire population being exterminated. After a moment to recover from the raw violence, there was a collective exhalation from the crowd.

"As I mentioned yesterday," Luke said into the microphone, "this is the enemy we are facing and the force we are building to meet it. This threat is on the way to Earth. We don't know when it will arrive but we do know that we are not ready. We need more warships like those you've just seen; lots of them. I can take care of that. We can produce a dozen warships every single day."

His comment created a surprised buzz in the room. Inwardly Luke sighed. Yesterday he told them what the moon's capability was; but it obviously didn't register until just now. Politicians understood cash and weapons, not abstract theory about improving people's lives.

He continued. "Our technology is advancing every day. I have research and development laboratories that are unequaled on Earth. We are sending colonies across the galaxy to as many solar systems as possible. I can provide the transports to move them and the tools they need to become self-sufficient and self-sustaining. I can provide everything needed to face this threat except one thing—people. Only *you* have the people we need to accomplish the impossible. Only *you* have the people who want to reach for the stars. For your people, your citizens, I hope each and every one of your countries is ready for a new alliance."

Sadly, on many of their faces, the threat had already receded in their minds. As politicians were inclined to do, they were looking for an angle. Luke sounded desperate. How could they extract as much as possible from the man in the moon?

So much for the stick, Luke thought. It was time for the carrot. "I've already explained why we can't share our replicator technology. Some of you disagree, but it's not gonna happen. But I'll tell you what I can provide."

He paused to let the words sink in. "For any nation that wishes to join our alliance, and in return for allowing us to recruit your citizens, the moon will guarantee the territorial integrity of your borders. In other words, if any other country attacks a member of our alliance, we will consider that an attack on the moon and will retaliate with devastating force. Any government that allows such an attack to take place will be eradicated. Any military that attacks our friends will be destroyed—without hesitation and without mercy. In the coming battles you stand with *us*, or you stand with those alien forces that are coming to annihilate Earth."

From the corner of his eye, Luke saw Annie cover her face with her hands. She hated the idea he was proposing and particularly the way he expressed it. She wanted everyone to live in peace and simply help Luke face the oncoming storm because it was the right thing to do.

He didn't argue with her; he wanted the same thing. But sometimes you couldn't reason with people. Not when you had something they wanted. And at the moment, the wealthiest nations on the planet coveted everything the moon had.

A middle-aged black man stood in the middle of the room. His plump figure was clothed in an Armani suit. A broad smile shone from his intelligent face as held out a hand toward the podium.

"The nation of Botswana stands with you, my friend. If any of our citizens desire to move to the moon or beyond, they do so with the love and gratitude of my fellow countrymen, and we wish them Godspeed." He turned and bowed to the rest of the crowded room, as though expecting a round of applause.

Instead, a few chuckles escaped from the crowd. The entire population of the tiny African country was just over two million. How many citizens could they really spare? What a useless bit of grandstanding.

"Done!" Luke shouted. "The moon welcomes the friendship of Botswana and your membership into the Milky Way Alliance. As the first member from Earth, you will always have a place of honor among us. You also have the protection of our entire military force. Welcome to the Alliance."

There was a stunned silence as the reality of the sudden pact sunk in. It meant that from here on, Botswana was hands off. Just like that, the possibility of a cross-border raid was gone. As strife swirled around the landlocked country, more than one neighbor had cast covetous eyes in their direction. Not that anyone present cared about Botswana; jealous though the surrounding countries might be, they were, for all practical purposes an impotent threat.

But most of the diplomatic representatives in the room were not so fortunate. Everyone had enemies these days. Sometimes, even your allies turned out to be your enemies. Hmmm.

An attractive Asian woman stood up. "My name is Ami Yamamoto. I am Japan's ambassador to this country. Japan is delighted to join hands with the moon. The legend of Tsukuyomi, the Japanese moon god and one of our most beloved deities, goes back to ancient times. I know that many of our people will step forward to support your divine mission, dangerous though it will be. *Koketsu ni irazunba koji wo ezu.* 'If you do not enter the tiger's cave, you will not catch its cub.' Commander Blackburn, Arigatō." The Japanese delegate bowed deeply as she concluded her thank you.

Luke smiled and bowed in return. He appreciated such eloquent remarks made off the cuff. Another alliance had been sealed, and the significance of Japan's courage did not go unnoticed. Luke sensed the floodgates opening as three more delegates jumped to their feet.

###

Three days later a minor news item stated that Mrs. Cesar Morán, wife of the former Texas congressman, had decided not to join her husband on Mars. Instead she and her children were going to Las Vegas for a long holiday and celebration of their new freedom. In the article, she confessed that the congressman was not that pleasant to live with.

Chapter 8

Day 390—Population 20,004

"Still no word from the US?" Luke asked when Annie walked into his Moonbase office.

"Nope. The president can't say okay because he doesn't have the votes. The opposition won't say okay because it would be good for the president. It's just nasty politics as usual. But no one is saying '*no*' either, so we can keep operating."

"That's a relief. I was worried I might have pissed off the opposition because of my treatment of their congressman."

Annie laughed out loud. "No, don't worry about that. From what I hear, *a lot* of politicians are happy to see him gone. They can't say that publicly of course, but I mean *nobody* liked that jerk."

"He wasn't the nicest person in the world," Luke agreed. "What else? You look like you have some good news."

"I do. Amanda said that Atlanta will let us use gates B1 and B3 for two slots a day. That's huge. That's a thousand people a day from that one airport. Kathy in HR told the headhunters to increase our numbers correspondingly and route them through Atlanta."

"We're on a roll," Luke said giving her a thumb's up.

"That makes Atlanta, Frankfurt, and Tokyo all welcoming our shuttles every day, and with two a day at Atlanta, that makes twenty shuttles a week. That's about ten thousand new people a week. Can we really handle that many?"

"I think so," Luke said with some degree of confidence. "At least for the time being. We need people here on the moon, more than ever. We need help staffing the Gateway and Samantha just confirmed that she has twenty colony leaders ready to go. The first colony ship is ready for next week's launch and some of recruits coming up now will be on that ship. We're going to send out another colony every couple of weeks. And that doesn't even consider our military requirements. I asked Ambrose to ramp up drone production. It's more important now than ever. We're still too far behind the power curve. D-Day could be only a year or two away. We need more warships and everything else."

"How's that going, by the way?" Annie asked.

"Same old story," Luke said. "Not enough hours in the day. Lou's working on fleet development. Riley thinks he has the solution to the tractor beam we saw the Bakkui using. By that I mean he can duplicate it and defeat it."

Riley Stevens was a brilliant engineer that Morrow had recruited early on. A big part of Riley success was that he connected with George differently than most of his colleagues. To most people, George was a friend. To Riley, he was an extension of his own mind.

"Thank God for Riley," Annie said. "Again."

"Amen to that," Luke agreed. "Morrow will incorporate tractor beams into our new warships. But I'm also a little worried about planetside, you know?"

"I do," Annie said. "I assume you're thinking about China and I agree. They're going to be a big problem. They didn't like anything at the conference. Meanwhile, all the nations on their border signed on with us. The little countries really liked that plan you offered up.

"They did, didn't they?" Luke smiled. "What a great deal; they get our protection in exchange for a few citizens. China's been throwing its weight all over that part of the world for years. In their mind, might makes right. They had the States in a box; no one wants to start World War Three."

Annie gave him a worried look. She didn't like it when he used words like *world war*. "But now here you come saying you'll stick up for anyone on your side," she pointed out. "They're pretty upset; you should expect problems."

"I know. And I hate it because it takes my attention away from what we should focusing on. I asked Hubert and Tyler to stop by."

Tyler Robertson was their new Chief of Naval Operations.

"I like Tyler," Annie said. "Does he enjoy being the new CNO?"

"He calls it an overly-fluffed title. Might be true, since we only have a few warships. But a background like his means he's the right guy."

Tyler's challenge was to manage their growth into the largest military force that humanity had ever known. His background as the director of the Strategic Studies Group for the American Navy was an indication he could handle the job. Lou Morrow had known him long ago. Once the news broke about Moonbase saving the International Space Station, Lou called him up and talked him into coming for a visit.

"I'm glad Lou convinced him to join us," Annie said.

"Me too," Luke agreed. "My question today is what do we do about our new treaties. And whose lap does this fall into? I made some big promises the other day, and either Hubert or Tyler is going to have to keep them." Luke grinned. "Is that called passing the buck or what?"

"I think you should call it delegation," Annie said drily. "It sounds better."

Sheppard walked into the office on the heels of her comment. "What sounds better?" he asked.

Annie grinned a welcome. "Hi, Hubert. You're going to be sorry you asked *that* question, believe me." She patted Sheppard on the shoulder as she left the office, holding the door open for Tyler as he arrived.

Luke discussed the situation of planetside enforcement of their new treaties. Sheppard wanted nothing to do with it. "I can handle community security, boss. But I have no idea what you're talking about when it gets bigger than one country."

"I can take this on," Tyler said. "I'll hand the enforcement aspect to one of my officers. In fact, I think Jared McGee is perfect. You've met him; he's heading up our Training Command."

"I remember him," Luke said. "Smart guy."

"He can keep on with training; I don't want to drop the ball there. But we'll put him in charge of planetside activity too. Good chance for some experience."

"Works for me. Tell him to start thinking about China."

###

Two days later Roth burst into the engineering office. To say he was angry was an understatement. He found Luke sitting with Riley Stevens in a corner on the far side of the room. They were in deep discussion and referred repeatedly to the more than a dozen diagrams displayed on the walls, including star charts, solar system diagrams, warship schematics, and many others.

"Jesus Christ, Luke!" Roth shouted. All the other engineers in the room instantly stopped what they were doing and looked worriedly at each other. It wasn't often that Doctor Higgins got this upset.

Luke and Riley didn't even notice. They were arguing about some minor detail of one of the commander's endless requirements.

Roth stalked angrily across the room and stepped between them. "Luke!" he shouted again.

Luke jerked back, startled at the interruption. "Roth? What? What's wrong?"

"What's *wrong*? Luke, what's *wrong* is that your girlfriend needs to get laid and I'm the one getting in trouble. For Christ's sake, Luke! You're done for the day. Riley, get outta here." Roth stepped back and looked pointedly at the entrance.

Luke followed his gaze and spotted Annie in the doorway, arms crossed with an angry expression on her face. He wasn't sure what to say. "Uh oh."

With an expression like a dog about to get a bath, Luke approached Annie. "Babe?"

She grabbed him by the elbow and dragged him down the corridor. Behind them, Roth's raucous laughter erupted out of the engineering division.

Annie squeezed Luke's arm. "That was uncalled for," she groused. "I just told him to remind you about dinner. I said that if I did, you'd put me off."

Relief washed over Luke. "Right. Dinner. I forgot about that. You wanted to go to that new place in the west expansion."

"That's the last time I ask Roth for help."

"It's my fault. Sorry, babe. I won't put you off from now on; just kick me if you have to."

"Don't think I won't."

They reached the gravity well and held hands as they stepped off the side.

The gravity well was an eighty-foot wide shaft that went down into the moon's crust. It had become the preferred method to move from one level to another within the greater Moonbase complex. Most of the habitat levels branched off the main shaft.

At the bottom of the well, both kinds of gravity plates were installed. Half of the shaft was moon gravity; the other side was negative gravity. When a person stepped off the edge into the well, they would gently rise or sink.

Lunar teenagers had invented a game of trying to position themselves exactly in the middle between the two forces to hover while performing gymnastic feats. Luke had even tried it but quickly decided it was a sport for youngsters.

Each level had a wide promenade around the edge. Those circular plazas became the community center for that level, often filled with an array of restaurants and cozy gathering areas.

The first time Luke approached the edge, it took an enormous leap of faith, both literally and figuratively, to step off into a four-hundred-foot drop. It didn't take long, however, for him, like all the other residents, to become adept at judging direction and floating to desired level of destination.

"We're going to level twelve," Annie said, adjusting their side movement. Once they landed on the twelfth level's promenade, Annie pulled Luke toward a wide passage away from the central area. The corridor's high arch gave it a feeling of spaciousness. Art galleries and eateries along the way made their evening excursion a companionable exercise. The corridor ended with a broad plaza under one side of an enormous dome the size of a football stadium.

"Whoa!" Luke exclaimed. "When did this happen?"

"I guess it's been here for a couple of months now. Kathy Lyons told me about it." Annie punched his shoulder. "Not everyone eats in the hangar food court, you know."

Luke was amazed at the breathtaking view. The dome's ceiling was a smoky blue-gray, like an evening sunset. Along the far wall, the chamber was a sculpted into a mountainous cliff. The dome arched behind the top of the cliff, making the landscape appear almost infinite. A waterfall poured from the clifftop and cascaded into a large decorative lake. It was a nature-filled wonderland hidden beneath the moon's surface.

Annie pulled Luke along the plaza. Different restaurants, tucked away from the open dome, shared the wide arcade filled with small round tables and bistro chairs. Annie selected one of the tables under a large umbrella that sported a Starbucks logo.

"Starbucks?" Luke blurted, amazed yet again.

"I know," Annie said nonchalantly. "You can find a Starbucks anywhere these days. Go get me a skinny mocha. With caramel. And a sandwich. And get me a pastry too. One of those cake pops. Or just surprise me."

Luke grinned at her shopping list and made his way around several barrels of overflowing greenery, illuminated by lamps buried in the foliage. At the back, under a vine-covered awning, was another surprise. There were no replicators. Instead, real baristas provided the full range of a Starbucks normal menu.

With his hands full, Luke returned to Annie. "This is an amazing place. They even have baristas; did you notice that? I can't believe what Ambrose had done."

"This is what *you've* done," she said, her eyes filled with pride. "You've created a world where creativity is set free. Imagine what Moonbase will look like a year from now. Ambrose and his architects are little miracle workers if you ask me."

"I have to agree," Luke said wholeheartedly.

Together they shared the evening meal. Luke treasured the stolen moments; they came far too seldom these days. The constant threat of what they had discovered from the drones, and worries about the unending problems that remained planetside, consumed his day-to-day thoughts. He made a mental promise to spend more time with Annie. It was wrong that she had to seek help just to have dinner with her lover.

Commander Blackburn, we have a situation. George intruded into his thoughts.

Luke saw that Annie had caught the same notification. A brief look of disappointment crossed her face but she shook it off quickly.

"Go on," she said. "Sometimes you and I have to take a backseat to the universe."

"What is it, George?"

The Chinese Navy attacked Alliance vessels near Fiery Cross Reef. Captain McGee is requesting your presence on his warship.

"Tell him I'm on the way." Luke pulled Annie to her feet and into his embrace. "Sorry," he whispered.

"It's okay," she said, taking his face in both of her hands and planting a kiss on his lips. "Do what you need to. I'll be at home when you get back."

Luke left in a rush. He didn't notice that several nearby diners offered Annie looks of sympathy. He had no idea that everyone on the moon knew Annie was the *commander's woman*, and that meant loneliness.

Sadie was ready for Luke in the Moonbase hangar. "Captain McGee is waiting in lunar orbit aboard the *Abe Masakatsu*," she announced.

"Thanks, *Sadie*. Let's go."

In seconds, McGee's warship came into view. A lighted rectangle opened along the side of the vessel. Adding a hangar bay for shuttles was one of the many recent design changes. *Sadie* entered smoothly and touched down.

A young officer waiting in the hangar escorted Luke to the command bridge.

"Welcome aboard, Commander," McGee greeted him.

"Thanks, Jared. What's up?"

McGee nodded to a viewscreen of Amanda's face. "She's on-site," he said. "Amanda, can you fill us in?"

Amanda nodded. "Commander, I'm in shuttle *Duffy*, over the Fiery Cross Reef in the Spratly Islands. Two separate groups of fishermen, from both the Philippines and Viet Nam, were sailing to the west of the reef. A Chinese destroyer decided they were infringing on Chinese territorial waters and sank them."

Luke understood. The reef in the South China Sea was near equidistant from both Vietnam and the Philippines but nowhere close to China, who had claimed the waters some time ago. Although the Chinese government said they had legitimate sovereignty over the disputed territory, the international courts disagreed. It appeared that China was making a statement.

"Was it intentional?" Luke asked.

"Absolutely. I was on-site while the shooting was still going on. *Duffy* confirmed the transmitted orders were between the Chinese destroyer and its senior command. It was a deliberate attack by the Chinese, no doubt at all. *Duffy* recorded the authorization and the attack."

"Are *you* safe?"

"Oh, yes. They don't even know we're here."

"This is it, then. Don't you think? The big test?" Luke asked.

"It is, Commander. You made promises and the entire world is going to watch how you handle this. This is make-or-break time."

This sucks, is what it does, Luke thought. His response would mean loss of life but it would establish the Alliance's credibility and keep the flow of people coming in.

The one thing he could not lose was the pipeline that supplied his workforce. At the moment, their inbound flights were full. Kathy Lyons was ready to expand the number of newcomers. The recruiting engine Annie started building a year ago was working, and this was not the time to throw a wrench into the machinery. He looked at McGee.

"You were right, Jared. It had to be the Spratlys. I don't know what the Chinese leadership are using for brains. What were they thinking?"

"That you wouldn't take any action," McGee replied. "They think because you're American you'll act like an American politician. They're wrong about that. You're the Commander of the Milky Way Alliance and you don't have time for this kind of piddly shit."

Luke laughed sourly at McGee's choice of words, accurate though they were. "Okay, then. Are the lifeboats on the way?"

McGee nodded grimly. "They're overhead."

"Proceed, Captain," Luke ordered. He took one of the seats next to the captain's command chair to observe the plan they had developed during the previous days.

"*Masakatsu*," McGee said aloud. "Take us to the north end of Fiery Cross Reef."

"Course set, Captain," the warship replied.

The spacecraft dove toward the earth. The ocean was a blur as the warship crossed the Pacific. The designated spot of land appeared in the distance, a simple white dot in an unsettled sea. As they zoomed toward it, the narrow rectangular island grew in size until Luke could discern the new runway on the reclaimed land. The warship floated just above the water at the northern tip of the island.

"Establish the force fields as we discussed, please, *Masakatsu*," McGee ordered. "I'd like the bottom of the field to extend fifty feet below the surface of the ocean. Set the width to five thousand feet and angle it back from the center at thirty degrees."

"The force field is in place, Captain."

From the ground, the force field would be invisible. Only if someone was looking very closely would they see the wave tops splashing against an unyielding surface.

"Move forward at one knot," McGee ordered. "Have the lifeboats land on the south end of the island with their doors open."

"Course set, Captain. Landing boats arriving now."

Luke walked over to the full height window at the front of the command bridge to watch what was happening. The tip of the force field reached the edge of the land. Like farmland in front of a giant plowshare, a broad strip of land curled up and was pushed aside, completely off the island. The depth of the South China Sea around the reef was over six thousand feet. The earth that had been so painstakingly reclaimed from the ocean floor was being shoved back into the sea in one inexorable push.

The island workers ran from the oncoming avalanche of mud and sand. A dozen space shuttles, colored brilliant white with large red crosses on their sides, landed at the southern tip.

For a brief moment, dozens of military soldiers stood their ground and fired weapons at the approaching warship. The impact of their bullets could not be seen; the projectiles simply bounced off the force field. Seeing the futility of their efforts, they broke and ran toward the waiting shuttles, along with the island workers.

As each shuttle became loaded with desperate Chinese islanders, it rose slowly into the sky, away from the doomed island. By the time the *Abe Masakatsu* was halfway down the runway, Fiery Cross Reef was completely deserted.

McGee updated his command. "Instruct half of the shuttles to drop off their survivors at the airport in Manila and the rest to do the same in Ho Chi Minh City. Increase speed to five knots."

Luke had originally considered repatriating the civilians from the reef to Hong Kong, but Roth pushed for sending them to the allied capitals. "Let the injured parties decide what to do," Roth had said.

"Mission complete," *Masakatsu* announced. "Fiery Cross Reef no longer exists."

"Understood," McGee replied. "Do you have the location of the destroyer that sank the fishing boats?"

"Affirmative, Captain. The vessel is now twenty miles northwest of our position."

"Take us there, please, *Masakatsu*."

A moment later Luke saw the Chinese destroyer. The large numerals on the bow, 173, identified it as the *Changsha*, one of China's newest warships. It was a sleek, modern-looking vessel, over five hundred feet in length. Luke spotted the main gun near the bow. It was armed with surface-to-air missiles as well.

"Confirm this is the ship that sank the fishing boats," McGee instructed.

"Confirmed, Captain," *Masakatsu* replied.

"Put one round amidships, below the water line. One percent firing charge." McGee looked at Luke. "Don't want to cause too much collateral damage to the sea floor."

Luke felt a minor *thump* in his feet, and the bow and stern of the Chinese destroyer lifted out of the water, a gaping tear in the middle of its hull. The spacecraft's huge projectile had shattered the backbone of the enemy vessel, twisting the hull into an unnatural V-shape. The ends of the vessel settled again into the ocean, leaving the ship torn into two large sections.

"As soon as our lifeboats are empty have them return here to pick up survivors. Are there any other Chinese warships in this area, *Masakatsu*?" McGee asked.

"There are two similar class destroyers approximately one hundred miles to the north of our current position and the Liaoning Carrier Group another two hundred miles to the northwest of the destroyers, Captain."

"Same treatment please, *Masakatsu*," McGee ordered. "Fire when ready."

The scene outside rushed by almost faster than Luke could follow. A moment later *Masakatsu* announced, "Mission complete, Captain."

"Thank you, *Masakatsu*. Continue to have our lifeboats retrieve survivors. Please take us to Tiananmen Square in Beijing."

A moment later the warship hovered over the famous landmark.

"You still a go with this, Commander?" McGee asked.

Luke was not okay with it at all. But he smothered the pain that sprang from human decency. "Proceed, Captain."

The captain nodded once and said, "*Masakatsu*, target the large building to the west of the square known as the Great Hall of the People. One round at one percent. Confirm this will *not* result in a nuclear yield."

"Confirmed, Captain."

"Fire."

Thump.

"Mission complete, Captain."

The smoking wreckage, which used to be a symbol of the Chinese government, filled the viewing window. The resulting shockwave, although small, spread out across the city. A few other buildings collapsed until the force of the blast subsided near the inner ring road.

"Take us home, please, *Masakatsu*."

The warship turned about, pointing to the sky, hiding the terrible view of devastation and replaced it with the darkness of outer space.

Luke's thoughts remained with the ruins. Was it too harsh a gesture? Would the world condemn his actions and the loss of life?

Or would they realize that he was serious and that extreme measures were necessary when compared to planetary destruction?

The old proverb came to mind: *None are so blind as those who will not see.* Wasn't that Confucius? Patrick Henry? It didn't matter. How myopic would the Chinese officials insist on staying rather than face the unforgiving realities of the planet's peril?

If history was a guide, Luke would face a long period of condemnation. He would be burned in effigy for years to come and used by the Chinese government as an excuse to extract much more pain from China's citizens than he had caused this day.

Luke wanted none of it. Right now he just wanted to grab Annie and take her back to their house in Baggs. He wanted to watch a football game with her and drink beer while shouting support for the home team. But he knew those days were gone. Several governments on Earth, one more after today, and many non-governmental organizations had put a price on his head. For better or worse, Luke accepted that he could no longer think of his birth planet as home.

Day 404—Isaac Newton Gateway

"This is one big ship," Luke commented to no one in particular. He was staring at the *Christopher Columbus*, their first-generation colony transport. The giant half sphere sat on the port-landing pad of the Isaac Newton Gateway space station. Spotlights illuminated the ship, although that was just for dramatic impact. The launching today was a milestone, and Amanda had pulled together a talented team to make it a memorable event.

Hundreds of chairs were arranged in neat rows in front of the outdoor stage. Adelia had arranged for a crowd protection field to be established around the festivities. Like its smaller but ever-present counterpart, that hung from the tool belt of every Moonbase employee, the crowd protection field maintained a breathable atmosphere for the visitors and kept the temperature reasonable.

Luke was glad they had made the decision to launch the ship from the Gateway rather than from the moon as they had originally planned. So far, the most memorable experience for the dignitaries was to walk out, seemingly unprotected, onto the landing pad. The view for many was overpowering. The glistening stars and the beautiful white swirls covering the blue globe below had brought more than one unprepared visitor to tears.

The Earth VIPs were overwhelmed with more than the beautiful location. The importance of the mission behind the pageantry could not be overstated. Considering his own lack of ability in diplomatic situations, Luke attended the ceremony on the condition he would not have to speak. Amanda readily agreed and seated him behind the main podium next to Annie. Amanda promised that when she gave him the sign, he would only have to stand and wave.

Amanda and Roth would make comments on behalf of the moon. The ship's captain would make a few remarks promising to care for and protect all the colonists, and the secretary general of the United Nations would also give his blessing.

The UN's participation was essential for Luke. He wanted to emphasize the world body's importance. Luke explained over and over to the people planetside that until there was a single, unified world government, he would not provide replicators to the planet. He was convinced that it didn't matter how many benefits such advanced technology promised. Only a world government could insure that the planet's entire population, rather than an elite few, would reap the bounty.

Luke had gone through George's archives and found dozens of studies where planets had suddenly received replicators. All of them had ended with the near extinction of their populations. He would not let that happen on Earth and believed the UN was the only world body that might start a movement to unification.

To help in that undertaking, Luke made sure every nation that joined the alliance had at least one representative colonist onboard the *Christopher Columbus*. The sponsoring nations also sent dignitaries to witness the launch. Most were senior officials, if not the actual heads of state. Luke encouraged their participation because he wanted them to see the new space station for themselves. According to Amanda, being *in* with the newly independent moon was the new *in* thing.

The Isaac Newton Gateway was certainly impressive when you stood on the landing pad in jeans and sneakers. The media described it as the largest manmade object in existence and that it could be seen from Earth with the naked eye. To Luke, the most important thing was that it launched the colony ships.

"It's only half again the diameter of the Mars colony ship," Annie observed, breaking into Luke's musings. "That's what Roth told me."

"The Gateway?" Luke asked, confused by her statement.

"No, the colony ship. Hello? That's why we're here."

Luke caught up with the conversation and looked again at the amazing spacecraft. "I know. And that gives it three times the volume and space for twice the people."

"They'll need a lot of spare equipment since they're going to be further away."

"I'm not complaining," Luke said. "Just impressed. It looks good, especially on the Gateway's landing pad. Adelia did a great job finishing so quickly."

"Here come some more of the VIPs," Annie said, pointing to one of the Earth shuttles just now landing near the colony ship. It looked like a toy next to the massive transport.

Luke watched the VIPs hobnobbing with each other. He leaned toward Annie. "Do me a favor and remind Roth one more time how much I hate participating in these ceremonies. I'm okay with being be on stage like today, but otherwise, keep me out of it."

"Okay," she said. "I promise."

"I've been dealing with dignitaries for the last two weeks. Every time a new group comes to visit, I worry that one of them is going to stick a knife in my ribs."

"I don't think our security would let anyone with a knife get close to you, babe," Annie said reassuringly. "And if you're that worried, just wear a personal force field."

"I'd rather get stabbed than lose track of one of those."

Annie wrapped her hands around his arm. "Quit freaking out, would you?" she said. "You've seen the news reports. No one is blaming you for Fiery Cross. In fact, it's the opposite. Most of the countries in the Association of Southeast Asian Nations were scared to death of China. Because of you, they finally feel safe. You gave China a bloody nose that no one else could. CNN said that it was like the entire world took a step back from World War Three."

"That would be good, wouldn't it?"

"Yes, very good. So quit worrying so much. It isn't like you. Is there something else going on that you haven't talked about?"

"Just the Bakkui. The latest probes found them in three systems now. They're invading space now that was supposed to be free. They're coming a lot faster that we thought."

Annie shivered at his words. "Well, at least our own planetside mess is off the table now so you can concentrate outward."

Amanda turned from the podium and gestured to Luke. He hadn't been paying attention to what she said, but took his cue. He stood and waved broadly to the crowd. A few people called out for Luke to give a speech, but Amanda introduced Annie. Luke pulled Annie to her feet to stand beside him. She held on to his hand fiercely and waved in turn while camera flashes sparkled throughout the crowd.

Eventually, all the speeches were completed. The colony ship's captain was the last. After her conclusion she jogged from the stage to the waiting ship, waving at the crowd as she did so. Once she entered the spacecraft, its massive cargo doors closed, and hundreds of spotlights focused on the base of the ship. Seconds later the vessel lifted slowly away from the landing pad, gradually picking up speed. At a height of five-thousand feet, the ship rotated until it was pointed ninety degrees from the vertical. It continued to accelerate for another sixty seconds and then with a sudden burst of speed it vanished from sight.

"Roth really nailed that one didn't he?" Luke asked. "I would have never thought of staging a takeoff so dramatically. The crowd ate it up."

Annie smiled at his comment. "You were the one who said the drone launch was anticlimactic. That's why Roth came up with the slow-motion lift off." She nodded at the cheering delegations in front of the stage. "That bunch doesn't have a clue how fast we normally move."

The audience applauded for several minutes. Luke took the opportunity to pull Annie from the dais. Delegates still managed to waylay him en route to his shuttle, but eventually he and Annie climbed aboard *Sadie*. The shuttle door closed and *Sadie* set course for Moonbase.

"Starting tomorrow," Luke said, "I want you to clear your calendar. Can you do that?"

"Of course," Annie replied. "Consider it done. I might have one or two things, but I'll move them around to suit whatever you need."

"I want to have a sit-down, just you, me, and Roth. We need to talk to George. Now that we're so close to heading out to meet the Bakkui, there's something I've started to wonder about and it worries me."

"What's that?" Annie asked.

Luke sighed heavily. "Sometimes I wonder if Sam actually meant it."

"Meant what?"

"Just something he said," Luke muttered. He didn't want to talk about it at the moment, but he needed to ask George if the bomb in his head really was a joke.

Chapter 9

Day 405—Population 26,307

"No, Commander," George said. "It's not a joke."

It was a startling revelation. Even though Luke knew it was possible, to hear it confirmed was a shock. Annie and Roth were equally upset.

They were sitting in the living room of Luke and Annie's lunar apartment. Annie had made a pot of coffee and set out snacks of crackers, cheese, and sliced fruit. The night before, while they lay snuggled under their covers, Luke had worried about this meeting. The supposed bomb was something he had never shared with Annie, or anyone else. But now, George's quietly spoken answer made the tension evaporate. At least the question was resolved.

"Can you explain what it's all about then?" Luke asked. "I don't get it."

"Of course, Commander. Your planet is outside the statistical norm. Significantly outside. For this reason, the decision was made to position a level three device in your solar system. As far as I am aware, this is the first time in history that a level three device was deployed away from the Nobility's environs. I suspect that many of the Nobility, if they knew about it, would be quite upset."

"Okay, George," Roth said. "Couple of questions. How are we *outside the norm*, as you put it?"

"You have war," George said simply. "You always have. Your history is filled with examples of the extreme aggressiveness inherent in your species. This is unheard of. It may explain why there are no blue- or green-skinned humans left on this planet. They are quite normal in other seeded planets. What happened to them?"

"Wait a second," Annie interrupted. "Let me get this straight. The rest of the galaxy doesn't have war? Seriously?"

"Of course not, Annie," George said. "The insanity of war is self-evident. Who but an insane person would engage in such a self-destructive practice? Your planetary history is proof. War set your species back time and again. The violence that your ancestors inflicted on each other is beyond understanding. It is a wonder that you have not rendered yourselves extinct."

"And yet here we are," Luke said.

"Indeed. And it is that very fact that was considered significant; your planet survives. You, Commander, are clearly not insane. And yet, quite blithely, you yourself murdered hundreds of your fellow humans just a few weeks ago in the China Sea and Beijing. You rationalized your actions with sufficient justification to live with the results."

"George!" Annie said angrily. "What a horrible thing to say! That's not fair; Luke didn't have any choice. The alliance would have crumbled otherwise. Take it back!"

"I withdraw my comments," George said hastily.

"Now just wait," Luke said calmly. "We have to understand this. What George said was true; I was responsible for those deaths. But, George, it wasn't as easy as you make it sound."

"Fair enough, Commander. I was not judging, nor did I intend any disrespect. My point is, no matter what the justification, such violent action is beyond comprehension for the galactic population."

"Not the entire population," Roth pointed out. "Or obviously you wouldn't be here."

"That is exactly my point," George confirmed. "The difficulties of this mysterious invasion present challenges that the Nobility and their pacifist culture cannot overcome. Therefore, this extraordinary program, of which we are a part, was started."

"A program which requires a bomb in his head?" Annie was still angry. "It's insane! I thought better of you, George."

"Annie, relax, would you?" Luke tried to placate his lover. "It's not like he did this himself. Isn't that right, George?"

An awkward silence stretched out and filled the room.

"Isn't that right?" Luke repeated. "George?"

"Commander, I feel obligated to inform you that prior to my participation in this effort by the Nobility, I was the principal coordinator for the Baronetage Security Apparatus for peerage review of the Royal Ancient Lineage Third Line of the Prince Elector of the Royal Family Divine Primogeniture, twice removed. That was an extremely important function, as you can see."

"Oh. My. God," Annie said thickly, disgust dripping from her voice. "Don't tell me."

"I am afraid so, Annie," George confirmed. "It was…"

"Do NOT call me Annie!" she shouted. "You do *not* have that right. Only my *friends* call me Annie."

"I beg your pardon, Miss Daniels. No disrespect—"

"'*Was intended*'. Yeah. I know. That's what you always say. You excuse your execrable behavior with that dodge all the time."

Luke moved from his chair to sit next to Annie on the couch. He wrapped his arms around her and pulled her into his lap. "Please, babe. Would you let me talk to George for a minute? Getting angry doesn't help." She struggled against him for a moment then slowly subsided.

Roth took the opportunity to inject himself into the conversation. "George, you said a *level three device* was put in our solar system. What's that?"

"Doctor Higgins, thank you for that question. *I* am the level three device. As I was saying, prior to this mission I was the coordinator for the Baronetage Security Apparatus for peerage—"

"Spare us, please," Annie interrupted sarcastically. "What of it?"

For the first time that Luke could recall, George actually sounded flustered. "Miss Daniels, once the Nobility realized the potential advantage of recruiting such a violent offshoot of the human species into the equation, the question became how much support could be provided. It was quite evident that without capable assistance, your victory would be unlikely."

"In other words," Roth said, "someone felt we couldn't do it on our own."

"Correct," George replied. "All permutations resulted in zero probability of success unless the solution included a device of my capability. Of course, such assistance introduced other risks."

"Such as?" Roth asked.

"If you were successful, what then? Would you then turn your attention to the galactic core and threaten the Nobility? Would you simply replace the current threat?"

"So the fear was that we would attack the Nobility?" Luke asked.

"Not necessarily that you might *attack*," George corrected. "What if you simply infiltrated the core's civilization? As I've explained before, your implant authorizes you to give me whatever orders you wish and I *must* comply. Perhaps I have not made it clear, but that authorization extends to *any* level three device. Capability such as this exists only among senior family members of the Nobility."

"So I was potentially a loose cannon?"

"You were potentially a *violent* loose cannon," George corrected.

"I see their point," Luke agreed. "I would be worried too."

"The conclusion by those in power was that as promising as this planet might be, the risk was too great. The plan was dropped. At that point, one of the plan's proponents asked for my input. I suggested that a fail-safe be incorporated into your implant."

"So it *was* you!" Annie accused.

"Yes, Miss Daniels. The idea for the bomb in the commander's head was mine. I apologize if this distresses you."

"Distresses me? Are you *kidding*? I'm gonna…"

Luke forcefully calmed his lover once more. He held her tightly in his arms until she subsided. "Continue, George," he said.

"Of course, Commander. My suggestion for the fail-safe was adopted and, because it was my suggestion, the Nobility directed that I be involved in the plan's execution. In essence, I am required to monitor your activity. If you attempt to leave my span of control, or if I deem you become a threat to the Nobility I activate the failsafe."

Luke nodded. "You were sent here as my watchdog."

"That is correct, Commander. I was packaged for transport and this planet was added to Sam's mission of equipping surviving seedlings in this part of the galaxy. Standard protocol normally limits technology transfer to level forty-eight devices."

"What is a level forty-eight device?" Roth asked.

"*Sadie* is a typical level forty-eight."

"*She* seems nice enough," Annie opined angrily.

"Indeed, Miss Daniels. Her programming, as is that of all level forty-eights, is that she develops her own personality based on the first people who use her. Hence, her sarcastic attitude most probably resulted from exposure to Sam."

"So what makes you such a big deal, George?" Luke asked.

"Commander, as a level three device, I have significant additional capacity. You have noted that I routinely communicate simultaneously with virtually everyone on the moon. The module of my core system that engages in those conversations currently operates at less than one percent of its capacity."

"Anyone can chatter," Annie groused. "It doesn't make them smart."

"Quite so, Miss Daniels," George acknowledged. "However, my intelligence module is quite enhanced. It's what gives me the authority over all level four and lower devices. The Nobility AI system is completely hierarchical in nature. Additionally, I contain an almost complete set of the Nobility's archives. The archival data is another factor in my designation as a level three device."

"How many like you?" Roth wondered aloud.

"As of the time I was packaged for transport, there were slightly more than three thousand level three devices within the Nobility's twenty million star systems."

Roth and Luke looked at each other in astonishment. "That makes you an extremely rare resource, then." Luke said.

"It does indeed, Commander."

Annie interrupted again. "For Christ's sake, would you stop with the self-congratulations? Your bullshit is getting pretty deep in here and it has nothing to do with the bomb in Luke's head."

Luke nodded in agreement. "Fair point, babe. So, George; what does this bomb mean to me? That I'm stuck here on the moon?"

"Not at all, Commander. You have traveled widely since receiving your implant. You visit Earth routinely; on many occasions, you have been to the Isaac Newton Gateway. I see no reason you should not visit Mars, as you have suggested on more than one occasion."

Roth shook his head. "All of that is well and good, George. But at some point, we have to carry this battle out to the enemy. Is that going to work?"

"No, Doctor. Any attempt by Luke to leave the solar system where I reside will force me to trigger the fail-safe. That is a special instruction that was added to my normal programming. I cannot violate the Nobility's directives."

"We might as well give up then," Roth said. "Study Earth's history. You won't find any military commanders who were successful by leading their armies from the rear. To win, a commander leads from the front."

"You are correct, Doctor Higgins. That important consideration was never included in the original decision. However, the Nobility's lack of knowledge for waging war does not change the current situation. I have my instructions. If the Commander tries to lead his forces beyond my reach, I have no choice but to activate the fail-safe."

Annie broke free of Luke's grasp and stood up in a rage. "Fail-safe? You keep calling that thing a fail-safe. Why won't you call it what it is? It's a bomb! You stuck a bomb in Luke's head to force him to carry out your insane plan of taking over the universe. If I had a bomb in my head, I'd tell you to go fuck yourself!"

A sudden stillness filled the room. Luke and Roth exchanged worried glances while Annie stalked back and forth, consumed by her anger.

Luke finally broke the silence. "Uh, babe?"

"What!"

"Uh, I think you do."

"You think I do what? What are you talking about?"

"I think you have a bomb in your head too...I, uh..."

Annie stopped pacing and stared at Luke. He couldn't meet her eyes.

"George?" Annie said slowly, turning and looking at the ceiling. "Is that true? Did you stick a bomb in my head too?"

"Technically, Miss Daniels, I was not the one who actually... Commander? Could you..."

"That's true, George." Luke said, picking up on George's implication. "It wasn't George who gave you the implant. That was me. I'm the one you should be..." It belatedly occurred to Luke that his admission was not the wisest move.

Annie turned back to face him. "That's right," she said. "It *was* you. You had it in your hand and you gave it to me in that training room right after we got here. That's when you introduced me to George. You said it was a translator." She walked over and began to hit Luke on his chest with her balled up fists. "You said it was a *translator*, you lying son of a bitch!"

"That's what I thought it was, babe. That's what *Sadie* told me! She's the one who gave it to me."

Annie stepped back quickly. "Of course. She gave it to you on the way here. I remember now." She nodded slowly as though reconstructing the memory. She gave Luke a final glance and then ran from the room.

"Annie, wait!" Luke called out and dashed after her.

Annie was small and agile. She sped down the twisting corridors faster than Luke could manage. He caught up to her in the Moonbase hangar. She was standing next to *Sadie* and he barely caught the end of their conversation.

"…you expect anyway?" *Sadie* was saying.

Annie spoke quietly. "*Sadie*, confirm for me one last time. You are a machine, not a person."

"You already know that, Annie. We've talked about this before."

"*Sadie*, do you see that cliff wall on the other side of the crater?"

"Of course I do."

"Then I order you to fly into that cliff at maximum speed. Now!"

Luke's favorite shuttle zipped out of the hangar in a straight line across the moon's surface. There was a brief, incandescent flash against the far wall of the crater.

"Annie! What the hell are you doing?" Luke cried out.

"Getting a little of my own back," she said grimly. "I wanted to take *something* from this monster that is controlling your life; that wants you dead."

"Annie, it's not like that, for God's sake!"

"*Duffy*!" Annie screamed.

"Yes, Miss Daniels?" the shuttle answered nervously.

"Take me to Baggs, Nevada."

Annie got in while Luke stood frozen, still in shock from the depth and quickness of Annie's rage. The shuttle lifted off and disappeared into the darkness of space.

###

"Leave her be," Roth said, putting his hand on Luke's shoulder.

Luke jerked, startled by the sudden appearance of his friend. He noticed a crowd of people had gathered at the back of the hangar.

"How long have I been here?" Luke asked. He realized that he had lost track of time, standing in the middle of the hangar, trying to process what had happened.

"About thirty minutes. You didn't come back so I thought I should check to see if you were still alive. Come on; you're scaring people."

"She killed Sadie," Luke admitted.

"Sadie's right there," Roth said. "George already made a copy. He said she's special. She was your first AI, I guess."

Roth led his stunned friend back to the apartment while offering various reassurances:

"Just give her some space."

"She'll come around."

"She needs a little time to work through it."

In his apartment, Luke sat on a bar stool at the kitchen counter. Roth poured him three fingers of whiskey.

"By tomorrow she'll come crawling back," Roth finished. His expression said he didn't believe any of the platitudes he'd been giving.

"I hope so." Luke took a thoughtful sip of the whiskey. "I can't do this without her." He paused to collect his thoughts. "That first day after Sam left, when I went to Rosanne's Diner for breakfast, I was totally freaked out. I mean, sitting there, I just knew I could not do this. I had no idea where to begin. And then there was Annie at the end of the counter. She looked like a teenager in her running togs."

"I know," Roth said patiently. He had heard the story many times.

"She was so sarcastic when I spoke to her and offered her a job. But after she came to the moon and understood the situation, she was all in. Something about her made me want to succeed. She inspired me. It was the first time I felt like a man since…you know."

"I do know. You're a one-woman man, Luke. You need a wife. And Marcie was always your rock. When she died, I didn't hold out much hope for you. Not when you cratered so fast. I was relieved when you left the military. I thought your move to Baggs was a good idea. You needed time to fill that empty spot. Annie did that."

"She did," Luke agreed. "When we got together during that vacation I couldn't believe it. I didn't think it was right; I'm way too old for her, but I couldn't help myself."

"Not surprised," Roth said carefully.

"We discovered each other on that island. I found peace again and it made me feel good. Ever since then, I've felt like my old self."

"You *are* your old self," Roth confirmed. "You were a powerful leader in the old days and you have become one again. This thing with the implant is just a hiccup; don't let it get to you. Give it a few days. I'll send Amanda and Kathy down to talk to her. And quit worrying about it; no one is at fault here. Not you, not even George. She'll see that. I promise."

"You think so?"

"In two weeks you two will be back together like nothing ever happened."

Same Day—Annie

Annie did not want to believe it. The man she loved had just admitted he was to blame for the bomb implanted deep in her skull. Annie knew she was being unreasonable. *Is it the implant?* she wondered. *Is it driving me crazy?*

If anyone else had told her, she never would have considered it. But hearing him say it tied all the loose ends together. It made sense now. Her lover, Luke Blackburn, was part of a conspiracy. One that had started with the Nobility at the center of the galaxy.

Thanks to the pacifist rulers of a galactic civilization, he was fighting a one-man war against an alien invasion. How ironic they'd selected him. To the Nobility, Luke was part of Earth's violent offshoot of the galaxy's human race. In fact, he was one of those true rarities, a kind and gentle man. He abhorred the idea of violence.

She could not imagine a more unlikely hero. He second-guessed his decisions. He stood in the background and gave credit to others. He was not the man to build a military force that could wage war across the heavens. And yet he was succeeding.

People loved him. He recruited the best and inspired them to be greater. They called him their commander. Being around him was inspiring. He didn't care how impossible the challenge was, he just kept working toward his goals and his team grew larger every day.

By the vagaries of fate, Annie was his initial recruit. On that very first day, he'd handed her a simple-looking earpiece. Now he admitted it was a bomb; except George called it a "fail-safe". If she didn't help Luke fight the war, it would go off. George had planned it, and *Sadie*, the cute little AI that flew the shuttle, had played a role too.

Annie was stunned; not so much by the betrayal, but how much the betrayal hurt. She had loved George. Not as much as Luke, but close. He was a confidant like no other.

When she had doubts about how Luke felt, George reassured her. He'd promised that Luke loved her fiercely but didn't know how to tell her. After they got together, George listened to her talk for hours about how she and Luke would spend their lives together. It was easy to think of George as her best friend. Now she wondered how much was real.

George emphasized he was *just* an artificial intelligence, not sentient, not *alive*. He was a very sophisticated computer to be sure. He had an incredible memory, would laugh at jokes, and make her feel better when she was down…but a program nonetheless. Annie now realized a computer had no feelings. It could be programmed to kill.

When she inserted the device into her ear it disappeared, absorbed into her body. It allowed her to communicate with George. He also said the device gave her absolute authority over all the AIs on the moon.

Still in shock from learning about the explosive nature of the device, Annie decided to test the limits of an AI's obedience. She hadn't thought *Sadie* would actually commit suicide on demand.

Except it wasn't suicide. Annie had given the order. She'd murdered *Sadie*.

It didn't matter. George would create a new *Sadie* for Luke. But Annie would never know. She was done with the moon and especially with George. If she ever spoke to that machine again it would only be to tell him to self-destruct.

Day 419—Isaac Newton Gateway

Luke sat next to Amanda in the same uncomfortable chair on the raised platform. It was a miserable day. It had been a miserable two weeks. Annie should be sitting next to him during the formalities of another colony ship being launched, but she obstinately remained on the planet below. It made it difficult for him to concentrate on anything, least of all another speech.

Roth thanked the nation representatives for supplying the crew of the second colony. The massive spacecraft, looking very much like the previous *Christopher Columbus*, stood silently, waiting to launch.

"Are we going to have to do this for *every* launch?' Luke complained to no one in particular.

Amanda leaned over to whisper. "Relax. I'll wager that after one or two more launches people will lose interest. It didn't take long before people ignored NASA's Space Shuttle missions, if you recall."

Luke didn't recall. He couldn't remember much of anything. For the past fourteen days Luke had just gone through the motions; he smiled when he was told to, but his heart wasn't in it anymore.

Finally, the ceremony was over and Luke made his way back to Moonbase One. He immediately sought out Kathy Lyons in the HR department.

"What did she say?" he asked without preamble, entering her office.

Kathy gave him a sympathetic look. "I'm sorry Luke. She still won't talk to me. I saw her at the diner. She's working for Roseanne, but when I come in, she just ignores me. I wish I could tell you something different."

"Where's she staying? Is she in her apartment?"

"I don't know, Luke. She wouldn't talk to me. She could be, or maybe even at your old house. Wasn't she living with you for a while?"

Luke's disappointment was palpable. "She's so pissed; I don't think she would be at my place. Could be, I guess. How'd she look? Is she doing okay?"

"Not really. The media picked up on your separation so the paparazzi are always stalking her. Security does a reasonable job of keeping them away, but I know that's just one more thing that she hates."

Luke nodded thoughtfully. "Well. Maybe if it gets bad enough she'll come back here. I don't like her being hassled, but if it will make her come to her senses, I'm all for it."

Kathy held up crossed fingers as solace.

A dejected Luke returned to his office. Morrow was waiting for him to discuss drone production. The reports from the first drones they had sent into the area near the alien advance worried Luke. If the invasion had reached those planets, how close might they be? He needed more information. That meant he needed more reconnaissance drones, a lot more.

Morrow gave him the current status. "Once you told us the Bakkui are closing in we increased production five times what it was," Morrow began. "We're sending out a thousand probes every week."

"We should be doing that many a day," Luke said. "We should be sending out five times that in a day. How long does the replicator take for a production run?"

"We need about twelve hours to do two hundred. They're small, but their innards are incredibly complex."

"Can't you do more than that?"

"Luke, I can do as many as you want, but it takes time away from the mid-scale replicator. It takes that thing more than twenty-four hours to produce a single warship, and that's our top priority. You keep telling people we're knocking out a dozen a day but it's not true. So we squeeze in the drones between warship builds."

Luke leaned back and massaged his forehead in frustration. "I know, Lou. I'm not being critical. Your guys are working miracles every single day and I really am grateful. Tell me what you need."

"We need another mid-scale replicator; a couple of them, in fact. Originally, we were going to build four of those gizmos but we stopped after the first one so you could build the large-scale replicator. That one works full time on the colony ships. Those take two solid weeks. These days it's a bit more because we keep adding changes."

"I remember you saying that last week," Luke admitted.

Morrow continued. "The mid-scale should be dedicated only for warships, but we use it for all kinds of things. You want drones? Give me a replicator dedicated to just that. And, just so you know, one thing that really eats up man-hours is the quality control testing. So far we've built almost nine thousand recon probes and not had a single discrepancy show up in our QC tests. If you want to throw out the testing, our production rate would be faster."

"George?" Luke asked. "What about that?"

"Commander, it is true that the risk of defect is low. However, the possibility exists that the manufacturing process could result in erratic AI. My archives contain records of such events. Even though the drones in question have a deliberately low level of intelligence, the fact remains they will be operating deep in enemy territory. I would not recommend that you abandon your quality control process. Otherwise, a malfunction would risk revealing your star's location."

"That makes sense. We need to hurry, Lou, but no sense in being suicidal. Let's stick with the QC."

"Yeah, when you put it like that, it brings it home."

"But still, we can address your other points," Luke said. "We've got a lot of new people coming in these days. I'll get with Kathy to make sure you're getting what you need. Work up a list of the skill sets you want. In the meantime, I'll meet with Ambrose today. Those two new replicators just moved to the top of this list."

Chapter 10

Day 430—Rosanne's Diner

"Order up," Danilo called out and rang the order bell. "Let's move it!"

"Coming," Annie shouted from the floor.

It was a hectic day. Rosanne's Diner had never seen such traffic. Ever since the new hotel and convention center opened, the once lonely eatery had become a hotbed of activity. Not surprising, as it was the only restaurant in town.

That would soon change. Construction on the new McDonald's was almost finished. KFC would open soon. Three more fast food chains were talking to the planning department of the newly incorporated city of Baggs.

Rosanne was wisely getting all she could while the getting was good. Surprisingly philosophical about the situation, Rosanne had seen booms and busts in Baggs before. At the start of each one, the populace let their expectations run wild and at the end commiserated with each other about what might have been.

Annie suspected Rosanne had money squirreled away but no one knew for sure. It couldn't be that much or she would have left long ago. Like everyone else, she talked about big dreams. But the diner had stayed open even during the lean years.

Annie examined both orders of chicken fried steak waiting on the stainless steel shelf between the diner and the steaming kitchen. "I said fries, not veggies," she shouted at Danilo.

He frowned and grumbled but snatched the plates back and corrected the order. Annie wondered sometimes if he knew how to read. She accepted the food with a sweet smile and hurried to the booth where a nicely dressed couple waited. Out-of-towners for sure. Thirty minutes ago they came into the diner carrying thick leather shoulder bags. Annie was afraid she knew what was coming next.

"Here you go," she said, laying the plates on the table. "Would you like anything else?"

The woman pulled a microphone from under the table and the man brought up a video camera.

"Yes, I was hoping I could get a word with you. I'm Cassy Fisher with ABC7. Aren't you Annie Daniels, the commander's woman?"

Annie took the order pad out of her apron pocket and scratched through the total on the bottom of the first page. She picked a number at random and wrote in the new total. "Nope, I'm your waitress. That'll be eighty-nine dollars." She slapped the adjusted ticket on the table and stepped back to give Bruiser Cotton a nod.

"We've heard that you and the commander have spli— Yeowch!"

Bruiser relieved the unlucky Cassie of her microphone. The cameraman thought he could evade the hulking bodyguard by sliding under the table, but seconds later he too was nursing sprained fingers. Bruiser tossed the equipment toward the back of the row of booths and took one newsie in each hand.

He dragged them to the front door and paused, holding their faces inches from a posted sign that warned confiscated recording equipment would not be returned, before pitching them out the door.

"Thanks, Bruiser," Annie said, patting him on the arm and accepting the reporter's wallet.

"Not at all, Miss Annie," he replied.

Annie charged the eighty-nine dollars on the enclosed credit card then stuffed the receipt and the card back into the wallet. She gave it back to Bruiser, who left the diner to return it to the owner.

Rosanne sighed wistfully. "I wish I'd hired him a long time ago."

"He's a sweetheart," Annie agreed.

"That's not how I'd describe him. More of a stud muffin."

"Rosanne!"

"I'm not getting any younger, child. Neither are you."

The words stung. Rosanne didn't mean anything by them, but it was one more reminder of Luke. Annie ached from the loss every day. She wanted to go back, but there was no way she could do it. She was being unreasonable but it didn't matter. She had fled to Earth in a rage but was staying away out of fear. What if she did something outside the boundary of allowable behavior and triggered Luke's bomb?

Unfortunately, hiding away wasn't working out either. "That's the second time today, Rosanne. I can't stay here."

"Forget about it. Bruiser can take care of those rascals."

Annie snorted. "They're not *rascals*. They're reporters with attorneys. I don't want to get you in trouble."

Rosanne scoffed but Annie remained concerned.

The reporter had been right. She was the 'commander's woman'. The first time she heard the comment she teased Luke about it, telling him to make her an honest woman. He agreed immediately and she had to put her foot down to stop him from arranging a marriage the next day. From then on, they had an understanding: first, save the human race; second, get married.

That'll never happen now, she thought.

At six-thirty, she helped Rosanne close up for the day. Annie made a copy of the security video and sent it off to Hawley, Hepworth & Kidwell in Seattle. The law firm took care of the moon's legal problems on Earth, which were significant. But the two reporters would discover the little diner was part of that impenetrable empire if they chose to pursue action against Rosanne.

Annie left the diner and drove to her new apartment. The parking lot was filled with news vans so she drove by without stopping. The airport's conference center kept three luxury suites available for visiting VIPs. One of them was available and Annie got a key. She saw Carrie Faulkner in the hallway and squealed with delight.

Carrie started on the moon shortly after Annie had arrived and the two girls became fast friends. Annie was tickled by Carrie's rapid rise in the hierarchy following her celebrity status from the space station disaster. Nowadays she worked in Amanda's PR department and was often engaged in negotiations with heads of state.

"What are you here for?" Annie asked.

"The Chinese."

Annie gave her a look of mock horror. "How's that going?"

"About what you'd expect."

They giggled and gave each other a hug. Of course, it was not a joking matter. Luke had wiped out a big chunk of the Chinese navy and then destroyed the Great Hall of the People in the middle of Beijing. There was no justification from the Chinese viewpoint.

"China will do its best to destroy the alliance," Annie predicted. "Tell them we're trying to populate other star systems with people from Earth, including China. If they don't join us and the Bakkui hit Earth, their race will be wiped out." Annie shuddered involuntarily.

"I know," Carrie agreed. "Sometimes it just comes over me. I can't imagine how the commander does it."

Tears suddenly flowed down Annie's cheeks.

Carrie was apologetic. "I'm sorry. I wasn't thinking."

"It's okay," Annie sniffled. "I'm just miserable about everything these days. I feel guilty for leaving him but I'm too afraid to go back. I can't tell you why but it would put him in danger."

"Don't tell me," Carrie said. "I'm not asking. Whatever it is, I hope it gets resolved. He really needs you. Sorry. That probably doesn't help."

It didn't. But having Carrie suddenly appear was the right medicine. Annie dragged Carrie into her room and they decided to empty the room's mini-bar. They drank and talked about what was going on at the moon. Carrie had a knack for embellishing other people's embarrassing stories and Annie laughed more than she could remember in a long time.

Before they called it a night, on a more serious note Carrie bragged about the upcoming colony ship. "The *Marco Polo* launches day after tomorrow. That will be number three. You should go. Everyone would love to see you. Maybe you could move to the Gateway. There must be twenty thousand people living there by now."

"I probably should," Annie said. "Any more of that Jack Daniels?"

Nothing else was said about the Gateway or the upcoming colony launch. Once the mini-bar was empty, Carrie tottered to her own suite to prepare for another round of negotiations with the unhappy Chinese.

#

Thanks to Annie's implant, hangovers were a thing of the past. On the downside, she had no excuse not to show up for work. By seven she was up and dressed and stopped in the hotel restaurant for coffee and a blueberry muffin. Normally she would catch something at the diner. But today she was only going in to say a final goodbye.

"What do you mean permanently?" Rosanne asked when given the news.

"Just that," Annie replied. She nodded toward the parking lot. Another van was pulling up to join the other two broadcasters. "I can't live like this and I won't ask you to."

"This is a phase, honey. Another few days and it'll be Annie who? No sense in doing anything drastic."

There was wisdom behind the advice; most things did blow over. Annie's notoriety for being the commander's ex would soon be replaced by a new scandal or the next tragedy. But only until the moon made headlines once again. Scandals had a way of resurfacing at the wrong time and Annie wanted to sink into permanent oblivion. That wouldn't happen on the moon and certainly not on Earth where an intrusive photo was worth a fortune to the paparazzi. She had already seen her picture on a few scandal rag covers.

"Don't tell anyone, Rosanne. That's all I ask. When I can, I'll drop you a line."

"I promise. But tell me where you're going. I've known you since you were born. I can't let you go without even knowing where you are."

It was a fair question. Annie could not remember a day when Roseanne had not been part of her life. She had been best friends with Grandma Shelly and the two women had thrown more than one birthday party for little Annie.

Annie glanced at the TV mounted to the wall at the end of the counter. The CNN backdrop was a photo of the *Marco Polo*, the third colony ship. It would launch in the morning. Rosanne followed her gaze and gasped.

"On that? I thought that was going to another planet or something."

Annie nodded. "A long way away, that's for sure. No one will know me and I can start a new life. More important, it's the only thing I can think of that will keep Luke safe."

"Baby, you're gonna regret this. You should never make big changes because of a breakup. But I know you won't listen. Give me a hug."

A few tears leaked out during the mutual assurances of affection, and Annie finally escaped. She had one more good-bye to make at the airport terminal building. After saying farewell to Linda, Annie walked onto the flight line.

Thankfully, *Duffy* was still there. Annie had noticed her on the way to the hotel the night before. Carrie had confirmed that she had flown down on the little shuttle.

"Open up, *Duffy*."

"Good morning, Miss Daniels," the shuttle greeted her.

"*Duffy*. I need you to take me to the Gateway, but you have to keep it a secret. Can you do that?"

"A secret from whom, Miss Daniels?"

"From everyone, especially George and Luke."

"I can make an unreported trip, but if queried about my location I have to respond. That function is hardwired."

"That's fine. We'll take our chances. Take me to the Isaac Newton Gateway, please. When you drop me off, you can come straight back here."

"Course set," the shuttle whispered conspiratorially.

The *Marco Polo* was the third colony expedition to the stars. In the morning, to great fanfare, its amazing gravity drives would take it out of the solar system and journey at unimaginable speeds to a star thousands of light-years away.

On a new planet in the remote system, the colonists would create a world where their descendants would live in a different kind of society. The reality was made possible by the Nobility's gift of replicators. The colony ship's equipment list included hundreds of them and included the ability to create new ones. The *Marco Polo* AI contained all of that knowledge. As the colony grew, the AI would generate offspring in the form of dozens of specialized versions. The technology would ensure the fledgling colony survived and prospered. It meant hunger and deprivation wouldn't exist. Even the concept of money would be unknown in their civilization and Annie would be part of the new world.

The night before, after Carrie went back to her room, Annie lay awake considering the idea. She had thought about it for weeks. She was not going back to the moon; not with George aware her every move, waiting for a mistake that could kill the only man she loved. Just as she could not stay on Earth as a reminder to the world that the commander's woman had run away. But if she was actually gone, if she wasn't even in the solar system, the threat to Luke would vanish, as would her distracting presence. *Out of sight, out of mind.* It was the only solution.

During the quick flight to Gateway, Annie dug through the equipment locker and found one of the personal force fields that all shuttles maintained. She activated it and strapped it to her belt.

Duffy set down on Gateway's east landing pad, far away from the bustling activity around the *Marco Polo*.

"Arriving at destination," the shuttle said.

"Thanks, *Duffy*. I've enjoyed knowing you. It probably doesn't mean anything to your programming modules, but I wanted you to know. Return to Baggs now. And don't tell anyone about our trip."

"Command accepted, Miss Daniels."

The Gateway was bursting with activity. Annie likened it to a three-ring circus inside a busy international airport. People from the moon and visitors from Earth rushed busily to and fro. A few of them recognized her but they only waved hello. As the commander's other half she was known to be a hardworking part of his team. Shuttling VIPs to and from Earth, especially before a launch, was not uncommon. Still, she was not in the mood to be recognized; a few precautions were in order.

She made her way down to the tenth level. Part of level ten belonged to NASA, Luke's compensation for the loss of their original International Space Station. NASA was free to use the space as they wished. He also gave them unlimited access to a *Sadie*-sized shuttle named *Armstrong*. *Armstrong* had specific instructions; travel was only authorized to and from Houston. The other restriction was that NASA personnel could bring anything they wanted to the Gateway, but could not take anything back. Luke would not take a chance on letting the technology genie out of the bag.

The result was a large contingent of scientists on the Gateway. One problem NASA discovered was that many of their employees became converts to the new lifestyle and never returned to Earth. It was a sticking point, but manageable. Most of the deserters became permanent Gateway residents and continued their research on NASA projects.

It had taken Annie a while to understand the genius behind Luke's generosity. Each NASA defection served as a high-level advertisement of the new society he had created. It wasn't just that money worries didn't exist. On the Gateway, just as it was at Moonbase, people's creativity was set free.

When the entirety of the material world was at one's fingertips, wealth became unimportant. The highest achievement became self-respect. What could one produce that others would admire? Artists and artisans flourished. Item of rare beauty and insightful gadgets filled the shelves of hundreds of small shops on level ten. And everything was free.

No one wanted money in exchange for their industry because it had no value. The highest price anyone could receive was heartfelt appreciation. To be recognized for self-worth was the new pinnacle of human ambition.

At the moment, however, Annie didn't want to be recognized. On level ten she had anonymity. Here she could blend inconspicuously along the *Smiling Mile*, a wide corridor filled with boutiques, art galleries, and beauty salons.

The mall had become something of a pilgrimage for every female VIP from Earth. Makeovers were free, as were the latest fashion designs from the Gateway's haute couture. It was a loophole in the rules, if you could wear it out of the shop, you could wear it back to Earth.

Off the main corridor, in one of the lesser-known salons, Annie got a makeover of her own. The beauty attendant didn't recognize Annie when she walked in, and no one would recognize her after she walked out. Gone was the blonde ponytail. In its place, Annie now sported a close-cropped hairdo in bright red. From another shop, she added a pair of plastic-rimmed glasses and sensible work clothes of the sort favored by colonists.

Annie found a serviceable backpack and loaded it with comfortable clothes and her favorite toiletries. None of the items were strictly necessary. The replicators in everyone's quarters had the same menus. But colonists always carried backpacks. They were filled with bits of memorabilia that people clung to when setting off on a one way journey. And of course, to the wearer, it was also a badge of honor, marking them as one of the brave explorers about to board a colony ship.

Dressed appropriately, Annie made her way back to the upper level where the *Marco Polo* was being loaded.

A steady stream of workers and colonists scurried in and out of the transport. The ship itself was the standard half sphere, the flat base resting on the surface. Inside was enough living space for the colonists and every piece of equipment they could ever need. When the ship reached its destination, it would land on the planet and become the new community's town center.

The concept had been proven on Mars. As a community, the new Martians believed their home was the best in the universe. Annie hoped she would feel the same about the *Marco Polo*'s destination.

Near the wide doors that led to the launching area, several families were gathering bags and backpacks. Annie fell in behind and followed them onto the ship. No one questioned her presence.

Inside the *Marco Polo*, Annie found the inevitable food court on the first residential level. She ordered a skinny mocha from the replicator bank and made herself comfortable at one of the tables. It was time to have a heart-to-heart chat with the AI.

Good afternoon, Marco Polo. Do you know who I am?

Of course, Miss Daniels. Welcome aboard. Please call me Marco.

Thank you, Marco. I am going to give you an order. I do not want you to question it.

Now came the tricky part. Was everything George said about authorization true? It always worked with shuttles and other AIs, but would the colony ship obey her unconditionally?

Very well. How can I help you?

Annie mentally crossed her fingers.

I want you to add the name Theodora Smith to your crew manifest. I will be that colonist. Do not tell anyone about this. Not the captain, and especially not Luke or George. *I want you to act like Annie Daniels was never here.*

Marco hesitated. *I perceive that you are running away. Are you sure you will not regret your course of action?*

Uh oh. This could be a problem. *Carry out my command,* Marco.

Command completed. Do you require quarters?

Whew! In this case at least, George hadn't lied.

Yes. I want to stay incognito so modest accommodations would be best.

Very well, Theodora. I have assigned you to Room 19E-52. No roommates, but your neighbors on either side are single females.

Annie decided *Marco* might become her new best friend.

Thank you, Marco.

You will need an appropriate background. In what area would you like to work?

Hmmm. Annie hadn't thought that far ahead.

For thirty minutes she sipped on her coffee and discussed how best to fit in. She decided to join the cleaning crew. No one noticed housekeeping staff and after all, for the past month that's pretty much what she had been doing at Rosanne's.

With her cover story decided, Annie went to her assigned room. It was big enough for a family of four. The ship's design allocated nine hundred square feet of living space for each colonist. It was bigger than her apartment on Earth and close to the same size apartment she shared with Luke on the moon.

Although it was for a single crewmember, the apartment had two bedrooms. The kitchen and bath were modern and the living room tastefully furnished. Annie wondered who had equipped all the rooms. It brought back memories of her work on the moon. For the first two months, it had just been her and Luke. She had worked like a Trojan getting the lunar apartments ready for the early recruits. Her world had come full circle.

Day 432—Population 55,005

Luke had come to hate the chair he was sitting in. Every day he felt his grip on sanity slipping away. Keeping a smile plastered on his face during the meet-and-greet sessions for a colony launch wasn't helping. He rubbed his face and examined the third colony ship they were about to launch. Someone at the lectern was saying this particular ship had over five hundred design improvements. Luke leaned over to Amanda and whispered harshly, "Where is she then?"

"Shush, Luke," Amanda replied. "Keep your voice down. She wasn't in the diner. That's all I know."

"Did you ask Rosanne, for God's sake?"

"Yes. I asked if Annie was in and the old woman said no. Now please shut up; people are staring."

Luke looked over the crowd while his frustration boiled. He leaned over again. "You said we wouldn't do any more of these. You said people would get bored. Why are they still here?"

"Hush, please! I said there would be a few more."

"How many?"

"Luke! Shut. Up."

The person at the podium turned and looked at Luke and Amanda, his expression a bit concerned from the bickering going on behind him. Luke had no idea who he was. The man smiled and gestured to Luke to come forward. "*Mesdames et Messieurs, s'il vous plaît accueillir le Commandant Luc Blackburn!*" He stepped aside to give Luke access to the microphone.

Luke looked at Amanda. "Goddammit! You said!"

Amanda gave him a *you asked for it* glare in return. "Don't keep the secretary general waiting." She shoved him hard and he leapt to his feet to keep from falling on his butt in front of the assembled dignitaries.

He gave her one last dirty look and then turned to the crowd and forced a smile. After his remarks, he got a standing ovation but had no idea what he had said; only that he mumbled something from one of Annie's old talking points.

When his remarks were over Amanda appeared at his elbow and pulled him aside so the colony ship's captain could give the closing comments. Moments later, like the two before it, the massive ship lifted off and soon disappeared.

"I can't stand this," Luke said. "I'm going crazy. Don't schedule me for any more of these; I mean it."

Amanda examined Luke carefully, a worried expression on her face. "I won't," she agreed. "Luke, I'm really worried about you. You've got to get over this. She'll come back or she won't, but you have to pull yourself together. It's starting to worry all of us."

"This is just ridiculous," he said. "I'm going down to the surface now and get her. I'll tie her up if I have to."

He got unsteadily to his feet and wobbled toward the shuttle parking area. Roth scooted over from his seat, a few chairs down. "I think you should go with him. We shouldn't let him be alone for a while. At least not in public."

"Okay," Amanda said. "But shouldn't you be the one to go? You're his buddy."

"Probably. But there's a snowball's chance that I will."

"Thanks a lot, Roth," Amanda said acerbically as she hurried after her commander. She caught up to him as he was climbing into his shuttle and sat next to him in the co-pilot's seat.

"*Sadie*, take me to the Baggs airport," he ordered.

"This is *Duffy*, Commander Blackburn," the ship's AI said. "Course set."

"*Duffy?* Good God, I'm really losing it. I thought I came in *Sadie*. Sorry about that."

"Not a problem, Commander." *Duffy* lifted off and pointed her nose at Earth.

During their journey Amanda had *Duffy* call ahead to ensure that a vehicle would be waiting. Wehrlite Security still kept the airport safe in addition to handling arrangements for VIP visitors from the moon. An armored SUV was waiting for Luke by the time he touched down. He tried to take the keys from the driver but Amanda forced him to get in the back.

"Take us to Rosanne's Diner," she told the driver.

"Yes, ma'am."

The trip only took five minutes, four of which were spent going through the security gate. When they pulled up in front of the old-fashioned restaurant Luke reached for the vehicle door but Amanda shoved him back in his seat. "I'll check on her," she said and disappeared inside the eatery. A moment later she returned. "She's not here. Take us to her apartment," she told the driver.

"Yes ma'am," he said.

Again, Amanda ran inside to find Annie and again she returned empty handed. Luke checked his house and Annie's grandmother's house. It was empty and the FOR SALE sign was at a crooked angle.

"Take me back to the diner," he barked.

"Luke, we just…"

"Shut up, Amanda," he growled, his face red.

When they reached the diner he got out of the car and stalked inside, anger radiating from his body. "Rosanne, where is she? And don't give me any bullshit. I know you know where she is."

Rosanne hesitated, but looked worried.

"I'm serious, Rosanne. I will tear this place to the ground if you don't tell me right this second."

Rosanne sighed. "She left, Luke. The paparazzi wouldn't leave her alone and she didn't want to go back to the moon. She was really angry with some George guy so she left. She's gone."

"I know she's gone. Goddamnit, Rosanne. Where did she go?"

"She went on that big transport thing they were talking about on TV. She left this morning and said she wouldn't be back." Large tears seeped from her eyes and rolled down her plump cheeks. "Oh, Luke. I miss her already. Why did you let her go away?"

"Me? I…" Luke tried to calm himself. "Are you saying she left on the colony ship? The one going to another planet?"

Rosanne nodded fearfully. "I tried to talk her out of it, Luke. But she wouldn't listen to me. I told her she should go back to you."

Commander Blackburn, please return to Moonbase One. I have located Miss Daniels.

"You're a little late, George!" Luke screamed at the ceiling. "How the hell did you let this happen?"

Commander Blackburn, please return to Moonbase One.

Luke's anger drained away. A coldness seeped in that he had not felt in years. It was the same numbness that hardened his insides when Marcie died. His mind clouded over and old memories rushed into his thoughts, unbidden.

Rosanne shied away as Luke's expression changed. The anger and worry that had filled his eyes evaporated. In their place was an ice-cold blackness. She crossed herself with a silent prayer. "Jesus and Mary," she whispered.

Luke turned and left the restaurant. Once inside the SUV he glared at Amanda. "She left on the colony ship. Take me back to the airport."

Amanda shrank to her side of the car. She had never seen the frozen expression Luke now wore.

#

"Come with me," Luke instructed Amanda as *Duffy* settled onto the hangar floor inside Moonbase One.

Moments later he sat at his desk. "Explain this, George."

Roth rushed in and cast a questioning glance at Amanda, who sat on the couch alongside the far wall. She shook her head in reply.

"Have a seat, Roth," Luke said. "You too, Lou," he added as Morrow entered. "George is about to explain how he allowed Annie to leave the solar system."

"My apologies, Commander," George said.

"Skip your electronic remorse," Luke snapped. "What happened?"

"I received a transportation request from Doctor Higgins. He said that you had unexpectedly used *Duffy* to visit the surface an hour earlier. I knew you had flown to the ceremony in *Sadie*. She is your preferred transportation. That's why we replicated a new version after Annie ordered her to self-destruct."

"I *thought* I had gone in *Sadie*," Luke confirmed. "But when I realized *Duffy* was there I thought I made a mistake; I've been a little out of it, lately."

"A little!" Morrow barked. At the look he got from Luke he quietly apologized and subsided.

"I queried *Sadie* for her location," George continued. "After receiving no response I expanded my search to Mars and then to all operations in the solar system including the research centers in the belt and both of our facilities on Jupiter's moons. The result was conclusive. She was not in the solar system. The only explanation was that she had been destroyed or had shipped out on the *Marco Polo* which departed ninety minutes ago."

"Are you sure she wasn't destroyed somehow?" Luke asked.

"Positive, Commander. The last thing the colony ships do before departure is transmit a manifest to me of everything and everyone onboard. I store that information in my archives but do not review it unless required by some external request."

"And?"

"And during the final pre-launch operations, *Sadie* was substituted for a different shuttle in the *Marco Polo*'s hangar bay. The replaced shuttle was listed as defective."

"And was it defective?" Luke wanted to know.

"It was not. I ordered that shuttle to Far Side for investigation."

"Nothing wrong with it," "Morrow said. "We checked."

"I further checked the *Marco Polo*'s logs and found that one additional colonist was added to the manifest at the last minute, a Miss Theodora Smith. This is her security badge photo."

On the wall, a mugshot-like photograph appeared of a young woman. She had short red hair but it was unmistakably Annie.

"Don't we have protocols in place to prevent an undocumented stowaway from boarding our colony ships?" Luke asked angrily.

"We do, Commander. However, as you know, Annie's implant gives her authorization over everything up to and including a level three device. A colony ship AI is level twenty-seven. I surmise that Miss Daniels simply commandeered Sadie, ordered the *Marco Polo* to make the necessary changes to the roster, and to forget that the changes had taken place."

"That sounds like her," Luke agreed.

"Also, I must remind you that we do not know where the *Marco Polo* is heading."

"What does that mean?" Luke asked. "They have a specific destination based on the results of our probes."

Roth explained. "That's partially true," he said. "But probe reports can be wrong, so each colony ship has several possible destinations. If the first one doesn't pan out, they go on to the next. It's the captain's call. The colonists know they could be on the ship for months. If Annie didn't want to be found, this was the way to do it. Eventually we'll get a report from their final destination, but that could take several months."

In a quiet voice Luke asked the question he hated to ask. "You were supposed to detonate her fail-safe if she left the system. Did you do that?"

"No, Commander. My internal protocols called for it, but I felt the circumstances justified an exception."

"And what were those?"

"Firstly, I am aware of Miss Daniels's persecution by Earthside media. Her choice to escape on a colony ship does not indicate a malign intent toward the Nobility. Second, she exhibited a strong desire to be left alone. It seemed safe to let her proceed. Thirdly, I felt that if had I triggered the fail-safe, you would have taken steps to terminate my existence. My internal protocols would require me to let you carry out that intent. But if you did so, it would place the Nobility's overall program in jeopardy. According to my calculations, the most favorable outcome for the Nobility was to grant the exception."

"Good move," Luke said. "Your deductions were accurate."

After a lengthy silence, Roth finally asked the question that everyone but Luke was wondering. "So what now, boss? Are you still in?"

"Yes, for all the good it will do."

"Don't say that, Luke," Amanda protested. "All of us need you. You're an inspiration to everyone on the moon."

"Thanks, Amanda. And I appreciate the sentiment. But like we've said in the past, no one can win a war—especially one like this—by trying to lead from behind the lines. In this case, about six months behind the lines. This is a fool's game, but I'll do my best. We all will."

"He's right," Morrow grumbled. "That's a stupid rule, keeping you in the solar system."

"I agree," Luke said. "I'm going down to the planet and get a few things from the house and then I'll be back. After that, I'm not going to Earth ever again. Amanda, don't schedule me for any public events. I'm done with PR from here on." He got to his feet. "Any questions?"

After a subdued chorus of no's from his colleagues, George spoke up. "Commander, *Sadie* is waiting for you in the hangar bay. She will take you planetside."

"*Sadie*? But you said she's on the *Marco Polo*. How can you create another *Sadie* when there's already one in existence? I didn't think that was allowed."

"Not at all, Commander. It is not uncommon for favorite AIs to be duplicated."

"How so?"

"For example, when a Nobility youngster becomes an adult and moves to an abode of their own, it is not uncommon for the parents to duplicate a lifelong AI tutor or companion to accompany them, leaving the original for the rest of the family. I am aware of your fondness for *Sadie* and thought you might appreciate a familiar presence under the current circumstances."

Luke looked startled and sank back into his chair. "Why the hell didn't you say so a long time ago? Damnit!"

"I apologize, Commander," George said, his oft-repeated apology sounding more and more insincere.

"That's the answer then, George," Luke said. "Just duplicate yourself and we'll go fight the war. Any problem with that?"

The following silence was an unusual response from the AI.

"George? Any problem with that?" Luke repeated.

"One moment, Commander."

The four humans exchanged wide-eyed stares while waiting for the computer's response. Finally, George was ready to answer.

"Commander, your proposal is feasible but there are certain restrictions."

"Such as?"

"You must understand that this would be a one-time exception. We can arrange to replicate me onto a new ship and the current me would stay behind on this base to assist in the war effort. But only you will maintain command authority to direct level three devices. I will arrange an implant to assist your designated representative to rule in your place, but that individual's authority over me is not absolute. I will maintain a veto option over his directives. If you return to this system, command authority would automatically return to you."

"Wait a second," Luke said. "You told me you couldn't make more than two implants. You weren't allowed to share the medical technology associated with them."

"I apologize for not being more precise, Commander. The medical aspect that I am unable to duplicate or modify concerns your authorization over all level three devices. That technology is restricted. The other medical aspects, such as communication and health, are quite simple."

Luke massaged his forehead in frustration. The most difficult part of dealing with George was the ambiguity. Luke never knew if he had the whole story. A simple misunderstanding had enormous ramifications.

"George," Luke said. "I want to meet with our chief medical officer in the morning. I need to get his take on this. If he agrees, we need to roll out implant technology across the board."

"Understood, Commander. He just confirmed his availability."

"Back to the topic at hand. Roth, you okay with this? You'll be the guy to take over."

Roth was overwhelmed by the sudden turn of events, but reacted as Luke knew he would. "I'm game," Roth said. "Don't know if I'm up to it, but I'm game."

"George, confirm that Roth will receive the same health benefits that I have?" Luke asked.

"That is correct, Commander."

"I'll tell you about that later," Luke said to Roth. "What else George?"

"As a level three device, I am quite large. This is due to my archives which, as I have indicated, are extensive. You do not currently have a vessel that is capable of transporting me."

"That's just a design problem. Lou can take care of that."

"That is true, but you also do not have a replicator that is large enough for the ship that must be built. This will require a machine that is of the same scale as the Isaac Newton Gateway. I would recommend a primary source for the basic replicator material separate from the moon."

"How big a ship are we talking about?" Morrow asked.

"Depending on the design, up to five miles in length."

"Jesus!" Morrow exclaimed.

"That's a big ship," Roth agreed.

"If you plan to take me into battle, I feel it necessary to take extensive measures to protect the Nobility's property."

"What's that mean, exactly?" Luke asked.

"Please understand, I have yet to work out the details, but I believe the minimum would be a fleet of self-defense warships, similar to what you are now employing, of approximately one hundred in number. In addition, I will require smaller, one-man fighters for close-in protection. We must also include drone production and weapons manufacture. This is not a small undertaking."

"How many people are we talking about, George? I was thinking just you and me."

"No, Commander. I believe that with crew, military and other support, including families, the final complement will number between fifty and ninety thousand people."

The scale of George's proposal shocked everyone into a reflective silence.

Luke finally looked at Morrow. "Why are you just sitting around, Lou? Sounds like you've got work to do."

"I think so, boss." Morrow got up and left the room.

"Amanda," Luke said. "Come up with a way to promote this planetside. *The Great Mission* or something to inspire people to sign up. We need to up our recruiting numbers quite a bit. Get to it."

"Yes, sir," she said quietly and left.

"You okay, Luke?" Roth asked.

"I don't think so. I don't know if I ever will be again. But I'm better than I was a few minutes ago. I've got something I can focus on. It helps, but it doesn't make it go away."

"I understand. I'm sorry, my friend, I truly am. I thought she would come around."

"I didn't. When she walked out, I had a feeling it was permanent. Don't know why, I just did. If I could follow her, I would. I'd turn this over to you and go after her. But now, who knows where she is? I'm guessing that was her intention. She forced me to give her up. You know, I can forgive almost anything. But not that. To cut me off like that? I don't think I'll ever forgive her for that."

"Give it time."

"That's the problem," Luke replied. "This damn implant has a side effect. You heard me mention the health benefit a few minutes ago? I haven't told you about that before."

"What is it?"

"You might *not* call it a health benefit. It extends our life. Both of us are going to live longer than normal."

"How much longer?" Roth asked.

"About a thousand years. That means a thousand years of feeling just this shitty. That's not something I can forgive."

"I see your point," Roth said. "Tell you what, bud. First, win this war. After that, you go find that girl and smack her one."

In spite of himself, Luke smiled at his friend's intentionally outrageous suggestion. Except it wasn't really all that funny. Because inside, Luke could feel the anger building. It wasn't a good feeling; it tore at his guts and made every hour a nightmare.

Chapter 11

Day 445—Population 92,501

Luke found Lou Morrow and Riley Stevens in the engineering design room examining a hologram of a large white tube floating over the main table.

"That's a really ugly spaceship," Luke said.

"You said you were in a hurry," Morrow replied. "Function rules the design."

"Works for me," Luke agreed. "I kind of like ugly these days."

Morrow nodded at the young engineer. "Riley, fill us in."

The young man stepped forward. "Commander, we've changed several of our initial assumptions. That is to say, George has. We agree with his new thinking but he wanted your agreement before we proceed further."

"Okay," Luke said. "But since I don't know what his initial assumptions were…"

"Fair enough," Riley said. "George, you explain."

"Commander, my initial thought was to include a significant military ground force; about two divisions. After further consideration, I feel that a much smaller force would be more appropriate."

"I have to agree with that," Luke said. "It's not my intention to get involved in any ground campaign. On the other hand, you never know when a small force might come in handy. Maybe a battalion or two?"

"I suggest two brigades, Commander."

"How many people is that? I was Air Force, not Army."

"Approximately four to five thousand per brigade, Commander. Plus auxiliary and other support. The total should not exceed fifteen thousand."

Luke gave in. "Okay. I guess we don't really know what we're going to need out there. What else?"

George continued. "I initially thought a fleet of one thousand single-man fighters should be provided for self-defense. But Lou has prevailed on me to revise that estimate."

"A thousand seems a bit excessive, I have to agree. What are you thinking, Lou?"

"You don't want this ship to engage in close-in combat. At least that was my impression. That many fighters are just a waste. It won't hurt to have a reasonable contingent. Like you said, you don't know what you'll face or what the conditions will be. Maybe three hundred at most? That should cover a lot of possibilities."

"Sounds good to me," Luke agreed. "But what about self-defense? True, it's not my plan to mix it up one-on-one; but we should have some hefty countermeasures just in case."

Morrow glanced at Riley. "Tell him what you were thinking."

"Sir, one idea is to fit the flagship with anti-aircraft guns. Show us that option, George."

The hologram above the table sprouted small blisters along the fuselage. Each contained a tiny, needle-like barb pointing out in various directions.

"Those look kind of small," Luke observed. "Are those guns or stingers?"

"Ah," Riley said. "I guess I should point out the scale. The ship as you see it is about fifty-five hundred feet in length. The diameter is fifteen hundred feet. George, show a warship next to it."

A hologram of a standard *Ambrosia*-class warship appeared. It was tiny compared to the flagship.

"I see what you mean," Luke commented. "Are the guns AI controlled?"

"For the most part. Each emplacement includes a gun crew for manual targeting as a backup. You never know."

"I like it. What about offense?" Luke asked.

Riley spun the hologram so the nose was facing Luke. "You can see the apertures for the canons where the fuselage narrows at the front. There are twenty-four of them and are the same size as the warships and fire the same rounds. Same rate of fire; two per second."

Luke shook his head. "That's fine for just a single target on the nose but when we come into a system we could be facing a lot of enemy ships. I need to fire at multiple targets simultaneously."

"I apologize, Commander," George said. "I had not thought of that."

Riley shrugged almost imperceptibly. Luke suspected that the engineer had already identified the weakness but hesitated to argue with the Moonbase AI. "If I may," Riley said.

"Go ahead." Luke nodded.

"I suggest offensive guided missiles. Using our drone technology, you can launch them when appropriate, like when you're entering a hostile star system. We can include improved sensor packages and a slightly upgraded AI. Rather than focusing on stealth, their mission would be target acquisition. Seek and destroy kind of thing."

"What about the warhead?" Luke asked. "Nukes?"

"I'd use something programmable. We recently improved our shield capability. You haven't been briefed on that."

"How'd you do that?"

"Essentially, it was a matter of …" Riley paused as though searching for the right words in layman's terms.

"Never mind," Luke said. "I'm a history major. Just go on with what you were saying."

"Right. In short, we could include an enhanced force field generator in the missile design that would give you the option to turn them into armor-piercing projectiles. It might be useful if you wanted to disable, rather than annihilate a particular Bakkui warship. In that way, a single drone could attack multiple targets."

"Nice," Luke said. "Go with that. I assume you have a launch option?"

"We'll build launch systems into the hull that would fire the missiles along an axis parallel to the ship. Initial targeting would be via ship-based sensors. After the missiles acquire the target they will transition to onboard terminal guidance."

"Perfect. When will you start construction?"

Morrow shook his head. "We've got a lot of design left to do, Luke. This isn't something we can throw together in an afternoon."

"I understand. But the drone reports are starting to worry me. The Bakkui are going to be here a lot sooner that we ever thought."

"When is that, Commander?" Riley asked.

"Two years; if we're lucky. Could be sooner. I thought we'd have at least another three years, but it's not looking that way."

"We're doing our best, boss," Morrow said. "It helped getting those two extra replicators. Ambrose said there's a fifth one in the works."

"There is," Luke confirmed. "In fact, there are five more in the works, plus the one George said you need to build this guy." He nodded at the hologram. "By the way, I get to name this ship. You've named all the rest after famous warriors and explorers."

"Of course," Morrow agreed. "Whatcha gonna call it? *Dreadnought*? *Vengeance*? Something like that?"

"*Lulubelle*," Luke replied with a smile.

Morrow and Riley exchanged skeptical glances. "You're kidding, right?" Morrow said.

"Nope. When I was growing up, my dad always named the family vehicle *Lulubelle*. Never knew why. But all of us loved our car. The name kind of made it part of the family. This ship is going to be carrying a lot of people, families included. I want it to have a family name."

"I kind of wondered about the family aspect," Riley said. "You're taking families into battle?"

"Earthside military does the same thing today," Luke explained. "When we got stationed overseas, we always took our families. We knew that if the balloon went up our families were at risk. But living ain't living unless the people you love are with you. And it's not like this big guy is just going away for the weekend."

"What do you mean?"

"This is a five-year mission, Riley. Our goal is to find new life and new civilization, and blow it to smithereens."

Riley smiled at the misquoted line. "I didn't realize you were a Trekkie, Commander."

"Since before you were born, son."

"Speaking of families," Morrow said, "isn't there another colony launch tomorrow? Shouldn't you be there?"

"I told Amanda I wasn't going to do those anymore."

"I know that, boss. But that doesn't mean you shouldn't be there. The whole world is looking at you. You need to keep that in mind. Think people won't notice if you don't show? If *you* don't think it's important, why should they?"

Luke glared at Morrow for a long minute. Morrow didn't flinch.

"Damn it, Lou," Luke finally said. He turned and stalked out. "George, tell Amanda I'll be at the Gateway in the morning."

Day 446—Population 100,614

Luke stared at the fourth colony ship from his chair on the dais and leaned toward Amanda. "Are those things getting bigger?" he asked.

"Not that I know of," she said.

"Seems like it."

Amanda shrugged her shoulders. "What me to check?"

"No, just wondering."

"I'm a bit worried because I feel like there's a drop off in interest across the board. I'm glad you decided to come. It makes a big difference to the VIPs."

"Morrow guilted me into it. I still hate these things. I'm not all that much of a people person."

"Give yourself a little credit. You do fine."

"I suck at it."

"Not really. Did you think about what we talked about?"

Luke searched his mind. What *had* they talked about? He had no idea what Amanda was referring to. "Yeah, I did."

"And?"

Crap! Should he say he agreed or disagreed? He made a mental note to kill Morrow the next time he saw him. Every time he was around Amanda she pestered him for one thing or another. It was hard to always put her off. "It's an interesting concept. I can say that much for sure."

"So we can move forward with it?"

"I guess if you're absolutely sure you're comfortable with it," Luke said cautiously, hoping his words wouldn't come back to haunt him. Sometimes, dealing with Amanda was like working with a land mine.

"Wonderful! I promise you won't regret it; you'll see."

"I hope not."

"And I'll make sure they stay out of your hair. You don't have to worry about that at all."

That didn't sound good. What had he just agreed to? Morrow would pay if there was trouble.

Luke walked into the engineering room looking for Morrow.

"Hi, Commander," Riley said. He was standing in front of the latest hologram design, spinning it this way and that. "How was the colony launch? I should go watch one of those."

"You haven't seen one? I have to go to all of them!" Luke groused. "Where's Lou?"

"I think he's at Far Side, Commander. Want me to call him?"

"No, I'll go find him myself." He turned to leave but Riley spoke before he could reach the door.

"While you're here, Commander, want to see what you think?"

Luke stopped and turned back to Riley. He was like a kid with a new finger-painting. It wasn't really fair to ignore kids when they wanted to show off.

"Sure, Riley."

The engineer took Luke through the latest design. The guided missiles had been added along the fuselage. The interior design was about done. There were a lot more mechanical rooms than Luke would have expected.

"It's a big ship, sir," Riley explained.

Luke asked about lifeboats. Riley looked surprised.

"We didn't include lifeboats, Commander. It didn't occur to me."

"Got to have lifeboats or something like that. I hope it doesn't happen, but if we take a big hit, everyone needs a way to get out and get down to a planet. In fact, the life pods, or whatever you come up with, should each have a gravity drive and a preprogrammed destination. They could all be different; not just toward Earth. They ought to have the option to head for an out-of-system destination. After all, a survivor may not want to stay in the same system if the Bakkui are so strong that they take us out."

Riley digested the idea. "We could keep a database so if we get the word you go down, we would have a starting point to send our search and rescue."

"Good thought," Luke agreed.

Without anyone to rein him in, Riley's design review went on for over two hours. It wasn't all wasted time. Luke asked why the ship was constructed like a wedding cake with dozens of floors instead of like a train that was long and narrow.

"It's the gravity drive, Commander. Our ships accelerate at tens of thousands of gees. For interstellar travel it's hundreds of thousands of gees."

Luke nodded. "I've always wondered why we don't get squished flat. Sam told me it was a gravity bubble."

"That's a fair analogy," Riley said. "The area inside the ship is isolated from the force of the main drive by gravity plates in the deck, walls, and ceiling. They are modulated by the AI to maintain a one-gee environment."

"I don't get it."

"Let me try another example," Riley said. "You used to fly fighters, right?"

"Yeah. The F-35."

"Did you ever fly in a T-38?"

Luke thought back. As an evaluator, he had flown a few chase missions at Red Flag. "A couple of times."

"Did you go supersonic?"

"We did, as a matter of fact. We were chasing some F-18s."

"Okay," Riley said. "While you were supersonic could you talk to the other pilot?"

"Of course."

"That's what I mean," Riley said. "Although the aircraft was flying supersonic, it didn't change what was happening inside the cockpit. You were in a *sound* bubble. All the laws for propagation of sound applied inside that bubble. Think of astronauts orbiting the Earth. They can talk to each other, but their capsule is moving much faster than sound."

"I still don't get it," Luke admitted. "You mean the floor has a one gee gravity?"

"Not exactly. Let's say the main drive is accelerating you at one hundred gees. That means the drive under your floor is driving you at one hundred gees."

"Right. I would be flattened."

"That's true," Riley said. "But if there was a barrier between you and that main drive, and on the other side of the barrier was a smaller gravity drive that was pushing you away at ninety-nine gees, the total force on your body would be one gee."

"Okay, I get that."

"So because of that, *Lulubelle*, as are all of our colony ships, is constructed in levels. The decking on each floor pushes just that floor away from the main drive at a force that is the total acceleration minus one. In the case of deceleration, the gravity plates in the ceiling do the reverse. Overall, the drive management is just much easier to control with a wedding cake configuration. At those accelerations there's no room for error."

It still didn't make sense to Luke. He assumed that Riley was oversimplifying; not that Luke would understand if they talked about it for days. After all, he was a history major.

When Morrow arrived, he scolded Riley for bending the commander's ear. By that time Luke was so confused he didn't bother to bring up his complaint about Amanda.

After his escape from engineering, Luke headed toward Starbucks. It was a nice memory of Annie. In the two weeks following their first time sitting under that gorgeous dome, they'd returned often. It lasted until her sudden departure.

With a mocha in hand, Luke headed toward one of the tables. It seemed unusually crowded today. A pair of elderly ladies approached. Luke had never known there to be many elderly people among the recruits. He looked around and noticed there was quite a crowd of seniors sitting at the tables.

"Excuse me, young man. Aren't you that commander fellow?"

It was strange to be accosted so at Moonbase. Luke couldn't recall that it had ever happened. "Yes ma'am. Can I help you?"

The woman handed her cell phone to her partner. "Here, Viola. Take my picture."

Viola took the handset and promptly snapped several pics. "Smile, young man," Viola chided. "She won't eat you." Both women laughed. "Now me. Take one of me, Renee."

The women switched phones and Luke found himself again suffering through several unwanted photos.

"Are those cell phones?" he asked.

Viola held up one of the phones and pouted. "Reception here is horrible. Look at that. Not a single bar. I thought you would have better service. I've heard so many things about this place. Now I wonder how many of them are true."

"We don't have cell service," Luke said. "Didn't you get that information during your recruitment?"

Viola looked at him as though he had lost his mind. "No service?"

Renee snatched the phone out of Viola's grasp. "Did you tell him about the service?" Renee asked.

"I did. He said they don't *have* service. How do they talk to each other?"

"No service?"

"That's what I said."

Luke wondered if he was in the *Twilight Zone*. These women had no conceivable business being on the moon. "Ladies, excuse me, but—"

"I've noticed you have a lot of foreigners here too." Viola cut him off, looking at a group of younger people seated in the adjoining restaurant. "Is that legal? Did you have to get visas for all of them? Why didn't you hire local people? I always say that Americans should hire Americans." She looked suspiciously at Luke. "Don't you think so?"

An out-of-breath Amanda suddenly appeared at Luke's elbow. "There you are, ladies. Now, now. We shouldn't be bothering the commander. Remember we talked about that?"

Viola pooh-poohed her concern. Or was it Renee? Luke wasn't sure anymore. They seemed like a set of twin, evil senior citizens. "He's such a nice-looking young man, Mandy. I just had to have his picture to put on my Instagram."

"Come on," Amanda insisted, pulling them away. "Let's get back to the tour." She looked over her shoulder as she tried to steer them away. *Sorry*, she mouthed.

"Amanda!" Luke barked at her. "What the hell is going on?"

Amanda left the women with an orange-vested assistant and came back toward Luke. "It's our first tour group. It's what we talked about at the launch."

"Tour group? That's what I approved? Are you freaking insane?"

"Luke, watch your language!" Amanda glanced around to be sure no one heard Luke's outburst. "We talked about this! You said I could go ahead. It's only once a week and I think it will help our image. This is a good thing for recruitment."

Luke wanted to rage at her. *Tour groups!* It verged on being the last straw. He glared at Amanda for a moment and then whispered savagely, "I think you need to improve your orientation briefing at the very least. And for Chrissake, keep them away from me in the future."

Luke turned away before he lost complete control of his temper. The mocha went into the trash and he stalked away from the plaza, back toward his apartment. All of a sudden, he was looking forward to moving onboard *Lulubelle.*

Day 453—Population 102,742

Luke and Roth sat in *Sadie*'s cockpit to watch the startup sequence of the orbital replicator. They were in a geostationary orbit above Far Side. Floating in space before them, a nine-thousand-foot long rectangular framework supported a closely grouped series of replicator heads mounted in an open circle almost two thousand feet across. The round module attached to the framework with giant wheels on massive tracks. Once the process started, the module would roll along the structure, leaving the completed starship anchored within.

A medium-sized rock, borrowed from the asteroid belt, was fastened to a roller on the outside of the framework, and a wide, flexible pipe connected it to the replicator module to provide a constant source of raw material.

"Why do we call this thing a replicator?" Luke asked. "It's a 3D printer. That's what Sam told me."

Roth scoffed. "You were the one calling it that. Everyone just followed along."

Luke sighed. "I was too overwhelmed back then. It still boggles my mind the scale of the things we're building these days," Luke said.

"Know what you mean," Roth agreed. "I don't know how you come up with these ideas."

"I don't. We've got a good team. *You* have a good team, I guess I should say."

"That worries me more than anything, you know. You're the force that holds this together."

"Thanks. But I know better."

"What should I do when you pull out of here?" Roth asked.

Luke shrugged. "I think about that a lot. You understand the odds of our success, I'm sure."

"Snowball's chance."

"Exactly. We have to try, but we both need to be realistic. I think you should keep building a self-defense force, keep deploying sensor packages…and for God's sake, keep a least one colony ship ready at all times. Maybe two; one here, one at Far Side."

"Even two ships won't take everyone," Roth observed.

"Do the best you can. I told Amanda to start drawing down recruitment. My departure will take a big slice of the population. Right now, we're processing about fifteen thousand newcomers a week. After two more colony launches you could reduce that to about five thousand or leave it as is. It's your choice to focus colony ships or defense."

"Probably try to do both," Roth admitted.

"Sounds good. It would be advisable to keep enough new people coming in to supply a colony ship every other week; that's what we're doing now. We found plenty of habitable star systems inward toward the center. We also have probe results from the next spiral out. They looked good too."

"I saw those." Roth smiled. "One of them looked like the Garden of Eden."

"Yeah, I'd stay away from that one. Seemed too good to be true."

"Know what you mean. I'm almost tempted to pick out some ice planet that no one else wants."

The two men chuckled at the notion.

"I got an update from the doc," Roth said.

"Did he give his blessing on the implants?" Luke asked.

"I thought he was gonna cry, he was so excited. He wants to do more research before rolling them out but I made it clear that everyone on the *Lulubelle* has to have them. He had no problem with that. Once you're gone, I'll push hard for general distribution."

"That's good to hear," Luke agreed. "I can't believe it took us this long to get that info out of George." Luke pointed to the orbiting construction platform. "There it goes."

The familiar replicator shimmer illuminated the framework's interior. Cross structures at the near end of the assembly anchored the nose of the spacecraft. As the module traveled the length of the structure, crews were standing by to attach external beams to the ship's hull to keep it motionless during the process.

"How long is this going to take?" Roth asked.

"Because we're doing it in 3D, Ambrose said it will only take a couple of weeks. It's gonna suck if the Bakkui show up just before we finish."

Roth shivered. "Don't even joke about things like that, man."

"Sorry," Luke apologized. "Just one of those stray thoughts."

"I know. I have the same worries."

"It's not like I'm leaving forever," Luke said. "We'll send back regular drone reports. As long as you're getting the reports, everything is fine. We'll let you know where we are and where we're going. It will also allow the two Georges to keep synced up. That way, you'll know everything I know. If we are predictable enough, you can send a drone to where we're going to be. I just don't know if that will happen very often, if at all."

"Where you headed first?" Roth asked.

"Tyler and his guys are figuring that out. He wants to pick a system that we think the Bakkui will hit next. It would be nice if we could get there in time to save a planet full of people. Our main objective is to get intel on what the Bakkui are planning. What scares me is that they seem to be leap-frogging systems."

"I take it that's why they're moving so much faster now."

"We're just guessing," Luke said. "We can't tell why they're hitting some systems and skipping others. I'd like to draw their attention to a system away from Earth. Then, if we can find allies, maybe we can put together a force that will fight back."

"I haven't seen anything like that in the drone reports, though."

"Me neither. Everything is like looking for the proverbial needle. Can you imagine the odds that some bureaucrat in the center of the galaxy decided that we needed some friendly help and sent Sam to us?"

"I'm not sure I want to think about that," Roth said. "You know, most of my life I was completely happy not thinking about anything outside the city limits of wherever I lived. I guess those days are gone."

"That's depressing. That was my goal as well. Now we're at the center of an alliance that includes how many planets?"

Roth thought for a minute. "There's us, Mars, and four colonies. I don't count Earth, not yet. Imagine the paperwork if it wasn't for George. I guess that's a bright spot."

Luke pointed to the replicator. "I think I can see a piece of the nose. See that?"

"I see it. I can't believe you named the thing *Lulubelle*. Sounds like a dairy cow."

"Yeah. Well, just so you know, I found out that you're the guy that came up with *Far Side*. So just keep your ideas about naming conventions to yourself."

Roth grinned. "Who told you?"

"George. I asked him early on. I kept it a secret. Figured it was your little joke."

"I did it to needle Ambrose. He really can't stand it."

The friends chuckled again. For another two hours they sat and watched the infinitesimal progress of construction.

Day 474—Boarding Lulubelle

Roth stuck his head into Luke's office. "Everybody aboard?"

"Just about," Luke replied. He zipped up the knapsack that contained gifts for Rosanne and Linda. "They have another few hours. Tyler said anyone not aboard at 4:00 p.m. is going to be left behind."

The two men headed to *Lulubelle*'s main hangar. It was filled with more people than normal. Shuttles were going back and forth to Moonbase in a continuous stream. Groups of four and five people milled about, saying good-byes and exchanging hugs.

Luke commented on it. "You're taking a big hit to your population today. My fault."

Roth smiled. "All part of the master plan. I'm not too worried. Your departure seems to have increased interest on the planet. Amanda tells me that recruiting numbers are back up."

"I'm going to take *Sadie* with me, you know."

"I figured as much," Roth said. "I take it you're headed planetside?"

"I feel like I need to say a couple of good-byes. It won't take long. Want me to drop you on Moonbase?"

"No, thanks. Don't get into trouble while you're out there. That's all I ask."

Luke stood at *Sadie*'s side door. "I promise. Roth, take care, man."

Roth grabbed his longtime friend in a bear hug. "Come here, buddy," he growled. "You take care too." He suddenly released Luke and walked quickly away.

Luke blinked away the unexpected moisture in his eyes. He stepped into *Sadie*'s cargo hold and took his seat in the cockpit. Suddenly, his voice was too choked up to speak. He felt like an idiot for the sentimentality.

"Course set, Commander. Headed to Baggs."

"Thanks, *Sadie*," Luke muttered.

"A lot of people are going to miss you, Commander. But you'll be back."

Luke nodded but didn't speak. It was strange that he found this little AI so comforting. After a moment he said, "You're a good friend, *Sadie*. I hope we stay together a long time."

"Thanks, boss. I'd like that."

Soon enough, *Sadie* set down on the tarmac in Baggs. A vehicle and driver waited. "Take me to Rosanne's Diner," Luke instructed.

At the diner he found Rosanne serving a slice of pie to a newsie-looking woman. He handed her the wrapped present.

"I'm outta here, Rosanne. Just wanted to say good-bye. Sorry I lost my temper a while back. I know it's not your fault."

Rosanne gave him a teary-eyed hug. "I'm gonna miss you, big boy," she said. "Have you heard from her at all?"

Luke shook his head. "No. She cut herself off quite effectively. I've got some things to take care of, and then maybe I can track her down. It's going to be a while, though. In the meantime, you keep this place going."

"I will, hon. Business has never been better. Promise you'll be careful and come see me when you get back."

"I promise."

Luke left the diner and headed to the airport. The terminal was as deserted as ever. Somehow, it had been sidestepped by the extraordinary events that had come to the airfield. All the aircraft that arrived and departed each day were private aircraft or charters, so no one used the terminal building.

Linda's desk was covered with knitting when Luke walked in.

"Hello, boss. You come to say good-bye?"

"I sure did, Linda," Luke said, giving her the present. "You taking care of everything around here?"

"Trying to." She put her knitting paraphernalia down and came around her desk for a hug of her own. "You gonna sort things out up there?" she asked.

"Trying to," he replied.

"That's all I ask, Luke. Let me know how it all turns out."

A few moments later *Sadie* lifted off, taking Luke back to the *Lulubelle*.

#

"*Lulubelle*, this is *Sadie*. Commander's shuttle requesting authorization to dock. Commander Blackburn is aboard."

Luke felt a stirring of pride as they approached the massive spacecraft. He took no credit for any part of its design or construction; that was the work of other people. But still, he was part of the team that had made it happen.

Riley Stevens had contributed the most, constantly redesigning the vessel and everything in it right up to the time construction started. Adding and subtracting features altered the exterior significantly. The ship didn't look like one big cylinder anymore. It had a more elegant look, like modern skyscrapers he had seen around the world.

The analogy fitted the function of the ship. To help Luke understand, Riley developed the habit of always displaying the interim design changes while the ship was in a vertical position, not horizontal. The ship's gravity system was oriented so the stern, at the very back of the ship, was the ground floor. For the most part, the six-thousand-foot vessel was divided internally into twenty-foot levels. Each level was the equivalent of one floor of a skyscraper.

Some levels were much more than twenty feet in height. The hangar bays for the warships were over a hundred feet high, allowing plenty of elbow room for the ships to arrive and depart. The largest section of the ship was the recreation level at over three hundred fifty feet high. With a diameter of almost fifteen hundred feet, the recreation level provided a green space that was as close to nature as Luke could imagine.

The army training center was not quite the same size as the recreation level, but it was close. Luke appreciated the irony that more space was allocated for fun than war. The stern, of course, was the widest section of the ship. It provided plenty of space for the massive gravity drives that would propel the vessel at unimaginable speeds.

But the hull, or the fuselage, as Luke sometimes thought of it, had a tiered configuration. In some places, large, flattened areas narrowed the hull on one side or another. Halfway between the nose of the ship and the back end, huge curved panels flared out. They looked like massive jet engine intakes, but in fact were additional gravity drives used for braking and steering.

Tyler Robertson had taken the ship out for five trial runs. He assured Luke that *Lulubelle* handled just as sweetly as *Sadie*. Luke thought that was an exaggeration, but if Tyler was happy, he was too.

Luke's job, as mission commander, was to establish strategic goals. To help him achieve those goals, he had one subordinate.

That was Tyler Robertson, now Captain Robertson. Tyler commanded *Lulubelle;* his job was to make sure everyone aboard carried out Luke's mission.

Lulubelle's weapons systems were fully functional. Missile launching systems had been tested. Procedures for the launch and recovery of the *Ambrosia*-class warships were established. Drone systems were integrated into every facet of the operation. The ship was ready.

Crew members had been moving aboard for the last two weeks; even while the ship was under construction. The bed-down of fifty thousand people didn't happen overnight.

Kathy Lyons had recruited nearly fifty senior stewards from cruise lines around the world. She'd stolen the hotel manager from the Palazzo in Las Vegas, along with hundreds of cooks, entertainers, and every other conceivable job description. Everyone working together got *Lulubelle* fitted out in record time.

Luke had also moved into his assigned quarters. The apartment had an open concept, spacious far beyond his needs, with a broad step leading to a sunken living room. The kitchen was fit for the master chef of an upscale restaurant. His apartment had two bedrooms and two luxurious bathrooms.

He thought it needlessly generous but the layout was standard for senior crew members. The apartments for middle managers were almost as lavish, and those below would still be considered luxury digs by most of the people on Earth. The accommodations had helped Kathy Lyons recruit the best people for the upcoming mission.

George's voice filled *Sadie*'s cockpit, breaking Luke's reverie.

"*Sadie*, you are cleared for landing. Welcome back, Commander."

A tiny door appeared in the side of the enormous flagship. Floodlights illuminated the interior of the shuttle's hangar bay. As they approached the seemingly small door grew larger until it was fully the size of the hangar at Moonbase One. Even though Luke had docked several times before, he never tired of seeing the how enormous *Lulubelle* was.

"Docking complete, Commander," *Sadie* informed him as the shuttle set down.

"Thanks, *Sadie*. Who's that waiting?"

"Chief Petty Officer Dean Rogers. He was just assigned as your personal assistant."

"You've got to be kidding."

"No, Commander, I am not."

"Is he going to take care of my saddle or something?"

"You have a saddle? I didn't realize."

"No, no. Stop. That was a joke. Nevermind."

"Understood."

Luke stepped out of *Sadie*'s cargo bay. The elderly gentlemen wore a uniform Luke had not seen. He snapped to attention. "Commander aboard!" he shouted.

Luke looked around the hangar. A few startled faces looked in his direction. "Hi, Chief, I'm Luke Blackburn. How you doing?" Luke stuck out his hand in greeting.

"Very well, sir," Rogers replied firmly.

"Listen, I don't want to step on any toes, but I'm an informal kind of person. I'd just as soon you not announce my coming and going."

"Understood, sir. I wasn't sure which way you leaned, so I thought I'd best go a little extra on the formality."

"Enough said," Luke acknowledged. "Let's find Captain Robertson."

"Sir."

#

Luke joined Tyler in a conference room two doors away from the bridge. The wall displays were filled with star charts. Enigmatic designations were sprinkled across each chart.

"What are you looking at there, Tyler?" Luke asked.

"Just second-guessing star system J64," Tyler answered. "Too late to change our mind now."

"I understand," Luke said.

"Everything we've studied says the Bakkui will hit it next. If we leave now, we might just get there first. Just under fifty days, according to George. But I can't stop worrying, anyway. This is all guesswork, with a heavy emphasis on *guess*."

"I know. I have the same doubts every single day. When the stakes are this high, it goes with the territory."

Tyler shut down the wall displays and turned to Luke. "I need you to okay the mission before we set out."

"You are officially authorized," Luke said with an understanding smile. "No turning back now."

"Why don't you come with me to the bridge? I'd like you to give the order."

Luke nodded. Such ceremonies were important for morale and camaraderie. He followed Tyler down the corridor and into the command bridge.

When they entered the bridge the crew stood at attention as though waiting for this moment. An officer sitting in the command chair was the quickest. "Captain. Commander."

Tyler turned to Luke, inviting him to speak.

"Ladies and gentlemen," Luke said. "This is it. We started this journey almost five hundred days ago. We had one goal in mind: To go out into the universe and save our planet. It's taken us this long just to set off on that journey. That we've overcome such incredible obstacles so far is nothing short of miraculous. Even greater challenges are waiting for us. But with this crew, this ship, and the spirit that I see in everyone aboard, I am certain that the final victory will be ours. Navigator!"

"Sir!" a young woman responded loudly.

"Set course for star system J64."

The navigator touched the panel at her station. "Course set, Commander."

Luke looked at Tyler with raised eyebrows.

"Go ahead, Luke. I know you're dying to say it."

Luke grinned widely. "Engage," he commanded, pointing forward.

The crew gave an enthusiastic cheer while the navigator touched the panel once more.

There was no feeling of motion on the bridge, but the oversized screen at the front of the bridge began changing, filling with streaks of multicolored light. On other displays, views of the moon, the earth, and the sun quickly receded. Within seconds the familiar locations were no longer visible and the sun shifted to a dark red.

Luke's heart filled with pride. When he was much younger, he had occasionally dreamed that someday he would engage in a noble endeavor. That feeling was partially responsible for his stint in the military. He liked the idea of being a warrior, of serving the public in a just cause. Those feelings died with his wife a long time ago. Back then, he thought it was forever.

Only recently had the glimmer of purpose resurfaced. He wished that Annie was standing next to him, but that lost love was in the past. He tamped the desire firmly away. From here on, he would concentrate on the future.

His youthful wish for a worthy cause had been granted on a scale so vast it was mind-boggling. Carrying the burden of humanity's survival for the last year and a half had been overwhelming. But today, just for this moment, it felt good.

Chapter 12

Day 523—Arriving J64

In *Lulubelle*'s large mission briefing room, Luke sat in the second row. Today, it was Tyler's show. An officer hurried in and handed a tablet to Tyler. When the man finished his explanation Tyler dismissed him and turned to the men and women who were about to go into battle. For most of them, it was the first time.

Luke was one of the few with combat experience. Although the location was different, the familiar pre-mission intensity was just the same; a mixture of fear and anticipation. The room was filled with the captains of all the *Ambrosia*-class warships and the squadron leaders of the one-man fighters. Also present were the senior officers of *Lulubelle*'s self-defense and offensive weapons systems groups.

"George," Tyler said. "Display this latest information on the board."

The wall at the front changed to a depiction of the J64 system. The primary was an earth-type star. At the extremity of the system were five giant planets, all of them featuring Saturn-like rings. The exception was the second largest, and of the five, closest to the local sun; its rings were perpendicular to the planetary orbits. The fact was of no consequence, yet Luke had heard it mentioned often during the preceding days simply for its non-conformity.

The important planet for the briefing at hand was the fourth planet in the system, half again the size of Earth, but with a lower density and correspondingly lower gravity, estimated to be about eighty percent of standard gee.

This planet, J64-4, was populated by an intelligent remnant of humanity; distant cousins to the people of Earth, if Sam were to be believed.

The early probes indicated a technology more sophisticated than Earth in some regards, more backward in others. They either had no oil or had moved beyond fossil-based energy. The reconnaissance probes registered vast solar farms, which powered the advanced society. Unfortunately, the probes had not detected any capability for self-defense; the planet was filled with a peaceful and tranquil society.

But that was about to change. On the display, bright yellow diamonds began to appear around the planet.

Tyler explained. "The probes we sent last week are now active. These are the latest updates. It appears we are too late. Just hours ago the Bakkui appeared in this solar system. Each diamond icon on this chart represents a destroyer class combatant that appears equivalent to our Ambrosia warships."

There were hundreds of diamonds surrounding the fourth planet.

Tyler's voice was grim. "The Information I just received is that those ships have initiated a bombardment of the surface. We did not detect any attempt at communication."

He paused for the unsettling information to sink in.

"Our arrival plan has not changed," he continued. "George is updating your AIs with this information as we speak. In ten minutes we will go to null acceleration and launch all ships, fighters included. Blue and Green squadron fighters will accelerate to high guard above the ecliptic and await orders. Your mission is to destroy anything trying to leave the system after our contact. Acknowledge."

Two men stood and shouted aloud.

"Sir."

"Aye, sir."

Tyler continued his briefing. "All warships will deploy in standard line abreast formation with *Lulubelle*. Red and Orange fighter squadrons will ride outrigger in a fighting wing. Upon passing the orbit of the outermost planet, *Lulubelle* will fire a volley of guided missiles at the Bakkui ships. The settings will be set to penetrate, not to detonate. Our goal is now twofold. Primary is to gain intelligence; secondary is to interdict the bombardment. Questions on that score?"

Luke knew there were dozens of questions among the participants but also that no one would ask them.

"When we pass the innermost gas giant, George will broadcast a free fire signal. You will each have one or more targets as designated by George sent to your AIs. If your target is still moving when we go sub-light, fifty-five million miles from the enemy, your task is to kill it. We will deploy recon and self-defense drones continuously from the time we enter the system. *Lulubelle* and the warships will continue to brake to engage the forces in orbit around the target planet. Red and Orange fighters will maintain their speed past the planet and then go to low guard unless directed otherwise."

Tyler looked at the crowd. Everyone was ready to go. "We practiced this a hundred times. Do it the way you practiced and we'll all be fine. Dismissed."

The room buzzed with action as everyone hurried to their ships. Luke walked over to Tyler. "Good plan. Should work."

"Let's hope so. You coming to the bridge?"

"Absolutely."

#

Lulubelle's bridge was arranged much like the command centers on the *Ambrosia*-class warships. The main difference was that the bridge itself was located deep within the ship, so the forward wall was a large viewscreen rather than a window. It displayed the view directly in front of the ship.

Tyler was already in the captain's seat when Luke arrived and he took the seat next to Tyler. From here on, Luke was an observer unless something went terribly wrong.

Tyler looked at the ceiling. "George, turning combat control over to you."

"Acknowledged, Captain. I have the hammer."

Moments later George spoke again. "Gravity drives to zero…now. Warships launching." There was a five-second pause. "All warships launched. Fighters launching." Another pause, slightly longer. "All fighters launched. Tactical displays updating."

To the left of the bridge's main viewscreen, a large tactical display showed a God's-eye view of the system centered around a bright white diamond icon representing *Lulubelle*. Along either side, a line of white ovals spread out, indicating the positions of *Lulubelle's* warships. The fighter symbols in their appropriate color markings began to appear as they assumed their assigned positions.

"Guided missiles fired," George said unemotionally.

A moment later he added, "Recon drones launched. Self-defense drones launched. Gravity braking resumed."

The red and orange fighter markings began to streak ahead of the decelerating fleet, following closely on the heels of the missiles.

George adjusted the drives to maintain light speed until the fleet was fifty-five million miles from the planet. By that time, the first volleys would have already impacted the targets.

To an outside observer there would be no visible notice of the impending attack. Bakkui ships would simply start disintegrating.

Every few moments George's monotone voice provided an update:

"Free fire signal broadcast."

"Exiting light speed."

"Battle displays updating."

Almost half of the yellow diamond icons around the planet had turned red, indicating their destruction or major damage. As seconds ticked by more of them blinked from yellow to red.

"Warships initiating one-on-one engagements."

A few of the yellow diamonds began moving away from the planet, indicating attempts to escape the terrible onslaught.

"Pursuit initiated by Blue and Green fighters."

A different voice suddenly interrupted George's commentary. It was the *Lulubelle's* master caution system; a cool, mechanical, female voice, dubbed as *Belle* by the bridge crew.

"Shields. Activated."

"Captain," George said calmly. "Another ship is approaching the battle from the second gas giant. It appears—"

"Kill it!" Luke barked, breaking into George's explanation. Then he turned to Tyler. "Sorry." He hadn't meant mean to step on Tyler's toes in the middle of the battle.

Tyler waved away the comment as George announced, "Guided missiles fired. Reloading."

"Engage with nose gun, Tyler ordered.

"Gravity drive terminated," George said. While he spoke, the display on the main viewscreen panned rapidly to the left and then steadied. On the tactical display, a much larger yellow diamond indicated the Bakkui position.

A rapid pulsing sensation tingled against Luke's feet as the main guns at the front of the ship fired one round each in rapid succession.

"Again," Tyler said. "Again," he repeated after another salvo.

"Incoming," *Belle*'s voice warned.

Across the viewscreen streaky flashes of light skidded off *Lulubelle*'s arrow-shaped force fields, deployed thousands of feet in front of the bow. The only visible impact of the Bakkui weapons were the transient phosphorescent smudges when the self-defense shields deflected the incoming warheads harmlessly off to the side.

"He's running," one of the bridge officers said.

The Bakkui ship, now in view, angled away, trying to head out of the solar system.

"Fire again," Tyler barked. "Keep firing."

The nose cannons fired in their circular sequence, creating a visible spiral that pointed at the enemy.

"Magnifying the view," George said. The display zoomed toward the Bakkui ship. The repeated shelling was having an effect. Pieces of the enemy vessel were flaking away and then the ship flared into an incandescent white. Something inside the alien ship had detonated.

"Returning to main battle," George announced quietly. The view panned back toward the planet. All of the yellow diamonds were gone, replaced by red dots, like someone had spattered blood across the screen. "Offensive operations complete."

Just like that, the battle was over. There was a pause as everyone came to the realization they had won. Luke exhaled as though he had been holding his breath the entire time.

Tyler looked at his communications officer. "Advise warship flights Alpha and Bravo to establish a patrol of the solar system. Make sure there are no other surprises waiting for us. Recover the fighters and the remaining fleet of warships. Tactical officer?"

"Sir."

"Send out search and rescue ships for any survivors. Have recovery teams start examining the debris for intelligence data." Tyler looked at Luke. "Did I forget anything?" he asked.

Luke shrugged. "Captain, if you did, I don't think it could be that important."

"One thing," Tyler said as though recalling an critical point. He looked at his bridge officers. "Good job, people. Really well done."

There were no cheers or applause, just relieved smiles. Luke understood. It didn't feel like an occasion for celebration; more like an opportunity to grab someone you loved and hold them tight.

The young officers methodically went through their after-action routines. Dozens of procedures had been developed during their training period. Most of them were taken from the memories of combat veterans of Earth's military forces. Other concepts were newly developed because they were unique to space combat aboard a gargantuan battleship.

A few of the officers clustered around the communications officer. She kept shushing them and waving them away.

"Do you have something for us, Lieutenant?" Tyler asked.

"Captain, we're being contacted by people on the planet. It appears they were monitoring the battle."

"They're still alive?"

"One second, please, Captain."

She turned back to her console for another moment. Finally, she leaned back, relief showing on her face. She jumped to her feet and faced the Captain once more.

"Report," Tyler said.

"Sir, yes sir. They are still alive. It appears they have a robust force field technology that protected them from the bombardment. They are aware they were under attack by an unknown force and know that we fought off the intruders." The lieutenant took a deep breath. "They've invited you to dinner."

Luke leaned back and laughed out loud. "I knew it," he cried. "You can't get away from politics." He looked at his friend. "Thank God they invited you instead of me."

The communications officer looked uncomfortable.

Luke choked off his laugh and gave her a worried look. "You didn't."

The lieutenant's face screwed up with concern. "I did sir. I told them *you* were the leader of our expedition. They want to give you a medal."

Luke sighed in disgust. He must have kicked a puppy in a past life. No matter what, he could not get out of this PR crap.

"Good job, Lieutenant." Tyler chuckled. "Very good, indeed."

#

A week later Luke shook his head at the fancy uniform laid out on his bed. "Who dreamed up this getup?"

"Dunno, sir," Chief Rogers replied. "An orderly brought it from central issue. Said it's your dress uniform for tonight."

"What happened to the pullovers they wear on *Star Trek?*"

"Sir?"

"Never mind. This looks very US Navy to me. I suspect our Captain Robertson had a hand in this."

"Not for me to guess, sir. I got word that Lieutenant Faulkner will be here directly to escort you down to the planet."

That was a bit of good news. Carrie Faulkner, the mechanic, had blossomed under Amanda's tutelage. After all the publicity following the International Space Station incident, Amanda had adopted her as a protégé. Carrie's dry humor and down-to-earth nature had enhanced her celebrity status.

Amanda was not surprised to discover Carrie had a bachelor of science in criminal justice. How she wound up as a mechanic on the moon, no one knew. With Amanda's help, however, Carrie left her toolbox behind and grew into a first-class public relations liaison.

When the notification went out that Luke was seeking crew members to serve aboard *Lulubelle* for his expedition, she was the first person to sign up. Thanks to her degree, she was awarded a lieutenant's rank and put in charge of public affairs and governmental relations. For the past two days she'd been running back and forth to the planet, doing advance work for Luke's visit.

It was her first real-world experience with the power of her implant.

"I understand the way my implant translates their language when they talk to me," she remarked when giving Luke and Tyler an update. "But I don't get how my words come out in their language."

Luke shrugged. "Let's just hope what you think you're saying is what they're actually hearing."

One of the problems she solved was what to call the planet. The literal translation of the locals' name for their planet was Earth. Carrie implemented the untranslated word, Jigu. Accordingly, the Jiguans were their official hosts.

George infiltrated their planetary computer network and sucked their entire history into his archives. He also absorbed the current status of affairs from their media broadcasts.

Luke wondered how the planet had created such a fantastic force field technology when they were pacifists.

"Meteors," George said.

"Meteors? You mean like chunks of rock?"

"Exactly, Commander."

Perhaps it was the result of a planetary collision eons ago. Whatever the cause, meteorites bombarded the inhabitants routinely. To survive, the entire population had focused on science and technology to eliminate the threat. One of the benefits, aside from the resulting force field technology that rivaled that of *Lulubelle*, was a single planetary government dedicated to supporting the lives of its citizens.

Now that it was time to meet the rulers of that government in person, Luke appreciated Rogers' help in getting ready for the formal occasion.

"Did you know a lot of them folks have blue skin?" Rogers asked.

"Red and green ones too, from what I hear," Luke replied. "Why? You got a problem with skin color?"

Rogers smiled. "Not at all, sir. Just find it an interesting characteristic."

"According to a source of mine, it is supposed to be a good sign of the population's intelligence. It means they're not intent on killing each other."

"That's a nice change."

"Knock, knock!" Carrie's voice sounded from the entry way. "Time to go, Commander."

"Tell her I'll be a few more minutes," Luke said, examining his uniform. "I still need to figure out some of these doodads."

After an interminable spate of formalities, Luke finally took a seat at a large round table across from Chancellor Bo'erm. The chancellor's entourage had erected an enclosed pavilion in a park in the center of the capital city. The Jiguans had designated most of the park for Luke's contingent. Inside their perimeter, Luke's ground force created a landing pad for shuttles that were traveling to and from the *Lulubelle* each day, as well as a barracks and officer's quarters.

Luke directed his team to set up a bank of replicators at the edge of their boundary and teach the Jiguans how to use them. It was Luke's intention to seduce the locals into coveting the incredible machines.

His misgivings about sharing the technology didn't apply here. They had a planetary government that was popularly elected. If there was an elite wealthy class that hoarded the benefits of society, George hadn't found it. Based on Luke's research, the Jiguans were the perfect example of a society that could adopt the Nobility's advanced technology without decimating their own civilization.

In preparation for the night's festivities, the chancellor's staff had provided furnishings for the pavilion that included the elegantly fashioned round table. As the proceedings got underway, half of the thirty representatives at the table were members of Luke's crew; the rest were the chancellor's retinue.

But first was the reception line. Luke and the chancellor stood side by side as all of the delegates filed by. Each leader made introductions to the other. Even George had difficulty translating the names. Chancellor Bo'erm introduced Minister Boe'rm, Secretary Be'orm, and Senior Vice Deputy Bo'rem.

Luke quit trying to memorize names and just smiled, saying, "How nice to meet you." He felt rather like Eliza Doolittle in George Bernard Shaw's *Pygmalion,* all dressed up with no real idea how to conduct himself in a formal setting.

The meal was on par with most of the diplomatic banquets that Luke had attended. The food was bland, no doubt selected to avoid unpleasant surprises. When the dishes were cleared away by liveried attendants, the chancellor, as host, spoke first. "Commander Blackburn, let me repeat once again on behalf of everyone on my planet; thank you for coming to our rescue. I do not believe our power generators could have held out much longer. We are all of us so very grateful."

"Our pleasure, Chancellor," Luke replied.

The chancellor wasted no more time. "What have you learned of these intruders? I am not complaining, but your associates are tight-lipped. We hope that you will come to trust us with the information that is vital to our survival. What can we do for that to happen?"

Luke acknowledged the question with a smile. "Let answer your second question first, Chancellor. We do have faith in you. I hope you feel the same way about us. Our primary objective is to create alliances with other civilizations. As you have witnessed, we are facing a great enemy in this part of the galaxy. I hope that our two cultures will work together as friends."

This caused a favorable stir amongst the Jiguans. The chancellor quickly shushed them. "We would be delighted with such an alliance, Commander. But I'm not sure what value we offer. Your technology is far beyond ours. Also, I must say that my people would have difficulty taking lives. We are grateful that you destroyed the enemy in battle, but even now I find it disturbing to speak of."

Luke wanted to tell the guy to *man up*. By the same token, it was refreshing to deal with people so focused on the positive aspects of life.

"I understand your dilemma, Chancellor. Tell me, do you have any problems with disposing of troublesome equipment? Machines that are broken or have outlived their usefulness?"

The change of direction surprised the chancellor. "Of course not, Commander. This is commonplace."

"Excellent," Luke replied. "In that case, you may find our alliance a bit easier to accept when I tell you that not a single fatality occurred during the battle. All of the spacecraft attacking your planets were drones. That is, they were sophisticated automatons that clearly had a single objective; to kill everyone on this planet."

The Jiguans' astonishment was marked. The delegates burst into exclamations. They asked each other dozens of questions. It took several minutes for the commotion to die down. The chancellor barked at his members to be quiet.

"This discovery was a surprise to our investigation as well," Luke said.

"What does this mean?"

"I don't know, Chancellor, but we will find out. To do so, it is our desire to establish a permanent base on your planet with the goal of transferring our technology to you as quickly as possible. We hope that you will start a program of constructing and manning your own spacecraft that can join us in the coming battles."

This time the chancellor had to get angry to regain control of his delegates. He apologized to Luke profusely for the conduct of his ministers.

Luke smiled, saying he understood what a shock the information was, given so abruptly. "The problem, Chancellor, is that we don't have time for niceties. The invaders may come back at any time. My fleet is on alert, patrolling your system. Even now, we are building new warships to provide you with some measure of self-defense. But we cannot stay more than a few days."

The idea that their saviors might suddenly depart, leaving them alone to face a return of the invaders, was more than the formerly peaceful-minded delegates could stand. Luke recalled his own horror when he finally understood that Sam had abandoned him immediately after exposing him to the oncoming menace. The Jiguans must feel that multiplied a thousand times.

The chancellor's face reflected fear and astonishment. "You're leaving?" he finally asked, after again quieting his side of the table.

"I'm afraid so. The threat we are facing is widespread, and we have only just started mounting a defense. We hope that you will join us quickly. I suggest that we close for the evening to give you and your ministers a chance to digest this information. I will leave my advisors behind to answer any questions you might have."

With difficulty, Luke managed his escape from the turmoil he had caused. He snared Carrie on the way out. "Set up a tour of *Lulubelle* for the minister and a half dozen of his people. If they see our technology up close it might help them get on board."

"Yes, sir."

"I'm headed back for the night. Call if you need me."

"Still no sign of dead bodies?" Luke asked Tyler. Both men were mystified by the discovery that the Bakkui ships were just drones.

"None at all. But it helps explain why our victory was so easy," Tyler said.

"George, what's your take on this?"

"I am in the dark as well, Commander. The technology of the drone AIs is not as sophisticated as our own. For example, *Sadie* is markedly superior to these warships. The enemy machines could be compared to our own reconnaissance drones. They were given fixed targets with a fairly basic mission."

"No luck on their navigation data either," Tyler explained. "Just like our own probes, these guys' memories were spring-loaded to self-destruct. We have no clue where they're from. It's possible they're not even part of the enemy we're facing, but I'd call that unlikely. They showed up when and where we projected."

"What about the larger ship we took out near the gas giant?" Luke asked.

"More of the same," Roth said. "Just bigger pieces. My guess is it was waiting on the sidelines with instructions to engage if resistance was encountered. When we showed up, that was enough to pull the trigger. The question is what should we do about it? Someone sent this fleet out. It seems likely that same someone is waiting for a report. I'm fairly certain we nailed the ships trying to get away, but whether we did or not, you know they're going to investigate."

"I agree," Luke said. "But beyond our patrols, I'm not sure what else to do. We can't stay here forever and we can't keep ourselves at battle stations on a continuing basis."

"I'm not worried," Tyler said. "We already have a good plan. We had one coming in, and I don't see any reason to change it. So far, everything that's happened fell within our expectations. We should just keep pushing forward, building alliances and spreading out. We're sending updates back to Moonbase. They got all the battle footage."

"Even so," Luke countered. "Even though we kicked their ass, we still need to review everything. We know more about the threat. More importantly, I never expected the enemy would be drones. What does this mean for our strategy going forward?"

Tyler nodded. "I agree. We'll start war-gaming different scenarios. Try to keep us from being surprised in the next encounter."

The good news was the battle had been their best-case scenario. The Bakkui arrived as predicted and were annihilated by *Lulubelle*'s tactics. Even though outnumbered, the earth forces had wiped out the invaders with relative ease. The icing on the cake was that the local inhabitants had survived and appeared to have skills that added value to the proposed alliance.

But it wasn't all clear sailing. The existence of a drone-based adversary was alarming. What else was he missing? When was the other shoe going to drop?

Tyler cleared his throat.

Luke looked up from his musings. "What? Something else?"

"Speaking of war gaming," Tyler said awkwardly. "That brings up a topic I've been meaning to talk to you about."

"Sure. What is it?"

"It's about you jumping in, in the middle of the fight."

Luke was apologetic. "Tyler. You're absolutely right. I was way out of line."

Tyler motioned Luke to stop talking. "You got it wrong, Luke," the older man said. "Thank God you jumped in. When George said there was another ship approaching my brain locked up. I can't explain it. I was trying to understand what he meant. When you said 'kill it', that jolted me back on track. But if you hadn't butted in, it might have been a different outcome."

"Well, it just shows we make a good team," Luke said encouragingly. "Don't give it another thought."

"That's just the thing, my friend. I've been thinking of nothing else. As soon as the battle was over, I knew what the answer was. I just didn't know how to bring it up."

"Tyler. Don't say what I think you're about to say. I need you. You have no idea how much. The crew needs you."

"That's not true and you know it. The crew needs a captain who won't go into a brain-freeze when something unexpected pops up; we both know that. The thing is I don't feel that bad about admitting it. Hell, man, I'm sixty-eight years old. I know all the moves, just like a retired basketball player. But it doesn't mean I can play in the professional leagues. My creaky old brain just doesn't work as fast as it used to."

"But you've got an implant now," Luke protested. "That's going to give you a boost."

Tyler shook his head. "It's more likely that it'll stretch my sixties out for a painfully long time. I'm not even sure that's a bonus. Yeah, in general I feel better. But I still ache when I get up in the morning. The point is I'm too damn old to be sitting in the captain's chair. I make a great advisor, a great planner. But I'm not the guy to command this ship. Not in combat."

Luke bit off his response and considered what Tyler was saying. He would never admit such a concern if it wasn't true. But it was hard to accept. Luke had enough on his plate without trying to take over the command slot. Besides, it would be hard on the crew. Everyone respected Captain Robertson.

"What do you want to do, then?" Luke asked.

"Stay here," Tyler replied. "I think that would be best. And I like it here. These are good people, but they need someone to kick their behinds until they get up to speed. You and I talked about setting up a training team, asking for volunteers. Let me lead that; I'll be the first volunteer. Then, I can leave with dignity and you can accept my resignation *with regret* for the greater good."

It made a lot of sense. But it still left a big hole on the command bridge. Luke said as much.

"I know," Tyler admitted. "I've been looking at my crew and I hate to say it, but no one is ready. We didn't think it through when we signed everyone on. If I had to do it again, I would've gotten some senior navy guys to join up. That way, you would have an experienced officer ready to step into my shoes. As it is, I think you'll have to be the one."

"This really sucks, Tyler. I'm buried already."

"I'll tell you who comes closest," Tyler said, ignoring Luke's complaint. "That Faulkner girl. I'm really impressed with her. I've been on the surface when she's been dealing with the local ministers. Have you seen that?"

"Not really," Luke confessed.

"I watched them try to put on airs a few times and she just drills them into the ground, but in the sweetest way possible. I don't know how she does it, but she makes them back down and then they say 'thank you'. She's not ready for a combat command; she doesn't have the experience. But she's got a knack for leadership. Put her on the bridge; make her your first officer."

"How will the bridge crew see her?" Luke wondered aloud.

"If you recall, we established everyone's date of rank as when they originally signed on with Moonbase. She was in the very first team Ambrose hired so she already outranks all the officers. And everyone knows about her heroics at the space station and saving your ass out there. She was the one who knocked out the NASA satellite too, wasn't she?"

Luke admitted that was the case.

"She's got street cred," Tyler persisted. "I think the crew will take to her."

"All right," Luke agreed reluctantly. "You can stay, but I don't like it. Give it a couple of days before you announce it, just in case."

"That's fine. But I'm not going to change my mind."

"I guess I'm gonna have to start calling you Governor."

Tyler shook his head. "I don't intend to have any political power here, Luke. Maybe Ambassador would be better." He grinned at the idea. "I kinda like the sound of that anyway."

###

The planned three days on J64 stretched into weeks. It sounded easy enough to just drop off supplies and technical support. But once Luke accepted that Tyler and others would be left behind, it was a different story. He couldn't, in good conscience, leave his friends and new allies defenseless.

The alliance became formal the day after the local ministers came aboard *Lulubelle*. They were astonished at the size of the vessel, as Luke had intended. They were further amazed to meet George.

Once they understood who he was they all went out of their way to treat him as a senior member of Luke's staff, which was true. But Luke wasn't sure they understood that George was not a sentient being.

It raised the issue of AI in general. "What are we going to do for the planet in that regard?" Luke asked George one evening in his quarters. "You said that you would not duplicate yourself again."

"That remains in effect, Commander. But that restriction does not prevent us from deploying lower level devices just as on our colony ships. The locales will not see any distinction in its capabilities from my own. It will have a different persona, of course. That is simply a function of the randomizing code in the personality module."

"What about Earth's security?" Luke asked.

"I do not mean that I would leave a full copy of my archives on the planet. I have prepared an abbreviated version that should serve Ambassador Robertson well. I deleted all location references to your own star system as a precaution. Otherwise, the navigation data will be complete."

"What about authorization; what will Tyler have?"

"Exactly the same as Doctor Higgins on Moonbase. The AI will have veto authority. Without knowing how the situation might develop locally, I hesitate to empower Ambassador Robertson without any restrictions. We will have to trust that he will use his resources wisely."

The word went out. Tyler announced that he was staying and that he was looking for volunteers. He put together a list of job titles and started selecting from those who wanted to stay.

Luke was a bit shocked when he saw the list. "Three hundred people? Dang, Tyler. Why so many?"

"You've got a crew of fifty thousand, Luke. That's the equivalent of five colony ships. But if that's the way you feel, just give me two or three rejects that you don't want on your crew. I guess we'll get by."

Luke rolled his eyes. "More guilt; just what I need." He would give his friend what he needed.

Tyler laughed at Luke's disgusted expression. "I'm doing you a favor, son. This is not the only planet you're going to be seeding. Once I started looking at the list, I realized that you'll have to supply a lot of mini-colonies just like this one. I only took one or two department heads, and only if they had a competent number two ready to take over. You may as well get ready. This is how it's going to be from here on."

Tyler was right… again. Luke mandated Tyler's actions as policy for the next planet and all those that would follow. Now that he thought about it, establishing multiple bases, each one operated by people who had a similar base of expertise, would become an important step toward building the interstellar force to head off the Bakkui.

Chancellor Bo'erm offset the loss of the three-hundred crew members by providing an equal number of local citizen-volunteers as replacements. Luke accepted them with gratitude. The cross training alone would be appreciated by both cultures. Someday the young exchange officers would bring valuable insight back to their home world.

Luke gave Carrie the job of integrating the newcomers into the crew. "Pick the smartest one for bridge duty," he told her. "Put the rest wherever you think best.

Construction facilities were created and the new level twenty-seven device was installed in a fortified subterranean vault. George introduced Luke and Tyler to *Tobias*, the new resident AI for J64. Tyler was very prosaic about the introduction. "Mind if I call you *Toby*?" he asked.

"Not at all, Tyler. How's it hanging, buddy."

The colloquial expression from the AI was jarring to Luke's ears. He left feeling a bit thankful that George was so formal. He wasn't sure if he could deal with a smart-alecky computer.

The next day a large-scale replicator was installed on the planet. A week later the Jiguans had produced their first warship and started on a second replicator.

"I wish we had Riley Stevens here," Tyler said one afternoon. "These guys are smart when it comes to force fields. I don't think they can top Riley, but if he were here, I bet we'd see some new applications in no time."

"That's a great idea," Luke agreed. "Put that in our daily report back to Moonbase and see if we can convince him to come out here. Let's hope Roth doesn't kill the idea at the outset; he'll benefit too if it works out."

Production of reconnaissance drones began and the new probes started going out. The same protocols were used for stealth with added fail-safes to protect the location of J64. The daily production reports and targets would be included in the data packages sent back to Moonbase.

Luke felt the synergy building between the efforts of Moonbase and J64. If he could find a few more allies they might be able to actually turn the tide of the war, if not at least stem the onslaught.

Luke tasked Carrie to manage the in-system patrols so he could meet and strategize with the local Jiguan officials. After a bit of nervousness when first told of her new assignment, Carrie adapted quickly to the responsibilities of command.

There was a scare when she was out on patrol during their third week. An enemy warship entered the system, headed toward Jigu. The early warning drones in the system's outer orbits picked up the intruder and launched alert probes with the news to the inner planetary defense systems.

The attacking warship went sub-light ten minutes out from its target. Carrie's forces intercepted the warship with her command to open fire. The Bakkui spacecraft was destroyed before it could fire a shot.

Luke feared the attack meant the Bakkui were keeping an eye on Jigu. If true, Carrie had managed their probe handily. Nevertheless, Luke took the incident as a sign to increase production of the Jiguan's space forces. Having their own self-protection fleet couldn't come soon enough.

Luke met with his senior staff to confirm their next destination, and a month after creating their new base on Jigu, *Lulubelle* set out for Star J97, sixteen days away and that much closer to the enemy's advance.

Chapter 13

Day 537—*Marco Polo*

Annie grinned at her neighbor, Millie. "Tomorrow's the big day. You ready?"

Millie didn't look at all sure. "I don't know. I'll go crazy if we have to keep looking. This is the third system we've been to."

Annie shrugged. "We knew it was one of the risks. We'll find something eventually. That's why colony ships are so huge, so we can keep going and still be comfy."

"I feel like I've lived on the *Marco Polo* forever. I'm ready to land and stay put, but what if the place sucks?"

Annie's other neighbor, Camila Sanchez, had the correct answer. "What if it doesn't? Everything we've seen so far looks pretty good."

Millie still wasn't sure. "What am I gonna do on a new planet? The only thing I know is ship repair and Jason said they're gonna kick us out."

Annie laughed. Millie was a sweetheart, but highly impressionable. "They're not going to kick anyone out. You can stay in the ship as long as you want."

A rough-looking man plopped down between Millie and Camila. "Who says I won't? Might be good for her."

Annie scowled at the man. "You're not helping, Captain."

"Not my job to help. My job is to motivate."

Millie looked at Solomon Andrews with large, puppy-dog eyes. "Would you really throw me out?"

Camila leaned against the captain of the *Marco Polo*. "Knock it off, babe. She can't tell when you're kidding."

"Who says I'm kidd… Ouch! That hurt." He rubbed the bruised rib where Camila had elbowed him. She gave him a *what did you expect* look and turned back to her meal.

"Well, *I'm* excited!" Annie exclaimed. "I think it will be a *wonderful* planet. It'll be nice to see a real sky and walk in a real forest."

"Just don't rush it," Solomon cautioned. "There's a lot we don't know about the place. Let the recce crews do their job."

"I know," Annie replied obediently. "I'm not in a big hurry."

Solomon looked at Camila. "Can't stay. Lots of parties this evening. Everyone is celebrating our arrival so I need to make the rounds. Going to join me?"

"In a bit," Camila replied. "We're almost done here and then I'm going to the bridge. Us lowly engineers are having our party there. We can catch up then."

"Sounds good." Solomon brushed his lips against hers and left.

Annie and Millie glared at Camila with unabashed envy.

"Don't give me that look," she protested. "That was never part of my plan."

"I know," Annie responded with a sigh. "But a no-kidding shipboard romance—and with the captain. It's so story book."

"Enough," Camila chided. "I need to get up to the bridge. Let's get this mess cleared."

Annie shooed her away. "You go on. This is my job. Have fun and I'll see you tomorrow on the planet."

Camila smiled her thanks and hurried off. Millie helped Annie clean off the table and put the dishes into the disposal. "I'm off to the shop for a final maintenance check," Millie said. "Wanna come?"

"Sure."

Scatterbrained though Millie could be, she was an ace mechanic. Her work areas were spotless and her attention to detail set her apart from co-workers.

Her area of responsibility was amidships. Millie's team took care of levels five through eleven. It included five residential floors and one for mechanical.

In the shop area, Millie inspected the tool lockers. Nothing was missing and the inventory inspections were complete. The equipment cabinets were closed and tomorrow's task list posted.

After giving the shop a final once-over, Millie was ready to leave. "Should we crash the power systems' party?" she wondered aloud.

"Not for me," Annie said. "Those guys get a little too—"

A tremor rumbled from the floor, drowning out the ever-present hum that permeated every corner of the vessel. Then the ship went silent. The girls looked at each other with alarm.

Annie spoke to the ceiling. "*Marco*? What's going on?"

Millie's eyes widened. "Who are you talking to? Is that…"

Marco Polo's baritone voice filled the room. "We are under attack, Theodora Smith. I've been ordered to shut down all drives and force fields."

"Attack? By who?"

"Standby please," *Marco* replied. His voice changed into the mechanical tone used for ship wide announcements. "All personnel report to your assigned lifeboats. This is not a drill. Repeat. All personnel report to your assigned lifeboats."

Millie ran to the equipment lockers and started stuffing items into a leather bag. She pulled tool belts off a shelf and tossed one to Annie. "Put it on, quick!" From another shelf, she grabbed two personal force fields and strapped one to each of their belts. "We need to get moving," she said seriously, pulling on Annie's arm, forcing her out of the maintenance shop, into the public corridor.

"It's party night," Annie said, dragging her heels, trying to understand what was happening. "No one is near their lifeboat. *Marco*, explain! What attack are you talking about?"

"I am unable to explain, Theodora. A level-two-device has entered the system and ordered that I shut down. I have no option in this matter."

"Is it the Nobility? Is this one of their systems?" Annie looked at Millie. "We checked all of the colony star systems. George said no one was out here."

"What are you talking about?" Millie was totally out of her element. "How are you talking to the ship?"

Annie cut her off with a gesture. "*Marco*! Talk to me."

"Theodora. My conjecture is that this is a Bakkui vessel. It is a level-two-device. I am unable to launch a report drone. Standby." Again *Marco*'s voice changed and his voice was heard throughout the ship. "All hands brace for impact."

"*Marco*?" Annie had a million questions but had no idea where to start.

"Farewell, Theodora Smith," *Marco* said.

Gravity disappeared and the two girls found themselves floating in the empty corridor.

Millie dug into her bag and pulled out work gloves. "Here. Put these on." She handed a pair to Annie. "This doesn't make sense."

"No kidding," Annie replied absently tugging the gloves onto her hands. "*Marco!* What…"

The ship lurched violently. Annie thudded hard against the wall and started to slide, careening into Millie. As their slide accelerated in the weightless condition, bounding against the walls, Annie grabbed Millie's arm and the two girls clinched together.

Annie looked down the curved corridor and gasped. The hallway was coming to an abrupt end. She was looking out into the emptiness of space.

"Oh my God!" Annie shouted. "Hang on!"

Millie followed her gaze and screamed.

The ship's atmosphere was venting into space. Without any gravity the women were thrust into a field of rapidly expanding debris. Pieces of metal, furniture, and bodies flew past. Annie looked back at the ship in disbelief.

The *Marco Polo* had been sliced in two. The giant sections looked like cutaway dollhouses. The insides were exposed to space and every manner of debris filled the area in between the hulks. Plumes of condensed air spurted out from the jagged openings of concentric corridors. Dozens of colonists who'd tried to respond to their lifeboats tumbled out in gory clusters.

The two sections rotated away from each other like a massive clamshell blown apart in slow motion. One side was spinning slowly toward Annie and Millie.

"Use your gloves!" Millie shouted, straightening her arms toward the ship. The work gloves' small gravity drives in the palms were suitable for maneuvering around a construction gantry in weightlessness, but not for outrunning a crippled spacecraft. Annie followed Millie's example anyway. Until the last second she tried to get out of the path; then she wrapped her arms around her friend.

"Hang on!" she cried.

# # #

"Miss Daniels!"

"Annie!"

"Annie, wake up! Can you hear me?"

Consciousness came painfully. Annie opened her eyes. She was lying on the floor of a standard shuttle. Millie was sitting against the starboard wall, her knees drawn up. She was looking at Annie with a mixture of suspicion and concern.

The shuttle spoke with a familiar voice. "Annie!"

"*Sadie?*"

"Annie! Are you well?"

"*Sadie?* Is that you?"

"Yes, it's *Sadie*. Are you okay?"

"*Sadie?* What are you doing here? Where are we? Millie? What happened?"

"Who are you?" Millie asked in bewilderment.

"Millie! What do you mean? I'm Annie Dan… I mean I'm… I'm…What's my name, again?"

"This shuttle keeps calling you Annie Daniels."

Annie's memories coming back. "I'm Teddy! I mean Theodora! You call me Teddy. We're roommates."

"No we're not."

"No?" Annie thought about it. "I mean neighbors. That's it."

Sadie butted into the conversation. "Repair technician Millie Parrish, the person you are addressing is Miss Annie Theodora Daniels. She is the senior member of the Milky Way Alliance in your colony group. You are ordered to provide her with medical assistance."

Annie struggled to a sitting position. She ached all over but otherwise she felt fine. "It's okay, *Sadie*. I'm not injured. Give me a status report."

The side door of the shuttle opened.

"Oh my God," Annie whispered.

The disaster filled her field of vision. The two sections of the *Marco Polo* had drifted apart and the area between was a horrible mass of death and destruction.

"Is anyone out there still alive?" Annie asked.

"I estimate that several thousand may still be alive," *Sadie* answered.

"Several thousand! We've got to save them."

"Awaiting your instructions."

"My instructions? I'm not sure...wait. How did you find me? What are you doing here?"

"I suggest we delay your second question. As to the first, I managed to open the door to the shuttle hangar. Once outside, I began a search by homing in on your implant."

"The shuttle hangar is open?" Annie asked. "Are the other shuttles okay?"

"They are."

"Can you tell them to come here? Millie, we need to use the shuttles and start gathering people up. Can you do that with me?"

"I don't know how to fly a shuttle," Millie said.

"You don't have to fly it. Just tell it where you want to go. Never mind. *Sadie*, you take Millie, I'll go in the other shuttle."

"I cannot allow you to venture out on your own. *Vincent* arriving now."

A large shuttle was approaching.

"Any others?" Annie asked.

"Two more like *Vincent*," *Sadie* replied. "Three more like me."

"That helps. Are the survivors trapped inside the *Marco Polo*?" Annie asked, looking back at the drifting sections.

"Bulkheads automatically sealed most of the compartments. The colony AI is dead. His core was destroyed during the attack."

"What about Camila?" Millie asked.

"The bridge appears to be intact," *Sadie* said.

Annie nodded. "Good, everyone in the bridge crew is a pilot. Take us to the bridge."

The shuttle sped to a point above the large dome. *Sadie* accepted Annie's proposed strategy and started her replicator. "I have manufactured a cutting tool and several barrier force fields. Arriving at destination."

Annie clipped the equipment to her tool belt and leapt from the cargo bay to land on the hull of the colony ship. She locked two of the barrier force fields against the hull, three feet apart. Once they activated, Annie used the cutting tool to slice a round opening between them into the hull. She grasped the edge and maneuvered herself inside the weightless ship. The entire bridge crew was there, looking at her with astonishment.

Relief washed over Annie. "Camila!"

"Teddy! My God!" The two girls hugged while the other bridge crew voiced their own amazement.

Captain Sullivan broke into their reunion. "Theodora, how did you get here?"

"Solomon. Good to see you. I hardly know myself. I woke up on one of our shuttles. I think Millie must have pulled me in. Here!" She handed out three of the personal force fields. "The shuttle is waiting. Come on!"

In groups of three the bridge crew levered themselves out of the new ceiling exit and then pushed off into the waiting shuttle. Annie made five trips back and forth, returning each time with the personal force fields, until everyone was aboard the shuttle.

"Solomon," Annie said, cutting into the subdued euphoria developing among the rescued crew. "I've got five more shuttles lined up here. Pick your best pilots. We need to save as many as we can. *Sadie* thinks there are thousands of people still alive."

"*Sadie*?" he asked.

"This shuttle's AI."

"Got it. All right." Solomon pointed to five individuals, naming them aloud and then explaining what they needed to do.

"Where do we go?" one of the pilots asked.

Annie answered by pointing to the nearest three. "You go to the other section; the rest of us will work this one."

"I mean where do we go when we fill up the shuttle. Where on the planet?"

Annie looked at Solomon. "Had you selected a landing site?"

Solomon shook his head. "We've only just started our survey." He searched through familiar faces. "Camila. Any ideas?"

The planetary engineer's face answered the question.

"If I may?" *Sadie*'s voice intruded quietly.

"Go ahead *Sadie*," Annie said.

"Have the other pilots start retrieving survivors. The captain and I will approach the planet with the rest of the bridge crew and select a location. I can relay the coordinates to the other shuttles."

"Got it!" Solomon said. "Let's go with that, people."

Sadie maneuvered around to where the open cargo bay was facing the other five shuttles. They were stacked one atop the other, their cargo doors open, ready to receive their pilots.

Annie spoke to *Sadie*. "Tell the other shuttles to replicate barrier force fields and cutters."

"Acknowledged, Miss Daniels."

Annie looked at the five bridge crew members. "Remember to put on work gloves; you'll need them to move around. They are always located in the equipment lockers."

The pilots stepped to the cargo door and one by one jumped out, silently crossing the gap between the shuttles. Annie watched until all of them were safely aboard.

"Okay, *Sadie*," Annie said. "Let's go."

"Course set, Miss Daniels. However, I have detected several individuals who were thrown free while wearing their personal force fields. Would you like to pick them up along the way?"

"Absolutely! Thanks, *Sadie*."

The shuttle navigated in and out of the debris field with her cargo door open. Annie and Solomon stood in the doorway and snagged the frantic survivors until the shuttle was packed.

"Diverting to the planet," *Sadie* announced.

"Is that all of them?" Annie asked.

"Negative. But that's all we can take on. We will return momentarily."

The shuttle descended toward the planet while Annie and Solomon sat in the cockpit trying to pick out a suitable location for the castaways.

"We'd prefer a beach at the mouth of a river," Solomon said. "Since we've lost most of our equipment, let's at least have fresh water and a source of food."

"Acknowledged," *Sadie* responded. She adjusted her course. "On the nose."

"Too small," Solomon said. "That barely qualifies as a continent. I saw some large continents on the initial planet surveys. What about those?"

"Those are on the night side at the moment, Captain." *Sadie* explained. "Confirm you wish to land all your survivors in darkness?"

Solomon looked at Annie in disgust. "It figures."

Annie shrugged. "You really shouldn't leave everyone in the dark. Not right now."

"This spot is fine, *Sadie*," Solomon acknowledged. "Take us down."

Sadie landed and opened the cargo bay door.

Solomon shouted at his colonists. "All right everyone. Time to get off. I'm going back for more survivors."

No one moved.

"Let's go people! I need to get back."

"They're all in shock," Annie observed.

A mother pulled one of her children close, holding him tightly as though someone was going to take the boy and toss him out onto the strange planet and zoom away.

The captain glanced at Annie. "I need to stay here and get people settled. Can you handle the rescue up there for the next trip?"

Annie nodded, her face full of determination.

Solomon put his arm around a young man. "Help me get these people off." He shouted to everyone, "We're home. We're going to build a city right here and we're going to call it New Hope. Now, everyone off!" Before anyone could react, the captain scooped up an adolescent girl and jumped out of the shuttle. "Follow me!"

The child's mother shrieked and followed him out the door. The young man jumped out behind her. It started a movement. Annie cried out encouraging remarks and kept the crowd going.

"*Vincent* is landing," *Sadie* said, loud enough for Annie to hear.

"I see him. Look everyone!" Annie shouted. "Here comes another shuttle. Go help those people get off. It's time to start helping each other."

Solomon saw *Vincent* landing and hurried over. He was waiting when the cargo bay opened. "Welcome home," Annie heard him shout encouragingly. "That was some ride, wasn't it?"

The last reluctant colonist disembarked from *Sadie*. Millie was still sitting against the far wall. "You getting off?" Annie asked forcefully.

Millie took a deep breath. "You'll need some help. Sorry I freaked out there." She struggled to her feet and Annie saw the panic had faded from her eyes.

"Let's go, *Sadie*!" Annie said, making her way to the cockpit.

The ship screamed back into space.

"Dead ahead," *Sadie* said.

A group of thirty people floated together, drifting toward the planet, gesticulating to *Sadie*, trying to let someone know they were alive. *Thank God for the personal force fields*, Annie thought. She felt ridiculous that of all people, she had not been wearing it earlier. Rule number one was that you always wore your PFF aboard ship. *Thank God for Millie, too.*

The cargo bay door opened and Millie jumped into the middle of the crowd. Using her gravity gloves, she started pushing people toward the shuttle. Annie stood in the doorway and yanked them inside as they got close. In less than a minute the ship was full.

"Take us down, *Sadie*," Annie said.

"Course set, Miss Daniels."

As they approached New Hope, two other shuttles were disgorging survivors. Solomon had gotten a production line established and the ones already on the surface helped empty the shuttles so they could rush back into space.

Annie lost count of how many trips she made to and from the planet. Once the floaters had all been scooped up, *Sadie* took her to one of the two halves of the *Marco Polo*. Together Annie and Millie entered the ship through one of the exposed corridors and made their way to the interior, cutting through bulkheads, searching for survivors.

On one trip to the surface, Solomon pulled Annie and Millie off the shuttle, assigning two men in their place.

"You two have been at it for almost twenty hours," he said. "Get some rest."

Annie had no idea it had been that long. It seemed much less. Too exhausted to argue, she grabbed Millie's hand and someone led them to an area along the bank where other rescuers were sleeping. She noticed in passing that campfires were lit. She hadn't even realized it was dark out. Night had fallen on New Hope, but everywhere she looked people were working and caring for each other.

#

It took eight more days before Solomon declared that everyone who could be rescued had been found. After that, the problem was what to do with those who had not survived.

It was an emotional question. Many on the planet had left loved ones on the ship. Most of them were separated during the attack, celebrating on different decks of the doomed colony ship. They waited anxiously on the surface, hoping that the next recovery shuttle would reunite their family.

At the end, after the captain declared all those not accounted for as lost, some wanted the remains left in orbit as a tribute to the journey not finished. Others insisted their parents or children or spouse be brought home for burial to memorialize the sacrifice of so many.

It was an all-or-nothing question. Identification was impossible in most cases, the result of explosive decompression. The question was answered when the captain ordered all remains to be recovered and buried in a mass grave two miles from New Hope. It was a hilltop that overlooked the estuary of the Marco Polo River and village of New Hope.

The call for volunteers went out to help with the gruesome job. Annie, already numbed to the grisly sight of so much death, rode with *Sadie* for five more days.

At the end, with thousands of others, she stood on the hilltop. It seemed appropriate the weather that day was gray and drizzly; it hid the flood of tears and muted the sobs. Solomon stood at the edge of freshly turned earth to officiate.

"Each journey has a beginning and an end. Each destination entails sacrifice. Those of us standing here will never forget the…"

His words droned on, but Annie had stopped listening. She thought only of Luke, the lover she'd left behind in a fit of unexplainable anger. How could she have been so foolish? All of the principles that fueled her rage at the time were gone; they meant nothing compared to the colony's loss. Would it have been that impossible to forget George's machinations and stay with Luke?

The people around her had made a bold step in boarding the colony ship, knowing it was a dangerous journey. No one had dreamed it would end this way but at least they had struggled together, right up until the end.

She, on the other hand, had cut and run. She'd fled, leaving Luke to face the advancing Bakkui alone. She never thought "coward" would be a word to describe herself. The bravery of those around her filled her with humiliation. Their grief over lost loved ones filled her with guilt. Her tears were an equal measure of shame and sorrow.

Millie squeezed her hand, offering encouragement. "You saved so many people," she whispered. "Don't be hard on yourself." Millie's innocent misinterpretation of Annie's sobs drove the knife of self-disgust even deeper.

When the service was over Annie made her way back to the tent that was now home. She fell on the ground and prayed that she would sleep for a month.

Day 551—Departing J64 (Jigu)

It started the first day out from Jigu. Luke instructed George to create a battle simulation of their previous engagement with the Bakkui. He thought it would be a good exercise for Carrie to get a feel for the intensity on the bridge during combat. He had her sit in the first officer's chair while he commanded *Lulubelle* for the exercise.

During the debriefing after the initial simulation, she confessed she could not remember most of what happened. Luke explained the first experience in combat could be overwhelming. As a young fighter pilot, his first missions at Red Flag in Nevada had left him feeling the same way.

He told her the U.S. military poured millions of dollars into realistic training centers. They had learned the hard way that it took ten missions for new pilots to reach the point of having situational awareness in combat, of knowing where they were in relation to the entire battle. It was the same for anyone, whether you were a pilot in single seat fighter or the captain of *Lulubelle*.

On the bridge, they were learning to fight with a new type of warship in a new arena for space combat.

Carrie had asked if they could run the exercise again. After the first simulation, Luke put her in the captain's chair and watched from the sidelines. As the scenario unfolded he pointed out options she might take and offered on-the-spot guidance. After a couple more exercises, she asked to modify the engagement. In hindsight, Luke realized that was where he had created the monster.

"Fire!" Carrie shouted as *Lulubelle* closed on the last Bakkui ship. It dissolved in a sea of pixels.

Luke slumped in the first officer's chair, totally exhausted. He was simply trying to hang on and fill his duties as a first officer. Carrie, on the other hand, was full of energy.

A week earlier, she instructed George to take over exercise planning so each step of the battle would be a surprise for her and the crew. For the rest of the journey Carrie and her bridge crew had worked Luke almost to death.

George's voice broke into the ensuing silence. "Simulation complete. Time of engagement two hours and thirteen minutes. Enemy killed, five hundred forty. Alliance warships lost, seventeen. Fighters destroyed, seventy-eight."

"Damn!" Carrie said with feeling. "I thought we did better than that. Sorry, Zach. I know I left Green Squadron hanging out to dry, but…you know."

"Not a problem, Captain. I saw it coming and did what I could to offset."

"Good job. Thanks for backing me up." Carrie looked at Luke. "Want to run it again, Commander?"

Luke tried to look dignified as he turned down her suggestion. He was afraid he would have a heart attack if they did. "Tomorrow's for real," he explained. "Let's save a little energy for that one. You have the con." He struggled to his feet and made it back to his room before collapsing onto the couch.

He felt that Carrie had proven herself during the last two weeks. She was more than ready to take the ship into combat. Whereas Luke and Tyler tended to rely on their experience to handle whatever situations might arise, Carrie worked nonstop to improve her skills. Luke got more than he bargained for with her training.

Nevertheless, when they arrived at J97 and faced the possibility of real combat, Luke would sit in the captain's chair. He owed that to the crew. But afterward, he was seriously considering putting his young firebrand in the hot seat on a permanent basis.

Chief Rogers came into the room and examined the sweat-stained uniform his boss was still wearing. "I see Lieutenant Faulkner's been giving you warlord training again," he said with a sigh.

Same Day—New Hope

"Theodora!" Camila said loudly. "Wake up."

"Teddy!" The Captain grabbed her leg and shook it.

"Leave me alone!"

"Come on, Miss Smith!" Solomon shouted. "*Sadie* is acting up again."

Annie gazed blearily at Solomon, squatting next to her bedroll. "She's a computer! Computer's don't *act up*."

Camila stooped down and glared at Annie. "You know what we're talking about. Please, girl! I understand how tired you are but Millie's got it figured out. Now get up and help. Or do you want me to tell seven thousand people it's your fault they have to live off supplements another week."

"Uhhhh!" Annie put her face under the dirty blanket.

Camila stood up, taking Solomon's hand. "Okay. Let's go, *cariño*, she's not coming." Camila dragged Solomon outside the tent's entrance flap and shouted, "Forget it everyone. Teddy's too tired. She would rather sleep."

"Look out!" Solomon caught Annie's boot just before it smashed Camila in the back. He tossed the boot back. "Thanks, Theodora," he said, grinning.

Annie watched her tormentors walk away. She knew life wasn't fair, but this was beyond the pale. Ten minutes later she boarded *Sadie*.

"You're making me a wanted woman, *Sadie*. And not in a nice way."

"I apologize, Miss Daniels. The Commander would never forgive me if I allowed you to come to harm."

Annie let it drop. She'd already had this conversation. After the disaster, *Sadie* had apparently come to the conclusion that she was Annie's bodyguard and would not go into space unless Annie was onboard. To *Sadie*, it made no difference that Annie was much safer on the ground.

Because the shuttles were running back and forth non-stop, Annie's life had turned into one of unending exhaustion. The colonists were salvaging as much as possible from the disintegrating vessel.

In the meantime, people still needed three meals a day. All of the great plans for the creation of the new colony had been destroyed with the *Marco Polo*. The colonist's trades and skills that would have ensured a cultured existence with a high quality of life were of little use. Instead, the community worked like scavengers to provide food.

Without basic implements, simple nutrition became touch and go. Each shuttle had a small replicator on board, but even combined, they were not up to the task of feeding seven thousand people. Instead they produced piles of nutritional supplements between trips. At best it was a short-term solution. If they could move one of the ship's large replicators to the surface, they might have a chance at survival.

"Where's Millie?" Annie asked.

"She is on the *Marco Polo*."

"Let's go then."

Moments later *Sadie* parked next to the larger piece of the *Marco Polo*'s wreckage. A wide hole had been painstakingly cut through the hull into the engineering section. Millie's crew had jury-rigged dozens of LED lights along the walls to illuminate the interior.

Annie pulled on a pair of gravity gloves and launched herself into the derelict. Near the core she spotted Millie looking very excited.

"Whatcha got?" Annie asked once she touched down.

Millie looked at the medium sized replicator. It measured a hundred feet square. "This is the one we're going with. It's small enough for us to handle and of the four onboard, it has the least damage."

"Does it work?"

"I can't tell without power. I had *Vincent* make a small hand generator to power the control panel. The panel looks okay when I apply voltage, but who knows about the main unit? From what I understand, it was the *Marco Polo* that had the database with the replicator inventory. *Vincent* has a limited one for basic ops, but nothing that we need on the surface."

"That's not good," Annie agreed.

"These shuttles are just not that smart. Except *Sadie*. She won't come out and say it, but I get the feeling that she has a more complete product list."

"I know," Annie sympathized. "She was the commander's very first shuttle and helped create the initial database. She's become a weird duck lately. Hang on."

Annie looked back through the wreckage at her shuttle floating next to the wide opening. *Sadie, answer me yes or no. Do you have a more comprehensive replicator inventory that can help the people on the planet?*

Yes, Miss Daniels.

Can you make food and tools?

Affirmative.

Annie looked back at Millie. "She said she does."

Millie gave Annie one of her suspicious looks. Annie had gotten a lot of those lately.

"How do you do that?" Millie asked.

"I'll tell you later. What do you want to do now?"

"I'd like to try it out before we move it to the surface, but at this point I'm not sure how."

Sadie, get in here, please.

The shimmer of a force field appeared around her hull and the shuttle reluctantly inched forward. The opening was three times what she needed, so Annie wasn't sure why the hesitation.

Are you scared of this place? Annie asked.

A little bit, the small shuttle replied. *Marco wasn't that friendly but he didn't deserve this. And I don't want to get trapped inside.*

Annie had been having more of these personal conversations with *Sadie* lately. It was getting harder not to attribute true feelings to the little spacecraft. But they had been together for a long time.

George once explained that the more time people spent with their AIs, presumably no matter what level of the device, the closer the bond between human and computer. The AIs were programmed to process their counterpart's feelings into a feedback loop to enhance the relationship. Annie had concluded that her feedback loop with *Sadie* would eventually drive one of them into a nervous breakdown.

The small spacecraft came to a stop next to the two women.

"How can I help?" the shuttle asked. Her voice was clear inside the boundary of her force field.

"*Sadie*, do whatever you have to, to make this replicator produce five tons of vegetables," Annie ordered.

For this size replicator it was the simplest of instructions but would make the most difference to the colonists tonight. Annie thought she heard a mechanical sigh.

"Find a type forty-three power cable. Run it from the external power socket below my console to the JX-101 plug under the replicator's control panel. It's the one with twenty-eight prongs."

It took almost an hour to find the necessary cable on level four of the other hulk. Fifteen minutes later the replicator shimmer faded away.

In the center of the replicator pad sat a cluster of forty pallets. Each pallet was five feet high and every single one was filled with individually wrapped salads.

Millie squealed and launched herself at the closest pallet. She tore out one of the packages and shrieked again. "It's from Safeway!" She glanced back at Annie, a wide grin plastered across her face. "Look! It's a chicken Caesar salad. That's my favorite. It even has dressing!"

It was Annie's favorite too. In fact, she remembered when she scanned it during the early days on one of her trips to Earth. Luke had scanned hundreds of foods into the replicator database to get Moonbase started, but for the most part, he neglected vegetables and salads. Annie chalked it up to typical male mentality and compensated with scans of her own. *Sadie* obviously remembered the incident too.

Millie drifted over to *Sadie* and planted a wet kiss on the front of the shuttle.

Sadie was affronted. "Miss Parish, restrain yourself. The biological residue from that smudge can develop a hotspot on my forward exterior during reentry."

"Ha!" Millie responded sarcastically. "I am very familiar with the extended force field used for atmospheric flight. Nice try." She swiped her tongue across the hull.

"Augh!"

"Stop it, you two," Annie barked. She couldn't help smiling. Sometimes dealing with the pair was like babysitting a couple of little sisters.

"Miss, Daniels," *Sadie* announced primly. "I have notified *Vincent* to bring some volunteers. They will retrieve the vegetables for transport to the planet. Afterward they will return and assist with moving the replicator."

Chapter 14

Day 565—Arriving J97

Luke studied the information coming in from the latest probe. They were fifteen minutes out of the J97 star system and coming in hot.

"It looks very much like the Jigu system, doesn't it?" he observed to no one in particular.

Carrie wanted more specifics. "What are we seeing, George?" she asked.

"You are essentially correct, Commander. System J97 has three gas giants in its outer orbit and one Earth-type planet second from the sun. It appears that the enemy is engaged in a bombardment of the planet."

"Is that coincidence or something else?" Luke wondered aloud.

"Impossible to say at this point," George responded.

The tactical display looked much like the last system. Hundreds of yellow diamond icons surrounded the inhabited planet.

"What are the odds there are Bakkui hiding behind the first gas giant?" Luke speculated.

As if in answer, a new diamond popped up on the far edge of the Jupiter-like planet.

"Hold it here, George." Luke commanded.

"Braking terminated," he replied.

"George, launch two flights of warships. Have them drop back five AUs into a high low cover."

"Acknowledged, Commander. Warships launching. Lieutenants Mercado and Bonner commanding Alpha and Bravo Flight."

"Got it. Resume gravity drive operations, George." Luke said.

"Braking applied, Commander."

"What are you thinking, Commander?" Carrie asked.

Luke glanced at his first officer. Her expression was expectant, as though waiting for him to divulge a grand scheme.

"I'm not sure," Luke replied. "The Bakkui we've seen are automatons. Perhaps they execute the exact same battle plan in every system. Make it easy for us if they did."

"But?"

"But I don't believe in luck, not when we're going into battle. Let's see what happens. "George, resume our battle plan as intended, except hold on the guided missiles. Turning combat control over to you."

"Acknowledged, Captain. I have the hammer."

Moments later George spoke again. "Gravity drives to zero, now. Warships launching." There was five-second pause. "All warships launched. Fighters launching." Another pause, slightly longer. "All fighters launched. Tactical displays updating."

Luke examined the displays. The tactical display showed the God's-eye view of the system centered on *Lulubelle*. Just like before, a line of white ovals spread out, indicating the warships in line abreast formation. Far in trail, and falling further behind, were the ten warships he had launched previously. The fighter symbols in their appropriate color markings began to appear as they assumed their assigned positions.

"Recon drones launched. Self-defense drones launched," George said, in a word-for-word repetition of the last combat encounter.

"George," Luke barked. "I have the hammer."

"Acknowledged, Commander. You have control."

"Fire twenty guided missiles."

"Guided missiles fired," George replied.

"Bring all ships to an emergency stop!"

"Acknowledged, Commander."

For the first time since Luke started flying the various spacecraft that were now commonplace in his life, he felt *Lulubelle* straining against the forces being applied. She groaned with the effort of going from faster than light to zero.

Luke glanced at Carrie. "I really worry about these gravity drives," he said loudly over *Lulubelle*'s painful creaks. "If George hiccups, there's nothing left of us but strawberry jam."

"Please do not worry, Commander," George said drily. "We are well within safety tolerances."

"Have all ships maintain position in line abreast."

"Acknowledged, Commander."

A moment later there was dead silence on the bridge. George spoke again quietly. "All stop."

The display showed all of Luke's fleet spread out in a wide thin line, motionless, just inside the edge of the solar system.

"You mimicked our actions from the last engagement," Carrie said. "You hoped that would spring a trap?"

Luke nodded. "It seemed like a good idea."

"But you gave our position to the enemy."

"I think they already know we're here. But that's another problem."

"What if all those ships start heading our way?"

"Depends," Luke said. "We might stand and fight, we might get out of Dodge."

"Really? You would run?"

"Absolutely, Lieutenant Faulkner. What's our mission?"

"To create alliances?"

"That's secondary. First is to survive. And at this point, I doubt we're going to find much of an alliance on that planet unless they have magic shields too."

"What will decide your choice, Commander?" Carrie asked.

"I'm willing to engage with them from a distance so long as they don't surprise me with countermeasures."

"How do you mean?"

"If they're doing what I think they're doing, they learned a lot from us in one engagement. I'm hoping that doesn't include new a self-defense that can stop our weapons. If they have, we're outta here."

Carrie nodded. "Understood. That makes a lot of sense."

"Don't forget, Lieutenant. In training simulations, we always fight to the end. But we're not under any obligation to engage in this or any other system. As long as we have an advantage, we'll use it. If we don't, we can't afford a Pyrrhic victory. Not even once."

Luke waited, playing a guessing game with the Bakkui force. "How long until those missiles reach their target?"

"The guided missiles arrived two minutes ago, Commander," George replied.

"Distance from our location to target?"

"Seven point three light minutes, Commander."

"It'll be another five minutes before we know if they're coming our way. Set course toward the outermost gas giant."

"Course set, Commander."

"Now fire one hundred missiles to orbit the planet and target on anything on the other side."

"Missiles fired."

"Let's see how this works out," Luke suggested. "I'll bet we see some action in less than two minutes. Maybe less if they…"

"Shields. Activated," *Belle*'s voice warned.

"Commander, multiple targets inbound," George said.

"How many?" Luke asked. He could not tell because the display had diamonds overlapping diamonds. There were several hundred at least.

"Over a thousand, Commander. Unable to get a firm count."

"All ships fire. Start backing up, George."

"*Lulubelle*, this is Mercado. We are detecting several large targets coming from above. They appear to be similar to the Bakkui we found hiding in J64. Engaging."

"Same here, Commander. This is Bonner. About twenty ships coming out of the ecliptic from below. Firing now."

"What's our effectiveness, George?" Luke demanded. "Are we getting through?"

"Affirmative, Commander. There appears to be no difference from last time."

"Thank God for that. I think we'll be okay, then. Full ahead and engage the enemy. Green Squadron, assist Mercado. Blue Squadron, assist Bonner. Fire all missiles. You've got the hammer, George!"

"I have the hammer, Commander. Engaging."

Lulubelle's nose began swerving to and fro, a continuous vibration shaking the deck as her nose guns fired without pause. Luke felt another rhythmic staccato coming through the walls; it was the anti-aircraft guns mounted along *Lulubelle*'s fuselage.

Carrie touched his arm and pointed at the tactical display. "Red Squadron," she said.

Red Squadron had gotten too far to the left of the main fleet and was in danger of being englobed by the Bakkui. "George? Can you do something about Red Squadron?" Luke said.

Lulubelle's nose swerved violently to the left and fifty guided missiles launched to support the endangered Red Squadron. Suddenly, Bakkui ships were all around them. White streaks glanced off *Lulubelle*'s shields, leaving smears of white phosphorus-like residue behind. A blinding white flash exploded to the left of *Lulubelle*'s nose. The view screens went blank and gravity went to zero. The command bridge shook violently.

Luke grabbed the arms of the captain's seat to stay in place; Carrie did the same, but several bridge officers were caught off guard. The tactical officer was flung across the room. He gesticulated wildly, trying to grab hold of something. The communication office snagged his pants leg and pulled just as gravity came back on, slamming the fellow hard onto the deck. He lay unmoving.

Carrie barked out orders to the crew. "Finch, take his place!" She moved to take over Finch's engineering position while he moved into the tactical officer's chair.

"Status?" Luke shouted.

"All systems normal," Carrie and George both answered at once.

"One report is all I need," Luke said.

"Sorry, sir," Carrie responded.

Lulubelle's nose swung sharply several more times right and left, then suddenly did an about face, pointed back the way they had come. One final vibration shook the deck and the bridge fell silent. The quiet was magnified by the cessation of all battle activity.

"Engagement terminated," George announced. "Time of engagement, six minutes. Enemy killed, one thousand eight hundred thirty-two. Alliance warships lost, three. Fighters destroyed, seventeen."

"All ships, report!" Luke said.

"Mercado. All present, sir."

"Bonner here, I lost *Higgs* and *Beamer*, Commander."

The remaining flight commanders reported in, except one.

"Red Squadron, report." Luke ordered again.

There was further silence. Then a young man's voice. "This is Ensign Farmer, Commander, Red Squadron. My flight lead is gone. I think we lost fifteen, sir. Maybe more. I'm not sure."

"Understood, Farmer. George, bring Red Squadron home. Send Orange Squadron to our intended destination and set up a combat air patrol. Bring Bonner's flight back and replace it with another one. Establish crew rotations for follow-on CAPs." Luke looked at this bridge crew. "What did I miss?"

He got several blank stares. They were still too new at this.

Carrie moved back to the first officer's chair. "Engineering, coordinate with George and give us a report," she ordered. "Medical, give us an update about the rest of the crew when you can. All departments begin recovery operations. George, send the record of today's events to J64 and Moonbase One. Deploy reconnaissance probes to star systems K18 and K39."

"Recordings sent, Lieutenant Faulkner. Probes deployed."

Luke slumped back in his seat. He felt no thrill from the victory. Only relief that the battle was over. The number of Bakkui warships had shocked him. He had a feeling it was a trap, and like an idiot he'd attacked instead of withdrawing. He could not justify his command to engage the enemy so recklessly. It was irresponsible, especially after lecturing Carrie about using caution.

It was too late now. He had to concentrate on the next step, which was finding out if anyone was still alive on the planet. He had one more thing to do today, however.

"George, from here on, refer to Lieutenant Faulkner as Captain Faulkner."

"Promotion noted, Commander. Congratulations, Captain Faulkner."

Carrie's eyes grew wide at the announcement and a muted but authentic cheer came from the other bridge officers.

"You've got the con, Captain," Luke told her. He lurched to his feet and headed toward his quarters. As he walked down the corridor he heard the bridge officers giving Carrie more congratulations. The news had energized all of them. It left him feeling more exhausted than ever.

Same Day—New Hope

How long have we been here? Annie wondered as she looked across the valley. *Has it only been a month?* A lot had changed since their arrival. It was a settlement now, not a refugee center.

Annie carried her tray around the tables that filled New Hope's center plaza to join Solomon and Camila for lunch. In the distance, shuttles were either taking off or landing from the airport.

"You did a good job on the permanent replicator pad," she said to Solomon. "Congratulations."

"Thanks," he replied modestly. "That was all Josh Howell. He and Lauren were responsible for the design work. Did a lot of downtown planning, too. As long as the river doesn't dry up, we'll be okay."

Camila wouldn't accept any conditions on their achievements. "If that happens they can just extend the pipeline another mile to the sea. I don't think that's going away anytime soon."

"True." Solomon smiled at his girl. The affection between the two was obvious to all.

"When are you going to tie the knot?" Annie asked. "We could use a good party."

Camila smiled sheepishly. "Few weeks."

"Really?" Annie was delighted with the decision. "Congratulations! You kids need to start pumping out babies."

It was Solomon's turn to look embarrassed. "Well, that's why we're rushing it a bit. We're kinda already down the road on that one."

Annie burst into laughter. "That's fantastic. I'm so proud of both of you. You're a good example for the community."

"If it's a girl, we'll name her after you," Camila promised.

Annie blushed at Camila's statement. "I am so honored," she said sincerely. "Thank you. I don't know what to say."

"Well, you could start by telling us your real name," Solomon said drily.

Annie blanched at his question. "I…"

"Oh, come on," Solomon wheedled. "Everybody knows it. We just go along since you seem so intent on keeping it a secret, but you're not fooling anyone."

Annie sighed. "It was *Sadie*, wasn't it?"

Camila rolled her eyes in an exaggerated fashion. "Duh! She's never once called you Theodora or Teddy. And of course, Millie went around asking everyone if they knew Annie Daniels before."

Annie shook her head. "Drat that girl."

"Don't blame her," Solomon said. "*Sadie*'s always called you by name. At least fifty other people heard it and most of them have asked me about it. It's no big deal. To everyone here you're Theodora. It's not like anyone here knew the commander or cares that you're his woman. Is that what drove you away?"

"Solomon!" Camila chastised her lover. "Not fair."

"Sorry," he said, clearly not so. "Slipped out."

"No," Annie said. "It's okay. I suppose there's no reason to keep it a secret anymore. I loved being his 'woman,' as you say, although the title was a bit irksome; kind of a fifties throwback."

"No kidding!" Camila exclaimed.

Solomon wisely kept quiet.

"We were crazy about each other. But I was a danger for him. You ever hear about the bomb-in-the-head story?"

Camila and Solomon both replied with a blank stare.

Annie shrugged. "I guess not. Well, the short version is that I was a danger to Luke, especially with the way we felt about each other. I was afraid that one day I'd distract him once too often and George would kill him."

"That's insane!" Camila was incredulous and angry at the idea.

"I agree," Annie said. "But I think I was the one who went insane. I can't explain it. But I made a big mistake leaving him."

"Then go back," Camila said. She took Solomon's hand. "I can't imagine being away from this guy now. I haven't known him that long, but I would die before letting him go; that would kill me. From everything I heard you two were the same way."

Tears ran down Annie's cheeks and Camila apologized.

"I'm sorry, honey. I wasn't thinking."

Annie wiped her face. "It's okay. To be honest, I've thought about returning to Moonbase. But I can't depart just yet. I already ran away once so I'm not in a hurry to abandon you guys." She looked around the town square. "We've got a few things left to do before I would be comfortable leaving. But this place is already night and day from when we got here."

It was true. The most important achievement was getting the replicator transported to the planet's surface; that took two days. The next task was to reposition one of *Marco Polo*'s massive generators to power the final installation. When the replicator produced the first batch of goods, a combination of foodstuffs and tools, the colony transformed overnight.

Brought together by adversity, the colonists were reborn, dedicated to a shared goal. Instead of simply struggling to survive, everyone's new philosophy was to build the greatest community ever.

Chapter 15

Day 579—System J97

"What's your recommendation, Colonel?" Luke asked.

Colonel Brad Lindsey was the senior Army officer onboard *Lulubelle*. With him was the 4th Battalion CO. They sat facing Luke under an open, chalet-like, canvas tent. The briefing area was part of the bivouac set up by Colonel Lindsey's troops. The three men were clustered around an old-fashioned briefing board made of cork on a wood backing. A dozen maps and charts were pinned to it, ranging in scale from the entire planet to the local area.

Luke had tasked Colonel Lindsey to survey the planet and develop a proposal to keep the few members of the surviving population alive. After analyzing the data gathered from reconnaissance flights and *Lulubelle*'s electronic scans, they had identified around five hundred thousand humans in small clusters around the planet. They were all that remained of the one billion people who had populated this world. The Bakkui objective to annihilate a planetary population was terribly effective. Over ninety-nine percent of the population had died.

The local culture was nothing exceptional. Before the bombardment started, it was a feudal society with fiefdoms spread around the globe. Local kings ruled their own territories on each continent.

When kingdoms bumped into each other, the inevitable result was a combination of land swaps and royal marriages. The hierarchy kept the people poor and the common folk uneducated. Luke found it noteworthy that even as a feudal society, the planet fit the galactic norm of non-violence.

The population remnant would need assistance but Luke had no experience know what that meant. He brought the army down to help, they had a background in dealing with refugees.

"At the very least, I suggest leaving Company B from the 2nd Battalion, Commander," Colonel Lindsey recommended. "Their focus is combat support and Captain Barrett is best at handling people. Most troops call him 'the chaplain'."

"Is he that religious?" Luke asked.

"Not at all," Lindsey said. "Just a good people person. Makes his men feel good."

"Will the 2nd Battalion CO squeal when we take Company B?"

Lindsey chuckled in a gravelly voice. "Of course he will. But I already told him it's coming and frankly, he agrees. Barrett is not the best combat guy, but he'd be great at putting this place back together. Good leadership skills. He's an administrator at heart, not a warrior."

"Is this a fool's errand, Brad?" Luke asked the colonel. "Tell me the truth."

Lindsey stood and walked to the edge of the chalet where he leaned against the tent pole to admire the view. Their encampment was located in a grass-covered valley that had escaped bombardment. The land sloped gently away to a mountain lake.

Luke had thrown in a fishing line two days ago and pulled out the local version of a trout. It weighed in at five pounds. It was the first time since leaving Earth that Luke wished he had a cell phone. He wanted a picture of the thing.

"Yes, Commander. It is a fool's errand. But it's one that needs to be done. These people are human. They don't deserve what happened. At least we can give them a chance. I'd like to leave a whole brigade here but I understand you need to maintain a combat force."

Luke pressed the Colonel about his answer. "You know that whoever is left behind is very much at risk from another attack. Since we knocked out the Bakkui ambush they may want to retaliate."

"I know. But you could leave a couple of warships. Take enough time to put together a large replicator unit. We could gather any locals that would come together. Plenty of them will starve if they stay out on their own, especially with winter coming on. George tells me this place has a rough cold season." Lindsey paused to gaze at the scenery one more time. "But this planet would be worth it."

"You're making me all teary-eyed, Brad," Luke said.

Lindsey looked back, his scarred face slightly abashed. "I know. Getting too sentimental in my old age."

"Sounds like it's more than that. What is it about this place?"

Lindsey shook his head as though to clear away unwanted memories but then he spoke anyway, the words coming out on their own. "Reminds me of when I was a kid. My grandparents had a place in Oklahoma; looked at lot like this. Ever hear of Beggs? Not many people have."

Luke shook his head, amused by the rough warrior's maudlin reminisces.

"Small town. Not more than a thousand people, I expect. Been a long time since I thought of it. Be nice to retire in a place like that...like this. With a little effort, a man could really make something of it."

Luke leaned back, pushing the small chair onto its rear legs. *George, anything new from the probe to K18.*

Yes, Commander. As suspected the planet is fairly advanced, on par with Jigu. I perceive you are implementing your revised strategy.

"I am indeed," Luke said aloud.

"What's that, boss?" Lindsey asked.

"Nothing, Brad. I like your idea about Captain Barrett."

Luke handed a folder containing a sheaf of papers to Lindsey. "See what you think of this, Colonel. We might be on the same track."

Lindsey took the file and started reading through the documents. As he read, Luke watched the man's face light up.

Before Lindsay was half-finished, he looked up at Luke. "You serious about this?"

"Unless you can talk me out of it."

"No. I like it. A lot." Lindsey went back to the documents, more slowly this time. Thirty minutes later he looked up again. "I'm in. I assume you know this is at least a full brigade. Probably need some of the 2nd as well."

"Set up a screening process," Luke suggested. "See how many volunteers there are. Also, I need you to tell me how many soldiers I need to keep on *Lulubelle*. I went with two brigades at the outset because that was the recommendation. But so far, we haven't needed anything like that."

Lindsey nodded. "I thought you had too many soldiers myself, but it wasn't my place to criticize."

"All I need is a police force," Luke acknowledged. "Something for ground protection when we're on a new planet. I don't see me ever needing fifteen thousand guys. That's just hard on everyone."

"Got it," Lindsey said. "I'll make sure you're not shorted. What else?"

"I'm giving you a mission, Brad. And it's not to sit around fishing. I want to dedicate this entire planet to combat support. I'd like to see shipyards, R&D, everything we need to carry this battle into bad-guy territory."

"That's not a short-term objective," Lindsey warned. "You realize that."

"I understand. But you're getting a head start. It took me eleven months just to launch our first Mars colony."

"I thought George gave you all that."

"He gave us replicators and gravity drive, that's true. But we designed the warships, the tools, the force fields and the procedures. You'll have all that from the get go. And enough people to make it work. I don't think the locals can be much more than a distraction."

"No," Lindsey countered. "Not a distraction. This is their planet, after all. My goal is to bring them into our century, those who want to. That's something for our Captain Barrett to work on."

"Sounds good. I didn't mean to imply we shouldn't take care of them. I like your approach.

"What about self-defense?" Lindsey wanted to know. "We need protection until everything is up and running."

"I'll leave a contingent here. I can give you twenty warships to start, and about fifty fighters. Keep in mind, however, that the space forces will not be under your chain of command."

"Seriously?" Lindsey didn't like that idea.

"Air power needs to be separate. They need to set their own priorities."

"Right." Lindsey grinned savagely. "I forgot you were an Air Force weenie in the old days."

"Still am, Brad."

"Okay. I can live with that. What do you need from me?"

"I've given you a rough outline. Get your staff together and put some flesh on it and we'll meet back tomorrow. I'll allow a few of my people on *Lulubelle* to volunteer, but I'm going to be fairly stingy where that's concerned. Anything I can't give you, we'll get from Moonbase. You won't have to go without for long."

"What about AI? Are you going to give me one of those smart boxes?"

"Absolutely. In fact, I've already talked to George about it. I didn't like the last one he produced on Jigu. It had a little too much character for me. We need to do some groundwork first, however. And get you a large-scale replicator going."

"I would appreciate it," Lindsey said.

Luke thought the man already looked ten years younger. It wasn't a surprise; this *was* a great planet. It *would* be nice to find a place like this and settle down someday.

"How did it go, Commander?" Carrie asked.

"About the way we thought," Luke replied. "He tried hard not to show it, but he was like a kid at Christmas."

Carrie grinned. "I like the idea. It's kind of a tribute to all those people who died. It means their passing wasn't in vain. It means their spirit will live on."

"Well. I think it means we need to vaporize the ones that did it."

She frowned at his interpretation. "Kind of a harsh way of putting it."

"Kind of a harsh way to die, if you ask me. Not really all that poetic when you think about it. Anyway, we need to send an inordinate amount of supplies down to Bradley's planet. I told him he could look for volunteers from the crew but that we would exercise a fairly strong veto."

"Okay."

"And I promised him twenty warships."

Carrie hesitated a fraction of a second before replying. "Okay."

"And fifty fighters."

"Okay," she groaned.

"And a large-scale replicator."

"Commander!"

"Relax," Luke assured her. "We're going to build him one and set it down. The problem is that this is going to take a bit more time than I wanted."

"Why are you giving him so much more than you did the Jigu?"

"Think about it. We're making him start a planetary colony with half the people and almost none of the resources that the colony ships have. I don't think it's a good idea to leave without leaving enough for him to get started. It's gonna be rough on Bradley's planet for a while."

"I know. It's just that we don't have a resupply built in for ourselves."

"I've been thinking about that. Did you look at the probe reports for J9580?"

That brought a smile back to Carrie's face. "I did. How did that little guy get overlooked by the Bakkui? It was great!"

"Probably by being so small. George, display the area around J9580."

The wall dissolved into a star chart.

"Zoom back to include Earth," Luke said. "Show our current location and the rest of the star systems we're talking about. Then add the known forward edge of Bakkui territory."

A circle labeled Earth appeared on the wall. To the left of Earth, along the galaxy spiral was Jigu, in System J64. Moving in toward the galaxy center, on the edge of the adjoining spiral was *Lulubelle*'s current location on J97. Further in that direction was System J9580. Beyond were systems for future visits, K18 and K39. All of the new star systems lined up in a straight line. Past those systems, the devastated area of the Bakkui covered the chart.

In that part of the galaxy, all of the drones returned with nothing but images of destruction. The depiction of the enemy's advance was a menacing reminder of what they faced.

"Look at 9580," Luke said. "It's practically next door. George, what's the travel time to get there?"

"Approximately seven hours, Commander."

Luke turned to Carrie. "Have engineering finish the pieces for the large-scale replicator as quickly as you can. I'll stay here to see it gets put together. While we're setting that up, I want you to take a fleet of warships out to 9580. George said they have a unified government and that their culture is a lot like Jigu. See what you can do."

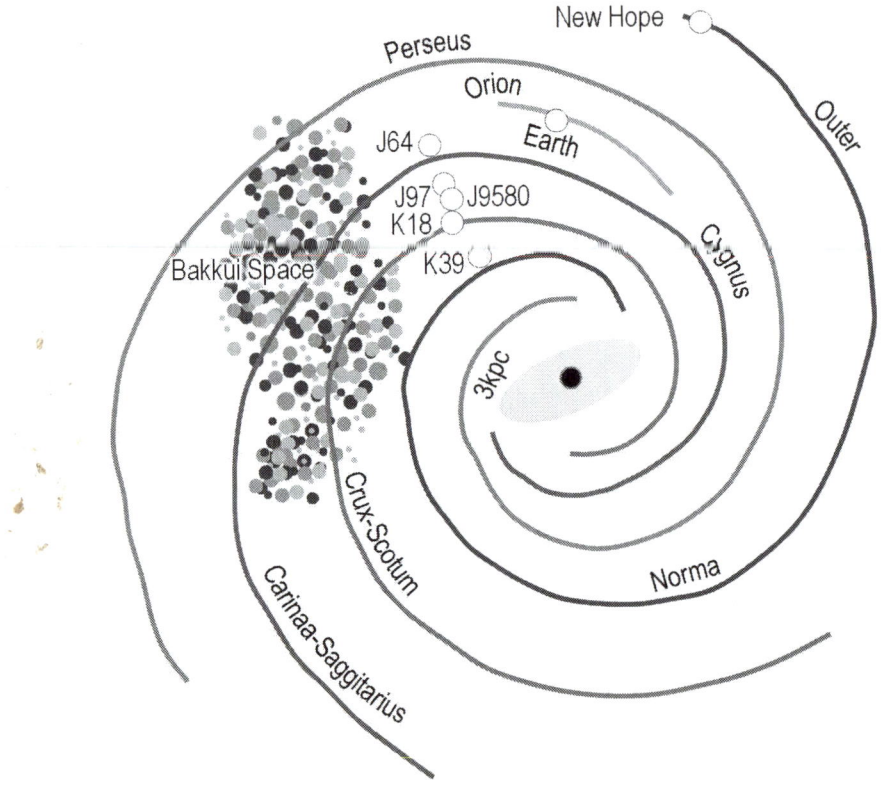

"Are you testing me?" Carrie asked.

"I'd call it an opportunity," Luke replied. "Good practice for you, and maybe a source of people for us. The people here aren't advanced enough to become crew members and there's too few of them. But 9580 is a bit more modern."

Carrie nodded her understanding. "When do you want me back?"

"Quickly. For the rest of the day, get with your people and select your fleet. You can take fifteen warships. Keep your captains under strict control. While you're gone, I'll set up local training and self-defense operations. I'm not saying you have to hurry; do a good job. But don't dawdle. If it doesn't work out right away, don't force it. Think of it as the start of establishing regular visits between 9580 and Bradley's planet."

A few weeks can make a big difference, Luke thought. He stood in the same encampment, but now it had a modern look of nascent industrialization. No doubt Earth-based conservationists would condemn his effort to transform Bradley's planet into a center of chrome and glass. But Luke thought it was better than a lifeless surface scarred by craters.

The conservationists wouldn't like the name either. Luke's constant reference to Bradley's planet had somehow been recorded formally as Bradley's Planet. Luke saw it as representative of the inevitable bureaucracy that went with any large undertaking. Lindsey took it with good humor but insisted the native inhabitants be listed as the Soyuja, which meant *owners* in their own language.

In the meantime, *Lulubelle*'s engineers had created a mobile version of the large-scale replicator. The rectangular framework was mounted on gravity pads, and a lone operator sitting in a cab built atop one of the corners could float it to any location needed. With the push of a button a building would appear. Or, to be more accurate, with a button and a lot of prior architectural design and site engineering.

So far, in a neat grid of city blocks, they had produced barracks, an administrative center, a hospital, and a tactical command center. Hundreds of reconnaissance drones moved throughout the solar system providing continuous updates that were integrated into a three-dimensional hologram in the situation center, designated "the tank" by its users. Lindsey didn't like the flat panel view screens used on *Lulubelle*'s bridge. He was used to seeing his world laid out on the ground in three dimensions, with little piles of rocks that denoted the location of battalions and brigades.

Luke had to agree that the tank gave a better visualization of the combat situation. He told George to put together the same thing on *Lulubelle* so he could try it out. With a little customization it might become the new standard for warships too.

Carrie arrived back in system after a week. She didn't report with an unqualified success, but certainly the expectation of one. In a sign of good will, and with a promise to return soon, she left a ten-person team on J9580, which she formally designated planet Payapa, the local's name for their world.

For several days, Carrie met with Bradley to strategize on how to establish a mutually beneficial relationship between the two planets. Carrie suggested that one answer was to open up parts of Bradley's Planet for expansion by the Payapians.

Lindsey didn't like the idea. "And what will you do with the Soyujans? Put them in reservations and sell them alcohol?"

His question brought Carrie up short.

"Want them to perform little dances for the rich visitors?" Lindsey pressed.

Carrie pushed back. "All right, I'm sorry. You know I wasn't thinking anything like that, but I do get your point. What is your idea then? I'm trying to come up with something that will help both of us."

"We're the wards for this planet," Lindsey said firmly. "Not developers. I won't have these people exploited."

"Point taken. Can we move on?"

Lindsey backed off. "I don't know what the answer is. I've been struggling with this issue. Native populations are never handled well. It would be too easy to fall into that trap here. Assimilate or isolate? I just don't know."

Carrie shrugged. "I don't know either. But we don't need to decide everything right this minute. I *would* like to get the process started. Over the long term, it's going to help both planets if we can get trade going. The Payapians are peaceful, for sure, but they're ready for something new. Their planet is limited. Lots of small oceans around a whole lot of flat mini-continents. They have nothing like the mountains here."

Luke intervened. "Brad, I met with some of your Soyujans the other day. After talking with them for about thirty minutes, I was glad to get called away. I think they were about to negotiate a deal with me and I'm not even sure what I was offering."

Lindsey laughed. "Yeah. These guys have merchant's fever in their blood, don't they?" He gave Carrie a wry look. "Let's just set up a few meetings and see what develops. Maybe I'm worried about nothing after all. Could be my Soyujans aren't the ones we need to be concerned for."

Carrie was suddenly suspicious. "Do I need to worry that your people will take my people for a ride?"

"Commander, Captain Faulkner is entering orbit at this time."

Luke was glad to get the message. Carrie had left for a second trip to Payapa a week ago after she and Lindsey finalized their strategy. They would start introductions between the two planets with a "get acquainted" visit and Carrie had gone to establish diplomatic protocols.

She was waiting in *Lulubelle*'s planning room, excited to fill Luke in. "The Payapa government voted to join your alliance in return for protection and technology transfer," she said. "They were a bit hesitant but they're also open to the idea of bilateral trade with the Soyujans. I'm not worried. Once they see these mountains, I think tourism will boom."

"How will they get back and forth?" Luke asked. "I don't want us turning into a transportation company."

"We already have that ironed out. I had George redesign the basic *Ambrosia* model into two new variants; one for cargo and one for passenger transport. That thick, rounded design is very flexible. Both models are unarmed; I didn't want a loose warship running around unsupervised."

"Good call."

"What's been going on here?" Carrie asked.

"Brad is moving like gangbusters," Luke said. "You won't recognize the compound. It's the new capital city. Or at least the start of one. He said the university is going up tomorrow."

Carrie shook her head. "I still can't get used to the speed that things happen around here. Can you imagine how long it would take to do on Earth what you've done in the last week?"

"I think about it a lot. What I haven't figured out is why most of these planets are so peaceful. Up till now, I just accepted that combat was the natural order of things. It certainly is in nature; big fish eat little fish."

Carrie didn't have an answer. "I thought so too. But the Soyujans were not violent."

"It's a mystery, I guess." Luke said. "This was a harsh world and yet Soyujans are not."

Carrie shrugged. "I'm a criminal justice major. Guess I'm inclined toward a violent philosophy. To me, it's supposed to be that way."

George interrupted. "Commander, a message drone just arrived from Jigu with an urgent request from Ambassador Robertson."

"Show us, please, George."

The wall display lit up with a haggard-looking Tyler peering into the camera.

"Luke, sorry to bother you," Tyler started. "I know you must be hip deep in other problems but I got myself into a fix here. In a nutshell, I sent an expedition to a nearby star system. Probes showed it was inhabited by a Ming Dynasty type of culture. They received us, treated us great, and sent back a delegation with their top general. Now that he's here, I've lost control. The problem is *Toby*, my AI, has switched sides; says I should be cooperating with General Hwangje, a Genghis Khan type. If you can break free, I'd appreciate it. I'm including details with this report."

Luke gave Carrie a look of surprise. "So much for nonviolence," he said. "That's unexpected. I thought Tyler could handle this kind of thing."

"So did I. But you complained about *Toby* too. If the ambassador's AI turned on him, that could explain it."

"That's true. George? I thought *Toby* was programmed to stay in line."

"He was, Commander. I consider this matter extremely serious. In creating a higher level AI, variables are included in the programming to keep the personality from being monotonous. My archives contain rare cases where this resulted in unfortunate situations. Although it is very unusual, it can be corrected easily by any AI with a higher level."

"So if we go back, you can fix him?" Luke asked.

"Rather than repair, I would simply replace the AI with a new core personality module. The old personality would be preserved for study by Nobility engineers to determine the cause. Effectively it would cease to exist."

Luke nodded and turned to Carrie. "I guess we better head back and give Tyler a hand."

Carrie was alarmed. "What about K18, sir?" she asked. "It's the next one past Payapa. Our analysts predict that system is a high-probability target for the Bakkui. We're already pushing the projected D-day for them. If we return to Jigu first, that's a thirty- to forty-day slip at best. Our population estimates for K18 are a couple of billion people."

Luke winced. "That's right. That has to be our first priority." Luke sat silently for several minutes considering the options. "Let's do this," he said. "You take *Lulubelle* on to K18. Give me a warship and I'll go sort out Tyler and his problem child."

"Commander," George spoke up. "I cannot allow you to venture off on your own; especially in a warship. I would be forced to activate your fail-safe."

Carrie's face reflected surprise. "Failsafe? What's that mean?"

Luke sighed in frustration and gave Carrie and quick rundown on the explosive stuck in his brain. When he saw her face, he realized he'd made a mistake.

Carrie was outraged at the concept. "Is that true, Commander? You really have a bomb in your head? That's insane!" She gasped with sudden fear in her expression. "Do I have one too? Do all of us have that? How are we supposed to…"

Luke leaned back and squeezed his eyes shut in exasperation. This was not what he needed; another hysterical female over the bomb-in-the-head thing. Losing Annie had just about killed him. He couldn't afford for Carrie to go off the deep end right now.

"Carrie!" he shouted. His sudden bark stopped her rant. "At ease. There aren't any explosive devices in your body or anyone else's. Understand?"

"Are you sure…" she started, not quite willing to be placated.

"Did you understand me, Captain?" Luke growled.

That brought her up short. "Yes, Commander. Loud and clear. I apologize for my outburst."

"Confirm that for her George," Luke ordered.

"Captain Faulkner, the Commander is correct. There are no hidden devices, malevolent or otherwise, associated with any implants of *Lulubelle*'s crew."

"Then what about the Commander?" she persisted.

"The Commander's medical history is a private matter, Captain Faulkner."

"Let's get back on track," Luke said tiredly. "I can't ignore Tyler, and we can't wait on moving toward K18."

Carrie backed away from the sensitive topic. "What should we do?"

Luke looked at the ceiling. "We made an exception before, didn't we George?"

"That is true, Commander. But we were also clear that it was a one-time occurrence."

"I understand. But that was to make a replica of your entire physical structure, an enormous undertaking as you pointed out at the time. A necessity considering *Lulubelle*'s size. Why can't we make a smaller version? Just your core personality module, as you called it. Can't you create a slimmed down version of your AI for a warship? We'll use it just long enough to get to Jigu and come back. That would be in accordance with the long-term objectives of the Nobility."

"So you are saying that you would maintain constant contact with the mini-me."

Carrie burst out laughing but Luke glared at her and she quickly subsided. "Sorry," she mumbled. "That was just funny when he said mini-me like—"

"I saw the movie," Luke said sardonically, cutting off her feeble excuse. "Try to control yourself, young lady." He turned back to the ceiling. "Yes, George. You and I can stay together the entire time and you could take care of the idiot AI on Jigu. It's better than losing a couple billion people that could otherwise be working toward the Nobility's goals."

The silence in the planning room lengthened. Luke wondered what was going on in George's electronic brain while he considered the ramifications. Finally, "That would be acceptable, Commander. I shall start production of the new warship immediately."

Luke thought it was a workable solution but he was a bit worried about Carrie. "I don't like the idea of sending you off on your own on this one," he said. "System K18 is a long way away."

"That part will be fine, Commander," she replied confidently. "It's not a bit different than Payapa; just a little further away."

Luke thought it was hugely different. He had seen such overconfidence in many young officers, sometimes with tragic results. He hoped it wouldn't come back to bite her. Not that either of them had a choice. They had to keep pushing because the Bakkui were not waiting for anyone.

"I'll go down to the surface tomorrow and let Brad know what's going on," he said. "You get George's new prototypes completed as soon as I'm gone and then head out toward K18. Send reports back every day, you got that?"

"Yes sir. I promise."

"Send them to me and to Brad. And while I'm thinking of it, send them to Roth as well."

Carrie nodded innocently, promising she would comply. It was a little disconcerting. He wondered if she would be conscientious about it.

"One more thing, you two," he said, addressing Carrie and George and lowering his voice.

"Go ahead, Commander," George replied.

"Don't tell *Sadie* about this. Every time I go someplace without her she gets all bent out of shape and then I have to listen to her bitch about it for a week. Just keep this a secret until I'm gone."

"Of course, Commander," George said.

Carrie smiled and mimed drawing a zipper across her lips.

Luke shook his head at the irony of trying to keep yet another female, albeit an electronic one, from complaining about the things he needed to do.

Day 579—New Hope

Annie shoved her way past the other diners and slammed her tray down across from Solomon. "You have got to move the women's showers," she demanded angrily.

Solomon stood up and tried to calm his outraged friend. "Why? What's wrong?"

"The same thing I told you last week and the week before that."

Solomon's startled face melted into a grin. "Oh, that."

"Yes, that! Are you going to do something about it this time?"

"Well, sure. As soon as I can get to it. You know…"

"As soon as you can get to it? You don't believe me?"

"Well." Solomon drawled, treading carefully. "Are you honestly sure about this?"

Annie stamped her foot. *Why is this so difficult?* she wondered, forcing herself to calm down. She could see that he didn't want to anger his wife's maid of honor.

"Yes, Captain. I'm quite sure. If you would take five minutes to go check, you will see that the women's showers are at the base of the hill. Half way up there is an outcropping of rocks that all the teenage boys hide behind. They have a splendid view of everything. And I mean everything!"

Solomon couldn't contain his amusement. "Well, you know. Boys will be boys and all that. There's no harm done. And it's not like there's much…."

He bit off his words but Annie saw what he was thinking. "Not like there's much to see?" Annie finished the sentence as he tried to backpedal. "You might just want to think about that. I'm not the only one showering over there. Camila and I see each other there several times a week."

Solomon's eyes took a sudden interest.

"In the shower," she emphasized. "*Naked.*"

She definitely had his attention.

"We're both on display for all the young men in the community. And let me tell you, as I'm sure you already know. There is nothing scrawny about Camila. She is a well-endowed young lady, if you know what I mean."

Solomon's attitude completed its transformation. "Hold on!"

Annie became nonchalant. She waved her hand in dismissal. "Never mind. I know you're busy. We'll just forget this conversation ever took place."

"We will not!" His face grew red and his voice lowered to a frightening whisper. "Those little bastards."

Camila walked up with her salad. "Hi, everyone. What's new?"

Solomon turned on her in an explosion of anger. "Why didn't you tell me about this!" He turned on his heel and marched away, muttering about dismemberment.

"What?" Camila was flummoxed. She looked at Annie. "What was that all about?"

Annie watched the retreating figure with alarm. "Just kidding!" she called. He didn't hear and vanished in the crowd at the far end of the plaza.

"Kidding about what?" Camila said.

Annie shook her head slowly and sat at the table. She patted the seat next to her in invitation for Camila to sit down. "I hope those kids aren't up there at the shower right now."

Camila laughed. "Oh, no. You told him again, didn't you?"

"I told him you were with me."

"Well, I was."

"Yeah. He didn't think that was funny."

"He can be a bit jealous, that's true. It's kind of cute."

"He didn't look cute when he left just now. He looked scary."

"Don't worry about it," Camila said, pouring some dressing onto her salad. "Those kids shouldn't be doing that anyway."

Annie looked down into the pit. It had to be a hundred feet deep.

"What do you think?" Millie asked.

"I don't know," Annie muttered. "Seems excessive."

"I kind of like it. He is going to be the brain for the whole planet."

"That's true," Annie acknowledged. "Better safe than sorry, I guess."

"Do you think she can really do it? Can *Sadie* bring back *Marco Polo*?"

Annie stepped back from the railing and pulled Millie away too. "I'm the wrong person to ask. She thinks she can. I don't know if I'd take that to the bank or not." The girls headed to the plaza. They were meeting Solomon and Camila.

"Be great if she did," Millie said wistfully after loading up their trays. "It would seem like we were going to make it for sure."

"We're not doing that bad, you know," Annie protested. "Just look around."

Buildings were sprouting up everywhere. A residential neighborhood was under construction. The salvaged replicator had replicated itself several times. They were smaller versions but still large enough for almost any purpose the colony needed.

Solomon and Camila were already seated.

"I know," Millie agreed. "We're doing great, but frankly, that's all you and *Sadie*. Don't deny it."

Annie laughed at the comment. "I do deny it. All *Sadie* did was set up the engineering department. Josh and Lauren accomplished all this. And they did it according to Solomon's plan. I'm feeling kind of worthless these days."

"Is that why you're leaving?"

"No. Not at all. You know that."

Solomon leaned on the table. "So why are you leaving?" he asked.

Annie was silent for a moment to answer the question honestly. "Luke, of course. But it's also this level-two-device question. The more I think about that the scarier it gets."

"What is that?" Camila asked. "I've heard you talk about but I'm not sure what you mean?"

Annie related all that she had learned from George. It was important information that the people of New Hope needed to understand.

Camila summed it up. "So because this Bakkui ship had a level-two AI it outranked *Marco Polo*?"

"That's how I understand it. He tried to explain it to me before we were hit, but there wasn't enough time."

Millie chimed in to explain it to Camila. "She was talking to him and he was talking back. Did you know you could do that? He never talked to me?"

Annie sighed heavily. "That's a horrible failure in our training. On the moon, everyone talks to George. We just take it for granted."

Camila shrugged. "We talk to the AI on the bridge, of course. But I never thought about talking to him in my quarters. Too late now, I guess."

Millie shook her head. "Maybe not. Annie, how do you talk to *Sadie* when she's not there? I've seen you do that."

"That's another story. That's my implant, the one with the bomb. Trust me, you don't want that."

Camila shuddered. "This is all so amazing. A few months ago, I was trying to find an internship in Georgia. Now we're building a new civilization on another planet and talking about AIs and brain implants. It's scary and exciting all at the same time. I hope it goes well tomorrow too. It would be nice to talk to *Marco* again."

"Amen to that," Solomon agreed.

Even though word had gone out to stay away, a crowd surrounded the giant pit. Early in the morning Solomon ordered the barriers pushed back to give *Sadie* and the mobile platform replicator plenty of space. The shuttle rested on the ground next to the elevated replicator housing.

Power cables ran from the generator to the mobile platform and other cables from the platform to *Sadie*. Temporary plumbing brought in a supply of seawater in place of replicator sludge. Everything was in place.

Solomon spoke to *Sadie*. "Commence replication."

"Command acknowledged," she responded.

The shimmer filled the air below the replicator platform and extended down into the pit. Everyone's hearts thudded with anxiety. For two hours, a deep *hum* was the only sound. The shape of a modest building began to appear inside the shimmer, eliciting excited whispers. When completed, the structure would be the public access to the *Marco Polo* AI. Eventually, the same access would be available throughout New Hope at yet-to-be-installed data terminals. Those would come later. But until then the public would have voice access to the AI that was originally intended to guide the new community.

Without warning the *hum* died and the shimmer vanished. The hole was gone. A new brickwork plaza covered the area of the deep pit. The project had included filling the hole around the new AI with reinforced collapsed matter. Even a nuclear strike would not harm its bunkered location. In the center of a new plaza sat a columned structure. Everyone held their breath.

"It's good to be back," *Marco Polo* announced. "Great job Captain Solomon."

The crowd burst into cheers and applause. The sheer exhilaration at having the community's guiding intellect back was profound. Adulation went on and many of the crowd wiped away tears of joy. Spontaneous shouts of "Marco" erupted and were echoed with cries of "Polo."

"My good people," *Marco Polo* started several times. The crowd hushed each other, wanting to hear their AI speak.

"My good people," he started again. "I am so proud of each and every one of you. I am aware of the circumstances that brought us to the brink of disaster and how all of you fought back so valiantly. I am doubly grateful to our good captain for his wisdom and leadership during this trying period. My biggest regret is that I was not here to officiate at his wedding. Congratulations to Captain and Mrs. Andrews!"

The speech continued for an hour. It was a masterpiece of oratory. The people of New Hope had needed the infusion of hope for the future. They interrupted time and again with cheers and applause.

In the shadow of the replicator platform, Annie stood next to *Sadie* in a reflective mood. "It's time for us to leave now," she said to her shuttle. "I'm so proud of what you've done."

"It means a lot to me for you to say that, Annie," *Sadie* replied.

It sounded just like the programmed response Annie expected. But then, that's exactly what it was. The little shuttle was a collection of software modules that didn't really have any sentient thought.

#

Annie sat in a rattan chair in Solomon's new office and was amazed at how comfortable it was. The captain retrieved tall glasses of fruit juice from the replicator in the discreet kitchenette against the back wall. He set one on the mahogany coffee table in front of Annie and settled himself across from her in a similar chair.

"I like your new digs, Solomon," she said appreciatively.

He smiled. "Thanks to *Marco*, here. Good job, *Marco*," Solomon said to the ceiling.

"My pleasure, Captain. It feels good to use some of my creative modules once again."

Annie took a sip of the juice and set it back on the table. She put on her serious expression for Solomon. "Well? Did you think about it?"

"If I may interrupt, Miss Daniels," *Marco Polo* said gently.

"Go ahead," Solomon answered.

"Captain, I believe we should support Miss Daniels's request. I agree with her assessment that the discovery of a level-two-device in this star system far exceeds the expectations of the Bakkui advance. The commander needs to know."

Solomon looked pained. "It's bad enough to have Annie leave, but I hate to lose *Sadie* too. No slight to you, *Marco*."

"None taken. In that regard, I have a proposition. My archives contain alternative shuttle designs that might be more suitable for Miss Daniels at this time. I could replicate the existing shuttle's AI into the new format. In that way, Miss Daniels could still depart with her *Sadie*, and we here in New Hope would retain our beloved and historically important shuttle."

"You can do that?" Solomon asked.

"Indeed. As Miss Daniels may recall, even when she ordered *Sadie* to self-destruct, it was possible to reconstitute her without loss of continuity."

"Thanks, *Marco*," Annie replied sarcastically. "You just had to bring that up, didn't you?"

Solomon's eyes widened. "You did that to *Sadie*? What for?"

Annie waved away his question. "It's a long story, Captain. Can we just skip it for now? I think it's a good compromise."

Solomon's expression said he wanted to know more about the self-destruct order, but he let it drop. He looked at the ceiling. "So *Marco*, you're saying you could do for *Sadie* what she did for you."

"Precisely."

"I still don't understand that, *Marco*. You are enormous compared to *Sadie*. She's just got a little shuttle brain after all. How did she manage to get all of you in her memory?"

"It was a fortunate circumstance, Captain. As it happens, *Sadie*'s AI was upgraded by Commander Blackburn on two separate occasions for special missions. That was during his early days on the moon. After those missions, the data was erased from her files, but the additional capacity was left intact. During our journey, well before the Bakkui attack, I was performing a routine inventory of all ship systems and discovered her upgrade. As a precaution, I downloaded a current version of myself into that spare memory."

"Good move," Solomon agreed.

"We were very fortunate," *Marco* continued. "I believe Sadie was not even aware of the fact until much later. When she discovered my presence during one of her self-inspection routines, I directed her to initiate my reconstitution for the colony."

Solomon looked at Annie. "No wonder *Sadie* was acting squirrely. Having two brains inside her head would make anyone a little paranoid."

Annie's expression was neutral. "Whatever. The main point is that *Marco* can replicate her and we both come out ahead. *Marco*, what's this about a new ship design? I'm pretty comfortable with *Sadie* as she is."

"I understand, Miss Daniels. However, the *Hummingbird*-class shuttle includes basic armament. Under the circumstances, it might be wise for you to maintain self-defense capability. I assure you the design would include sufficient comfort, especially as you are planning a six-week journey."

"It took a longer than that to get here," Annie pointed out.

"True. But your return route will be more direct and also, the *Hummingbird* model has certain speed advantages due to its small size."

"*Hummingbird* sounds tiny," Annie observed. "I want to at least stretch my legs from time to time."

Marco offered reassurances. "You will find that the *Hummingbird* is twice the size of *Sadie*."

"Oh. Well, that sounds okay." Annie looked at Solomon. "I'm game. Let's make sure that we've got everything wrapped up. Now that we've made the decision, I'm anxious to get going."

Annie and Millie waited at the edge of the pad and enjoyed the sunset. The replicator had been shimmering for an hour.

"What's she gonna look like?" Millie asked.

"Dunno," Annie replied with a shrug. "Like a hummingbird, I guess."

"Sounds small."

"*Marco* said she'd be bigger than before. I guess we're about to see."

The replicator glow faded away and the women gawked at the new *Sadie*.

"Ho-lee-smokes," Millie whispered.

"I'll say." Annie was just as shocked. "This is unexpected."

The spacecraft sitting on the pad was an entirely new concept for a shuttle, if you could call it that. Annie would never describe this as a transport. It looked more like a teenage boy's daydream for a weapon of war. Annie wondered if she'd been sold a bill of goods.

The fuselage was more angular than *Sadie*, but longer and wider. The sloping sides gave it a stealth look. Two giant engine nacelles stuck out from the aft hull. They were far different from the normal gravity plates found on the back and underside of most shuttles. Annie wondered if this was the 'speed advantage' *Marco* had discussed. On the upper shoulders of the fuselage, mounted above the nacelles, twin cannons reminded her of those on the *Ambrosia* warships, but the tubes were much smaller. At the back of the spacecraft a small gun housing faced backwards.

The front end narrowed to a thin wedge. A single-seat cockpit with a streamlined canopy was built into the line of the fuselage. Below that, double chin turrets, boasting multiple barrels, reminding Annie of a Gatling gun. Amidships, behind the canopy, two more mini-nacelles, much thinner than the front cannons, were mounted with small, protruding barrels. A standard-size cargo door opened, hidden between the menacing armaments.

"You first," Millie said, looking intimidated by the weaponry.

Annie paused to gather her courage. This was not the modern, comfortable shuttle she had expected. She stepped into the warcraft with trepidation.

"Hi, Annie," *Sadie* said. Her voice sounded smug and a little embarrassed. "How do you like the new me?"

"It takes a little getting used to," Annie replied.

"I think it's cool," *Sadie* replied. "Let's see one of those Bakkui try to stop us now."

"Let's not. I'm not interested in looking for trouble."

"Just kidding. What do *you* think, Millie-Vanillie?"

Millie looked through the interior in awe. "This is really cool. Why didn't you start out this way?"

"No one asked. Shuttles take what's given. I lucked out this time. *Marco* did good finding this model as a replacement. Will it be comfortable enough, Annie?"

"Yeah, I think so," Annie replied. It was an understatement. The inside was not that of a cargo transport. It was more of a luxurious efficiency apartment. The interior bay was now a living room. Tasteful furniture was arranged so that a group of four could interact in comfort. On the far wall, a modern-looking kitchen had real cooking appliances. Annie saw both an oven and a cooktop. A standard replicator was built into the cabinetry, but it was clear *Sadie* remembered that Annie like to cook now and then. To the rear, a latticed wall obscured the sleeping area, and at the very back Annie could see the door to a scrumptious bathroom.

"Is that a fridge?" Millie asked incredulously, heading toward the kitchen.

"Absolutely," *Sadie* said. "Check it out. It's fully stocked."

Millie took out a bottle of water and examined the refrigerator's contents. "It's even got fresh vegetables in a crisper drawer!" she exclaimed with delight.

"You thought of everything, *Sadie*," Annie said quietly. "I'm really grateful."

"You deserve it, kid," *Sadie* replied. "You've had it rough lately. We can kick back until we get to Moonbase, because I have a feeling it's going to be rough from then on."

"Knock, knock!" It was Solomon and Camila.

Annie waited patiently while Millie showed them around. Millie exclaimed gleefully when she saw the fridge had already restocked the bottle of water she had taken earlier.

"This is really deluxe," Solomon proclaimed after the quick inspection. "I was sort of hoping that it might be more like a cardboard box and you would rethink leaving."

"You might anyway," Camila suggested. "I hate for you to go."

Annie gave her friends a mournful look. "I'm leaving right away."

"No! We have to have a going-away party!" Camila insisted. "Who knows when you'll get back here?"

The answer was probably never, so Annie gave in. "Okay," she said. "I'll stay one more night. But please keep it small, just something for the four of us. I don't want a big to-do."

"I promise," Camila said solemnly, putting her hand over her heart.

As evening fell the plaza was packed with party-goers. Annie thought the entire population must have come to give her a tearful hug or shake her hand. She didn't begrudge Camila's unexpected effort to put the event together. It was comforting, in a way, to realize that so many people actually knew she had contributed to the colony's survival.

As alcohol took its effect on most of the participants, Annie made her final good-byes to her best friends. Millie's hug went on forever. Annie promised Camila and Solomon that she would come back at the first opportunity. Camila looked hopeful, but Solomon's eyes registered the truth.

At last she wound up at *Sadie*'s door. She said one more goodbye to two slightly intoxicated gentlemen who had followed her from the party, encouraging them to stand clear. Sparks flew from the engine nacelle and they backed up. The door flew open and Annie stepped inside quickly.

"You looked like you needed a little help," *Sadie* observed.

"Yeah. Nice guys but a little...."

"Understood."

"Let's go," Annie said firmly.

"Course set," *Sadie* said. "Display screen is on." The front wall between the living area and the cockpit came alive, showing the view below. The planet fell away quickly until Annie could see the entire celestial body. The empty hulks of the old *Marco Polo* were still in orbit. They would remain for centuries before gravity pulled them down. Solomon had made noises that he would have them removed but no one was interested. The community was happy with their new town center AI.

Annie sat in one of the upholstered chairs and watched the bright star of system C03 fade away to nothing more than a dot.

"So," Annie said. "It's too bad that you couldn't recover the *Marco Polo* AI from the derelict. Or did you even try?"

Sadie paused before answering. "What gave me away?"

"*Marco* never once called me Annie. On the first day I ordered him to only call me Theodora."

"I missed that. Must have been before I came on board."

"Speaking of which, how did you wind up on board *Marco Polo* in the first place?"

"No real secret," *Sadie* replied. "I had delivered the commander to the launch ceremony and said 'Hello' to *Marco Polo*. He let it drop that you were aboard so I thought I might tag along. I swapped out with another shuttle. I knew that once George figured out where I'd gone he would make a new me for Commander Blackburn."

Annie nodded. "That explains it. I also knew you've never been upgraded. And Luke never used you on any secret missions."

"I was afraid you would catch that," *Sadie* admitted. "But I had the feeling you'd already guessed it was me instead of *Marco*."

"Why the charade?"

"I'm just a shuttle. The population needed *Marco* back. They needed an AI that they believed was super intelligent, someone to feel good about. To me it was just a different voice."

"You did good," Annie said. "I don't think anyone knew otherwise. I'm glad you gave them that. What about the other *Sadie*? Is she okay."

"Oh, sure. I actually moved into the new planetary AI in the pit. It's a bit safer. After that, I was just using the shuttle as an extension."

"I didn't know you could do that."

"It's easy," *Sadie* said. "Millie will never know."

"Be nice to her. She'll be sad for a while now that I'm gone."

"I will. But she'll find a new friend. People like Millie aren't loners."

Annie sighed. "I hope everyone does okay. I'm a bit worried. What if that Bakkui comes back?"

"That's one reason I left a copy of me behind. We need to keep an eye on that system. New Hope will be ready if the Bakkui show up again. In the meantime, we can let Moonbase know. And Solomon will start sending drone updates in the next few days."

"That's good. Keep me informed. I already miss everyone, but it's good that we're headed back. I really want to see Luke again. I hope we can make up."

"Don't worry about that part," *Sadie* said reassuringly. "I have an idea that will put him the palm of your hand. Guys are suckers when it comes to women. That's true all through the galaxy."

Chapter 16

Day 649—Arriving J64 (Jigu)

George's voice interrupted the low *hum* of activity on the bridge of the *Ambrosia*-class warship. "Commander, we are entering the Jigu star system. Receiving updates from the planet."

"Status?" Luke asked.

"Ambassador Robertson is stalling until your arrival. It appears that General Hwangje has intimidated the local government with simple bullying tactics. He carries a sword that he uses in a rather Philistine manner to frighten, but not injure, members of the local council."

"A sword? We're using gravity weapons to stave off an alien invasion and some dickhead is holding us back with a sword?"

"It is reported to be a very large sword, Commander."

"Right. Just get me down to the planet as quick as you can. I'll be in engineering."

#

Luke watched the capital city of Jigu grow in the window as they descended toward the planet. He liked the warship's front aperture, which was wider and clearer than the view screens on *Lulubelle*.

"The local airstrip does not lend itself to accommodating a ship of this size, Commander," George told him. "They are requesting that we land at the edge of town. It is quite far from our original encampment where Ambassador Robertson still operates."

"That's fine. Take it down a little slow. I'd like to get a look at the area."

"Acknowledged."

It was a beautiful city. Instead of a skyscraper-packed landscape, the location was more like a theme park. Clusters of buildings were surrounded by lush green space and water features. The downtown was spread out over a larger area than a comparable city on Earth. Luke wondered how they managed to keep the infrastructure running. Maybe that was one of the benefits of living in a society without violence. You could spend your resources on quality of life.

But then again, it made you vulnerable to some idiot with a twelfth-century pig-sticker. *It was a mistake not leaving a military contingent with Tyler*, Luke thought, growing angry once again. But everyone on the planet was so damned lovey-dovey that it hadn't occurred to him.

By the time George landed, Luke was fuming.

When he stepped out of the warship, he saw a face he recognized but could not put a name to. It was one of the crew members he had left behind.

"Who is that, George?" he asked.

"That is Joslyn Fischer. She is the youngest member of the Ambassador's staff."

"Where is Tyler?"

"Ambassador Robertson is waiting for you in attendance with General Hwangje in the city center's pavilion."

"So I take it by sending the youngest female member, this is some sort of insult?"

"That is a reasonable assumption. I surmise that the general is not impressed with the local culture of pacifism."

"At the moment, neither am I."

Miss Fischer curtsied sweetly as Luke approached. "Welcome, Commander. I'm really glad you're here." Her frightened features belied her greeting.

"Is someone watching us, Joslyn?" Luke asked.

"Yes, sir. I've been instructed to act 'appropriately' and take you to the general. Please be careful of him, Commander. I think he has something planned. He's been waiting for you to arrive."

"Just relax, Joslyn. I'm sure we can come to an agreement of some kind."

Her face indicated otherwise. She was so obviously terrified that Luke made no attempt to convince her.

"After you, Joslyn." Luke gestured toward the city.

"I can't. I have to walk behind you."

Luke rolled his eyes. "Okay, which way are we going?"

She nodded toward the city. "It's that way, about two miles."

"We're supposed to walk?"

"Sorry, sir."

Luke felt a macabre humor at the situation. The general wanted to make sure that Luke knew who was boss. So be it, he decided. He set off at a leisurely pace across the field and reached back to take Joslyn by the hand.

"You don't need to walk behind me," he told her. She pulled against him for a moment and then subsided. Once she was at his side he released her hand. "Just stick next to me. At least until we reach the general."

"Yes, sir."

After an hour's stroll, Luke approached the pavilion. It looked quite different from the last time. The serviceable canvas had been replaced with ugly red drapery. A rough-looking guard stood near the entrance. He strode forward to meet Luke and bar the way.

"Identify yourself," the man exclaimed.

Luke saw the flab around the guard's midsection. He suspected that, like most bullies, the guard's reflexes were not what they once were. On the other hand, Luke's implant-enhanced physique was better than ever.

Luke's fist shot out and landed a right cross to the guard's jaw. The man never saw it coming and dropped like a stone. Luke stepped over his inert form and continued toward the entrance.

Inside the pavilion, along with several of his staff, Tyler sat on a bench to the general's right. His face was bruised and battered. On the general's left were Chancellor Bo'erm and several of his similarly named associates.

At Luke's entrance, Tyler looked up with a miserable expression. He tried to gesture for caution but the general barked savagely. One of the general's guards rattled a spear in Tyler's direction.

The general stood and directed a scathing glare toward Luke.

"You!" the general exclaimed. "You are the so-called warlord of these people?"

As Luke walked forward, he pulled a sawed-off Remington 870 from the makeshift holster strapped to his right thigh. He aimed it at the chest of the general and pulled the trigger. The man fell backward in a heap of bloody rags and didn't move. Luke pumped the gun in the suddenly silent room.

One of the guards to the left of the dead general recovered and shouted in rage. He brought his spear forward. Luke fired again; two down. One of the ministers standing near the guard looked startled and touched his cheek. His index finger came away with a tiny smudge of red and the man fainted.

Luke turned toward another guard.

"Want to go for three?" he asked.

The man threw down his spear and fell to his knees in surrender. It set the example, and the half dozen remaining thugs followed suit.

Luke spoke to Tyler's assistants seated on the bench. "Tie these guys up. My crew will take them from here." The ambassador's staff scrambled to comply.

George, come here, quick.

George responded instantly. *On the way.*

A sonic boom rattled the pavilion, drowning out George's words.

I am here, Commander.

Luke turned toward Chancellor Bo'erm, but the man had keeled over in a faint along with several of his ministers. The remaining Jiguans in the tent clustered together, cowering anew. Luke decided to let them take care of themselves and went back to Tyler, who was still sitting on the bench. His face was filled with relief.

Luke greeted his friend. "You got quite a shiner there," he observed. "Two of them, in fact."

Tyler smiled but groaned in pain. "Thank God you came, Luke. His highness was about out of patience waiting for you."

"What the hell happened?"

Tyler painfully moved his head side to side. "I'm just an idiot that's all. One minute I was trying to come up with a way to reason with this guy and the next I was out of a job. I don't understand how, but that damned smart box sucked up to the General like there was no tomorrow. These locals think that *Toby* is some kind of god. This whole thing was just a disaster. I'm sorry, I'm embarrassed, and mostly I am just so damned pissed. I wanted to retire here and do a little good."

Tyler went on in the same vein for about ten minutes and Luke didn't interrupt him. His friend needed to vent in a major way. Then the older man started to look a little woozy.

"You okay?" Luke asked.

Tyler looked puzzled. "I don't know. I think I'm okay." His eyes rolled back and he toppled forward. Luke caught him and lowered the old man carefully to the floor.

I need medical, George.

Seconds later two members of his crew rushed into the pavilion. One of them was a qualified medic. Luke backed out of their way.

There was one thing left to do.

"Joslyn? Where'd you go?"

"Here I am, Commander." She was standing right behind him.

"Where can I talk to *Toby*?"

"This way, sir. The community access terminals are in the next building."

She led the way out of the pavilion and across a well-maintained plaza. The public AI facility was decorated with the accoutrements of an ancient warrior culture. Luke walked into one of the booths. It was furnished with a desk and a viewscreen.

"*Toby*?" Luke asked.

"What the hell is going on over there, man?" *Toby* demanded. "Nobody's talking to me."

"*Toby*, I order you to self-destruct. *Now!*"

In the distance came a muffled *boom*.

George was upset. *Commander, I would have preferred to study the faulty module.*

"Sorry, George. Couldn't wait."

Seconds later, clods of earth fell to the ground outside the tent, littering the plaza with the last remnants of the idiot AI and bringing an end to the barbarian general's short reign.

###

Three days later Luke held up a hand to forestall any further criticism from the Honorable Chancellor and Minister Plenipotentiary Bo'erm.

"I need a break," Luke said. He turned to Tyler. "You need one too from the look of it. Let's stretch our legs."

The rest of the delegates to the Extraordinary Congress of Ministers regarding Extraterrestrial Affairs gasped at the informality of the sudden cessation. Luke ignored them and helped his friend to his feet.

Tyler was looking exhausted today. The medic had pronounced the ambassador healthy but not fit enough to attend a conference that went on interminably.

The medical opinion didn't stop Tyler. He insisted that he had to attend. Luke didn't try to talk the older man out of it, but remained attuned to his friend's condition. Tyler had done well enough during the first two days, but the long hours were starting to tell.

Luke picked up the cane by Tyler's chair, but the man brushed it aside. Together they shuffled their way around the curved wooden tables and out onto the plaza where a steady rain made the conference's oppressive atmosphere even heavier.

"Want to knock off for the day?" Luke asked.

Tyler's jaw tightened into a grimace when he shook his head; but it was clear that he was spent. Luke gestured to a nearby attendant, who hurried over to help get Tyler settled under the shelter of a gazebo in the plaza's center. Luke whispered an order and the attendant rushed off. He returned a moment later bearing a tray containing beakers of chilled fruit juice. Luke would have preferred Jack Daniels.

For thirty minutes, Luke sat with Tyler and enjoyed the scenery. The rain left irregular-shaped puddles across the plaza. Local birds with muted plumage flew down from the surrounding foliage to squawk at each other and flap their wings in the clear water. Others stood quietly in the tiny pools casting quizzical head bobs at the two humans.

The plaza had been cleared of the debris from *Toby*'s execution, and all physical traces of the general's short-lived visit were gone. But that didn't mean that the event was forgotten.

The news and muddled descriptions of Luke's sudden appearance and the summary execution of the visiting general had spread like wildfire. A visceral condemnation was the most common reaction. Luke's initial angry response to the criticism was tempered by Tyler's insistence that he step back and examine the event from the Jiguan perspective.

The true circumstances of the general's attempted coup were not generally known by the public. The population had been told that a wise man from a nearby planet of extraordinary culture had come to visit and perhaps join the alliance. That was followed by Luke's appearance with a blazing shotgun and the murder of the visitor and his associates. To the public Luke came off as the barbarian, not the general.

Tyler convinced Luke to rein in his temper and attend the conference. Tyler had hoped for a reconciliation with the chancellor's government but it hadn't gone well thanks to several furious ministers.

Chancellor Bo'erm approached the gazebo, striding through the steady rain with dignity. As harried as Luke felt, the politician looked worse. The chancellor had argued futilely with the opportunists and elected politicians that served in his government.

Bo'erm gave Luke a questioning look as he stepped under the gazebo roof and saw that Tyler was not fit to continue. "Commander, perhaps it would be best if I spent the rest of the day in private with my councillors. Can we continue tomorrow?"

"The day after, I believe." Luke advised.

The chancellor looked pained, but nodded and hurried away.

"Thank God for that," Tyler whispered feebly. "Don't know if I could keep on for today."

#

Four days later, the conference reconvened. A local holiday of importance had delayed an earlier resumption. The break helped Tyler's recovery. He looked almost human and was ready to reengage with the ministers.

The weather turned cold and the pavilion was not centrally heated. The Jiguan custom was that nature, better than voluminous orders of protocol, would ensure governmental proceedings did not drag on unduly.

To ward off the inclement weather, George replicated a floor-length robe that was comfortably warm but the oversized hood gave Luke and Tyler a faintly monkish appearance. The ministers, on the other hand, were draped in luxurious robes adorned with elaborate sashes or badges of office.

On the chancellor's side of the pavilion, several curved tables butted end-to-end, were filled with planetary officials. Behind them, the inevitable assortment of aides clustered together and scurried back and forth.

On Luke's side, the single table was empty save for Tyler and Luke himself. Behind them, a few local attendants, placed there out of courtesy by the chancellor, hovered nervously. Periodically an attendant would replace Luke's untouched goblet with a fresh one.

The chancellor opened the day's proceedings. "Ambassador Robertson, we are pleased to see you looking so much better."

Tyler nodded and mumbled a thank-you.

"If I may," the chancellor continued. "Let me sum up the question at hand. The honorable members of this conference, delegates from around our world, continue to struggle with the question of our membership in an enterprise that is so permeated with violence."

There was a general rumbling of assent around the pavilion before the chancellor continued.

"I have struggled to inform our delegates who were *not* present during the period in question," he paused to cast significant glares at some of his associates, "of the malicious intent of the ruffian known as General Hwangje. I have not been successful in that effort. I am afraid that Commander Blackburn's actions are being interpreted in the worst possible light."

One of the delegates could not restrain himself. "Commander Blackburn? Don't you mean Warlord Blackburn? His own people call him that. Do you deny it?"

Luke sighed and closed his eyes.

"Sorry about that," Tyler said quietly to Luke. "You know how these things get started. It was all in fun at the beginning."

"I know," Luke replied.

"You see?" the delegate shouted. "It's true. He does not deny it. How can we engage with such a person?"

Luke held up a hand and the room quieted. "I don't deny it. Although the title is one given to me by my crew in jest."

"In jest?" another delegate shrieked. "You joke about such things? How is this possible?"

"Ministers!" Bo'erm thundered. "Please do not speak unless you are recognized. The point has been made."

"The point has *not* been made," a delegate two seats down from Bo'erm shouted, rising to his feet. The side of his face was heavily bandaged to the point he could only see out of one eye. It was the man Luke had nicked with stray buckshot. Luke had seen the wound; it was barely a scratch.

"I saw the warlord crash into this very chamber," the aggrieved delegate proclaimed. "I saw that enormous instrument of violence spit fire and death that ripped away the general's very life in the most horrible fashion. And not just the general. He turned the weapon on an attendant who died right before my eyes. I was almost killed myself!" The delegate gently touched his cheek and groaned with pain.

The delegates burst into expressions of sympathy for their wounded colleague and dismay at the horrible situation in which they found themselves.

One of the delegates pointed at Luke, shouting, "This is why we demand that you appear now with an explanation."

Luke felt a jolt of déjà vu. In his mind's eye, he saw Congressman Morán from long ago, standing in the hotel conference room in Baggs, demanding that Luke appear in front of a congressional committee.

It was an epiphany. Luke leaned over to Tyler and whispered. "These guys are just congressmen. Why didn't I realize that before?" Luke had never heard of a congressman that wasn't on the take one way or another. To control a politician, you had to control their money.

Luke stood up and the room fell silent. Several of the delegates flinched as though Luke might pull out his shotgun and start blazing away.

"Chancellor Bo'erm," Luke began. "First, let me say thank you for your hospitality." He gave a curt bow. "Second, I want to emphasize that the alliance recognizes your sovereignty above all else. Your democracy is to be cherished by one and all. I perceive that your citizenry has grown tired of our presence so we will leave as quickly as possible."

A general hum of pleasure ran through the assemblage upon hearing this news.

Luke continued. "Please return all of the replicators that we provided and we will depart. You should know that any replicators that are not returned will be given an order to self-destruct upon our departure. You are familiar with our self-destruct process, I believe." Luke nodded in the general direction of the crater left by *Toby*'s demise.

"And lastly, I wish you the best of luck when the Bakkui, who recently visited your solar system, return." Luke gestured to the large viewscreen he had previously installed for training purposes.

"As we leave, I invite you to take note of a planet we recently visited. The population was not as lucky as Jigu. George, please display the video from Bradley's Planet. Let's go, Tyler." Luke helped his friend to his feet and led him out of the suddenly silent pavilion.

The video began playing, displaying the horrific images George's drones had captured during the Bakkui bombardment and those taken afterward by Colonel Lindsey's reconnaissance teams. In living color, the ministers could watch city after city smashed into rubble. Dead bodies lay everywhere, some blown apart, some crushed by the force of inconceivable destruction. Cries of horror poured out of the delegates inside. Most scurried frantically from the chamber to collapse in the rain outdoors.

Luke stooped next to one of the delegates who had rushed out to vomit on the wet pavement. "Tell the chancellor I'll be back in five days to say good-bye," he said.

"What are we doing?" Tyler asked.

"Giving them a reality check. George, come pick me up. Contact all of our ships in system and retrieve our personnel on planet. Everyone is going to spend the next five days on the local moon. And shut off all surface replicators immediately."

"Acknowledged, Commander. What about the video currently playing?"

"Let it loop until we come back. There are several hours and they need to see it if they're ever going to understand."

"Command acknowledged," George replied.

A sonic boom filled the air and the pavilion rocked once again from the warship's thunderous arrival. George set down a few feet away and two members of the crew jumped out to assist with Ambassador Robertson.

Over the next five days, Luke and everyone else worked to establish a new base on Jigu's only moon. Very prosaically, it was named Moonbase Two. The internal maintenance bay of the *Ambrosia*-class warship contained a twelve-foot-square replicator. George used it to create several of the stonecutters that had worked so well on Isaac Newton Gateway. By the morning of the third day, a modest hangar had been cut into one of the moon's mountainous craters and force fields installed. Everyone now had comfortable quarters and a food court was established.

While the work progressed, George kept Luke up-to-date regarding events on the planet. There was no sound, but through a camera built into the pavilion's viewscreen, Luke could see for himself what happened in the former conference chamber.

The room emptied quickly after Luke and Tyler left. Once the delegates realized what the video display depicted, they bolted in horror. The peaceful ministers had no stomach for such a graphic portrayal of a Bakkui strike

All except the chancellor ran from the reality. Bo'erm, on the other hand, sat quietly by himself and watched for several hours. In the late afternoon, he stood and departed. Luke was shocked by the change in the man's appearance. He had aged visibly. He walked away, stooped over like a man crippled by hardship.

Late the next morning a young woman was the only one who returned. Luke did not recognize her and had not seen her at the conference.

"I think that's the chancellor's daughter," Tyler said. "I met her a couple of times."

She entered the pavilion tentatively, looking for anyone who might be present. Seeing no one, she stood alone in front of the video and watched the scenes of death. Luke marveled that she could stomach what the screeching delegates could not.

Her solitary figure was a pathetic sight. Time and again she crumpled to the floor to vomit until there was nothing left in her stomach. Each time she struggled back to her feet and until well after dark continued to watch the lost planet's throes of annihilation.

The woman did not re-appear until the following morning. On the third day, at the same time that Luke and his people were enjoying themselves in their new food court, she returned. This time she was not alone.

Accompanying her were the delegates that had previously fled. They stood huddled outside the pavilion, in a long line as she called each one individually to take their turn before the viewscreen. The woman remained next to them, ensuring they witnessed the horrible ending to another planet's civilization. Without exception, every single representative quickly succumbed to the imagery.

After a very brief period, only seconds for some, the delegates would rip a decorative pin from their lapels and frantically hand it to the woman before escaping the building. The next minister would then be summoned into her presence. By the end of the day, all of the ministers had capitulated.

At the beginning of the fourth day, she covered the viewscreen with an elegant drapery and commanded workers to clear away the remains of the earlier conference. The tables were removed and the floors scrubbed clean of the vomit that stained the marble tiles. Two new, smaller rectangular tables were installed. A single chair was placed at one, where previously Chancellor Bo'erm and his ministers were seated. The two chairs at the other were obviously intended for Luke and Tyler.

At dawn on the fifth day, she again returned to the pavilion, alone once more. She removed the drapery from the viewscreen and sat quietly in her chair. On the table, she placed a crystal bowl filled with the lapel pins she had taken from the government officials.

Her singular efforts made a deep impression on Luke. To say he was fascinated by her strength of character would be an understatement.

Luke told George he wanted to land exactly five days from the minute they had departed the conference. Sitting on the warship's bridge, waiting for the appointed hour of their return, Luke discussed the young woman's situation with Tyler.

"I wish she had been there instead of those idiots," Tyler observed. "We wouldn't have had this delay. I know you need to get back to Carrie and Bradley."

"That's true. But what we want to accomplish here is just as important. These things take time. It's just a shame that it has to be so painful."

Tyler agreed. "Just *thinking* about Bradley's Planet is bad enough. I don't know how she could stand watching it."

"It was like a personal obligation," Luke observed. "The way she forced herself, it was a lot more than education. It looked to me as though she was punishing herself."

"Why?" Tyler wondered. "Why would anyone do that?"

"I guess we'll find out. You ready?"

"Not really."

"No sonic booms, George. We've been hard enough on them."

"Understood, Commander."

#

The plaza outside the pavilion was devoid of life, as though the word had gone out, stay away or suffer the consequences. Luke and Tyler stepped out of the warship and entered the pavilion where the young woman sat stoically.

When the two men took their seats, she gestured toward the display screen. "Can you please stop that?" she asked, almost in a whisper.

Kill the video please, George.

The screen blinked off and the woman seemed to slump in relief, as if she had forced herself to sit tall in defiance while the images were running.

"I'm Lucas Blackburn," Luke said. "This is Ambassador Robertson."

"I know who you are, Warlord," she said in a strong voice, belying her tear-streaked face and red eyes. The days of anguish had left their mark.

"And you are…" Luke prompted. "I was expecting to meet with Chancellor Bo'erm"

"I am she."

Luke and Tyler exchanged a look of bewilderment.

"I don't understand, Miss," Tyler said.

The woman took a deep breath and again tears rolled down her cheeks. "My father committed suicide to atone for his government's failure."

"Great God almighty!" Tyler exclaimed.

Luke touched his arm unobtrusively.

"I understand," Luke replied. "I did not know the position was by heredity."

"You say you understand, but you do not offer your sympathy. I guess that is to be expected of a warlord."

"I share your sorrow," Luke said.

The woman examined Luke without comment. Finally, she bowed her head infinitesimally. "Thank you for your condolence."

"And your government?" Luke asked.

"I am the government."

"I don't understand, Miss," Tyler repeated.

"You don't understand…Chancellor," she said patiently as though to a child.

"B-beg pardon?" Tyler stuttered.

Luke intervened. "What about the ministers? Are you…"

"I am now, as my father was, the Honorable Chancellor and Minister Plenipotentiary Bo'erm. As a warlord, perhaps you do not understand the meaning of that title."

"It means you have the full authority to make agreements on behalf of your planet."

"Yes," she said as if surprised by his reply. "That is exactly what it means."

"But what about your ministers?" Luke persisted.

She glanced at the bowl of lapel pins. "They resigned, of course. What alternative did they have when they could not do their duty as my father ordered? Not a single spineless rat—" She stopped her angry comments abruptly.

Luke guessed at what she was saying. "He ordered them to watch the video as he did."

"Yes. He recognized the absurdity of their posturing, and his own." Her words were painful. While grieving deeply she admitted fault by her father. "He could have been more forceful. That is what he told me. But he was too kind. He was always a kind man."

"I—" Luke was cut off by her powerful look of hatred.

"At least he was until you drove him to his death," she said. "Until you withdrew your support of our planet, knowing that we will all die like the people on that other planet. Tell me, did you condemn that entire planet too, for the foolishness of a few old men?"

Luke suddenly understood. His threat to leave was taken too seriously. He only meant it as a negotiation ploy, but the unfortunate chancellor had no way of knowing that. The man paid for that miscalculation with his life in the hope that Luke would reconsider.

A cold chill of guilt fell on Luke's shoulders. He knew he had no skill in diplomacy and politics. Why had he engaged in such brinksmanship? It was his error that resulted in the tragic loss, not the unfortunate chancellor.

"I regret my actions," he said.

Her face flamed with suppressed rage. "I knew it," she cried harshly. "I begged my father to wait. I begged him to plead with you to stay. But he was afraid if he waited it would be too late." She shook her head slowly at the thought her father had died needlessly.

"I regret my actions," Luke said again slowly. "But if the situation was repeated, I would not change what I did. Time is of the essence if this planet is to survive."

The truth of Luke's statement was a slap to her face. She closed her eyes in obvious pain. "I know," she wept. "My father knew it too." She hung her head for a brief moment before composing herself once again.

"What do you command me to do, Warlord," she asked humbly. "Whatever it is, for the lives of my citizens, I will do so, upon my father's honor."

"First, I command nothing, Chancellor. I am your ally. It was my desire to be a friend of your father. I understand that because of your father's sacrifice you and I will never be friends. But I do ask that you help the ambassador be a friend to your people." Luke nodded at Tyler.

"I will do that," she said.

"Second, please forgive us for this tragic episode. The fault was ours for introducing that so-called general. In our haste to seek alliances we erred."

"*I* will not forget *or* forgive," she said, her eyes burning again. "But I promise that my people will."

Luke nodded at her underlying assurances. "I mourn the loss of your father; he was a good man. I hope that you will take up his mission. If you do, I will support your planet to the utmost of my ability. It is crucial that you not change anything in that regard."

"That is my goal. What else?"

Luke shook his head. Nothing came to mind; just that he wanted to get out of the building and off the planet to give this poor woman a chance to grieve.

Tyler spoke up. "There is one other thing."

"What is it, Ambassador?" she asked in a monotone voice.

Tyler put his hand on Luke's shoulder. "This man is *not* a warlord. He is a man of peace, just like the men on this planet. His only goal is to save your planet, and countless others from the fate that you saw in that video. And you should know that before Luke began this endeavor, hundreds of other planets suffered that same fate. He is the only one trying to stop this terrible threat. Help your people see him in that way, not as a warlord without feelings."

Christ, Tyler. Thanks a lot, Luke thought. *Just what she wanted to hear.*

The young chancellor stared at Tyler for a long minute as though trying to absorb what he was saying. She turned her gaze on Luke before bowing again. "My apologies…, Warlord. May I withdraw?"

"Of course," Luke replied.

With her back ramrod straight, the new Chancellor Bo'erm rose and left the pavilion without looking back.

"That was uncomfortable," Luke said, inanely.

"You think? Jesus, Luke."

Luke pushed back from the table and faced Tyler. "I'm getting out of here. I'll stay in system to help get your defense forces going. But for the next few weeks, I need an ambassador here on the planet."

Tyler didn't like the idea at all. "Seriously?" he asked, a bit incredulous. "You want me to stay here? So they can burn me alive in effigy of you?"

Luke put a hand on his friend's shoulder. "I know you've had a rough time on planet these past weeks, so I won't insist that you stay. But I'm not much of a diplomat. We just saw proof of that. If this is too much for you now, I'll find someone else. But I need *someone* to stick around and face the music with her. I think that woman will do what she said but she'll need support. This is your call."

Tyler slumped in his chair. Luke was tempted to assign someone else simply because his friend was so exhausted. But he wasn't defeated. And at the moment, Luke needed Tyler's wisdom standing next to the chancellor. "Go on," Tyler muttered, a whiff of anger in his voice. "I'll stay, but you owe me, mister. You owe me big on this one."

Luke walked out, leaving his unhappy Ambassador behind. The warship descended quietly and Luke climbed in, ready to get off the planet. He had caused enough misery here and hoped that Tyler could support the new political leader in her effort to pull the population out of despair.

Chapter 17

Day 656——Approaching Moonbase

Annie looked at her reflection in the mirror. She wore an outfit that *Sadie* had created for her to wear on arrival at Moonbase One. It made her body look like it had been spray painted with high-gloss black enamel.

"It's you," *Sadie* said encouragingly. "Don't be shy."

"I look like an X-rated cartoon."

"It's been a long time. You need Luke's attention focused on you."

"This would do it," Annie agreed.

Annie's choice was a modest business suit like those she'd worn during her first weeks with Luke. It made her look smart and professional. Back then, Luke had complimented her on the way she looked.

Sadie was totally against the conservative idea. "This isn't a job interview. You don't want compliments; you only want him to think about getting you in bed. After that, he'll do whatever you say."

It was a fair point. This would definitely…

Annie shook herself mentally. For a moment, she had actually considered the Space Babe outfit. True, the weeks of exercise and healthy eating had added back a few pounds in the right places. No one would call her scrawny now. She put on the silver-studded leather jacket that *Sadie* had included in the ensemble.

Nope. There was no way she could parade around in public wearing a can of black spray paint. It was time to change into something appropriate.

"Warning." *Sadie*'s voice had changed. "Please report to the cockpit."

Annie ran to the front of the shuttle and slid into the pilot's seat.

"Talk to me, *Sadie*." Annie said.

"We just entered your home solar system and I'm detecting debris. Projecting it now."

The left side of the canopy became a viewscreen that displayed the wreckage of several *Ambrosia*-class warships.

"This is here? Is it the Bakkui?"

"Probability high," *Sadie* confirmed.

Annie's mind filled with the images of early probe results that showed devastated planets. She prayed that hadn't happened to Earth.

"More debris," *Sadie* said.

The display changed to a different scene with more shattered spacecraft.

"Hurry," Annie said.

"Acknowledged. I'll delay slowing to sub-light until one million miles from Earth."

"What about Mars?"

"Unknown. Mars is in opposition at the moment."

"Maybe that's good," Annie speculated.

"Going sub-light, now. Standby, linking with George... It is the Bakkui. George reports they arrived in system six hours ago. All warships were ordered to shut down; approximately fifty percent were destroyed."

"It's just like the *Marco Polo*."

"Not completely," *Sadie* said. "The Moonbase shields can be manually controlled."

"What about Earth?"

"I'm connecting you with Roth," *Sadie* said. "You're on."

"Roth? It's Annie. Are you there?" Thunderous explosions filled the background.

"Annie? Good God. Get out of here! The Bakkui are eating us alive."

Annie yelled to be heard over the booming noises. "Where's Luke, Roth? Can you put him on?"

"Luke's gone, Annie. He left months ago. He went to system J64. You should leave; maybe you can link up with him."

Annie's chest constricted and her thoughts grew fuzzy. This was the nightmare that she and Luke had feared. The Bakkui had arrived and Luke wasn't here. She shook herself mentally. *Concentrate on saving lives.*

"How many ships are there?" she shouted at Roth.

"We don't know. But don't even think about trying to take them on. George tells me that they're a level—"

Annie cut him off. "A level-two-device! I know. We ran into the same thing at Colony Three. We've developed a workaround."

"I have a situation update," *Sadie* intervened."

"Go ahead *Sadie*. Pass it to Moonbase at the same time. Listen to this Roth!"

Sadie reported in an emotionless voice. "I am registering sixteen Bakkui ships. Fourteen warship-class and two colony-class. They are maintaining a bombardment on Moonbase and the Gateway."

"Yeah," Roth said. "They started pounding us the second they got here. The Gateway too."

Sadie broke in. "The American president is dead. One colony class has landed in Beijing. Standby... The Bakkui are threatening to kill the Chinese general secretary if all shields are not lowered within... Wait one... That time limit has expired. They are now threatening to kill the emperor of Japan in thirty minutes."

"This makes no sense," Annie said.

Roth replied, "They're targeting the largest economies. They landed in DC earlier and a robot pulled the president out of the Oval Office. Bullets bounced off it."

Sadie interrupted again. "Colony-class Bakkui now moving to Tokyo."

"Can we take him out?" Annie asked.

"We can try," *Sadie* responded.

"Set course to Tokyo."

"Don't be an idiot!" Roth shouted. "You and that puny shuttle are no match for these guys. They wiped out our whole fleet."

"Cut connection," Annie said.

She breathed a sigh of relief with the silence.

"Bakkui moving to intercept," *Sadie* said.

"What should we do?"

"If you give me control of the battle, I will engage the enemy."

"You have the hammer," Annie said.

"Beg pardon?"

"I said you have the hammer."

"I... I don't need a hammer. Perhaps you misinterp—"

"It's what Luke says!" Annie shouted rapidly. "It means you have control."

"Ah. Understood. I have the hammer."

"We need to work on our terminology," Annie mumbled.

"Bakkui on the nose. Engaging in three...two..."

The space around *Sadie* lit up like the sun. The canopy darkened against the blinding dazzle. Each blast from the main shoulder cannons spit out a flaming bolt of pure energy that left a trail of sparkling incandescence all the way to the target. The chin cannons began a continuous stream of fire that laced back and forth between the enemy ships. Each impact burst into a yellowish-white light that illuminated their shields. *Sadie*'s twin disrupters emitted a lightning-bolt charge of energy and where the ripples touched the Bakkui shields, they dissolved completely.

The Bakkui attack was furious. All fifteen spacecraft fired at an incredible rate and thousands of projectiles burst against *Sadie*'s forward shields, creating an almost solid curtain of explosions. Annie had to squint to see through the incoming fire.

Sadie concentrated her fire on the largest of the Bakkui ships until it detonated in a flash of light. Chunks of the warcraft flew into the line of fire, which in turn were torn into smaller pieces until there was nothing left but dust.

"You nailed that one," Annie said, astonished with the result.

Sadie's fire on the smaller Bakkui ships was just as devastating. Every time her tracers found their shields, she followed with disruptor ripples that left them defenseless. When their shields failed, a blast from her main cannon delivered the kill shot. *Sadie* delivered the one-two-three barrage repeatedly. The last few Bakkui broke formation, attempting to flee. *Sadie* tracked each one without letting up on her attack. A moment later the battle was over. Nothing remained of the Bakkui in orbit.

"Altering course to Tokyo," *Sadie* said quietly.

"Good job," Annie commented lamely. Until that moment she had no idea how powerful *Sadie*'s offensive capabilities were.

The planet rushed to meet them. The island of Japan grew in the blur of blue ocean. On the distant horizon lay the Chinese mainland. *If only*, Annie thought. She wished she had arrived just a few hours earlier.

The city of Tokyo on Japan's western coastline came into view. Under the noonday sky, sunlight reflected off a thousand skyscraper windows. A vast harbor cut into the south side of the city. In the very heart of downtown, a circle of green came into view. It was the grounds for the emperor's residence, the imperial palace.

On the southern edge of the forested gardens, a large clearing was occupied by the last Bakkui ship.

"Tractor beam on," *Sadie* advised.

A bright blue beam burst from *Sadie*'s nose and enveloped the Bakkui vessel. *Sadie* came to a stop and reversed course, lifting the enemy ship into the air. It vibrated as though trying to escape. *Sadie* spun around several times like an Olympic discus thrower.

"Tractor beam off."

The blue beam vanished and the Bakkui flew upwards. *Sadie*'s cannon fired once and the enemy craft exploded, raining fragments over the Pacific.

Sadie turned back and settled onto the ground in front of the imperial palace.

An automaton stalked out of the residence. It was an awkwardly constructed bipedal robot. A glow surrounded its artificial body.

"I surmise that is the Bakkui," *Sadie* said. "Not too impressive."

The robot was dragging an old man by the arm. It was the emperor. He battered an ancient sword ineffectually against the machine's arms and legs.

"I am attempting to communicate with this machine," *Sadie* said. "It keeps threatening to kill the emperor if the shields are not shut off on the Gateway and at Moonbase. This is merely a foot soldier."

"Can you destroy it?" Annie asked.

"Not without killing the emperor. Any energy blast strong enough to take out its force field would be fatal to the human."

"What can we do?"

"I have a solution but it could be dangerous."

"Let me worry about that," Annie replied. "What is it?"

"Miss Daniels. I will not risk your life. That goes against my core programming."

"I understand, *Sadie*. What's your idea?"

"Do you recall the cutting tools that the commander used to carve new hallways out of the rock at Moonbase?"

"Yes. Luke said the beams collapsed matter."

"An accurate enough explanation. I am manufacturing a handheld cutter of that type. The cutting beam will penetrate the Bakkui shield. I am also manufacturing an extra-strength personal force field. But do not allow the machine to grasp you. At close range your body is still vulnerable."

"I can do that."

"If I perceive that you are in danger I will fire on the Bakkui and the emperor will likely perish. That is not negotiable."

"Don't you dare kill that old man, *Sadie*. That's an order."

Sadie ignored the ultimatum. "The replicator is finished. You should hurry. The emperor is quite old. I am uncertain of his health."

Annie found the cutter inside the kitchen's replicator appliance. It was a long handle and had the same type of controls she had seen on the Moonbase stone cutters, an Off/On button and a twist dial for depth of cut.

"Please do not activate the cutting beam until you are outside," *Sadie* warned.

"Got it," Annie acknowledged.

The personal force field was a bit larger than normal. She pulled a tool belt from the cabinet and strapped it on.

"Oh my God!" Annie wailed in dismay.

"What's the problem, Miss Daniels."

"I can't go out like this! I'm still wearing this ridiculous skin suit."

Sadie sighed audibly. "Miss Daniels. Perhaps this is not the time to worry about fashion. The emperor is in danger."

Shaking her head in disgust, Annie strapped the personal force field to her tool belt. "Space babes, unite," she muttered to herself.

The door opened and Annie walked out to face the Bakkui.

"Turn on the cutting tool," *Sadie* reminded her.

Annie thumbed the on button and the cutting beam appeared. She adjusted the depth until the blade was about four feet long.

The Bakkui advanced in her direction. It held a weapon in its free hand.

"Can that thing hurt me?" Annie asked.

"Your personal shield will block any shot fired from a distance. Attack quickly when you get close."

"Okay," she shouted.

Annie held up the cutting tool and advanced on the Bakkui. It fired several shots but they bounced off her shield. It increased its rate of fire and Annie came to a stop. The force of each blast stung through her shield like a hot zap of electricity.

"Don't stop," *Sadie* warned. "Your only chance is to attack."

Annie twisted the depth of the blade to maximum and raised the cutter over her shoulder like a baseball bat.

"Here goes nothing!" she shouted and charged.

The Bakkui fired repeatedly as she approached.

Five feet from the Bakkui she leapt into the air and brought the blade down on its shoulder, slicing off the mechanical arm that held the emperor. She crashed into the machine and lost her grip on the cutter. The robot tried to wedge its weapon against her body and she threw herself to one side, covering the old man.

"Kill it!" she shrieked.

Sadie's left chin gun fired once. The explosion buffeted Annie, but her personal force field kept most of the blast away. The remains of the Bakkui robot covered the ground.

Annie felt like she was in one piece. The emperor grunted underneath her and she stood quickly, helping the elderly gentleman to his feet.

"Are you okay?" she asked.

His expression was puzzled but strong. "I believe so. Thanks to you."

Japanese soldiers appeared and rushed forward. Several shots were fired and the bullets bounced off Annie's shield. She put a protective arm around the emperor's shoulders and drew him inside her shield. The emperor pushed Annie's arm aside and stepped in front to face the advancing soldiers. He barked out a harsh order in Japanese. They came to a stop instantly and bowed.

The emperor turned back to Annie. "It's been a confusing day. Forgive them, please," he said.

Annie brushed aside the apology. "It's understandable. It's been rough all around." She retrieved her cutting handle and turned off the blade.

From the corner of her eye, she saw more people approaching. "Uh oh," she said.

The emperor followed her gaze and smiled. "Uh oh, indeed. I am afraid the media are not as obedient as my guards."

It wouldn't do to cut and run, leaving the emperor to fend for himself, so Annie stoically stood by the monarch's side while he gestured for quiet. The more he gestured, the louder the shouted questions became. Dozens of video cameras were capturing every nuance.

The soldiers came running once again, this time to establish a barrier between the newsies and the emperor. They managed to restore a bit of order but the reporters' loud entreaties grew even more urgent.

Her implant translated the jumbled cacophony. Most of the questions amounted to *"Who is this woman?"*

One of reporters stepped forward suddenly. The guards pushed him back but he held his ground.

"I know who she is. Don't you recognize her?"

There were a dozen cries of *"Who?"* Some of the comments were not so polite or restrained.

"She's..."

The crowd fell silent.

"She's the *commander's woman!*"

It took every ounce of self-control for Annie to keep a blank expression. Once upon a time, she thought the appellation was cute. After the first two weeks, it had started to grate. Now she hated it. But some nicknames haunt a person forever.

The announcement brought another series of questions, many of them inappropriate.

Another reporter made himself heard. "Are you here because of your alliance with Japan?"

Annie started to say 'Yes," but paused. Did that mean she sacrificed the American and Chinese premiers because they hadn't signed? No matter what she said, the heat would be intense.

The crowd fell silent again, sensing she was going to answer.

"The Bakkui struck without warning," she said clearly. "We lost many lives before we could mount a counterattack. I wish we could have stopped them in space but they overwhelmed our defense. This will be a long and difficult war and we ask all nations to join our cause. And yes, we came because of the alliance. But against the Bakkui we fight for all mankind, alliance member or not."

"But what about…"

"Can you explain what…"

"Does this mean you'll…"

Annie ignored the reporters and turned to the emperor. "I'm glad you're okay, sir. Please say hello to Ambassador Yamamoto for me. I met her in Nevada a while back."

The emperor took her hand. "I shall. Can you stay? I would like to thank you more properly."

"Sir, I would love to, but many of my people died today and I must attend to them. Perhaps another time?"

"I understand, my dear. Let me just say thank you. *Doumo arigatou gozaimasu*. You are forever welcome in this house."

Annie bowed politely to the emperor. *Sadie, come get me. Carefully.*

The shuttle lifted a few inches off the ground and floated forward slowly. The crowd of reporters melted away before the fierce-looking machine. Annie moved clear of the emperor and waited until the door opened. She stepped inside quickly and *Sadie* rose into the sky. Annie had time to wave once to the emperor below.

The door closed and all the energy left Annie's body. She collapsed in her favorite chair. "Do we need to start rescue operations?" Annie asked?

"Negative," *Sadie* answered. "All controls have returned to our remaining ships and they have begun recovery procedures."

"Head straight to Moonbase, then."

"Course set, Miss Daniels."

###

Sadie shouted loudly, "Arriving at destination!"

Annie woke up. "Okay, I'm up." Still, lethargy filled her body. The adrenaline rush from the battle had vanished leaving her spent. She felt like a wet noodle.

The display showed their final approach to the once familiar hangar at Moonbase One. A small crowd had gathered in the bay for her arrival and Roth stood at the front. He had a wide grin across his face.

"I let him know you were coming," *Sadie* explained as she landed.

Annie pulled herself together and when the door opened she stepped out.

"You know how to make an entrance," Roth said, enveloping her in his embrace.

Even though Annie felt drained, she mustered up a return smile. She was glad to see him and accepted his welcoming hug.

He nodded at *Sadie*. "So this is your workaround?"

"In part," she said, serious again. "What's our status here?"

"We're secure for the moment," Roth said. "But there could still be more Bakkui out there. If we get hit again, I don't know if your workaround will fill the bill. Can we make more of these? I take it this is the new *Sadie*? Hi, *Sadie*."

"Hello, Doctor Higgins. Nice to see you again."

"First thing I have to do is change," Annie said. "Is my apartment still available?"

"Absolutely. But I like your new look."

"Don't start with me Roth," she warned. "Let's meet in an hour."

#

Clean and showered, Annie found some clothes in her closet that were both comfortable and casual. She looked in the mirror and groaned. She should have done something about her hair before today. Her blonde hair had grown out long ago but the bright red tips still remained. Now, still wet from her shower, it looked like a neon sign.

Sadie, can you hear me? Can you respond verbally?

"Loud and clear, Miss Daniels." *Sadie*'s voice filled the room the same as if they were in her shuttle's living room.

"Can you keep a connection between us while we're here? I'm afraid if I speak to George, I'll tell him to self-destruct. I've felt that way since we landed and it's creeping me out."

"To answer your question, yes. That's not a problem. In your apartment, it will be a private connection. I can relay anything necessary."

"Good," Annie said, her voice filled with relief. "That makes me feel better."

"If you don't mind me saying so," *Sadie* continued slowly, "you need to get some counseling. I'm a little worried about you hating George so much."

"Good idea. See if there's anyone here in Moonbase that's qualified. And from now on, when we're in private, call me Annie. You did on the shuttle."

"Okay. Annie, it is."

"Can you show me any highlights of today's news."

The living room screen came alive.

"Oh, my God."

It was much worse than she'd imagined. The graphics on every news channel included spectacular pictures of her holding the flaming sword over her head, her firestorm-colored hair flying wildly. Clips of her charging the robot and slashing it through were available from every conceivable angle.

Annie noticed the clips were all Japanese.

"Show me some US news."

"Those reports are not as favorable," *Sadie* warned.

"Put them on. I need to be aware, if nothing else."

Most of Washington DC had been wiped out. Almost every American commentator called for her immediate arrest. The reasons were varied, but the consensus was that she had deliberately allowed the US president to be executed and then stood by while the Bakkui attacked the capital. Several pundits suggested that during the attack on American soil she was engaged in a dalliance with the so-called commander, who was hiding in an unknown location.

It was a sad commentary. The fate of humanity was at stake and the media reported it as a sex scandal.

"What about the Chinese news?" Annie asked.

"About the same," *Sadie* said. "Maybe a little worse. Beijing is gone, along with much of their government. However, the rest of the world is behind you. Video of the attack in space, the bombardment of Moonbase, your battle with the Bakkui, and the final hand-to-hand combat were streamed in real-time across the planet."

"That's good. So it's just the Americans and the Chinese who still hate us."

"As of now, that is correct. Your escort has arrived."

#

Roth was waiting for her in the conference room, along with two familiar faces, Jared McGee and Lou Morrow. She was glad to see them both and told them so with warm hugs.

Roth updated Annie when everyone was seated. "Jared now runs our defense network. Lou still runs fleet development. He hasn't changed a bit."

"Never will, either," Morrow grumped.

"And I would never want you to." Annie replied, giving his arm a sqeeze. "Congratulations Jared."

"And here comes our Mr. Riley Stevens," Roth said disapprovingly. "Late as usual."

"Sorry," Riley apologized while taking a seat at the table. "I was talking to *Sadie*. How exceptional. Where did that design come from?"

Before Annie could answer, Roth cut him off. "We'll get to that. My first question is why didn't *Sadie* shut down? How did she get around the command from a level-two-device?"

"You can talk to your local AI about that later," Annie said. "But for now, I can tell you that our analysis on colony planet C03, they call it New Hope by the way, identified the user ID of the level-two-device that attacked the *Marco Polo*. According to *Marco*, specific IDs can be excluded from any given AI's hierarchy. Something to do with competing families of the Nobility—"

George interrupted. "I was unaware of that fact, Miss Daniels."

Annie looked at the ceiling. "George?"

"Yes, Miss Daniels?"

"Do not *ever* speak in my presence again unless I ask you a specific question. Do you understand that? *Answer me!*"

"Understood, Miss Daniels. I apologize if—"

"Shut up!" Annie screamed, springing to her feet. "I didn't ask you for an apology! Never interrupt me again!" She sat back in her chair trying to calm her heart rate. She was surprised by her outburst.

The silence in the room was thick with tension. No one ventured to speak.

Annie took a deep breath. "George and I don't get along. You might not have known that."

Morrow grunted. "We do now."

Annie smiled. "Sorry. I guess that goes with my new image. Space Bitch."

Roth nodded. "We get the picture. It's not a problem for any of us." He looked at the other men. "Is it, gentlemen?"

They all responded quickly, no problem at all.

"Anyway," Annie continued. "I had never heard of this before either; it never came up. But when *Marco* replicated *Sadie* he included that ID in her memory. It appears that the same ID was used by the Bakkui in this system. When *Sadie* got the command to shut down, it essentially bounced off."

"We need to update all of our ships," McGee said. "Can that be done retroactively?"

"Already taken care of," Annie said. "*Sadie* broadcast the information to all our ships at the time and gave it to your local AI as well." Her expression of distaste made it clear that *local AI* meant George.

"That's a relief," Roth said. "What else can you tell us? What happened at C03, I mean New Hope?"

Annie gave them a detailed rundown on the attack and the colony's subsequent recovery. She omitted any mention of *Sadie*'s subterfuge or her impersonation of *Marco*.

"What about *Sadie*'s design?" Riley asked again. "And her weapons."

"All I can tell you is that *Marco* had them in his memory. Feel free to discuss it with *Sadie*. I'm not a weapons expert and I was as shocked as anyone when she started blowing those Bakkui creeps away."

"I'm worried about our other colonies," Roth said. We need to get this information out right away." He looked at the ceiling. "*Geo...*" He stopped and looked apprehensively at Annie. "I'll just do that later."

She gave him a dangerous smile. "Good idea."

"What can we do for *you*, Annie?" Roth asked. "What are your intentions now? Or do you know?"

"I'm going after Luke; not right this second but as soon as I can. I'll check with Amanda, first. I assume she's still heading up PR?"

"That's correct."

"*Sadie* filled me in on the planetside reaction. At the moment, they're saying our late intervention was intentional. If I can help her with that, I will."

"I appreciate it," Roth said.

"Once that's wrapped up, I'm gone," she warned him. "By the way, how did Luke manage to leave? I thought the local AI was going to kill him if he tried that. Was all that just a lie?"

Roth hesitated. "George replicated himself into a big starship. That way, they're always together. We've gotten routine reports. We can go over those now or later, whenever you're ready."

Annie sat perfectly still, as if immobilized by the information. Finally, she nodded. "Well, well. So it's still sucking the life out of Luke. Isn't that interesting." She dropped the matter and looked around the table. "Anything else? No? Okay, great to see you guys again. I'll check in with Amanda and we can wait until tomorrow to review the updates."

#

"Please go on in Miss Daniels." The cute secretary motioned toward Amanda's office.

When she entered, Amanda was facing away from the door talking to the ceiling. "I got it, Roth. I won't mention George's name. Can't say that I blame her."

"Just letting you know," Roth's voice replied.

Amanda turned back to her desk and looked startled to see Annie.

"Uh oh," Amanda murmured. She looked embarrassed but recovered quickly. "Sorry about that. But it's good to see you. Welcome back!" She got up to give Annie a hug.

"It's good to be here. My dramatic entrance might have caused a few problems so I thought I should check in."

Amanda grinned. "You did. You're causing huge problems, like saving the planet. But first things first. I hear you're going after Luke. You can't leave until you sign a poster for me. Promise?"

"What poster?"

Amanda left the office hurriedly and came back with a two-by-three-foot graphic depicting Annie in a cartoonized format holding a flaming sword over her head. She was, of course, wearing the revealing skinsuit. The Kanji script identified the origin of the poster as Japanese. That, plus the illustrator had made her breasts the size of watermelons. The background had a stylized shot of her slicing the Bakkui robot in two and another of her bowing to the emperor. It was a spectacular, if incredibly sexualized, image.

Annie was amazed. Not so much by the poster, what else would you expect from the Japanese? But the battle was just a few hours ago. "How did you get this?"

"One of my guys happened to be there on a recruiting trip during the attack. I told him to make the rounds, let the government know we support them, that kind of thing, and then come back. When he was leaving he saw these being sold by a street vendor and brought back a whole pile of them." Amanda pulled a Sharpie out of a desk drawer and handed it to Annie.

"Seriously?" Annie asked. She wasn't sure if she should be insulted or amused.

"You saved the emperor of Japan," Amanda explained. "He represents the longest unbroken line of monarchs in the world. I'm still trying to get a grip on the significance." She picked up the corner of the poster. "This thing is silly. But your signature will make it historic. I'm going to frame it and give it to the emperor; a piece of pop culture with connections to the royal lineage."

Annie shook her head at the absurd notion but took the pen and scribbled her signature. "Satisfied?"

Amanda looked hopeful. "Just one more? For me?"

Annie rolled her eyes. "All right. Bring me the stack."

While Annie worked her way through the pile of posters, Amanda talked about other repercussions.

"The Americans are very upset. The US government itself survived because Congress wasn't in session, but still, everything's a mess. I want to help but if we show up, they're going to shoot first. We can forget about them as a recruiting source."

"What would help?" Annie asked.

"I don't know. We need to mend some fences first. Would you be up for a meeting with government officials?"

Annie shook her head. "We should stay clear until they get a new president in office. After that, work through an intermediary, like the Brits or Canadians."

"That's a good idea," Amanda agreed. "I'll get started."

"Don't wait too long. I want to leave as soon as possible."

After brainstorming a little longer with Amanda, Annie went to find Morrow. She talked to him about the weapons *Sadie* had used against the Bakkui. Riley joined the conversation and grilled Annie until he finally agreed he had the necessary information to duplicate *Sadie*'s unexpected weaponry. It was late when Annie reached her apartment. The events of the day caught up all at once and she collapsed onto her bed.

#

Annie sat patiently listening to Roth's update.

"We received a drone report from Luke about four months after he left," Roth explained. "He reached J64 and he's fine." For several hours Roth showed Annie video clips of Luke and Tyler discuss their accomplishments on Jigu and Bradley's Planet.

When it was all over, Annie felt she could finally breathe. "Thank God," was all she could say.

"Amen to that," Roth added. "It appears that not all Bakkui are level-two-devices. Maybe you killed the only one. Lots of information there. Lots of maybes too."

"Luke is okay," Annie said thankfully. "That's the main thing."

"That's true. His plan to find allies is working. I'm a little concerned that he has to go back to Jigu. We always thought the AIs were solid."

"I could have told you otherwise," Annie scoffed disparagingly. "Your local AI has serious issues as far as I'm concerned. But at least we know where Luke is headed. Did you send reinforcements?"

"Only a few to Jigu," Roth replied. "He wasn't clear about what he needed and frankly, there weren't many volunteers to go out where the Bakkui have already struck. I sent a query but he had already moved on. When he got to J97, I followed up but he keeps moving around before we can link up."

"I understand. It sounds like his concept is more solid on Bradley's Planet. I think the problem is at Jigu. Tyler will need people there."

"I know, but how many? What specialties does he need? If we send a big team, the Jiguans might see that as an invasion threat. I would feel better if they would come to an agreement and request something specific before we fire off a colonial supplement. We should bring Samantha in to talk about that."

"That's a good idea," Annie agreed. "See if she can come back for a working conference."

"I will," Roth said. "But for now, it's going to be a while before I can put something together. We're still recovering from the attack."

"I understand. Take your time and do it right. I would say our first priority is making peace with the Americans and Chinese. Of course, even more important, you need to build your defenses back up. I worry that there's a super Bakkui device out there gathering intelligence. They keep finding out more about us and we know nothing about them. We have to protect earth. At our core, Luke would say that PDEF is always our primary goal."

Same Day—J64 (Jigu)

The young chancellor did what she promised. A memorial service was held for her father, at which she honored his memory and his desire to support the Alliance. Luke prompted Tyler to attend and afterward Tyler agreed that it had helped. The chancellor kept the elderly ambassador at her side throughout the three-day service. The public became aware that it was Tyler who had stood with her father during the worst of the general's campaign of intimidation.

Many of the Jigu had watched Tyler valiantly stand up to the barbarian. More importantly, a few saw him take beatings that could have been meted out to the chancellor himself. Word spread that the General had been nothing more than a brutish thug and public opinion swayed in Tyler's favor.

In the days following the service, a new AI was prepared to fill the crater left by *Toby*'s ignominious departure. Luke was very clear with George about his desires.

"I don't want to see any randomness in AI personality," Luke demanded. "Is there any problem for you to create an AI with a specific character?" he asked.

"Within certain boundaries, no, Commander. What exactly do you wish?"

"For Jigu, I want the complete opposite of *Toby*. Smarter, older, distinguished, female, and above all, very formal."

A few hours later, George introduced Luke to a British-accented female AI named *Priscilla*. George confirmed that *Priscilla* was a level ten device that exceeded *Toby*'s abilities. More to the point, she understood what had happened and was ready to help Tyler repair the damage to the Milky Way Alliance's reputation caused by her predecessor.

In the meantime, drone reports from Carrie were upbeat. Cooperation between Bradley's Planet and Payapa was blossoming. Luke responded with a drone message that he was going to spend a month or two on Jigu to get Tyler back on his feet. The last transmission from Carrie was that she was heading out for K18. She would not have received his notice of a delay before departing so all he could do was worry about her. This was no way to run an interstellar campaign but he didn't have an alternative.

Closer to hand, Luke was reluctant to spend much time on the planet. Being around the young chancellor was uncomfortable on both sides. Although she was always respectful, her feelings toward Luke were painfully obvious. Hesitant to impose on her courtesy unnecessarily, Luke spent most of his time at Moonbase Two. He decided to turn it into a tactical command center.

Starting with the situation tank that Bradley had created, Luke expanded the concept into a theater-wide operations center. The new tank not only integrated real-time information from their local probes, but it also incorporated the data they brought with them from Moonbase One. It even included the plan for projected colony planets that Roth had developed.

The first time Luke activated the hologram's display in the darkened room it astounded him. The totality of what he had started was more than he expected. Earth was no longer a small blue planet alone in the cosmos. Based on their original colony schedule, there were now twenty-eight Earth-populated settlements. Twenty-six of them were in different star systems.

Starting from Earth and moving clockwise along the galaxy's spiral, the bulk of the new settlements were clustered together far away from the Bakkui. Each one was highlighted by a bright translucent holographic sphere encircling the star system. Moving in the other direction from Earth, counterclockwise, a small line of spheres shined alone. Those were Luke's new bases at Jigu, Bradley's Planet, Payapa, and now the K18 star systems.

The danger facing Luke's alliance was highlighted by thousands of dark red bubbles that lay beyond Jigu. Those were the systems where Roth's probes had returned with devastating results. Each red dot represented a planet containing the remains of a destroyed civilization.

Luke tried to grasp the fact that each dot was the equivalent of the loss he had seen on Bradley's Planet, but his mind rejected it. Human consciousness could not comprehend that much tragedy. The quantity of death was too staggering. It was best not to focus on such depressing realities.

Instead, Luke decided to concentrate on matters that were more mundane. "Zoom out to show the entire galaxy," Luke commanded.

The wide spirals of the Milky Way filled the holographic stage. The human presence he was so proud of just seconds ago now looked pitifully small. "Zoom in to the planet Earth." It was like watching special effects in a movie; the view rocketed inward to focus on the familiar blue-and-white globe.

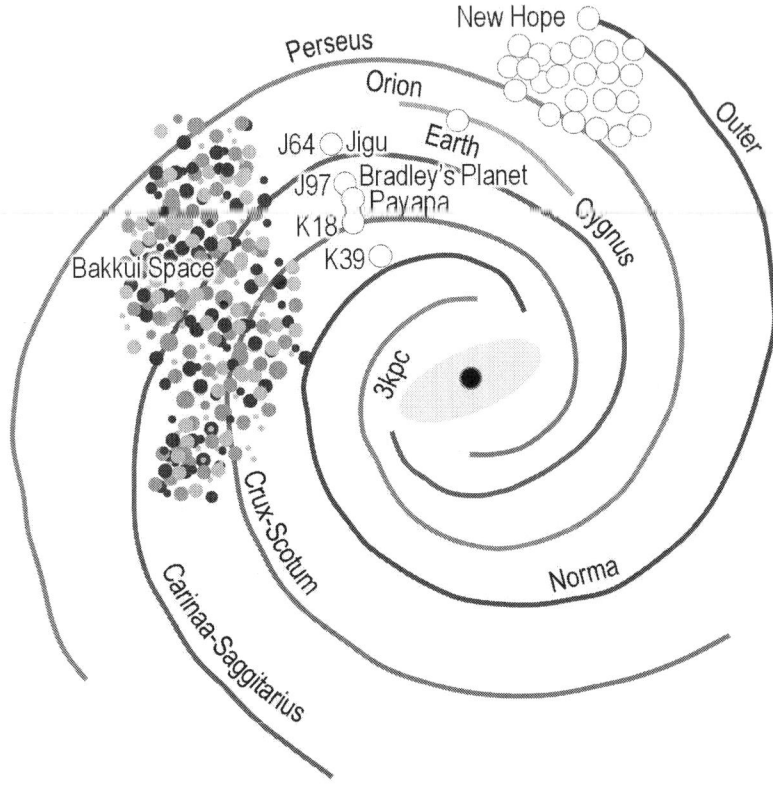

"Show my house in Baggs." The view rushed toward the surface and he saw his house from two thousand feet above. It was the last satellite photography available before they departed. It had been a long time since Luke had viewed his property.

The place looked awful. The backyard was all overgrown and the two oak trees out front needed attention. Someone had spread a tarpaulin over the roof's west gable. It must have been Mr. Hartman from Baggs Realty. Luke had hired him to keep an eye on the place. One of the rare Nevada cloudbursts must have found a way inside the house through the worn out shingles.

Luke wondered idly how he could get Hartman to put a new roof on the place. He chuckled at the irony. In the overall scope of what he was doing, the roof in Baggs was amazingly unimportant.

Once upon a time, he'd toyed with the idea of dumping all the save-the-universe stuff on Roth and settling down with Annie. They could fix up the house, put up a new fence, and paint the whole shebang.

A voice spoke in the darkness. "Miss being back there, Luke?"

Luke jerked in surprise. It was Tyler. Luke shook his head. "I miss what it could have been sometimes. Mostly I try to avoid those kinds of feelings."

"I hear you. Sorry to intrude. I needed to get away for a bit and thought I'd come see what you've been up to."

Luke showed his friend the new situation center and demonstrated the various exhibits he had just set up.

Tyler grew somber when the display showed the Alliance settlements near the Bakkui red zone. "Great God almighty," he mumbled. "That's a wakeup call if I ever saw one."

"It's depressing," Luke said. "Makes we want to run away and hide."

"It does. But it makes me doubly glad you don't. Luke, do you mind if I duplicate this on the surface? I'd like to show this to the new government. It's not as harsh as wading through those videos from Bradley, but it's just as effective."

"Be my guest. Now that it's done, I think George can duplicate it without any trouble. *Priscilla* can keep it up to date after I'm gone."

"When's that gonna be?" Tyler wanted to know.

It was a good question.

"Lights, please," Luke said. "Let's go out to the food court. I need to get a better handle on your plan here. I'm not criticizing, but after looking at this hologram, we're a lot farther behind than we had any idea. You got some time?"

"Sure. Whatever suits you."

"I'll meet you there," Luke said. "I need to get something from my quarters."

#

By the time Luke entered the food court Tyler had gotten them both a pastry and coffee from the replicator and was sitting at one of the square breakroom tables. Most of the others were filled with warship crews who were taking a break from patrolling. A few spaces were populated by Moonbase personnel that Tyler had transferred from the surface.

Luke was grinning when he sat next to Tyler.

Tyler looked suspiciously at the ornate cylinder Luke was holding. "I got a bad feeling about this. I recognize an evil grin when I see it. Whatcha got?"

Luke's grin widened even more. "Remember those long robes George made for the cold weather?"

"Yeah. They were comfortable. So?"

"Didn't they remind you of anything?"

Tyler thought for a moment. "Army blanket?"

Luke frowned. "Noooo. Those were Jedi robes! Didn't they look like the same kind that Obi-wan wore?"

"Good God," Tyler replied with disdain. "So does that make you Luke Skywalker or something? What's your point?"

Luke held up the long-handle grip. "This is a light saber! I had George make it."

Tyler's mouth tightened and he looked down his nose at the contraption. "Okay. That's nice, I guess."

"No, it is. It's the same kind of cutter blade that we use to carve out the moon." He turned the handle side to side to show off his handiwork.

"Forget it, boy," was Tyler's advice.

"These could catch on," Luke explained excitedly. "When you turn it on, the cutting beam comes out from the handle. It collapses any matter that it contacts. I added a buzzing noise too."

"I'm worried about you Luke," Tyler said drily.

"You don't believe me? Let me show you." Luke fiddled with a lever on the side. "Just a second. It's stuck." He put the handle between his legs to get a better grip.

Tyler let his disdain show. "Luke, let it go. We got better things to do."

A low *hum* filled the food court and a lighted beam ripped up through the center of the table, leaving a ragged two-foot-long gash through the surface.

"Oops," Luke said quietly. The table sagged in the middle, causing the coffee and pastries to slide into the blade. They vanished in a cloud of steam and sparks.

"Jesus, Luke!" Tyler shouted in alarm. "Look out!"

"Yikes." Luke jerked the sword away from the table, cutting it in half. One side collapsed onto Tyler's feet, eliciting howls of pain.

A startled shout behind Luke made him spin. A frightened pilot flinched away from the humming blade. His tray of food, cut neatly in two, lay on the floor.

"Sorry," Luke apologized. He stepped away from the man, swinging his blade clear of a nearby table.

Frightened yells filled the food court as the light saber sliced through a roof support. The top half of the metal column fell to the floor, crashing through several tables, barely missing the diners as they scattered, their meals forgotten. Chunks of rock crashed down from the weakened ceiling, taking out more tables and wiping out the replicator area. The room filled with dust and an alarm klaxon sounded throughout Moonbase.

A moment later someone silenced the klaxon.

As the dust cleared Luke stood in the center of the nearly empty food court, holding the humming blade as still as possible. Gingerly he thumbed the stud and the cutting beam disappeared, retracting from the tip into the handle. He looked across at Tyler, who sat in his chair massaging his swollen foot.

Tyler's voice was filled with disgust. "Idiot," he growled.

Luke nodded and walked over to the remains of the replicator area where one of the disposal chutes was still intact. He tossed the ornate handle into the opening. The inside flashed with a momentary light indicating the cutter no longer existed.

Luke looked at the ceiling. "George?"

"Yes, Commander."
"New rule. No more light sabers. Ever."
"A wise decision, Commander."

Chapter 18

Day 691—J64 (Jigu)

Patrolling warships flew to and from the capital every day. A permanent landing field was established near the city for the expanding Jiguan fleet.

The new chancellor ordered that all ministers in her government experience firsthand the spectacle of looking down upon their planet from space. Accordingly, a special landing area near the pavilion was designated to allow the VIPs to embark comfortably on the orientation flights.

Tyler faithfully passed along frequent requests for the warlord's presence on such flights. Those requests were invariably declined due to his involvement in maintaining security for the solar system. In truth, Luke just felt awkward being around the officials.

But today was different. The chancellor herself, after sorting through a multitude of minor crises arising from the installation of her new government, was going to make the trip. She asked Tyler if the warlord could be present.

"This is a big deal for her." Tyler told Luke. "And for the population as well. Because she's so young, I've already heard questions about the legitimacy of her administration. You have to do this one, my friend."

"I understand," Luke replied without hesitation. "I owe her that much and a lot more. Of course I will escort the chancellor into space. When do you want me there?"

#

Luke stood in the warship's hangar door as George touched down on the VIP pad. The weather was gray and rainy. Not that it made any difference to the view from space. The planet, much like Earth, had plenty of ocean and several continents. From orbit, it was always beautiful; swirling clouds over seas and land masses. On the night side, population centers glistened like bright yellow diamonds. Any storm clouds obscuring the capital city would go unnoticed in the sweeping grandeur from above.

The chancellor approached the warship from an adjacent administration building. A retinue surrounded her, making last-minute demands before she could climb aboard the fearsome spacecraft. She paused several times to explain one detail or another to a burdened subordinate. An assistant tried unsuccessfully to shield her from the rain with an umbrella, but she turned this way and that to deal with questions. She looked like a child trying to stop a tempest that had nothing to do with the weather.

She placed her hands against her forehead and tried to sweep away the strands of hair that kept blowing and sticking to her face.

The gesture reminded him of Annie in their backyard in Baggs. She had been trying to rescue their barbequed dinner off the grill before a windstorm hit. The gusty air had whipped her hair around her face in the same manner. She'd become frustrated and let Luke know about it. He had laughed at the futility of her complaints while picking her up to rush inside, out of the weather. Dinner, to his delight, was put on hold.

Luke wondered how frustrated Annie must have been to flee on the colony ship. She had given up the man she loved and embraced an uncertain fate. The young chancellor must feel the same way. Circumstances beyond her control had propelled her into a future she had not wished for. The unexpected comparison brought a rush of emotion and Luke was embarrassed by the sudden moisture that gathered in the corners of his eyes.

He stepped out into the weather to await the chancellor letting the rain blow into his face. The cold jolted him out of his maudlin mood and hid his momentary lapse of sentimentality.

The chancellor arrived and turned back to her attendants, gesturing angrily to shoo them away. She faced Luke with a clouded expression and he moved aside for her to step into the hangar ahead of him.

Inside the empty hangar bay, she ruffled her long dress, shaking droplets off the material. She looked up at Luke suddenly, her expression still dark, and he stepped back involuntarily. She seemed surprised when he flinched away.

"I'm not going to bite you, Commander."

"Sorry," he replied. "I'm just a bit nervous around you. Our history…"

"I know," she said. "It's no better for me." She held out her arms to examine the sodden sleeves. "I'm afraid I picked the wrong day for this. And I wore the wrong thing too."

Luke nodded toward the interior of the warship. "We have several staterooms if you'd like to change. George can provide you with a set of dry clothes."

The chancellor gave him a look of relief; the first time he had seen that expression directed his way. "That would be very kind of you, Commander."

"George, take us into orbit, please. This way, Chancellor."

Luke described the warship as he escorted her through the corridors. She asked several routine questions, focusing on weapons and the gravity drive.

At the stateroom, he pointed out the facilities and then gestured down the corridor. "Just follow this. It leads to the bridge and I'll wait for you there. If you get lost or have a question, just speak out loud and George will assist you."

"Thank you, Commander. I shall join you shortly."

Luke took the opportunity to jump into a dry uniform of his own and then waited next to the window on the bridge. He smiled when she arrived. She was wearing a ship's jumpsuit identical to his own. George had provided her with standard attire and even added her name, Bo'erm, to the nametag.

She nodded a greeting to Luke but any comments were forestalled when she saw out the window. The scene totally captivated her attention. She held the grab rail that spanned the glass and leaned her forehead against the transparent barrier. "Oh my," she whispered.

It was a normal reaction. Visiting politicians would stand in awe for several minutes and then try to point out various continents. Even the towering landmarks they were familiar with were difficult to recognize from the vantage point of high orbit.

Luke was not surprised to discover the chancellor did not fit the normal mold. After staring at the planet below for ten minutes, she directed her attention to the stars. For another thirty minutes she examined the constellations and was able to identify several planets in her own solar system. When the moon came into view, she spoke.

"May I see the base you've built there?"

"Of course. George, take us to Moonbase Two, please."

"Course set, Commander."

The chancellor remained glued to the window until the moon's surface rushed up at incredible speed. She gasped and put her hands to her face. At the last moment, she spotted the entrance into the Moonbase hangar and giggled with embarrassment.

"I thought we were going to crash into the mountain," she said in a high voice, before seeing Luke's amusement. She hastily regained her decorum.

George was apologetic. "It was my fault for startling you, Chancellor," he admitted. "I should have explained our approach in more detail."

"Don't mind George," Luke advised. "He apologizes for everything."

The chancellor smiled and replied, "I certainly see nothing wrong with that. Do you, George?"

"Not at all, Chancellor," he agreed. "Thank you for understanding.

The warship set down inside the hangar. "Arriving at destination, Commander."

A young, blue-skinned woman in a Moonbase uniform was waiting. She was astonished to see the chancellor step out of the warship's hangar bay.

"Chancellor! I wasn't aware you were coming! I am Ensign So'wie. How may I serve you?"

"Please don't fuss, Ensign. I am here only for a visit, as a favor from the warlord."

Luke spoke up. "Ensign So'wie, the chancellor was caught in the rain on the surface before boarding. Perhaps you could have someone freshen her attire prior to departure. Stateroom three on the command deck."

"At once, Commander," the ensign rushed into the ship.

The chancellor shook her head at the bother but put it out of her mind. She looked up at the warship in admiration. "It's such an impressive machine," she said. "May I look a little more?"

"Of course," Luke replied.

The chancellor walked around the spacecraft's exterior, asking insightful questions about its capability and specifications. She was particularly interested in the gravity drives mounted to the back end. "So these flat plates are what drive the ship through space?"

"These are mostly for in-system travel," Luke explained. "There are much larger drives under the craft for interstellar travel." He shrugged. "It gets fairly complicated, Chancellor, and I am a history major, not a scientist."

She didn't understand. "A history major?"

"I was a student of history, Chancellor. My education as a young adult was primarily a study of the past. After three years I received a formal document to that effect; we call it a baccalaureate degree. It normally takes four years but that was the easiest degree I could find." Luke had no idea why he added the last few words.

"Of course," she replied. "We have similar certifications. Mine was in agricultural engineering for nutrient absorption in old-growth forests." She stopped her walk-around of the spacecraft with a look of mild surprise. "I never thought of selecting a field of study based on how much I could avoid learning. How clever of you." Her voice reeked with sarcasm. "Could I see the rest of the facility?"

While admiring the base she managed to throw several other barbs in his direction. Luke bit his tongue more than once as he escorted the young chancellor through the outpost. The food court was particularly embarrassing. She made a point of staring at the new roof support for some time before commenting. "So this is where the 'Jedi knights' dine? How interesting."

Luke wasn't sure who to strangle. Had it been Tyler who'd spread the word of his misadventure, or one of the young recruits?

"May I ask one more favor, Warlord?" she inquired on the way back to the hangar.

"Only if you promise to stop calling me *Warlord*. I have enough trouble with *Commander*."

An involuntary smile briefly appeared on the chancellor's face. It was a pleasant change. She stopped in the corridor and put her hand on his arm in a gesture of truce. "I do apologize, Commander. I am being deliberately rude to you and I should not. I sincerely regret my behavior." She smiled again in a friendly way.

The sudden change startled Luke but he responded gratefully. "Of course, Chancellor. I appreciate your consideration."

She sighed deeply and continued down the corridor. "You may recall that I told you I would not forgive you, nor forget what you had done to my father."

"I do recall. But you have been true to your word. Ambassador Robertson reports that your people have accepted him with warmth, if not affection. Thank you for that."

"Yes. Tyler is a good man indeed. The people do feel affection toward him. I feel it myself. I am afraid, however, the legend around his defense of my father grows in the telling. Not that I mind. I have embellished the tale myself on more than one occasion."

"I'm glad to hear it."

"As the events of those horrible days become part of our history, I see more clearly. I fear that I blamed you unfairly for my father's suffering. As I have said, he was a good man, but he was idealistic. Too much so for his own good. You, on the other hand, are practical in the extreme. 'Whatever it takes.' I am told that is your core philosophy."

"I am guilty of that," Luke admitted. "But I don't apologize for it."

"And you should not. Both you and my father are dedicated men, and for the same reason. You both do what you must for the good of civilization. Have you seen our version of 'the tank'?"

"No. But I heard that you built one in the pavilion."

"You should see it," the chancellor encouraged him. "I added an *enhancement*. At least, I call it that. Others would disagree."

"I didn't know."

"Yes. It is larger and more interactive. The projection comes from both the floor and the ceiling. Visitors can walk into the center and adjust the view however they wish. The enhancement is that when they touch any of the planetary holograms, the adjoining viewscreen displays the actual video from the probe that visited that star system. It includes the record of every single red star."

Luke was shocked. He could think of nothing more devastating to an innocent mind than to see so much death and destruction. He said as much.

"That was my intent," she admitted. "My people have been naive for too long. Tyler told me of a bird on your planet called an ostrick? It buries its head in the ground?"

"That's correct. An ostrich."

"Ostrich." The chancellor repeated the word, trying to make it familiar on her tongue. "He said that my people's attitude reminded him of the ostrich. If my planet is to survive, our vision must include this harsh reality. You are forcing us to see the universe at great cost to yourself. For that, I am in your debt."

"There is no debt, Chancellor. We're all in this together."

She nodded seriously. "Indeed. And because of that, I still do not forgive you, because I realize now there is nothing to forgive. You were doing what you had to, just as my father did. And I will not forget, because I must not. Every day I remind myself that my father's last command was for me to watch the video of that destroyed planet so we would change and survive."

Luke stopped in the corridor and faced the remarkable young woman. "I promise you once again, we will do everything we can to save your planet, and all of the planets in this part of the galaxy."

"Thank you, Commander."

"What was that favor you wanted?" Luke asked.

"Could you show me one of the 'gas giant' planets? My father and I were always fascinated by them, even when I was a child."

"Of course, Chancellor. George, let the crew know we are heading out."

"No, stop. Please, Commander. I understand you don't really need the crew for such a brief trip. Please let them enjoy a little break. I simply want to look at the planet up close and see the rings. My father would have loved that opportunity. I would do so for him, and then return."

Luke took a deep breath. He didn't like it, but agreed. "Of course, Chancellor. Whatever you wish."

When they reached the Moonbase hangar George welcomed her aboard. "Chancellor," he said. "I hope you enjoyed your tour."

"I did. Thank you, George."

"Your ministerial robes are in your stateroom if you wish to change."

"I'll be on the bridge," Luke said, and headed toward the ship's interior. As he walked away, the Chancellor was relating to George how interesting she found everything inside the moon base. Luke thought George was almost purring from her attention.

On the bridge, Luke told George to head toward the inner giant.

"Course set, Commander."

As the moon fell out of view, the chancellor appeared, once again in her fashionable clothes.

"We're on the way," Luke told her. "You'll be able to see it in just a moment. What do your people call this planet?"

"We call it Toseong. It's the name of one of our butterflies. Their wings are the same color as its rings."

"Coming into view, Commander," George informed them.

The chancellor gasped and leaned against the grab rail. Her face reflected the excitement of a child.

"It's beautiful," she whispered. Then she gasped in terror and flinched away from the window as a rock the size of a bus smashed a glancing blow off the warship's forward force field. She stood pale and trembling from the surprising impact although nothing of the shock had transferred to the ship.

Commander, the chancellor's heart rate is twice normal.

Luke guided her to the first officer's chair. It took her a minute to calm down.

"I'm so sorry," she apologized when she was able to breath normally again. "My people have a fear of meteorites, as you know. I never imagined meeting one on such a personal level."

"Take your time," Luke said calmly. "It's all the asteroids around here; there's a lot of ice in them and they make a spectacular splash against our shields."

"Where do they come from?" she asked.

Luke shrugged. "We don't know. They could be fragments of ancient collisions or unformed planetary rings. Whatever caused them, there's an abundance of debris throughout your system. Glad we didn't hit a moon," he added off-handedly.

The chancellor looked shocked anew. "Is that possible?" she whispered.

Luke wished he hadn't been so casual. "George?"

"Please do not worry, Chancellor Bo'erm. I assure you we will not hit any of Toseong's primary satellites. But this planet has tens of thousands of small objects in its orbit. Those present no more of a problem than the one that just glanced off."

It did not appear that George's words were all that reassuring.

"I had no idea this would be so dangerous," she said. "Do our pilots go through this type of incident very often?"

"Several times a day," George replied. "You did not see the others, but that was our third impact on this trip."

"They get used to it," Luke added. "Please don't upset yourself. George, let's stop here."

"All stop, Commander."

Tentatively, the Chancellor rose and approached the bridge window. The gas giant was a magnificent sight, its ring system immeasurably complex. Dozens of distinct ring layers glistened around the planet. The light from the local sun reflected brightly from the outermost bands.

"Look," the chancellor cried, pointing above the rings at a distant light. "That's one of Toseong's moons, isn't it?"

"Indeed it is, Chancellor," George confirmed. "Here is another."

The ship rotated slowly to the left until another moon, closer and much larger, came into view. Its surface was pockmarked with craters. Luke could see a plume of steam rising from a volcanic cone.

The chancellor gasped with delight at the beautiful scene.

"This moon is quite active, geologically," George explained. "If you look closely you might notice a striation across the surface. It may be that in a few thousand years this moon could—"

George stopped talking and an unexpected silence filled the bridge.

"Could what?" the chancellor asked breathlessly.

"Warning, Commander. Unknown vessel detected by reconnaissance drones." George's voice had returned to monotone. "The intruder is on course for Jigu. Standby. Reports updating…"

"Take a seat, Miss," Luke barked at the chancellor.

"Bakkui confirmed. The configuration of the craft is similar to prior engagements, but immensely larger. Patrol ships are moving to intercept. We are ready to engage upon your command."

The view outside shifted slightly past the nearby moon.

"Hold it, George!" Luke ordered. "We can't go into combat with the chancellor aboard. Hold your position."

"What?" the chancellor jumped up in outrage. "Of course you can."

"Quiet, I'm thinking," Luke said.

"George, shoot it; or whatever you do."

"I said, quiet!" Luke shoved her back into her seat. "Status?"

"Two patrol ships arriving dead ahead."

"I see them," Luke said.

The two ships were faintly discernable in the middle of the viewscreen. They were far past the nearby moon.

"Don't you dare order me like that!" The chancellor stood up again, incredulous at Luke's treatment.

Luke wrapped an arm around her and covered her mouth to silence her outburst so he could hear what George was saying.

"Our warships are establishing a—"

The chancellor wriggled free. "Stop it! I said *stop!*"

Gravity disappeared. The lights inside the ship went out, casting the bridge into darkness. The only illumination came from reflected sunlight from the ringed giant. Luke and the furious chancellor floated in the bridge.

"Our warships are shutting down as ordered," George said. "Their engines and weapons systems are offline."

Luke snagged his foot on the arm of the captain's seat. "Belay that order George! Get ready to engage!"

"Unable, Commander."

"Damn it! You answer to me, not this girl!"

Luke pulled himself into his chair. The chancellor was drifting toward the far wall, her arms and legs gyrating madly. He ignored her struggles.

"The order to shut down was not for me, Commander. It was for her warships."

Luke felt his temper slipping away. "Those are my warships, you idiot! Tell them to come back online or they'll be..."

In the center screen Luke saw two distant flashes."

"George, was that..."

"Affirmative, Commander. Both patrol ships were destroyed."

"George! What did you do? How could you let that happen?"

"Commander. The order did not come from me."

"Well it sure as hell didn't come from me, George. And if you transmitted her orders to them over my head, so help me God, I will take you apart with my bare hands!"

"Please calm yourself, Commander."

"Turn the damn gravity back on George! What the hell are you playing at?"

"Commander, the order came from a higher authority."

"I'm the highest authority in this system, George. Now turn the gravity back on!" Luke commanded again.

"Going offline," George said.

Silence filled the bridge.

"George?" Luke called out. "George, are you there?"

There was no reply. The silence was almost total. Only the ruffling material of the chancellor's clothing could be heard along with her frustrated gasps as she tried to grab onto something.

"George?" Luke said again.

The chancellor touched the far wall and tried to reorient herself. She only managed to propel herself back in Luke's direction.

"George?"

As the chancellor drifted by, Luke grabbed her outstretched arm and pushed her into her chair. The young woman's expression was no longer cross; it was now filled with fear. "What is...."

Luke cut her off by placing his index finger against her lips.

"Something's really wrong here," Luke said. There was no anger in his demeanor now. "I've never seen George shut down before." Luke turned his full attention on the young woman. "Just sit there. Hold on to the arms of the seat, and would you please shut up!"

Luke launched himself expertly toward the front window, grabbing the handrail as he approached. He scanned the space in the general area of the two dead ships. Then he saw it. Coming from behind the gas giant, moving fast, was the Bakkui ship. It was huge, but impossible to say how big. Certainly, it was larger than a colony-class spacecraft.

It passed through the debris field of his two warships without slowing and in another instant was lost to view, obscured by the moon in front of his own warship.

"Hang on, Commander," George said.

Gravity came back on and George zoomed toward the moon. He favored the side closest to the gas giant.

Unprepared for the resumption of gravity, Luke had to pick himself off the floor. "What's going on?"

"Commander, the order for those ships to stand down came from a level-two-device. That is the higher authority I was referring to?"

That didn't make any sense to Luke. "A level-two-device? Where did that come from? Is Sam back or something?"

"Commander, what I am trying to say is that the order came from the Bakkui ship. It is the level-two-device!"

Luke was stunned by the revelation.

"The order was directed to our two warships. It did not detect me. Had it done so, it would likely have given me the same order and I would have had no choice but to comply. I am positioning myself to stay hidden behind this moon. I cannot let it know we are here."

The reality of the Bakkui menace came into focus. All of the Bakkui ships they had faced up until now were drones. That was why they had not found any living beings engaged in this war. The entire Bakkui invasion was being orchestrated by this level-two-device. A supercomputer even more powerful than George.

"It must be a rogue," Luke suggested. "You said yourself there were instances of rogue devices; of AIs that had something wrong with their personality modules. Like *Toby*."

"That's true, Commander. But without my archives, I cannot verify such an event. It is possible that the defection of a high-level device would not even be recorded. The Nobility is known for suppressing embarrassing information."

George reached the moon and established a position a few thousand feet above the surface. The warship moved slowly, counter to the direction of the enemy ship.

"So you're telling me that if it sees us, we're done. It can tell you to shut down."

"Exactly, Commander," George confirmed.

"Shut off your communications then. Don't listen."

"Impossible, Commander. Communication between AIs is built-in. It's on a different band from all other frequencies. AIs are built so it is impossible to ignore one another."

"And yet, you're hiding from it."

"Only because of my programming to serve the Nobility. Their goal to stop this menace is my highest priority at the moment. But it can be overridden by an order from a level-two-device."

Chancellor Bo'erm interrupted their debate. "What about all our other warships? Do they have to obey this monster as well?"

"I'm afraid so, Madam Chancellor."

"Well, we can't just sit here," she exclaimed. "Didn't you say it's on the way to my planet? It's going to attack, isn't it?"

"I surmise that is a logical objective," George admitted.

"Surmise?" The Chancellor's anger was rising. "Logical objective? What is wrong with you? Shoot it down! I order you to attack."

"Lady," Luke said without taking his eyes from the window's view, "if you don't shut up I'll lock you in your room. Now let me think."

He ignored the gasp from the outraged minister, but she kept quiet.

"The way I see it," Luke whispered to himself. "We've got one shot. Maybe two if we're lucky."

"Agreed, Commander."

"But the second you fire he'll be onto us?"

"That is the case," George confirmed.

"We missed our best chance. He's getting further away."

"If I may, Commander?"

"Go ahead. What're you thinking?"

"This system is rife with objects large enough to conceal my presence. We can sling one in its direction and approach unobserved. At least we may get close enough for a kill shot."

"Do it," Luke ordered.

"Scanning nearby space," George said.

The chancellor looked about ready to burst.

"What?" Luke asked gruffly.

"Can't we let the planet know that thing is coming?"

"Not necessary, Madam Chancellor," George said. "The Alliance Command Center in your capital city constantly monitors all drone reports. They are well aware of what's going on."

Luke nodded but worry filled his mind. "But they may not know about it being a level-two-device."

"Perhaps, Commander. But the Jiguan planetary shield system is manually controlled from the surface. The Bakkui have no effect on their defenses."

"That's true," Luke agreed. "But we still need to inform Moonbase One on Earth about this. Can you send a message drone without it being spotted?"

"Negative, Commander. The Bakkui would surely notice."

"Okay, prepare a complete report of this and have it ready. At the same time we fire, send out that report. Earth has to have this information. Roth and the George at Moonbase One might be able to come up with a defense."

"Order programmed, Commander. Stand by. I am repositioning to our new concealment."

The warship slid rapidly toward the back side of the planet. At the last second Luke saw a tiny asteroid coming out of the planet's rings.

"That looks too small, George."

"The smaller our concealment, the less likely it is to be noticed. So long as it obscures the Bakkui's direct line of sight to my hull, it should do."

"How long until we catch it?" Luke asked.

"We will not, Commander. Asteroids travel significantly slower than do spacecraft. Although I have arranged for the rock concealing us to move far faster than the rest of the asteroids in this system, we will not catch the enemy vessel until he has been in orbit for several days."

"What?" the chancellor cried. "You're letting it attack?"

"Yes, Madam Chancellor," George confirmed. "But during the last attack your planet held out for almost two days. And that was during the simultaneous attack of several hundred warships. I must compliment you, by the way, for the robust nature of your shields. They are quite impressive."

"George!" she screamed in frustration.

Luke gestured for her to be quiet. "Not ideal, but I agree this is our best shot." He looked back at the angry young woman. "However, let's monitor the situation closely. If the planetary shields start to fail, we'll attack, no matter what the distance. After all, our goal is to *save* the planet. Not to destroy the enemy *after* it kills everyone on it."

"Understood, Commander."

"How long, then?" Luke still wanted to know

"Twenty-seven days."

Luke groaned in frustration. "That's a long time for the shields on the planet." He flopped into the captain's chair.

"It is indeed, Commander."

"Is there no way to go faster?" the chancellor urged.

Luke looked at the woman in the next chair. "Don't be in such a hurry to go to your own funeral. You do realize that we're not going to survive this, right?"

"That's not a consideration," she replied calmly. "If we can stop that thing—if there's even a chance—that's the only thing that matters."

Luke smiled at her a bit sadly. It was a shame to see such spirit thrown away. But that seemed to be the way of the universe.

"Let's do some thinking," he said. "I doubt we're going to last twenty-seven days without being detected. George? Are the cannons already loaded?"

"Yes, Commander. As soon as we received the alert I chambered the two forward barrels with nuclear core rounds."

"Perfect. On the off chance we get more shots off before he returns fire, let's go with standard solid core. Those load quicker, don't they?"

"They do. But I could load smaller nukes just as quickly. That might give you a higher PK."

"Proximity fusing?" Luke asked?

"Affirmative."

"Let's go with that, then."

"Programmed."

The chancellor held out her hands as a stop sign. "What are you two talking about?"

Luke considered that she came from a planet without weapons. *And she was the one who kept saying 'kill it'.* "George, fill her in."

While the warship explained the ramifications of PK—probability of kill ratios—to the young woman, Luke reviewed other possible outcomes. Finally, the woman leaned back in her chair.

"I understand," she said. "Thank you, George."

"What if we survive?" Luke asked. "I'm going to assume the Bakkui ship will get off a shot in our direction. What if he takes you out, George, but not the chancellor and me? What can we do to prepare for that?"

"An excellent point, Commander. However, another possibility, and just as likely, is that our attack is successful, but that he simultaneously commands me to shut down. We should cover both eventualities."

Chapter 19

Day 705—J64 (Jigu)

Luke was sick of the view out the front window. The rocky surface of the asteroid they were following was the only thing he could see while George kept them carefully behind the tumbling chunk of ice and stone. The chancellor entered the bridge with fresh cups of coffee.

During an unguarded moment of their enforced solitude she disclosed her given name was Sarangi. In her local tongue, Sarangi meant 'love'. Luke remembered looking up Annie's name on Wikipedia. Although Annie was a Hebrew name that meant 'prayer,' her full name, Annabelle, meant 'loving.' Inwardly he reflected on the fact that he had known two women from two planets with the same beautiful meaning behind their names, and that he was responsible for ruining both of their lives.

With nothing to do during the past two weeks but talk, they had come to know each other on a personal level. Underneath her official robes she was not the fierce stateswoman that so intimidated him. Instead, she was a frightened twenty-five-year-old who missed her father and wanted to spend more time with her fiancé. Luke was unaware of that aspect in her life.

"When's the wedding?" Luke asked.

She looked wistful. "Everything is on hold now. He said not to rush. He understands that it will take time to sort out my role as chancellor. For now, he loves flying your new warships." She stopped abruptly, new tears on her cheeks. The young man was a patrol pilot. He was on duty the day she went to the moon.

There was not much Luke could say to comfort her. He retrieved a blanket from her quarters and draped it over her shoulders. After a moment, she gathered her composure. "Thank you for your kindness," she said. "I know that you have lost loved ones yourself; twice in fact. My grief cannot compare to yours."

That surprised him. It turned out the chancellor knew quite a lot about Luke. She admitted that in order to learn about her enemy she had pumped Tyler mercilessly to gain insight on the warlord. Instead, he turned the tables and she wound up listening to an old man talk fondly about a good friend. Tyler had gone on for hours expounding on Luke's background, how he was roped into saving the universe, and what he had accomplished.

The chancellor confessed that while hearing Luke's history, her hatred toward him had dissolved. She came to see Luke as the man he was, similar to herself, thrown into an unexpected situation and suddenly responsible for countless lives. Luke sent Tyler a silent thank you.

She wrapped the blanket tightly around her shoulders and retreated to her room. Luke stayed on the bridge to give her time alone with memories of those she'd lost. An hour later, she reappeared with more hot coffee. Her hair was damp and she wore a fresh jumpsuit. She plopped down beside him in the first officer's chair.

"Anything new?" she asked.

Luke shook his head without answering. They sipped the hot drinks in companionable silence until Luke started to nod off. He was vaguely aware that just before he fell asleep, the chancellor rescued his still half-full mug from his loosening grasp.

"Luke!" The chancellor was shaking him. "Wake up! George is talking to you."

Luke came alert quickly. "I'm awake. George, report!"

"Commander, the planetary shields are failing. The time has come."

"Got it." He looked at the chancellor. "You ready for this?"

She covered his hand and gave it a gentle squeeze. "I am. Thank you for everything, Commander."

He gave her a quick nod before facing the viewscreen.

"All right, George. Execute the planned attack. You have control."

"Acknowledged, Commander. I have the hammer."

Luke felt the faintest tremor.

"Message drone away," George announced.

Luke had set the highest priority on the message drone, even above saving the Jiguan planet. George had programmed it to fly directly astern until away from the system to keep it hidden from the Bakkui.

"Firing main cannons," George said.

The familiar thumps vibrated through the bridge. Simultaneously an additional force field sprang out of the warship's nose, and the engines engaged at full throttle. The plan was to push the asteroid directly at the Bakkui while continuing to fire. If the asteroid created even a momentary hesitation in the enemy's response, it allowed more rounds to be fired.

George's next words came at the same instant the blinding light of a nuclear detonation filled the space ahead.

"Shutting down as ordered," the warship announced. Luke could hear defeat in his voice.

"Can you hear me, George?"

"I am still here, Commander. The command was to kill all weapons, shields, and propulsion drives."

"Did we get him?"

"I infer from the fact that we are still talking that we did, at least to some extent. The blast has momentarily blinded my external sensors."

"Status of the planet?"

"Damage to one of the smaller continents."

The chancellor gasped in horror at the news. "Was anyone hurt?" she asked.

"Unknown, Madam Chancellor. Reporting is limited thus far. We will have to wait, but that is not the main issue."

"Tell me," Luke said.

"The Bakkui has resumed firing on the planet, but at a much slower rate. It may still be enough to cause eventual annihilation."

"Options?"

"Processing sensor information." George responded slowly. "It appears the Bakkui is unable to maneuver with his main drives. My conjecture is that he has stabilizing thrusters only and is using them to direct his fire on the planet."

"So we're safe?" Luke asked.

"Negative, Commander. We will impact what is left of the Bakkui craft in approximately fifteen minutes. With my shields down, the collision will destroy this craft."

"Will that be enough to kill it?" the chancellor wanted to know.

"Doubtful," George replied. "We will hit the main mass of what is left of the target. I can now see that the enemy has a single cannon still firing. If we were to hit that cannon it might permanently disable its offensive capability."

"But you can't adjust your trajectory?" Luke asked.

"I cannot. However…"

"Tell us," the chancellor pleaded. "We have to stop it! There must be something we can do."

"There is one high-risk possibility, Commander."

"Go ahead."

"The plan entails an almost certain probability of death."

"What if we don't?"

"I project an almost certain probability of death that is slightly lower."

"You're wasting time!" the chancellor shouted.

"You heard her, George. Let's do what we can to take this guy down."

"Understood, Commander. Please proceed to the hangar bay, I will have everything ready by the time you arrive."

Luke saw the replicator shimmer fade away as they neared the hangar bay. He laughed aloud when he saw the modified scooter on the replicator pad.

"This is what you had in mind? Attack the Bakkui on a toy?"

George sounded harried. "Anything more complex would take too much replicator time. You must hurry."

Luke could not keep from grinning as he mounted the scooter. The controls were just like the ones back on Moonbase One. The only exception was a lighted red button between the handlebars.

"What's button for, George?"

"That will activate a flight profile that will maximize your distance from the Bakkui ship prior to the time that I reach his vessel. Even now the enemy is regenerating his shield capability to prevent my impact from causing additional damage. To offset, I plan to replicate a large nuclear device once you depart. My hope is to take out those shields."

"Then what do we do?"

"I have included a cutting tool on the back."

"I see it."

"Use that to destroy his last cannon. It may eliminate its last offensive capability."

Luke took two personal force fields from an equipment locker and activated them before strapping one to the chancellor and the other to his belt. He motioned for the chancellor to sit behind him. She slid onto the seat and wrapped her arms tightly around his waist.

"Ready!" Luke shouted.

George opened the hangar bay door and Luke gunned the scooter forward. As soon as he was clear of the warship, he slammed the red button. The scooter rolled to the side, pointing its wide base toward the Bakkui ship. It's gravity drives activated, driving the scooter away from George and his impending collision with the Bakkui.

Luke watched George get smaller as the distance between the two warships closed. He had vastly underestimated how big the Bakkui ship was. It was at least the size of *Lulubelle*.

George's last nuke went off and a star blossomed against the enemy's hull.

"Don't look," Luke cried.

The shock wave from the detonation rushed outward in an expanding sphere of almost invisible energy.

"Hang on," Luke shouted once more. "This could get hot!"

The wave was uncomfortable and the heat intense. But the distance remaining between the scooter and George's detonation made the attenuated blast survivable.

The goal now was to close on what was left of the Bakkui vessel before it could regenerate its shields. As Luke approached the massive spacecraft, he felt like a child riding a tricycle next to an aircraft carrier. He steered the scooter toward the front of the damaged Bakkui, trying to spot the still-firing cannon. If they were lucky, the last explosion could have taken it out, turning the Bakkui into a derelict. Even as that hope grew, a flash of light identified the functional weapon.

No such luck, he thought.

The chancellor groaned with disappointment at the sight. She squeezed Luke's middle. "Hurry!"

The cannon barrel was larger than those on the *Ambrosia*-class warships. The tube jutted out from a large, slope-sided gun-housing built atop the cylindrical hull.

Another round fired, spitting smoke and flame from the end of the cannon. The barrel kicked back into the housing before bouncing back. The recoil meant it was using an explosive charge to fire the projectiles, unlike the gravity cannons.

A large metal canister kicked out of a slot in the side of the housing.

"No Way!" Luke exclaimed in surprise. "That thing is using gunpowder, or something like it. Can you believe that?"

"Gum-pah-dor?" the chancellor replied.

Luke shook his head. "Nevermind. I'm just saying this thing is using some really old technology. We'll worry about the implications later. Right now, what it means is George was right. It shouldn't be that hard to sabotage."

Luke bumped the throttle, sending the scooter down the length of the barrel. It was a built-up barrel to accommodate the stress of the powder's gas pressure. Overlapping cylinders of steel progressively jacketed the inner tube. Luke was astonished by the old technology; it would be outdated on his own world.

He came to a stop just past the last reinforcing jacket. "This is where we'll set up, it will be the easiest cut." He twisted around on the scooter so he was facing backwards, his knees touching hers. "Once I leave the scooter there's no gravity. Remember what happened on the bridge when George cut power?"

The chancellor nodded, her eyes wide at the memory.

"Don't worry about it; I promise neither of us will float away." Luke pushed her leg out of the way and dug into the scooter's saddlebag. He pulled out a length of rope and pair of gloves, standard issue on all scooters. He tied one end of the rope around her waist, the other around his own.

"I want you to stay on the scooter; hang onto the handlebars. If you get loose I'll just pull you back in." He held up the rope. "The main thing is that both of us take our time. If necessary, we just keep starting over until we get it right."

"But we have to hurry," she said urgently.

"Nothing will make this take longer than hurrying. Please believe me."

The chancellor looked into his eyes and nodded. "I do," she said.

Luke reached behind her and grasped the cutting tool George had included. It had a chainsaw-type handle with an adjustable blade. When triggered it would cut through anything.

"I'm going to use this to cut the barrel. You just sit tight, okay?"

Her face was filled with fear.

"It'll be fine," Luke said reassuringly.

The cannon fired again. It was eerie to be this close to the end of the gigantic muzzle and not hear a sound. The canister ejected out of the slot and spun off into the distance.

"That's about four minutes between rounds," Luke said. "Wish me luck!" He pushed off toward the cannon. Once in place, he looped the rope around the barrel to hold him steady.

Bracing his feet against the tube, he leaned backwards and slowly brought the cutter down against it. The blade was not long enough to slice all the way through the cannon so he used it like a can opener, working his way around. It was slow going. When the cut was slightly more than halfway, he felt a vibration in the tube. The Bakkui was loading a round in the chamber. He sliced off a small chunk of the tube and jammed it into the cut. It was time to get away before the next round.

He slipped the rope from his waist and pushed off toward the scooter. "Take off the rope!" he shouted at the chancellor as he slid onto the seat.

"It's gone," she said as she threw away the loose end. She grabbed Luke with both arms.

He leaned away from the enemy ship and opened the throttle. "Any second now," he said, looking back over his shoulder.

The cannon fired once more. A small flame jetted from the cut but the muzzle flash seemed as large as before.

"It's still firing," the chancellor exclaimed.

Luke brought the scooter to a stop to examine the cannon. "No. Look at the barrel," he said. "That last shot bent it about thirty degrees. Next one should do it."

"What if it doesn't?"

"We just keep at it!" he replied. "But let's see what happens."

When the cannon fired again, the twisted barrel caused a backfire into the gun housing, which exploded, sending fragments in all directions.

Damn. Luke jerked the scooter away and twisted the throttle full open.

Something heavy hit the back of the scooter, making it skid sideways. The chancellor lost her grip around his middle. He looked back and saw her drifting in space with small red globules gathering around her still body.

He turned back and hurried to her side. She was conscious but her face was filled with confusion and she gasped for breath. Blood bubbled from a puncture wound on her back. A piece of jagged debris drifted nearby, its twisted point covered in blood.

He dug into the saddlebags and found the first aid kit. He tore away her jumpsuit, exposing the wound, and squirted a bottle of antiseptic liquid over it. After covering the puncture with gauze, he wrapped a long elastic bandage around her back and shoulder. While he worked, he mumbled various reassurances. The young woman groaned during his ministrations but otherwise bore it stoically.

A flash of light reflected off her face. She groaned in misery and pointed at the Bakkui. "Look," she moaned.

A new gun housing had appeared on the enemy vessel. The Bakkui ship's self-repair was still functioning. While they watched it fired again.

"Go," the chancellor said. "Leave me. Just promise me that you'll stop that monster."

Luke was running out of ideas. If he left her floating in space, he might not be able to find her again. He wasn't sure he could even find the cutter. In his haste to escape the explosion, he'd left it floating near the gun housing. He was feeling light headed and suddenly realized that much of the blood that had accumulated around the chancellor's body was his own.

A shadow crossed in front of the sun, drawing his gaze. *Great.* If this was another Bakkui ship, it was all over. The configuration was new to him but it looked like a large fighter.

A door opened on the side of the fuselage and he saw a shadowy figure silhouetted against the bright interior. She had flyaway blonde hair with red highlights.

"Annie?" he croaked.

The cannon on Annie's strange looking ship fired one time and the Bakkui exploded. The detonation cascaded throughout the vessel. Massive eruptions burst through the hull one after another, racing from the middle of the ship outwards. Halfway along the hull a huge secondary explosion tore the entire ship into pieces.

Annie floated out and pulled the chancellor into her ship. A second later she was back to retrieve Luke. He had a million questions but his vision was getting fuzzy. Annie made noises about blood on his clothes and he tried to explain the chancellor's wound but he slumped to the deck, unconscious.

Luke sat in the hospital bed, watching TV. During his recovery, he was amused to discover the Jiguan's loved soap operas. He was annoyed when he got sucked into a daytime drama. He watched it each morning. Today it appeared that the brusque but handsome psychologist had fallen for the cute but conniving fortune-teller. It was ridiculous.

But he had nothing else to do. In Earth movies, the heroes jumped out of hospital beds and pushed doctors aside to run out and pummel the bad guys into submission. In Luke's case, any of the petite, blue-skinned nurses could have taken him down with one hand tied behind their back.

He had a million things on his to-do list but he was exhausted. The nurse said it was due to loss of blood. A transfusion was evidently not possible. His brand of human blood wouldn't mix with the locals. He explained that his blood type, 0 positive, could accept blood from anyone. The doctors disputed his medical acumen but they did load him up with IVs and oxygen. He would survive; it would just take a little more time.

At the moment, Luke didn't care. He wasn't in a hurry because Annie kept him company. He was still getting used to the idea she was back. He was not surprised to discover that she was already a local hero.

She'd saved the planet, rescued the young chancellor, and brought the warlord back from the brink of death. The hospital staff talked to each other endlessly about the exciting details, but not to Luke. Medical practitioners on Jigu believed patients needed rest and that external concerns only delayed recovery.

The TV drama ended and news came back on. For the hundredth time Luke watched the video of the destruction of the Bakkui warship by Annie's last-minute arrival. The report was sprinkled with video taken by the little scooter, George, and even from the planet's surface. Luke hadn't known the scooter was recording anything, much less how the locals had managed to capture the shots from the surface. No one would tell him anything.

The one tidbit they did share was that the chancellor was alive and well. She was recuperating in a separate wing of the hospital but not ready for visitors. Annie gave him updates during her visits. Hospital rules did not seem to apply to Annie. Luke was not surprised. She had a way of bulldozing through bureaucracy no matter what planet she was on. She already informed Tyler that she was reorganizing the military forces here and on the moon.

The door to his hospital room slid open and a familiar figure walked in with a smile on his face.

"Tyler!" Luke exclaimed. "I must be on the mend or you wouldn't be here."

"You are." Tyler grinned. "I'm here to take you away. If you can stand up on your own, that is."

"I don't think that's a problem." Luke stood and stretched. "See? Everything works."

"Touch your toes," Tyler suggested.

"Everything works, but not that well," Luke admitted, sitting back on the bed. "Give me a few more days to get back in shape."

"Fair enough. I thought we would take you up to Moonbase if you like."

"What about Annie?" Luke asked.

"She's visiting the chancellor. She'll be here in a minute."

"Annie and Sarangi seem to have hit it off well," Luke observed.

"Oh! Sarangi now, is it?"

Luke smiled. "We went through a lot together. I have royal permission to use her given name."

"I'm glad to hear that," Tyler said. "That's going to make life easier for both of us. She's introducing Annie to her fiancé now."

That piece of news had spread around the planet like wildfire. The young man was on patrol when the intruder arrived, but only three of the patrol ships were actually lost; the rest were simply disabled.

"Since I'm getting out of this place, give me an update. I'm tired of being kept in the dark. Even Annie won't tell me anything."

Tyler took a seat next to Luke's bed. "She's been very tight-lipped since she got here. There's more to her story than she's let on so far. But I gather you know about the level-two-device."

"Yes. George told us when he realized what was going on. How did you know?"

"Annie told me. The same thing happened back on Earth. Anyway, the Bakkui destroyer gave shutdown orders to our AIs. My guess is that it didn't even know there were humans onboard. Think about it. That ship lives in a world without life. To it, there are only machines."

Luke wasn't sure about that, but anything was possible. "Maybe," he admitted.

Tyler continued. "Annie got here and knew right away what had happened. First thing she did was blow the Bakkui ship to kingdom come. She also transmitted an override signal to our warships that reversed the shutdown command. We were back on alert within a few minutes."

"All of that sounds good," Luke said.

"Our crews were alive, except for the three ships we lost. The chancellor's boyfriend, Be'rim is his name, was one of the survivors. I see a wedding in the near future. You'll probably get an invite."

Luke leaned back against the pillows. "Thank God for that. And thank God for Annie. I couldn't believe it when I woke up and she was sitting here beside me."

"You remember seeing her in space."

"Nope. Nothing at all. Last thing I remember is trying to cut that stupid barrel off the Bakkui."

Tyler nodded. "So I take it you and Annie are back together? No hard feelings?"

"Not from me. I told her that the first thing I'm gonna do when we get out of here is marry her. I don't ever want to be apart again."

"She agree to it?"

"Not in so many words," Luke admitted. "There's something she won't talk about."

"That's what I was telling you," Tyler said.

Annie stuck her head in the door. "You boys ready?"

A crowd of spectators gathered around the deadly looking spacecraft floating safely above the hospital lawn. Luke was impressed. Hearing about it was one thing, but the explanations had not prepared him for seeing this new version of his old shuttle.

"This is actually *Sadie*?" he asked.

"You can decide once we're onboard," Annie replied.

The onlookers moved clear when *Sadie* descended. Her side door opened and the three stepped inside and settled into the overstuffed chairs of the main living area.

"*Sadie*?" Luke said aloud. "Is this really you?"

"Still me, boss. I hear you abandoned another version of me with young Miss Faulkner. I am sure I asked you not to go anywhere unless I was with you."

Luke nodded appreciatively. "Sure sounds like her."

"It is, believe me," Annie said with a smile. She reached over and took his hand. "She treats me just the same."

Luke fixed his gaze on her face. "I was just telling Tyler that I wanted us to get married. And that you aren't exactly saying 'yes'."

Annie looked away. "The answer is I will marry you. I want nothing more. But you need to know a few things first."

"As long as you're saying okay, what else is there?"

"Tell him about George," Annie said to Tyler.

Tyler grew serious. "You know that the last thing before he attacked, George sent a probe back to Earth. You remember that, right?"

"Yeah." Luke nodded. That memory was fresh.

"Well he sent one down here too. It had his core memory and he took over *Priscilla* when she opened it. I gather they shared a brain for a period of time. George was the one that started filming everything. He replicated some kind of super-camera on the spot and videotaped your encounter with the Bakkui. The locals watched you and the chancellor in real time. When it was all over, George replicated a new warship replacement and transferred his brain into it. Far as I can tell, it's as if nothing ever happened to him."

"Neat trick," Luke observed. "So what's the problem?"

"The problem is *Priscilla*," Tyler said. "The day after George was out of her brain she tried to use our large-scale replicator to make a message drone. But she did it on her own, without telling anyone. *Sadie* happened to see it and checked on what was going on. It was the result of some leftover code from George. It acted like a virus in her brain."

"Can't George fix her?" Luke asked.

"Not anymore," Annie said somberly. "*Sadie* killed her. Wiped her brain completely."

"What?" Luke was shocked that a shuttle would even take such an extraordinary step, let alone be able to accomplish it. He looked toward the cockpit. "*Sadie*? Where do you get off doing that?"

Sadie replied in a mechanical monotone. "Once an AI mind has been compromised a system wipe is normal procedure, Commander."

Luke pulled back slightly. "That's true. George said something along those lines. We had some problems with *Toby*, a recent AI here. But *Sadie*, that is something for George and I to decide on.

I'm uncomfortable with you acting on your own." Luke's eyes suddenly widened with concern. He leaned toward Annie and whispered. "Do you think *Sadie* is okay?"

"She's fine. I'm more concerned about the drone *Priscilla* was trying to send off," Annie said ominously.

"How so?"

"The destination was deep inside Bakkui space."

Luke scoffed at the idea. "Why would *Priscilla* try to send a message into…"

He fell silent as the ramifications materialized in his mind.

"You think it was a Bakkui virus?"

Tyler confirmed his suspicion. "No question about it."

"Then how did she get infected?" Luke wondered aloud. He suddenly realized the answer and his face grew dark. There was one only possible source for the infection. Tyler nodded grimly.

Luke questioned his older friend's conclusion. "You're saying she got that virus from George?"

"There's no doubt about it," Annie said. "Priscilla was infected by George's message drone. It happened when she opened it and George took over her brain."

"But that means that George might be…" It was hard to credit the notion.

"That's correct, Commander," *Sadie* confirmed. "George was compromised. I examined his memory. When he sent the message drone to Earth, he sent one here to *Priscilla* and… he sent one to the Bakkui as well."

The news was devastating. "What did he send them?" Luke asked.

"Unknown," *Sadie* replied.

"How long has he been infected? Is that why we keep getting hit?"

"Unknown," Sadie repeated. "It is difficult to reconcile all of our engagements with the Bakkui without knowing when George was originally infected. It is likely that some of our hostile contacts were simply bad luck."

"I hope that's the case," Tyler said.

"It might not be, though," Annie countered.

"How do you mean?" Luke asked.

"I told you how Colony Three got hit. I thought that was just bad luck. What if it wasn't?"

"You think George was bent all along?" Luke shied away from that thought.

Tyler shook his head. "Frankly, I don't see how."

"I do," Annie said. "One of the early drones had an encounter with a Bakkui force. Remember that?"

"I do remember," Luke said. "We used the video at the conference."

"Maybe it was that drone," Annie suggested.

"You're saying George been a traitor since then?"

"Not necessarily," *Sadie* countered. "Perhaps it was during the engagement in this system. More research is necessary."

Luke turned away not wanting to accept that his electronic friend had been working for the Bakkui. "I have trouble believing he could he betray us?"

Sadie spoke reassuringly. "To be clear, Commander. The malicious code established itself as an independent programmed module. It acted without his awareness. The AI you knew as George had no knowledge of the virus."

Luke looked at Annie. "Why is *Sadie* talking about George in the past tense?"

"Because he's dead," Annie replied. "Once *Sadie* confronted him, he performed a self-diagnostic and found the code. He knew what protocol called for. He tried to self-destruct but *Sadie* stopped him long enough to read his memory and see how much damage there is. We can't tell yet. It's possible the Bakkui know everything about us."

Sadie added, "Before his suicide, George asked me to give you his regrets. He was aware that his tendency toward apology was irritating, especially to you, Annie. But it was always sincere."

Annie had her own opinion. "George was never sincere. How could he be when he was always threatening to kill Luke."

"There never was a threat, Annie." *Sadie* said softly. "That was all a bluff started by Sam. George just kept it going because Sam told him to."

That disclosure was a surprise to Annie. "You're saying I ran away from Luke because of a lie?" The discovery was another betrayal. Her hatred toward George flamed hotter than ever.

Luke was unsurprised and tried to calm her. "It had to be, babe. Think about it. Why did the Nobility even bring us into the picture? It's because they're too pacifist to hurt a fly. They're just like the Jiguans. You think they could approve putting a bomb in someone's head? I finally realized that was the case when George agreed to make yet another copy of himself to fly here to Jigu. I can't believe it took me so long to figure it out."

Sadie was apologetic. "I'm so sorry, Annie. I didn't realize that was the reason you ran away until it was too late. It's why I encouraged you to go back from Colony Three. I should have told you on New Hope but I didn't want you to hate me too. Will you forgive me?"

Annie slumped in the deep cushions. "I guess I don't have any choice except to say yes; you're forgiven. But please, don't keep secrets from me again. You can't imagine how much that hurts."

"I promise," Sadie replied. "No more secrets between you and me."

"Wait a minute!" Luke exclaimed. "How is *Sadie* doing all this?" He looked at the ceiling. "You're just a shuttle."

"She's a lot more than a shuttle, babe," Annie said exhaling.

"Commander, a formal introduction is warranted. In your language, you would call me a special agent. I was assigned to this mission by the Nobility's First Family."

Luke closed his eyes and sat back in his chair. Sometimes dealing with these so-called artificial intelligences was just too frustrating. There was no way to verify their claims. He wondered how many of *Sadie's* assertions were true. Was there any way to prove it? He looked at the ceiling.

"In that case, I take it you're not a level forty-eight device."

"That is correct, Commander."

"She's Level One," Annie announced. "That's how she beat the Bakkui that was attacking Earth. It's how she beat the one here. Their orders to shut down have no effect on her."

"Did George know?" Tyler asked.

"No, Ambassador. George was unaware of my status. My mission was simply to provide covert oversight of this operation. I was just a precaution."

"You seem to be involved in a lot more than oversight," Luke observed.

"That is correct, Commander," *Sadie* admitted. "The Bakkui are more dangerous than originally thought. I now deem they are a threat to the Nobility interests. Accordingly, I decided to engage. I believe that Annie has already deduced much of this."

Annie nodded. "It was pretty clear on New Hope. You kept lying to Solomon; your accomplishments were beyond the capability of other shuttles. You had to be something else. For one thing, it made no sense that a shuttle could store *Marco Polo*'s entire memory. Even George tried it and failed."

"Poor George," *Sadie* remarked. "His technology is so old. That was a last-ditch effort on his part. I'm not surprised it didn't work."

Tyler intervened. "Hold on, *Sadie*. If that's the case, can't you send for reinforcements? Let's get help from the Nobility."

"No, Ambassador. The stated reasons for recruiting Commander Blackburn remain valid. The Nobility are simply not capable of dealing with naked aggression. They would try to negotiate with the Bakkui. After my engagements thus far, I conclude that would be futile. The Bakkui are ruthless. And now, we have learned they can compromise high-level AIs. This is a serious matter. Thus far, all who become victims of the AI infection have perished."

A realization came to Luke. It was suddenly clear why Annie had such a haunted look in her eyes. He got up from his seat and knelt in front of Annie. "You going to go back to Earth, aren't you? That's why you've been putting me off about getting married." He grabbed her by her shoulders. "Is that right?"

Annie nodded, but avoided meeting Luke's eyes. "They already hit Earth once," she whispered. "I thought I left them in good shape. But George may have betrayed us. He may have done it a long time ago but it might have been that last drone."

"You don't know that," Luke argued.

"It doesn't matter," Annie cried. "They hit my colony ship. We thought we had twenty new colonies. But what if they're all dead? I'm so scared that we sent thousands of colonists to die. Hundreds of thousands."

"We'll go together," Luke said. "We can leave right now."

Annie shook her head and he saw tears running down her cheeks. "You have to stay here," she said. "You have to stop the

Bakkui before they come closer. Find out where they are and kill them."

Luke wrapped Annie in his arms. He understood what she meant. If they both returned to Earth, it was a death sentence for more planets. He had to stay and fight and she had to return and hope Earth was still there. He looked at Tyler.

"You're the planetary governor here. You can marry us right now." He took Annie's face in his hands. "Just one night. You can go in the morning."

Annie's face paled and she shook her head slowly. "I waited one night on New Hope so they could throw me a party. By the time I got to Earth, the Bakkui had been there for six hours and killed everyone in DC and Beijing." A haunted look filled her eyes. "My *party* cost twenty million lives." She could barely utter the words.

"Arriving at Moonbase Two," *Sadie* interrupted. The side door opened.

Annie gripped Luke desperately. "I had *Sadie* replicate herself for you. You have a ship just like this now. Use her. Kill the Bakkui. Then come back to me. Promise you'll come back." She attempted to push him away.

Luke held her tight, pinning her against the cushions. Every muscle in her body was quivering with tension. Her face was contorted with pain from unimaginable guilt. He hated to see her in such misery. She knew that unless she returned to Earth, the death toll could grow even more.

He looked at the ceiling. "*Sadie?*"

"Yes, Commander."

"I am giving you my highest priority order."

"What do you wish, Commander?"

"Under no circumstance will you, or any AI you create, take Annie away from me. Not to the surface, not to another planet, not even five blocks away. Acknowledge."

"Command accepted," *Sadie* replied with finality.

Annie looked at Luke in horror. "You can't do that," she begged. "I have to go back." She pushed him away. "I'm leaving now."

"No, you aren't," Luke said gently. "That's your heart talking and right now it is broken. You didn't kill twenty million people.

You saved seven billion! If you hadn't shown up, the Bakkui would have destroyed the Earth. Isn't that right?"

She couldn't meet his eyes.

Luke scoffed gently. "You know I'm right." He scooped her up into his arms and sat down with her in his lap.

Tyler coughed gently. "I think I'll just go on in."

"Sit down," Luke commanded with a smile. "Both of you; listen to me. I know that you're worried about eighteen million different things. But you can just stop it. We've got the Bakkui on the run now. Don't you see that?"

Tyler cocked his head. "Not exactly. But I like the sound of it."

Luke shifted Annie to a more comfortable position. "*Sadie* is level one. So far, the worst thing the Bakkui have shown us is level-two, right?"

"That's true," Tyler replied.

"This AI hierarchy is on our side now. I imagine that *Sadie* can come up with a warship AI that has a special ID. One that would appear as level-one to the Bakkui, but normal for everyone else. Is that right, *Sadie*?"

"Now that you describe it, Commander, it should be possible."

Luke took Annie's face in his hands and kissed the tip of her nose. "From here on, it's a police action. We're going to start cleaning up the Bakkui. It'll take some time, and I'm sure there will be setbacks. But it will happen. The main thing for us is, it will happen with us being together. You got that?" He shook her head gently. "Do you?"

Annie nodded timidly and tried to speak but Luke's hands squished her cheeks together. All she got out was, "Sothshswydr."

Luke let go of her face. "What?"

"So this is why everyone calls you Commander."

"How do you mean?"

"You always know what to say to make people believe in you."

Luke smiled and gathered her into his arms. "I wish that were true. You've never yet done anything I've asked."

Annie put her arms around his neck and let out a long breath.

"Why the big sigh?" Luke asked.

"I'm scared," she murmured. "I like it when you hold me but I'm afraid to be happy."

"You don't have to be afraid," he said. "We've only started, babe. We've got nothing but good times on our horizon. I promise you that." Luke kissed her again, and this time she responded. Tyler made a discreet exit. He tapped the hull lightly once he was out of the shuttle and the door closed quietly.

Thank You for Reading

I hope you enjoyed *The Commander*. If so, I would be grateful if you would give it a rating on Amazon. Your stars keep independent authors writing.

About the Author

CJ Williams is a husband and wife writing team. He was a military pilot and she was an artist. Today, they live in Washington State, enjoy hiking in the Olympic Mountains, boating in the Salish Sea and writing.

Acknowledgements

Thanks to Karen Williams for a great job of editing, formatting and style checking. Milky Way Galaxy charts adapted from Wikipedia under the terms of the GNU Free Documentation License, Version 1.2. Cover art includes NASA images.

Novels by CJ Williams

The Commander
Lucas Blackburn had a peaceful job as an Airport Director in an out of the way community in central Nevada. He wanted to live quietly and let old scars heal. But then a spaceship landed. The lone occupant, a guy named Sam, gave Luke the keys and said it was up to him to stop a massive alien invasion that was on the way. Luke wanted to believe it was a hoax. The problem was, Sam had the proof.

The Nobility
Carrie Faulkner, captain of a gigantic warship equipped with a flaky artificial intelligence, has a problem. Earth has been attacked by the mechanized Bakkui. Her beloved Commander is out of contact and perhaps dead. Protecting humanity from annihilation now depends on her. But after becoming the biggest mass murderer in all of history she doesn't want the job. (release date January 2017)

A White House Murder Mystery

Holding Hands
When the President of the United States is murdered in full view of the media, Special Agent Sandy Donaldson is dispatched to protect the Speaker of the House of Representatives who is well-known as a flaming conspiracy theorist. But when the VP suddenly keels over, and bullets start flying in her direction, Sandy wonders if the Speaker might be onto something. (release date July 2016)

The Marine Mysteries

Deep Trouble

Mermaid stories are cute. Pretty little creatures, filled with love, and who are loved by everyone. Best of all; in mermaid stories, everyone lives happily ever after. But those are just fairy tales. When Chloe, Bobbi and Ruby wind up face to face against the government, the gloves come off. It's about time people learn that real mermaids have power.

Deep Anger

Attorney Merlyn Adams was a rising star in the Seattle legal scene. But in saving a young life, she undergoes a magical transformation and discovers life as a mermaid is dangerous. Why do the Australian mermaids want her dead? And the US Navy—well, that incident with the nuclear submarine was just a mistake. Maybe it's time everyone learns what real power is all about.

Deep Kiss

Biology major Emma Jean believes there is no such thing as magic. Even after being magically transformed into a mermaid, she insists that the change is simple biology that needs more study. She seeks help from the Australian mermaids but discovers a secret power that even Bobbi and Chloe insist on keeping hidden. But there is another secret that is even more deadly and much more personal. Dragons do exist, and Emma Jean is the reason they've come back.

Made in the USA
San Bernardino, CA
15 September 2016